Mold my Future

AMI BELLA

To those who dream. Follow your heart—don't stop
until you reach it.

Playlist

"Rosas"—La Oreja de Van Gogh

"Simplemente Amigos"—Ana Gabriel

"Como La Flor"—Selena

"2NDO CHANCE"—Becky G, Ivan Cornejo

"Shameless"—Camila Cabello

"La Vie En Rose"—Emily Watts

"TUYA"—ROSALÍA

"El Beso"—Mon Laferte

"Suerte (Whenever, Wherever)"—Shakira

"Bidi Bidi Bom Bom - 1994 Version"—Selena

"Two Weeks"—Grizzly Bear

"BESO"—ROSALÍA

"Para Enamorarte"—CNCO

"Loba"—Shakira

This book contains content that may be triggering to some readers. Please heed warnings before continuing.

Content Warnings:

Explicit sex, anxiety, mentions of unhealthy eating habits, violence, stalking, child abuse, parental neglect/abandonment, suicide, cancer, parental death, mentions of drugs and prostitution, incarceration, and racial discrimination.

Chapter 1

Rosie

"Mom, I don't have a boyfriend!" The teenage girl next to me shouted into the phone as she stared at her mother's eyes through the protective screen. "I don't!" She repeated. The older woman's silence was enough for me to understand the glare she aimed at her daughter—giving her the "you definitely do" kind of look.

I silently side-eyed them, deciphering their expressions and making up my own hypothesis on how this conversation was brought up in the first place.

The daughter showed up for the visit in a turtleneck. Her mother spotted it and assumed the obvious. Was she wearing it because fall was starting, or was she hiding a huge hickey?

Who knows. My attention shifted when I heard the buzz of a door. I moved in my seat, the coldness of the metal chair sending goosebumps up my spine. I wrapped my purple cardigan tighter around me, and my fingers wrung together as my knee bounced. I shook in anticipation until a head of black hair fell into view, and I relaxed as my sister appeared.

She sat in front of me and reached for the phone with a smile. I mimicked her movements, pressing the phone to my ear just in time to hear my nickname fall from her lips, "Rosita."

"Bee, hi," I pressed my hand against the glass, wishing it wasn't there. My life had never been the same since I started visiting this prison seven years ago. Every other Saturday I would take the bus from Chicago to Greenville, trying to keep my relationship alive with the only family I had left. "I know I missed our last visit. Business is out of control," I sighed, sorrowful for not being there for her. While I loved my job, there were moments I wished it didn't keep me away from her.

Hecho de Hilo was the yarn shop I owned. I started it six years ago after graduating from high school, and it's what keeps me afloat while I await Bianca's release. As much of a distraction it was and a great gateway for my future, it tended to push itself to the top of my priorities list.

"Don't apologize," she scolded. "You're out there living your life. You don't need to hold back just because of me," she raised a brow, a knowing look on her face. She was four years older, and moments like these only reminded me of that.

I nodded, keeping my gaze down to not endure another lecture from her. It was true that I couldn't hold back living just because hers was on pause. I've done so many things in the twenty-four years I've existed. Like graduating high school, opening and owning my own business, and teaching people something I love. Yet, it still felt like I had so much left to do—things I wanted to do.

Like opening up my ceramics shop and studio.

Ceramicá de la Vida would be its name. I've had the name jotted down on a piece of paper since my second pottery class in high school, kept safely in a shoebox in my closet. The people closest in my life knew of this dream, especially Bianca, but no one knew what I wanted it to be named. For now, that was for my eyes only.

I hoped that when the day came, Bianca would be there during its opening. She would hold the scissors with me, cut the red ribbon, and we would hug, celebrating a wonderful moment, finally having her by my side. For that to happen, I knew I needed to work harder to ensure I got a good lawyer to get her out of this hell just in time.

"Now tell me what was keeping you so busy the last three weeks," she hummed, pulling my attention back into the conversation. Straightening up in her seat, she rested her elbows on the table, attentive and ready to listen.

I inhaled deeply, thinking back to all the tasks I needed to complete the past few weeks. There were so many things to say, yet I couldn't think where to start. I pressed my lips together, leaning back in my seat as my eyes darted around the rest of the visitation room before catching on the color of a woman's coat.

It was a light periwinkle color, and I noticed her nails matched it. She was clearly put together, and it reminded me of a recent addition to the shop. Amor y Fe. This cozy blend of blue and purple, perfect to get the last touch of summer as the seasons began to change.

"We got a new color of wool," I recalled. "We've been experimenting with dyes, and customers have loved it. It's our best seller!" I began, toying with my charm bracelet—a grown habit of mine.

Creating such a vibrant color was risky, considering warmer shades were popular during the fall. Thankfully, it was working out.

"We ended up running low on the wool, so we had to go back to the farm to get more," I recounted. "I wish I could've stopped by then, but we needed to get back to open up shop."

Owning an ethically sourced yarn shop was unpredictable, but after its opening, it's been a favorite of the locals since. However, despite its popularity, we still struggled to scrape by to the other side of a success story.

"It's okay," she reassured me. "I've been occupying myself with Luna's book. It's become really popular among the crowd here," she wiggled her brows, tapping her fingers on the surface.

Luna Garcia has been my best friend since middle school. She's been there when my mom died, when Bianca and I were on the brink of being homeless, and when Bianca got arrested. She held the title of second-in-command at my shop, and through all of her support and hard work, she's established herself as a published author of the fantasy/romance genre. I was beyond proud of her and was so excited to be there when she published last month.

"She wanted me to send the message that she's starting her second book," I said.

Her face lit up. While she was clearly happy, showing emotions of excitement, it didn't reach her eyes. For a long time, those emotions never did. Ever since she got sent to solitary a few years back.

I tried to ignore it most of the time. What could I really do anyway?

The prison rarely ever cared for loved ones enough to keep them aware of what was going on inside. We were only knowledgeable about things based on what those inside told us. Sometimes, they hid certain information because they believed it was better to be in a bubble of ignorant bliss.

I still shake at the memory I came here to visit her like every other Saturday, but they refused to let me in. Claiming she was unavailable. They threatened me with forceful removal after I refused to leave, demanding to know where she was. I ended up having a panic attack on the curb in the parking lot and had to call Luna to pick me up. It was pouring rain when she arrived, but I hadn't noticed until I was in the car. I didn't hear from Bianca again until a week later when she finally called me, letting me know what happened. Now it was like looking at a flashback as I stared at her.

Her hair seemed more untamed, her waves frizzier and unruly. The same shine wasn't there like before. Even though she's been in prison for seven years, she managed to find a hair routine that did the job. Scanning down to search her eyes again, it was more obvious now. The bags under them were darker and more prominent.

"Bianca, what's wrong?" I furrowed my brows, pausing.

"What do you mean?" She tilted her head.

"It's hard to see right away, but you don't look okay," I started to worry. My heart rate picked up at the thought that she could be in trouble or that she was in solitary while I was gone. "What's happening? Please, tell me," my eyes were wide, my nostrils flaring as I took big inhales. I pressed my hand against the glass like I was clawing for the truth.

"Okay," she inhaled, closing her eyes. "There are a few new inmates that have been causing some issues with me and my friends," she tucked a strand of hair behind her ear. "We've been protecting each other, but one of them is insane," she whispered, cupping her hand on her temple to create a barrier around her eye as she stared at me.

"What do they do?" I gulped, shifting in my seat.

"Weird shit like leaving her underwear and used tampons on my bed, staring at me constantly, following me around even though she's not even in the same bunk as me," she breathed out, fisting her hair. "Two weeks ago, she was watching me while I slept," she chewed on the inside of her cheek.

"And you didn't tell me because it's not like there's anything I can do," I realized, glancing down at my lap, biting down hard on my lip, tears filling my vision.

"Exactly. I didn't want to worry you; you get in your head, and you don't need that," she defended, raising her hand to mirror mine. "I'll just keep my head down like I always do," she forced a smile, waiting for me to return it, but I didn't. "I'll be fine. Now, please. I only have an hour. What else is new?" She changed the subject.

I chewed on the inside of my cheek, nodding slowly. I wanted to push, but Bianca always felt more at ease when I told her about my life, so I continued.

"Hecho de Hilo got an invitation to Romano Tech's grant benefit. That party where small businesses gather and they grant solar panels to a winner for their business, the one with the list I've been trying to get on for the longest time," I explained.

Her smile returned, her features softening as she leaned back in her chair, crossing her arm over her chest before she moved, leaning forward.

"Isn't the CEO like *really* hot?" She rested her chin in her palm, a smirk spreading across her face, a genuine one this time. "Maybe wear a dress with a deep plunge, get yourself a billionaire," she licked her lips like she just ate the most delectable dish out there.

"*Bee*," I warned.

She brushed me off.

"First of all, I don't even know what Victor Romano looks like, and second of all, he runs a billion-dollar corporation. I'm just a feeble small business owner who barely profits fifty thousand a year. I get into a relationship like that, and he could destroy me in an instant," I snapped my fingers.

She sighed. "Or he could help you out," she shrugged. "Don't close your heart to love," she reaffirmed, hiking her shoulders up as her gaze cascaded with a hopelessly devoted look.

"Let's just forget it," I exhaled. "I don't even know why we're talking about it like he's there waiting for me to date him," I shook my head, kidding myself. "The point is that Hecho de Hilo got invited. The three of us are going to go tonight," I grinned, getting back on track. "If we win the grant—" I was cut off by her.

"It would change *everything*," her eyes widened as she mocked me. She burst out into a chuckle when I frowned at her. "You've been talking about this for the last three months. As proud of you as I am for that, Rosita, I want to know the juicy parts of your life," she wiggled her brows. "Anyone I should know of?"

Here we go again. Bianca loved nothing more than some good gossip—or, as we like to say, *chisme*—especially when it related to my love life.

"Bianca, honestly," I rolled my eyes, leaning back and looking away from her. I worried about her safety a moment ago, and now I was annoyed. "I'm not looking for a relationship, at least not for a while," I rubbed my arm.

"All I want to hear is that my sister is happy with someone. We're not getting any younger, and it'd be nice to know someone is looking after you while I'm here," she gestured around her.

I let out a defeated sigh. "I don't need anyone to protect me, I'm twenty-four years old, and I've been on my own for the last seven years—you better not blame yourself because we both know it wasn't your fault," I butted in before she could even say anything. "What I'm trying to say is, I'm happy right now, and I don't want anyone to mess it up. The last thing I need is a distraction," I defended my stance, but I was met with a soft smile from her, one that said, "Oh, you're so naive."

"Love can't mess anything up; it only makes you stronger—we both know that," she winked, causing me to huff out a laugh. "I've been stuck in this place for the last seven years, and I will have spent more than a decade here by the time I get out. Our love is what keeps me going, Rosita. You're my rock," she pressed her lips together, gleaming.

"But that's different," I argued, disagreeing with her entirely, and this time she rolled her eyes. "I'm your rock because I've stuck beside you. I don't want to let someone random in my life, and for what?" I shrugged.

"For love," she mused, but I shook my head, pinching the bridge of my nose. "Eternal, 'let's have a future' type of love," she sighed, gazing up with a goofy smile.

"Sounds like a distraction," I countered.

She sent me another look, a disappointed one.

"Eight more years until I'm out of here, and I can finally find my little sister a good man," she joked.

"No," I deadpanned. "You are not going to find me a man. Once you're out of here, we can move past *everything*," I glanced at her, and for a second, I saw a glimmer of hope in her eyes.

"Eight more years," she repeated.

We talked for the next hour, and the minutes flew by until the guard eventually announced that visiting was over.

I waited until Bianca was on the other side of the door before I got up and left. Other families of inmates walked alongside me before we went into our cars. Parents, spouses, children, siblings, and other relatives were all here to see their loved ones. We were all different, yet we shared the same desire for them to be okay.

Eight more years.

Chapter 2

Rosie

After a four-hour drive back to the city and a quick nap, I finally made it to the shop. Saturdays were surprisingly our slowest day of the week, with Sunday taking the busiest. But it was the day when our regulars came in, including my favorite customer, *Señora Rivera*.

"I hope you get the grant, Rosita," Señora Rivera smiled as I scanned her yarn. "It would be so nice to see this business grow," she thanked me when I handed her the bag. "Maybe you can even open your ceramics studio," she raised her brows in excitement. She was one of the few people in my life to know about my dream, and would always say she would be my first customer.

She wasn't Hecho de Hilo's first customer but was our most frequent. Every week, she stopped by the shop for a restock of yarn, which prompted her to show me her latest project, which took up more than half the space in her purse. Then she gave me her phone filled with photos of everything she made for her grandkids—usually a sweater for her oldest granddaughter. She was such a stereotypical grandma who loved her grandchildren more than her own kids and smelled like cinnamon.

"*Ay, mija*, I forgot to show you the cardigan I made Lucia," she hurriedly pulled her phone out of her purse—*just in time*—and shoved the screen in my face.

Wearing a sage green cardigan with daisies on it was a teenage version of Señora Rivera. I could tell she loved it based on her beaming smile, not the awkward ones you made when your parents made you take photos.

"*Tan hermosa*, your grandkids must love you a lot to wear your sweaters," I joked.

She responded with a laugh as she put her phone away.

"It's your yarn. Lucia never complains about the texture," she pointed at me.

I blushed.

"Plus, you always add fun and new things to your classes so that us *viejas* know how to make, *ay, como se dice*," she paused, head tilting up as she thought about the word. "Trendy clothes," she remembered.

I nodded, aware that most of my classes cover tutorials in a more modern approach, giving *abuelas* a chance to make something other than itchy Christmas sweaters.

"We actually know what they would wear," she hummed.

It was nice to hear that our work was continuing to be received well.

"Nothing better than an *abuela* gifting clothes that match their style," I shrugged, gesturing to the red and blue patchwork sweater I had on. "I'm glad that I can help," I smiled proudly. "But then again, Señora Rivera, you're the one who led the class that time."

It was true.

I had been struggling with the pattern even after practicing two weeks before. I attempted to lead the class, but noticing my uneven petals, she jumped in to save the day. It reminded me why I always called her for help when I was stuck on a commissioned piece. It was safe to say she's been crocheting way before I was born.

"*Ni me acuerdo, mija,*" she brushed off. "I'll be back tomorrow with a cake to celebrate," she stated.

My face scrunched in confusion.

"For winning the grant," she shook her head and waved her hands like she couldn't believe I didn't understand what she had said.

"But I haven't even won," I responded.

"Mija, you will," she patted my hand from across the counter, saying goodbye as she walked towards the exit.

I smiled, muttering a soft "thank you" before the bell chimed, signaling her departure. The shop was empty now, and even though we didn't close for another two hours, I knew I had some downtime.

I drummed my fingers on the counter before walking to the computer to check some emails. Might as well do something while I waited for Luna or Summer to show up. Scrolling through pointless emails, my eyes scanned over a familiar name. I quickly clicked on the email, my heartbeat picking up.

To: Rosie Martinez
From: Miles Jones (Plains Acres)

Hello, Miss Martinez! I hope you are doing great today! I wanted to talk over the phone but I know you prefer email, do get back to me when you get the chance!

I have some bad news to tell you…I'm selling the farm. I know it's a big shock, but it won't be finalized until the end of the year. So I'm giving you a chance. I'm willing to postpone selling, but I want you to prepare a presentation for me. Show me that Hecho de Hilo is worth holding out a little bit longer. You have until the end of November! Make me proud!

Sincerely,

Mr. Jones

I reread the email over and over again. There was no way.

The aching throb in my chest, the pressure building in the back of my eyes, that tightness in my throat, and my knuckles straining as I squeezed my hands into fists—I was panicking. I stepped back and found a chair to sit in as I counted my breath. After a few minutes of breathing, I stopped and glanced around the store.

It was a quaint shop, nothing like big-name yarn shops. Just a few aisles and a workstation. Walls painted in a tangerine orange matched the primary color of our brand, and hardwood floors were scratched and scuffed just from the overall wear and tear of running a business. Well, except for that one time Luna dropped a dolly, which left a nasty scuff on the floor right by the entrance. None of that really mattered, but it was sentimental, like the wall to my left, filled with photos from Hecho de Hilo's endeavors. It was a journey throughout the last six years, and it hurt to think it might all be gone.

Glancing back at the computer screen, I frowned, contemplating what could cause Mr. Jones to sell the farm.

Mr. Jones owned the alpaca farm where our yarn was sourced. Without him, no more yarn, no more store, and no more money. We were struggling as is, and now this was happening? It took me three years to find an ethically raised farm that was reasonably priced and local. How could he do this to me?

I tried not to think too extreme, taking a last calming breath before I stood up. I replied to him before I closed out of the window. I needed time to think before going in with a plan.

~

"What do you mean he's selling the farm?!" Luna yelled, eyes wide as she sat up from the couch in the living room of our two-bedroom apartment.

"My reaction exactly," I responded, a lot calmer now that I had a few hours to process the news I had received.

"He's known us for the last four years. He wouldn't drop a bomb like that on you without giving you a warning," Summer offered, confusion written across her face.

Summer Hernandez has been my employee for the past five years. Making her way through art school to get her Master's, she's been a huge help when it came to design. She was positive, bubbly, and creative. Only two years younger than Luna and me, she knew a lot more about pop culture and social media scandals than I did. Tie that in with her impeccable style, and she was the cool little sister I always wanted.

"He's giving me three months to make a presentation showing him the business is worth keeping the farm," I explained.

They both let out a sigh of relief.

"See?" Summer gestured with her hand, already grasping onto the positive of it. "It's like a sales pitch. You've done it before when you leased the building, and when you sourced the yarn in the first place, this is second nature."

I nodded. "You're right. It's just that my anxiety gets the best of me," I sighed, plopping down on the loveseat. "I have a few ideas swimming in my head," I threw my head back against the pillow.

Ethically and locally sourced, Latina-owned small business.

I kept repeating my small list in my head. It was a start.

"But right now, I just want to focus on the grant," I closed my eyes and clasped my hands over my stomach.

"When we win, do we all get to use the car?" Luna asked.

I peeled one eye open.

"Technically, yes, but my name is on the paperwork, so I'm the only one who can use it for personal use." I made sure to read over the fine print a million times over. There was no way I would enter into a billion-dollar company's grant only to be scammed.

"Does this mean that you're pushing the opening for the ceramics shop back?" Luna popped another question as my eyes shot open. "If we win the grant, shouldn't the money we save from expenses be put towards saving Hecho de Hilo if all goes downhill?" She seemed worried as the words slipped past her mouth.

"I haven't even thought about that," I gulped. "I don't know," I answered truthfully. "There are a lot of things we can do with the money," I began to wonder about all the possibilities.

The prizes for this grant were grand. A brand-new electric car and solar panels with a lifetime warranty, on top of the twenty-thousand dollar check the winner received. The cash prize wasn't limited to business use, meaning I could use it for anything if I win.

But that led me to wonder what I should do with it—keep Hecho de Hilo afloat until we no longer can, close Hecho de Hilo when the farm is sold, or focus on opening my dream.

None of it was a win-win situation. If the farm is sold, I would have to let something go.

"Like the Winter Drive," Summer butted in.

I sat up in realization. "Oh yeah," I slouched, resting my face in my hands, feeling entirely overwhelmed.

The Winter Drive was a charity event we hosted yearly for five years. Customers donated coats and other clothing while I made hats, gloves, and scarves. It was an entire day. We helped families in need in our community, and some local restaurants donated or catered food. It honestly felt like a party. It was one of the most rewarding days of the year.

"I didn't think we could do that this year. Would we put the money towards that?" Luna jumped in, crossing her arms over her chest. "It would be a good idea to close out with a bang if it ends up being our last one."

"I don't know," I sighed. What do I choose? My business, my community, or my dream?

Hecho de Hilo was my baby, but it was just a stepping stone to get to Ceramicá de la Vida. As much as I loved crocheting, I didn't find my passion until I took my first pottery class in high school. I still have the first bowl I made as a catchall for my keys right by the front door. Ceramics became my future, opening a studio accessible to anyone wanting to learn.

Only problem?

It was fucking expensive. The clay, the kilns, the glazes, all the materials. Crocheting was the more sustainable and logical option in the beginning. It was a piece of the puzzle to get me where I wanted to be. I just didn't think it would take this long.

And now, with another boulder blocking my goal, I knew I needed to prioritize what's essential—the Winter Drive. My studio could wait just a bit longer, I guess.

There was a long pause in the apartment, Luna and Summer staring at each other before one got up.

"Don't worry too much about it now," Luna came up behind me, rubbing my arms soothingly. "We'll go out tonight and worry about the things with Mr. Jones tomorrow," she kissed my cheek and squeezed my shoulders lightly. "*Tranquilla.*"

"Yeah, let's just focus on tonight," Summer got up and reached her hand out for me. "Help me with my makeup?" She tipped her head to the side, causing me to break out into a grin as I got up.

Putting my dream on hold was the right thing to do, right?

Chapter 3

Victor

"Leaving so soon already?" I walked past my assistant Ari's desk as she logged out of her computer, grabbing her water bottle and laptop.

"Well, I only have an hour and a half to get ready for tonight's grant benefit. I'm guessing you won't be in attendance as usual?" She cocked a brow, throwing her bag over her shoulder.

Ari Cho was my stubborn, level-headed assistant. She never cared how she spoke to me, always opting for snide and sarcastic remarks. Sometimes, it felt like she was my boss, but maybe that's how I liked it. Because of her, I never missed a meeting or a deadline.

"Do I even have to answer that?" I glanced over my shoulder at her, stopping when I reached my office door.

"I still don't understand why you created the grant if you're not even going to show up," she shook her head, reaching down to straighten the Spider-Man figurine on her desk before she walked down the short corridor towards the elevator. "I feel like your logic throws itself out the window," she deadpanned.

"You know I have an aversion to people who are only in it for the money," I stated matter-of-factly.

Ideally, I'd be there, but I despised being a spectacle for people who only got into business either to get rich quick or were second-generation mom-and-pop shop owners. It was easier if I stayed away and supported them silently.

"Says the multi-millionaire," she rolled her eyes.

I smirked. According to the media, I was a billionaire. The company was, not me. Unless I wanted to underpay my employees and stop running half of my non-profits, then maybe, but I don't see myself doing that anytime soon.

I started Romano Tech after I graduated college. It took me six years to build this empire—an environmental tech company designed to reduce the negative impact this planet has caused on the environment. It has been a dream of mine since I was a kid, and it's been working. Now, I was searching for my next dream. Whatever that may be.

"You know what I mean," I glanced at her.

She sucked on her cheek in thought, most likely deciding if she should say the snarky remark sitting on her tongue. "I'll see you on Monday, Victor," she responded instead, right as the elevator doors opened.

Stepping onto the floor was my best friend and COO of the company, Luis Sosa. Charismatic, witty, and brilliant was how I would describe him. He was my backbone while building this company and, honestly, during the roughest points in my life. I'd take a bullet for him.

"Ari, I'll pick you up at eight, okay?" He asked, passing her before he placed a kiss on her cheek.

She smiled, placing a hand on his upper arm before she stepped onto the elevator.

It amazed me how gentle she was with him. I always guessed it was his charm because if I did that, I'm sure she would have bitten my face off.

"Don't be late, Sosa." She flashed him a look before the doors closed, and that's when I saw the true Ari shine through.

"She loves me," he waved off, turning his attention towards me. "We're going to be scouting a date for Ari at this thing, wanna join?" He followed me into my office, sitting in the chair across from me.

"I thought I sent you there to represent the company. You're one of the people who vote for the winner. You shouldn't be scouting dates for my assistant," I squinted at him, wondering how he managed to get this position in the first place, even if I had hired him.

"Yeah, but there's something called multitasking. I find a nice girl for Ari and I vote on the winner, easy peasy. Besides, it would look good for *Romano* Tech if Victor *Romano* was actually there!" He pointed out.

I resisted the urge to roll my eyes.

The last time I went to this benefit was probably five years ago. After shaking many hands and fake smiling all night, I had enough. I decided to shut away from all publicity, only opting to appear at a few galas during the year. I never had a problem since most of the tabloids couldn't place a face to my name. That was how I wanted it.

"You're terrible at multitasking," I furrowed my brows. "Anytime you tell me a story, it takes you ten minutes to get the first sentence out because you're too busy staring at your phone," I pointed out as his face scrunched in offense. "And nothing about this grant has anything to do with me being there," I huffed as I logged into my computer.

The Renewable Energy for Businesses Grant was one of my ways of doing charitable work for others. Once a year, small businesses of all sorts were invited to this event. They spend their night talking up our executives, and then, at the end, one winner was announced. The winners received their prizes, and the company got good publicity.

"You found the grant. How could you not have anything to do with it?"

He furrowed his brows, questioning my logic like Ari did a few minutes before, but it didn't matter. I didn't need to make sense. I just didn't wanna go.

"I'm not going," I answered, hoping he got the message. He smirked, and I mentally prepared for whatever he was plotting.

"I figured you'd say that, so here's a proposal," he straightened, pressing his finger to his lips. "Show up tonight, mingle with some business owners, and chance will choose the winner. Don't show up, and I'll have no choice but to convince the other board members the grant should go to Tickle Me Sweet," he shrugged.

I immediately stopped typing.

While the name was cute and cheesy, their owner was far beyond it. A nosy, ungrateful, ignorant woman who had no business selling cupcakes for a living. I've tried to remove her from the invite list, but too many people loved her business, and the headache from the backlash was just not worth it.

"Fine, have fun finding Ari a girlfriend then," I replied, clenching my jaw. I knew the longer I thought about it, the more Luis would've added conditions to that so-called "proposal."

"Great. I'll let Ari know she owes me twenty bucks," he tapped his hand on my desk before making his way out the door.

I suddenly remembered why he's the COO.

~

I still couldn't believe Luis managed to get me to go to the grant benefit.

Yet, here I was.

I walked down the dark corridor, fixing my suit jacket as I navigated to the ballroom. It was always best to go through the back, avoid the crowd, and not have people bombard me immediately.

Fixing my cufflinks, I shook away all the negative thoughts and composed myself as I turned the corner when something hit my chest hard.

"Ow," a soft voice spoke, my heartbeat quickening as I repeated their angelic voice in my head. "I'm sorry, I didn't see you there," they took a step back, allowing me to see their silhouette. The light feeding in from the venue shone just enough to see them.

Long raven hair cascaded down their shoulders, their tan skin radiated beautifully against the pearl color of the dress they had on.

She was the most beautiful woman I've ever seen.

Breathtaking.

"Sir?" Her brows furrowed.

I blinked, not realizing I was staring.

"Are you okay?" She wrung her fingers together.

My heart tugged at her shyness as I opened my mouth to speak. "Yes, thanks for asking," I said, passing her a reassuring smile, which she returned. I felt that leap in my chest again. Clearing my throat, I ran a hand over my lapels, attempting to calm my nerves.

"Are you going to the event down in the ballroom?" She pointed in its direction.

I nodded.

"Me too," she smiled lightly.

I could catch the tiniest blush spread across her cheeks in the dim hallway.

She shifted in her step, staring down the hallway hesitantly.

"I'm assuming you're part of a business that has entered for the grant," I slipped my hands into my pockets, pacing a few steps away to give her some space.

She followed my movements, pivoting in her spot to face me.

Now, standing in front of her, I ran my gaze over her figure.

She was beautiful, the smooth silk of her dress draped over her body. Any movement of her legs made the fabric ripple elegantly.

"Yes, Hecho de Hilo. We're a small crochet shop located right outside Pilsen," she answered. The way the words rolled perfectly off her tongue when she spoke was enchanting. "What about you?" She glanced up at me. Her head reached my shoulder, but she was wearing heels, so I figured she rested at an average height.

My mind couldn't help but wonder how she would fit nestled underneath my arm.

"I'm just here to network," I shrugged.

She nodded.

"What were you doing back here anyways? Shouldn't you be brushing up against the highest executive to win the grant?" I raised a brow, causing her to laugh.

If her voice was enough to cast me under a spell, then her laugh would make me sell my soul.

Fuck me.

"I should, but I came here to think. It's much quieter," she rubbed her hands together before wrapping her arms around herself as she gazed down with a solemn look.

I felt a pang in my chest, the tug on my heart sending signals to my brain as I felt the urge to know why she was sad.

"What were you thinking about?" I leaned my back against the wall opposite her. I didn't hesitate for a moment. I needed to know what was going on.

"I don't think I should let out my feelings to a stranger," she shook her head, but she mirrored my movements, her hands clasping together in front of her and her eyes running up to meet mine again.

"Why not?" I shrugged my shoulders, tipping my head to the side. "I won't judge," I offered her a small smile, which worked as her eyes glimmered, lips cracking into a slight grin before she opened her mouth.

"I want this grant more than anything," she said, her gaze brightening even in the dark hall. "I never thought we'd be invited to enter, and now I'm not sure what I have to do to win," she sighed, covering her face with her hands.

"Why do you want this grant so much?" I furrowed my brows and licked my lips, contemplating how to help.

It was unlike anyone I have ever met to be hiding away and possibly ruining their chance of winning instead of making themselves known. To not be screaming from the rooftops about their story or telling how much they've struggled the past few years. Instead, she was holding back, like she was ashamed of what people would think or afraid she didn't belong.

I couldn't pinpoint her reason for hiding, so maybe that's why I asked.

She uncovered her face and looked at me in shock before a self-deprecating laugh slipped from her mouth.

"Why don't I? The grant includes an electric car and solar panels. Gas expenses are cut, and solar panels are expensive as fuck, but they lower the cost of electricity. If my business gets this, we could put the money we save towards something that matters," she said.

"Like what?" I studied her.

She paused for a moment, looking frustrated with herself. I was about to tell her she didn't have to answer before her eyes widened, almost like an idea appeared.

"Every year during the holidays, we host a winter drive. I spend the entirety of November crocheting all the necessities—hats, sweaters, mittens, scarves, blankets. I get some help from volunteers and other businesses in the area, and we make an entire day out of it: good food, hot chocolate, *pan dulce*. Everyone brings something. It's one of my favorite days of the year, but honestly, it bites us in the ass with all of the expenses. This year might be a struggle," she inhaled deeply, rubbing the back of her neck.

"So then, why do something that will hurt your business?" I straightened a little, inclined to know more.

She wasn't worried about her own well-being. She was worried about how she was still going to help others even though she was struggling. If I could give her the grant right now, I would. I just needed to push her a little more to get out there. As much as I wanted to tell her she didn't have to prioritize others over herself, her community obviously meant a lot.

That spoke volumes.

"Because families need it, Chicago winters are cold, and unfortunately, many families don't feel safe going to shelters. Whether it's language barriers or just because they're scared, I want to be able to bring a safe space to them," she stated.

My chest rang with that warm feeling again when our gazes met again.

"Plus, the kids love it when they get something with little designs," her face softened while she gestured with her hands.

"You're passionate about this," my lips curled upwards.

She nodded sheepishly. "My business is my life," she rested her head against the wall. "And without my community, I don't think I'd have one," she added.

"If you believe that, then your life will get better," I straightened up, pulled my hands out of my pockets, and readjusted my jacket. "Get out there and tell everyone what you told me. Good luck tonight," I said before I walked away.

She stayed behind, shouting out a "thank you" as I turned the corner, unable to wipe the grin on my face.

I'm so fucking glad I came tonight.

Chapter 4

Rosie

I walked back into the ballroom, quickly finding Luna and Summer. I shook off the jitters that were bubbling in me before and after I bumped into Mystery Man—the name I decided suited him.

I was nervous about this grant benefit as is, but my nerves only inflated when he literally walked into me. I tried to stay away from the opposite sex. If I got attached, it would be a distraction from my business and Bianca. Something I didn't need at the moment. But fuck, he was by far the hottest man I ever laid my eyes on. Seeing him in the hallway was a little challenging, but I could gather that he was tall and handsome.

He was also strong, his hard chest almost breaking my nose when I face-planted into him. The pain that spread through my face was understated, but we spoke for a bit afterward. Even after our departure, he still lingered in my mind.

My stomach fluttered at the thought of his beautiful dark eyes, those long lashes, his deep baritone voice, his perfect smile—he was gorgeous.

But he was also kind. He helped me understand what I was aiming towards with winning the grant and for my business.

It was a genuine gesture that made my face blush and eased my nerves because my thoughts were in order.

Walking back to my friends, Luna handed me a glass of champagne once I reached them. I downed it, and the bubbles eased my remaining nerves.

"Are you okay? You kinda snuck off," she rubbed my arm, Summer doing the same on the other side, concern written on both of their faces.

"I am now. I just needed to catch a breather," I reassured them.

They understood.

Having social anxiety and being required to attend social events was not a good mix. But I had my girls to support me. They're there when I have a panic attack and when I need to talk. I couldn't ask for better friends.

"We haven't been able to grab the attention of the COO, but rumor is the CEO is here," Luna whispered.

My eyes widened. "Victor Romano is here?" I stumbled out, glancing over my shoulder, trying to spot the man.

I did my research on Romano Tech, and I learned two things after reading many articles: there were no photos of him online, and his employees described him as kind. Not many CEOs had that quality.

"Should we split and try to find other executives?" Luna asked.

"No," Summer quickly pulled her back, looping our arms together. "White executives love nothing more than a small business run by three Latinas, especially if one of them is Black," she smirked, referring to herself at the end. Her father was born and raised in Guatemala, whereas her mother was born in Ethiopia and raised in the States. They met and had three children who, by their mother's words, were a handful. "We'll find whoever is available and attack," she studied the room.

"Quick, Owens just walked away from that cupcake lady," Luna pushed us in his direction.

I couldn't even compose myself until we were right before him.

"Ladies, it's a pleasure that you're here tonight. It's about time we finally invited more insightful entrepreneurs to this event," he smiled, gesturing at us with his champagne glass. "Not to cause some drama, but I'm hoping to get Rachel off the list next year," he whispered as he leaned forward, all of us stifling laughs.

It was no secret no one liked the Tickle Me Sweet lady. She was nothing but a bigoted, money-hungry bitch.

"We're really grateful we got on the list this year. You have no idea what the grant will do for us and our business," I pressed a hand to my chest. The opportunity truly meant so much. I don't think I've been this excited for anything besides the day I signed the lease for Hecho de Hilo's building.

"I'd love to stop by one of these days. My son would love your shop! He and his wife are currently expecting, and he's been so nervous that the poor boy can't do anything but crochet!" He cackled while the three of us melted at the thought.

"That's adorable. I hope he's making clothes for the baby," Summer cooed.

"If he needs something soft for the baby, we have a great selection of baby yarn," I said, making sure to insert self-promotion. That's precisely what we're here for, after all.

"Of course! Thank you for the yarn the other week. My wife can't wait to show them the blanket she made for the little bundle of joy. She was raving at how soft it was," he complimented, sending a toast our way.

Obviously, we needed to impress the board of execs, so a few weeks ago we sent each one a small gift as a way to say thanks. It was a good thing it was paying off now.

Every time my business got a good review, I exploded with pride. I knew my ideas would sell.

"Hmm, crocheting must run in the family, ever thought about picking up the hook, Mr. Owens?" Luna shot him a look, a playful grin on her face.

"Oh, dear, with my arthritis, I don't think I'll be able to," he glanced down at his hands.

"Nonsense, we have a book at the shop that tells you all about how to crochet with arthritis. There may be a little struggle, but there's no reason you shouldn't try," I shrugged, raising my brows in a suggestion. "Besides, I bet Mrs. Owens would love crochet date nights."

"I bet she would, much more than attending events like these," he pondered before he nodded towards a middle-aged woman with short-medium blonde hair and pale skin sitting at the bar, looking rather unamused.

These events do seem unamusing if you spent the entire night sitting.

"Oh, she looks bored," Summer pouted. "We shouldn't keep you much longer. Go spend time with your wife," she smiled.

He nodded, agreeing. "I will. It was nice talking to you, ladies. You certainly have my vote," he winked before walking towards the bar.

"Okay, one down, who's our next bet?" I pulled them around the cocktail table, giving another once over the venue. I began to listen as Summer listed off more people, but we narrowed it down to the people we had our best shots with. As I made my mental list, I landed eyes on Mystery Man again.

There he was talking with Luis Sosa, the COO. A smile poured over his face, and I was blinded by that award-winning grin, his teeth pearly white and his dimples poking in his cheeks. I could get a better look at him now, and he was breathtaking. His features were so chiseled and strong, his dark hair styled so elegantly with it slicked back, yet it was long enough to give some oomph. If he were a sculpture, he'd be made of the highest-quality clay, with hours spent ensuring all his perfections were captured.

I would love to sculpt him.

Just as I couldn't stop staring, he lifted the glass to his lips, his eyes locking with mine at that moment, and I froze. I did the only thing I could think of and offered him a genuine smile. One that he returned.

"Do you think he could be the CEO? He looks Italian," Luna followed my gaze.

I was glad she assumed I was scouting out and not drooling over him.

"Who knows?" Summer shrugged. "Let's go find out." She quickly grabbed my hand and pulled me along in his direction. I could not turn back without making a fool of myself, so I braced myself as we introduced ourselves.

~

Victor

"So, nine executives have already placed their vote. Myself and a few others are still scoping out our options," Luis said. "I'm partial to the crochet business. They're doing well for what their business stands for, being eco-friendly and all," he explained. "I have a feeling they might win," he hummed.

I nodded, barely paying attention after I met eyes with that woman again. After getting some intel from Luis, I found out her name.

Rosa Martinez.

It was fitting, a rose symbolizing beauty, and she was everything and more.

"Are you even listening?" Luis asked.

I looked at him. No, I was not, but I wasn't going to let him know that.

"You were talking about Rosa's business and how they're in the lead right now," I responded calmly.

He narrowed his gaze.

"I was, but I asked if you're coming on Sunday. My mom and sisters miss you, plus we're having a carne asada before the weather starts getting colder," he raised his brows, a smile flashing over his features.

"It's been a while since I've gone. I don't want to intrude," I brushed off.

The last time I went to a Sosa family dinner was in a little more than a year. I could come up with a multitude of reasons why I hadn't shown up, but knowing how witty the entire Sosa family was, my excuses couldn't cover the lies anymore.

"Look, I know you don't want any concern," he began.

I gave him a look.

"*But*, you've been putting too much of your time into Project Regenerate," he voiced. "It's been a year, and we're making progress. Don't you think it's time to cut back and let the deal work itself out?" He explained.

Project Regenerate was the stepping stone to bring Romano Tech to the top in the world. I hope to start its year-long production by the end of the year. There will be an entire campus dedicated to producing and curating solutions that will fight to end climate change. It'll bring the best minds from around the world to one place. It's a plan I've set my heart on to give the planet one last chance to reverse the harm we caused it.

Though, it'd be selfish not to admit I've neglected the people who cared and loved me. I didn't think I was obvious about it.

"Why didn't you ever say anything?" I took a sip of my drink.

"Because you're probably the most stubborn person I've ever met. You never do things people tell you to do even if it's good for you," he chuckled when I rolled my eyes. "Anyway, you need a refresher. That one day you take off every year isn't cutting it. Being with family will do you good. You know your seat will always be waiting," he patted my shoulder and offered a small smile.

"Luis Sosa, always offering a heartfelt thought after an insult," I placed my glass down, sending him a look.

"Victor Romano, never knowing when to say thank you," he retorted.

"Thank you," I said, lacking any emotion.

Luis opened his mouth to make another remark but wasn't given the chance as a light-hearted voice interrupted.

"Mr. Sosa, good to see you again," a young woman with a curly brown afro wearing a dark red dress came into view, very excited to see the two of us. Two women were beside her; one had shorter, wavy hair, and she was wearing a green dress. The other, well, it finally connected once I met her gaze.

It was Rosa.

Luis had been so distracting that I wasn't even given the chance to be blessed at the sight of her walking towards me, but at least she was here right now.

"The Hecho de Hilo team, are you enjoying your evening?" Luis jumped back into his COO voice, booming power and respect in one.

"This night has been amazing," Rosa said, taking the lead. All attention was drawn to her, and there was no doubt that she was the owner just by how she held herself. "Thank you again for this opportunity," she grinned at Luis, her gaze meeting mine quickly before she turned away, her cheeks changing to a hint of pink.

"It's always our mission to bring more opportunities to small businesses, but we really wouldn't be here tonight if it weren't for our CEO," he slapped my back hard, causing my muscles to tense.

My plan tonight wasn't to be outed by my own best friend as CEO. And based on the look on Rosa's face, my hopes for whatever we could have came crumbling down.

"You're Victor Romano," her eyes were wide, her hands gesturing towards me. "It's an honor to meet you. Thank you so much for giving our business a chance to grow," she reached her hand out.

I relaxed slightly as I felt my mouth curve upward. "After hearing how passionate you are about your business, this is more than just chance," I said as I shook her hand, goosebumps rushing up my arm and back at her touch.

Her skin was soft, and our hands molded perfectly against each other. She licked her lips, suppressing a smile as she pulled away. Her hand reached up to tuck a loose strand of hair as she struggled to meet my gaze again, darting between the floor and the centerpiece. But after a short pause, her face was beaming again, a smile worthy of everything.

"Thank you. I'm hoping tonight you and the rest of the board are able to see how hard we work," she pulled her lip between her teeth.

I swallowed. My gaze focused on her mouth and the way her plump lips were glazed with a gloss I was desperate to taste. The dazzling sheen, clearly visible under the chandelier light, made it even more tempting. The more I stared at her, the more beautiful I found her.

"We don't want to keep you. We're sure you have many other businesses to talk to, so thanks again," she linked her arms with her two friends before we could stop them.

I shared a look with Luis, and he just shrugged.

"They're just being cordial," he summarized before walking to the bar.

I shortly followed him, the owner of Tickle Me Sweet finding us. If only she could find it in herself to be cordial. I looked around the banquet hall before I found Rosa again. I caught her staring at me before she glanced away, her two friends distracted as they were talking to another board member. I laughed to myself, finding her shyness amusing.

She was cute.

The rest of the night, Rosa and I passed glances at each other. Sometimes, I caught her, or she would catch me, but during this excruciating night of listening to owners talk up their business in half-assed ways, those secret moments created a game between us.

Throughout the night, instead of her turning away in embarrassment, I found Rosa holding my stare for a few beats before glancing away, a shy smile adorning her features.

Anticipation filled me the closer it came to announcing the winner. With the votes counted and the winner right in Luis's hand, I asked him who it was. Whispering the winner in my ear, I stared at the envelope, and before I could even second-guess, I ripped it from his grip, making my way to the stage. My presence made the audience whisper in shock, although I couldn't find a shit to give about it.

After listing off the most formal nonsense about coming here and thanking the board and businesses, I finally was able to get to what everyone was here for. To what I was excited to announce.

"It would be my pleasure to announce the winner of this year's grant," I paused dramatically, the audience growing with anticipation. "Rosa Martinez, owner and founder of Hecho de Hilo," I announced, the crowd clapping in congratulations.

I watched from up on the stage as her friends had to coax her to move. The one in the green dress appeared more aggressive when she gave her a slight shove. I walked over to the stairs and met Rosa to help her onto the stage without falling in her heels. The same electric sparks shocked me across my body when our hands met again.

She held her dress in one hand and let go of mine as she raised her hand to cover her mouth in shock, staring at what awaited her behind me. At that moment, many award presenters came out from behind the curtain.

Two carried out a giant check for twenty-thousand dollars, another held the keys to our newest electric car with the car spinning on one of those cool displays, and a lovely glass award to tie everything together.

I saw her hands shake when they handed her the award. Her lips pressed together as she tried to suppress the happy tears. I stayed in the back while another presenter guided her to the microphone.

"I've dreamed of something like this," she began, her voice cracking. "This is the break that I've been working towards," she ran her hand over the plaque. "As small businesses, we struggle, we fight, we dream. Some days, we want to question why we still struggle if we work hard," she hummed, licking her lips. "But then you look and remember why we still choose to endure that pain—*hope*. We never seem to run out of hope. And when people like the board at Romano Tech offer us an opportunity, we realize there's still enough. Enough to keep fighting for our dreams. Thank you, Romano Tech. Thank you, Luna and Summer. Thank you, Bianca. And thank you to all the customers and supporters of Hecho de Hilo," she said, ending her acceptance speech with the crowd cheering.

I couldn't stop the smile from forming as I clapped along.

She was guided behind the stage where the following paperwork process began. As she walked past, she met my gaze and mouthed "thank you."

I nodded and wished I could tell her she had nothing to thank me for. This was all her.

I threw my keys on the table by the door, shrugged off my clothes, tired from the night, and utterly relieved Rosa's business won the grant. Another year without Tickle Me Sweet winning meant it'd be a great year.

I went through my night routine before I made my way to my office to check on any unseen messages from the day. I knew how bad it was to look at technology before bed, but nothing was more comforting than knowing everything was completed.

Clicking on my screen, I opened my inbox, finding only one email awaiting me.

To: Victor Romano
From: Miles Jones (Plains Acres)

Good afternoon, Mr. Romano! I hope you're doing well! I'm confirming our meeting next week and checking in to ensure I have the most recent copy of the contract. I'm looking forward to discussing the future of Plains Acres with you!

Sincerely,
Miles

I took a deep breath.

I thought back to Luis's words about me being too tied up with Project Regenerate, but staring at the email in front of me only confirmed that what I've been doing has been right all along. I'm one step closer to making this project a reality.

Buying Plains Acres was the last piece I needed.

Two thousand acres of land would be turned into the base campus for Project Regenerate. Everything will operate right in the state exactly as I've always imagined it.

Leaning back in my chair with a satisfied grin, I momentarily glanced at a photo on my desk. My heart melted at the sight of my mom.

It was me and her, flour-dusted everywhere on the counter, our clothes, and our faces. I was five in that photo. Her smile radiated with life and love, and at the time, mine did the same. She was helping me roll out the pasta dough we had made. It was my favorite memory.

Ten years since she's been gone. A bittersweet taste was left in my mouth, knowing she'd be proud of me, yet I wish she were here to witness this herself. It didn't hold any better with the knowledge that he could. If he wanted to be here, he could.

But he made a choice not too long ago.

I've learned to live with that choice. Now, I'm living my best life without him. The email in front of me only proved that.

Chapter 5

Rosie

Even after a full night of celebration, I still woke up in denial. From meeting Victor Romano and winning such whirlwind prizes—the memories lumped together in my head, my brain attempting to process everything. I don't think I began to go through what had happened until this morning.

Right after I was presented the award, I was whisked away to sign paperwork finalizing my ownership of everything. Then Luna and Summer took me out to eat at my favorite restaurant. We felt fancy walking in our black-tie attire compared to most clientele dressed in sweats or pajamas, but the food was delicious. After dropping Summer off at her house, Luna and I crashed.

It was one of the best sleeps I had.

This morning, news swarmed around, and it was nice to wake up to a handful of heartfelt messages from everyone before I got ready for work to open the shop.

Señora Rivera was there waiting for me with a cake like she promised. On top of a few customers in a line. Nothing unusual for a Sunday morning, but it didn't stop me from feeling so good. Everyone told me I deserved to win and that all my hard work had paid off. But deep down, I felt like I still had a few steps until I reached that point.

Once the morning rush settled, I could leave Luna and Summer to it while I took my lunch. That's when my phone rang, and I was pushed through to my sister.

"Guess what?" I grinned.

"You got the grant?!" Bianca shouted into the phone in disbelief.

I laughed.

Her words of congratulations piled all together in one swoop.

"How did it go?"

"The board members loved my ambition and passion," I inhaled, recalling the ones who told me themselves last night. "I won the majority vote, and we're getting everything delivered today!" I squealed, unable to contain my excitement.

While it was great that I could share this moment with her, it didn't feel as monumental as it should without her physically being here. It was hard not to let guilt consume me just for celebrating an accomplishment.

You should feel bad. It's your fault she's in there anyway.

"I swear, the moment I get out of this hell, we're going on a road trip in your brand-new electric car," she said.

A smile appeared on my lips as I pushed my guilt to the back of my head. "The moment you get out, I'm throwing you a huge party and cooking all of your favorite foods," I grew excited at the thought.

"I've been adding things to my list," she began. I could picture her twirling the phone cord around her finger, similar to how she twirled her hair. "One of the girls was talking about seeing Niagara Falls on her honeymoon. I'd like to go there. It's also close to New York City so maybe we could do both in one trip," she suggested. "Though you know I really want to spend our first Christmas together in New York City, so we'll figure it out," she rambled.

I stifled a laugh. "I could never forget, you've been wanting to go since before I was born," I hummed, that guilt plaguing me again. "I know you want to do all of these things, Bee, but I don't want you to have high expectations when you come home. It's no prison, but I'm not living in a penthouse overlooking Lake Michigan either," I chewed on my lip, not wanting her to lose hope on her living her life once she comes out, but I didn't want to give her unrealistic expectations either.

She sighed. "*Mira Rosita*," she sucked in a breath. "You're my little sister who's been busting her ass for as long as I can remember. My only expectation when I get out of here is for you to be there. We can worry about spending Christmas in New York later," she reassured. "For once, can I be the big sister in this relationship?" She asked, her tone lightening.

"You've always been," I pressed my lips together in a small smile.

"*Cuidate*, okay?"

"You too," I inhaled. "I'll see you in two weeks," I said before I hung up. I shoved my phone back into my pocket before I directed my attention to my computer.

A spreadsheet with all the shop's current expenses was opened on the screen. Another tab had all the expected costs for opening my ceramics shop.

Before Bianca called me, I gathered all the finances to calculate the remaining amount after expenses in case Mr. Jones decided to sell the farm. Even if it was a predicted amount, it was clear that having the Winter Drive would push us under more in the following year due to the cost of materials (which is a lot when you're supplying local eco-friendly alpaca wool), closing the store for an entire day, and closing early the day before to clean up and clear out space.

Little things like that add up quickly for a small business.

I was about to give myself a break from looking at spreadsheets until I paused, remembering I needed to start on that presentation for Mr. Jones. I massaged between my brows before I sat back in the chair. Worry rang through me, but I shook the feeling out, pinching the bridge of my nose. I didn't have time for that right now. I needed to stay calm.

Think positive.

If all goes well with Mr. Jones and my presentation moves him so much he decides to keep the farm, then I'll be able to use the money from the grant and my savings to finally put a deposit down on the building and the one next door. I could save Hecho de Hilo and have enough to start bringing Ceramicá de la Vida to life.

I sat down in the desk chair, opening a new tab. The last time I made a presentation was for my AP Seminar class. I still remember my eight-minute speech on why we should save the bees. It was some of my greatest work. If only I could replicate: "Why You Should Save The Bees." I chewed on my lip, typing the same title on the first slide, figuring it could work.

Why You Should Save Hecho de Hilo:
- *Ethically and locally sourced*
- *Latina owned*
- *Community-based*

I sat back, satisfied. All I needed to do was create a slideshow presentation and an in-depth argument that my business was worth not selling the farm.

A knock disrupted me, and I glanced up to find Luna standing in the doorway.

"Was wondering where you were," she smiled, walking over to see what I was working on, but I closed the window.

Even though she knew what was at stake, I didn't want her to stress about it as much as I did. This was my fight to win.

"Whatcha doin'?"

"Just running through some inventory for Mr. Jones. He wanted to make sure he wouldn't run short," I lied, but she bought it. "Is everything fine?" I asked.

"They're here to install the solar panels, but they need the key to the roof," she pointed up. I nodded, reaching for the carabiner clasped around my belt loop. "Also, Victor Romano is here," she said while I handed her the key.

The key almost fell out of my hands from shock. "What?! Why?!" My heart rate increased. I was nowhere near prepared to meet with the CEO again. I unconsciously brushed my fingers through my hair, hoping it looked presentable. "Why did I wear this today?" I looked down at my outfit, an orange cardigan I crocheted worn over a white tank top and jeans.

Atrocious.

"Rosie, stop," Luna placed her hand on my shoulder. "You look hot as hell, the tank top makes your boobs look great, and the cardigan will only show him how much you love the craft," she reassured me.

I took a deep breath, nodding. "You're right," I wiped my hands on my thighs. "But what do I do? Do I give him a tour or something?" I stood up.

She looped her arm around my shoulders, rolling her eyes. "Rosie, you've talked to many higher-ups before and wooed them over. If impressing rich white men was a career, you'd be a millionaire. So go," she grabbed my arms and pushed me out of the office.

"But," I inhaled. "He's different," I leaned against her to prevent her from pushing me even further. "He's not egotistical or arrogant. He seems like a CEO who cares," I said as I played with my nails.

I wanted to impress him. Clearly, my business meant something to him if he was here, and I wanted to show him that winning the grant won't go to waste. And maybe I could get to know him better, seeing as I did all the talking last night.

"That's even better because if he cares, then he'll see just how much you care," she turned me around to look me in the eye. "Remember how you said talking to him last night was so easy?" She raised a brow.

I glanced down.

I told the girls about how I had a run-in with Victor. The imposter syndrome in me kept telling me the only reason we won was because I talked to him first. But they both promised it wasn't the case. He didn't vote that night, but he did present the award.

"Stop telling yourself he lied about the win. If he did and your name wasn't on the card, I'm sure those board members would've trampled him onstage. There's nothing they hate more than an overpowered CEO," she smirked.

I'm not even surprised she knew what I was thinking about.

"Okay, thanks, Luna." I gave her a quick hug before turning around to walk out the door.

I made my way through the small aisles while I heard Luna shout to the installers to follow her upstairs. I waited until they cleared when I made my way to the front.

And there he was.

He stood beside the counter talking to Summer and a customer. Summer was multitasking, engaging in conversation while ringing up the customer's yarn. Once I approached, the customer was gone, and Victor's gaze reached up to meet mine.

"Mr. Romano, it's so good to see you again. I knew the installers were coming today, but I'm surprised you're here," I offered a kind smile, linking my hands in front of me.

"Victor is just fine," he raised his hand and returned the smile. "Besides, I always like to visit the business that won the grant to make sure the installation process runs smoothly," he explained. I couldn't help but feel that he wasn't speaking the truth, but it amused me that he would make such a silly lie.

"Well, how about I give you a tour in the meantime?" I gestured around me.

His eyes brightened. "I'd like that."

Chapter 6

Victor

For once, I was actually pleased to make my mandatory appearance at the winning business, mainly because I got to see Rosa again. Usually, I would show up, congratulate them on the grant, and ask them a few questions about their journeys as owners. I was proud to see their business evolve, even if I'd rather watch it from the sidelines.

With Rosa, though, I wanted to be front and center.

She offered to give me a tour of the small yarn shop. I surprised myself with how happy I was to be shown around.

So she began.

"Welcome to Hecho de Hilo. That is the proper name; we don't translate it into English," she warned, earning a smile from me. She walked backward, guiding me along as she gestured around her. "We're a small business owned and founded by me, and we specialize in all things crochet," she said, her eyes gleaming. "Here, you can find anything and everything to do with crochet," she rested her elbow on one of the shelves, pointing to a selection of books. "New to crochet? At our establishment, we offer multiple books guiding you through beginner tutorials, basics, and how-tos," her voice was strong, *elevated*.

I grabbed one of the books and ran my fingers over the cover, noticing the attention to detail.

"If you're an expert and need some inspiration, you can select from our intermediate and advanced ideas books for more. Our books range from the beginning to the end of crocheting, written by our lovely second-in-command, Luna, and illustrated by our wonderful assistant manager, Summer," she pointed to the two girls behind the counter who waved rather enthusiastically at me. "You can check out physical copies, but e-books are also available online," she smiled, tipping her head to the side.

I acknowledged the two girls before flipping through the book I held in my hand, realizing how much talent and thought was put into this book. It was good to know she had a wonderful team and friend group as support.

"Are these books made by hand?" I lifted my gaze, carefully placing it back in its place. There seemed only to be one or two copies of each. While they looked like regular old books, they had a handmade feel to them.

"Yes, the bookstore owner we partnered with was kind enough to create the books for us," she explained, grabbing a book off the shelf and opening to a page with an embossing in the corner, showing it to me. "Only a few customers actually check them out, but we have them just in case," she closed the book, placing it back.

"It's a smart choice to check them out, reducing waste compared to printing multiple copies," I stated. "Most businesses take the easy way out. It takes an inquisitive mind to find a solution," I smirked, glancing at her.

She faltered, her cheeks tinting pink as she tucked a strand of hair behind her ear and played with the sleeve of her cardigan. "It takes one to know one," she hummed.

My lips curved upward.

Her smile grew wider, and the atmosphere shifted, a magnetizing pull that had me following her even when she didn't tell me to.

"Now, onto the best part," the energy in her voice remained, and the warmth on her cheeks faded away. "Our yarn is made from the softest alpacas you can ever find in Illinois," she grinned, yanking a light blue yarn off the shelf. "Right now, our best seller is our new periwinkle color, *Amor y Fe*. It's selling like crazy no matter the yarn size," she handed it to me.

The softness of it was unreal. It felt like a cloud in the palm of my hands while also feeling like a mother's hug. It brought back joyful memories that placed a smile on my face.

Her voice pulled my attention back to her, the soft, angelic tone entrancing me. "Speaking of, we offer a huge selection of yarn, from making blankets and clothes, or if you even dabble in amigurumi," she moved alongside the aisle, referring to different kinds of yarn labeled in English and Spanish.

I furrowed my brows at the last word. She seemed to find my look rather amusing before she elaborated.

"It's making stuffed animals out of yarn, originated from Japan," she stated, running a hand over her chin. "It's a bit trickier, but it's totally worth it in the end because they're adorable!" She beamed, a blush spreading across her cheeks.

I stared at her eyes, noting the dark brown of her irises. The sunlight streaming through the windows made them gleam a striking hazel. It felt like drowning in an abyss. It was a perfect way to describe how her eyes lit up as she spoke, and my heart exploded with a new sense of passion— something that made me feel complete.

"Your eyes light up anytime you talk about your business," I voiced, smiling brightly. "It's cute as much as it's charming."

She stopped in her tracks, brows raising in shock before she let out a light laugh. "Thank you," she ran her fingers through her hair. "Is it part of your job to compliment the owner?" She cocked a brow, a teasing smirk on her face.

"No, just something I noticed," I shrugged, shoving my hands into my pockets, licking my lips as I grinned.

"I'll keep that in mind then," she nodded, rubbing her hands together before backing into the next aisle. "We keep all crochet tools in the back, making it easier for stocking," she gestured at the wall while shuffling on her feet, pulling down the sleeves of her cardigan, and fixing her hair.

She was flustered.

"All materials are recyclable; no plastic is used," she explained, the corners of her mouth curving upward at me. After a beat, she nodded towards the back of the shop, the jangle of her charm bracelet sounding as she moved. "Lastly, over here is our workshop. Not only do we sell materials for you to crochet, but we also offer custom pieces to be commissioned, usually made by me," she pressed her hands to herself.

It was a small section of the rest of the store with a big workbench in the middle and shelves of different yarns stacked on top of one another behind it. On the opposite wall was a chalkboard with a flow chart of how to order a commission. The adjacent wall was a collage of photos and art, ranging from her and the other girls posing with some small children and, whom I assume were their parents, to different fictional characters.

She stepped closer than expected next to me as we began browsing through the photos, her sweet floral scent wonderfully invading my nose again.

Raspberries and jasmine.

"This is our wall of memories. Some are drawings from children who want their dream stuffed animal to come true. Others are from the Winter Drive and our crochet classes." She pointed at each photo, her arm brushing against my shoulder as she reached forward accidentally.

It was subtle, but the contact made time slow down.

"Which we also offer on Tuesdays and Thursdays," she trailed, eyes glancing up at me. "In both English and Spanish," she added, a sheepish smile appearing on her features.

Even noticing the proximity, neither of us moved.

"You know your way around adapting your business. I'm impressed," I inhaled, gazing down at her.

From the books to the yarn to representing and putting her community first. There wasn't one thing she missed.

It caused that feeling to open in my chest. Which was something I hadn't felt in a while. The warmth, the comfort, the security…I was catching feelings, and nothing could be done to stop it.

"Well, it wasn't easy, but I love it," she said. "Crocheting is timeless in a sense. You ask someone, and they share stories about their grandmother crocheting their Christmas sweaters. Now, the younger generation can enjoy the craft, too. Whether it's through making your loved ones a gift or sharing your talents online," she pushed the front pieces of hair out of her face.

It was captivating how they fell, framing her features perfectly.

She looked so effortless.

"It's the impact you make that makes it all worth it," I said, running my gaze down from her hair to her eyes, stopping at her lips momentarily.

She blushed, breaking out into a grin.

"Yeah, it's the people that make the biggest difference, in my opinion," she pressed her hands together. "Like Señora Rivera," she pointed to a lady in a photo, posed next to a girl who looked like a young spitting image of her. "She spent her entire life working at a bread factory to make ends meet for her family. Now retired, she loves providing for them in another way—crocheting," she rolled her lips together before forming a smile. "That's her granddaughter. She loves sweaters and cardigans."

In the photo, the granddaughter wore a blue sweater with strawberries.

"She learned how to make that pattern in one of our classes. I think Lucia has like ten of them," she laughed. "But my point is that customers like her are why Hecho de Hilo can exist. She knows what we stand for and knows we want to help our community. Without her and others, we'd just be any other business," she shrugged.

"I can see why you won the grant, Rosa. No one but you deserved it," I complimented.

She blushed even more. "I'm sure you had something to do with it since I was the only business to talk to you," she raised a brow. "I still can't believe I didn't recognize you," she mumbled more to herself, but I still caught it.

I'm glad she didn't know who I was when we first met. The first impression she had of me was the stranger in the hallway. Not the CEO, Victor Romano. She was raw in her emotions and her treatment towards me. I was able to get to know her for who she truly was and what she stood for. Something I can't seem to get these days. I will always respect her for it.

"Actually, I had nothing to do with it," I stated. "Because I'm the CEO, the execs and I agreed I would have no part in voting. The decision was theirs alone," I explained.

Her eyes widened.

"Don't doubt yourself. Hecho de Hilo is an impressive business. Romano Tech is grateful to be servicing you. As am I," I stated.

"It's something I still can't believe," she shook her head, glancing down. "Never in my life did I think I'd win a grant that would give me a boost," she sucked in a breath. "Thank you, Victor," she looked at me appreciatively.

"It's nothing," I shook my head. "If anything goes wrong with the panels or the car, just call the office, and we'll get everything fixed," I stated, both of us making our way to the front.

She blushed. "Bye, Victor, and thanks again," she stopped right before the door as I opened it.

The bell above the entrance rang in my ears as I waved goodbye. As I walked to my car, the only thought in my head was wishing one of the panels broke just so I would have a reason to come and see her again.

Chapter 7

Rosie

Before my mother unveiled the narcissist she was, she taught me one thing—*das gracias cocinando comida*. You give thanks by cooking food. From sending a dish to our neighbors after babysitting us or bringing it along to an event, she considered it rude if we didn't show our appreciation.

So here I was, waiting in Romano Tech's lobby to show my appreciation for Victor a few days after the solar panels had been installed. And partially because I wanted to see him again. I was drawn to him, deeper than a level of attraction or even admiration from a business perspective.

He called me *cute*, for crying out loud.

Even if it was mindless flirtation, I knew I needed to investigate.

"Miss Martinez, Mr. Romano's assistant will be here shortly to escort you to his office," the receptionist hung up the phone as they spoke to me, gaining my attention before I thanked them. Then the elevator doors opened, a ding sounding through the lobby.

"Rosa Martinez?" A young Asian woman with straight, long black hair greeted me. Her sharp, blush-colored pantsuit radiated elegance and professionalism, but her kind smile was welcoming. "I'm Ari Cho, Mr. Romano's assistant," she said as she walked towards me and offered a hand.

"It's a pleasure to meet you," I smiled, shaking her hand. Her grip was firm enough to make me wonder if her smile was genuine or just for show.

"Please follow me," she walked me over to the elevator. "Mr. Romano just left a meeting, so he will be here soon. He's been notified of your presence and insisted I bring you to the office myself," she explained.

I nodded, watching the doors close.

"Why would he go through all that trouble for me?" I thought out loud.

Ari chuckled like it was a stupid question.

"Mr. Romano tends to take good care of his business partners. He expects nothing but the best," she hummed. She stood straight with her hands folded neatly in front of her, reminding me to fix my posture.

"That's nice of him, but I'm only here to thank him for the grant. It's not often that you receive an electric car as a prize," I trailed off. "Or twenty thousand dollars and solar panels for your business," I muttered.

The luxury of the prize only showed how loaded this company was with all the power it held to give away such lucrative items. It was so much to wrap my head around.

"No, but it's all part of it. You work hard for your business, and Mr. Romano returns it by making your life a little easier," she said, turning to face me slightly. "I've read your profile. I know everything about you, Miss Martinez. Let me tell you this grant is very deserving of you," she complimented.

My brows raised in shock, but they relaxed as a heat spread across my face when I thought back to his words.

"Mr. Romano did heavily imply it yesterday," I blew out a breath, feeling that self-doubt set in again. "But it's nice to hear it from you," I pressed my lips together with a smile. "Unless he told you to say that," I second-guessed again.

"You're funny," she hummed a laugh.

I responded with a shy smile as the doors opened, and we walked onto a spacious floor.

"You can wait here. Would you like to have anything to drink?" She gestured towards a section of plush sofas while she asked.

I respectfully declined her offer, but part of me wished I had said yes just to see what kind of beverages this place offers.

The entire wall to my right was full of floor-to-ceiling windows with an amazing view overlooking the northern part of Lake Michigan. Navy Pier could be seen from the seating area. The ceilings were high, and the vents and ducts were exposed, yet the office still had a sophisticated look. There were numerous meeting rooms with glass walls, except half of the glass had fancy privacy screens, making them look foggy. In the middle of the floor were cubicles, again, not the dull, I'm-trapped-in-a-dead-end-job kind, but the modern ones built with wood and the same foggy technology on the glass. The entire space screamed "renewable tech." It was sleek, with warmth incorporated.

"Rosa, welcome to Romano Tech," a familiar voice greeted me, and I turned around to see Victor. "I see you're taking it all in," he smiled, standing before me with his hands shoved into his pockets.

He wore a navy blue suit with a white button-down underneath that had the first button undone. He shouldn't be this hot, but he was.

I had to take two deep breaths to cool myself down.

"Hi, Victor. It's an amazing place. I've never been in an office setting before," I explained, tucking a strand of hair behind my ear. "It's very bright in here," I grinned, glancing up at the lights.

"Bright environment for bright minds," he shrugged. "Why don't you come to my office?" He nodded in the direction before I smiled, falling into step beside him.

We walked down a small corridor, which reminded me of the night we met. This time, I could see his handsome face, which only added to the butterflies in my stomach.

"I bet your employees love working here; it's so nice," I said, admiring the place, trying to distract my mind from his attractiveness. I noticed his employees at work and wondered what they were doing. Were they devising a plan to run the country on green energy or finding a way to stop all plastic production?

"I'm sure they enjoy it as much as any other employee," his lips tipped into a small smile.

I agreed on some level. Sometimes, work was work.

"After you," he held the door to his office open. My mouth dropped open when I stepped inside.

There were white walls with fancy abstract art hung on them, a spacious lounge section with a black leather couch, two grayish-blue suede loveseats, and a TV mounted on the wall, plus another section with bookshelves lining the wall. The view was impeccable, completely taking over the rest of it once your eyes laid upon it. The sun radiated through, lighting up the desk that sat perfectly centered.

"You definitely have taste," I sucked in a breath, walking over to the window to take a look at the view.

The cars driving along the street looked like ants and you couldn't even make out the people walking on the sidewalks. Everything was so tiny up here.

"Unless this was the work of an interior designer," I glanced over my shoulder.

"I made some requests. They put it together, though," he answered, smiling shyly. "So, what do I owe the pleasure?" He shut the door behind him.

I felt something in me stir.

The action caused my lower belly to flutter. The possibility of what could happen between us in his office. So secretive, so forbidden, so *hot*.

"I brought you a gift as a way of saying thanks," I pushed those tainted thoughts to the back of my head and placed the bag on his desk. "It's a dish I made. It's pork in red sauce with rice and beans. I hope you like it. I just wanted to bring this up after everything you've done for me and my business," I shrugged, the heat returning to my cheeks. "I know it's a stretch, but I enjoy cooking for others as a way of saying thanks," I explained, hoping I didn't look crazy for bringing him a home-cooked meal.

"You didn't have to, but it smells delicious. Thank you," he grinned, and his eyes were longing. "I haven't had someone cook for me in a long time."

I couldn't help but feel my heart pause—what did he mean by "someone"? Could it have been his ex? No, I was overthinking; he could be talking about a relative or a friend. It wasn't any of my business, even if it was an ex.

Calm down, Rosie.

"I'm happy to have done this then. Nothing's better than someone making food for you," I smiled as I rubbed my hands against my jeans.

"Yeah, nothing beats that," he hummed, a pause engulfing us.

I rolled my lips together in thought. I didn't want to go, and I wasn't sure if he was being polite by not saying anything, but then he opened his mouth to speak.

"How are the upgrades doing?" He asked.

I relaxed, glad to know he wanted to keep the conversation going. "Great! Everything is running smoothly, and I estimated our expenses for the following year, so I'm hopeful we will save a lot," I nodded. "It's amazing what your company is doing for small businesses alike. I hope to work with you again one day," I grinned, ignoring the trickle of doubt in my mind.

"It's a pleasure doing business with you, Rosa," he stretched out his hand.

I shook it before gazing up at him. He was warm, but the feeling he caused in me was heated. "Please, call me Rosie," I swallowed the shift in my stomach, correcting him.

His gaze softened, the corner of his lip curved up. "Rosie," he repeated.

I felt my heart skip a beat, hearing him say my name. I slowly pulled my hand away, but his warmth lingered. My thumb rubbed against my palm in an attempt to engrain his touch into my skin.

"I hope to see you again," he said, shoving his hands into his pockets.

I smiled at him before I turned and walked out of his office. Making it back into the elevator, I let out a heavy breath at the intensity that hit me.

One touch from him, and he was already convincing me to stay. To throw everything I've said about not wanting a relationship and only focusing on my business and my sister—but fuck he was making it hard.

I leaned against the wall, contemplating that even if I wanted to give in to my feelings for Victor, it wasn't the right time.

~

Victor

I watched as Rosie left my office. A warm feeling spread across my chest.

She was sweet to bring a meal as a way of saying thanks.

I smiled to myself before my phone began to ring. Confused about who could be calling at this hour, I read the contact, my brows raising in suspicion before I answered.

"Mr. Jones, I wasn't expecting a call from you so soon. How are you?" I sat back in my chair.

"Mr. Romano, I'm doing well."

"I hope you're calling because you decided to sell your farm to Romano Tech," I raised a brow, the excitement bubbling in my stomach at the thought.

"You crack me up, Victor!" He cackled.

I furrowed my brows, unsure how I was being funny.

"I'm only calling because I need to postpone our lunch for tomorrow," he said. "My niece is flying in earlier than expected, so I've got to pick her up at the airport. You understand, family always comes first," he sighed.

I stared at the photo on my desk, a heavy weight on my chest. "No need to explain, Miles, I understand. I'll forward you to Ari. She'll have everything in order," I said before redirecting the call.

Sitting back in my chair, the guilt couldn't be hidden. An earlier flight made him put a pin in an eighteen-million-dollar deal, whereas I would've done the opposite. And I have.

I missed birthdays, dinners, recitals, competitions, and graduations— all because I got roped up in work.

Maybe Luis was right.

I frowned at his face in the photo, knowing he definitely was.

The picture was taken at Luis's sister, Isabella's, quinceañera last year.

The last event I attended.

It was an emotional day. Luis cried when he saw Isa in her poofy red dress for the first time, and his mom scolded him about staining the fabric with his tears. Isabella spilled that her older sister hooked up with the older brother of one of the *chambelanes*—a secret I haven't told anyone—and watching Isa celebrate womanhood was heartfelt.

The memory put a smile on my face.

I lifted my gaze, staring at the bag of food Rosie had brought me. I glanced at my watch and figured I could take my lunch now. I reached for it and realized it was still warm. Taking off the aluminum, I felt my heart skip a beat when I gazed at the food.

Luis's mom used to make this all the time. It was one of my favorite meals and a comfort, especially when I didn't have time to cook.

Knowing I couldn't neglect my loved ones any longer, I dropped the foil and sighed, reaching for my phone. A few rings later, Luis picked up.

"Is that invitation still open for Sunday?" I asked.

He paused. "Of course, you know you don't have to ask. My mom and sisters are gonna be thrilled to have you there again," he chuckled.

I felt my lips curl. It would be good to see the people I considered my family again.

~

I listened to my car beep as it locked, a few bags of chips in my hand. I made my way up the walkway and stared at the vast craftsman-style house.

When Luis got the position of COO, he was able to buy this house so that his family could live in it. He moved them all into a wealthy suburb in the southwest part of the Chicagoland area, something he was proud to do after all the hard work his parents did.

"Nervous?" Luis came up behind me.

I shrugged. "Haven't been here in a year, don't know how the girls will react," I inhaled before he opened the door.

"Well, you kinda deserve it, so go," he gestured.

I gave him a look before I went into the house.

It was surprisingly quiet as I made my way inside. The grand entrance was clean as ever, and I stared up at the staircase when the sound of footsteps reached my ears. I set the bags down, knowing who it was.

"Victor! I had a feeling you were coming today!" A little girl with tan skin and black hair came rushing down, immediately jumping towards me before I caught her.

"Woah, Elena, you've gotten so big!" I grinned, holding her up in the air as she squealed. "How long was I gone?" I set her back down.

She counted on her fingers, a thoughtful look on her face before she stopped to stare at me. "An entire year, Victor!" She placed her hands on her hips for emphasis.

I laughed, kneeling so we were at eye level. "I know, but the important thing is that I'm back," I pinched her cheek. "Will you forgive me?" I softened my gaze, hoping she would accept my apology.

"Mhmm, maybe, ask me again in an hour," she shrugged before walking away.

"She's the smallest, but she's so feisty," Luis spoke up from behind me, carrying bags in his hands.

I agreed.

"C'mon, the rest of the girls are gonna be thrilled you're here," he nodded toward the backyard, where I could smell the meat cooking.

"Luis, *tráeme la salsa y el guacamole*," Alma said with her back turned to us, not recognizing my presence yet.

Alma was the matriarch of the Sosa family. Tough, loyal, and generous, she was the closest thing I had to a mom. She was also my mom's friend. Their friendship grew when Luis and I befriended each other when we were nine.

"*Ay, mama*, I'm busy right now. Ask Victor to do it," he scoffed.

Her ears perked before she even registered what he had said.

"*¿Qué dijiste? No me vas a hablar así*," she snapped the tongs together and turned to face him before her eyes widened in shock to see me. "Victor! *¡Mijito!*" She threw her hands in the air before she quickly approached me with a hug. "It's been too long! Where the hell have you been?" She pulled away and shoved my chest.

I winced from the impact, but the joy I felt from being here diluted it. "I'm sorry, but I've been distracted with work. Thankfully, I finally realized how important these gatherings are to me," I smiled, holding her hand in mine.

"Oh my goodness," she gasped, covering her mouth with her free one.

I furrowed my brows.

"You've met someone," she said.

My eyes widened. I was going to dismiss any assumptions, but I couldn't open my mouth before Luis could shut his.

"Her name is Rosie. I've never seen him smile more in his entire life than in the past week, Ma," he grinned.

Alma audibly melted.

"Luis," I gritted, shooting him a look.

"It's okay, *mijito*, I know being in love for the first time can be scary," she patted my chest.

I shook my head. "No, I'm not in love with her. We met a week and a half ago," I shoved the words out of my mouth as fast as I could.

"All it takes is a second to know they're the one. That's how long it took me to know about my Javier," she grinned.

My heart warmed when she talked about her late husband.

Javier was the love of her life and father to their six children. He passed away five years ago. I did my best to be there as they were for me after my mom died. Especially Luis. Call it internalized *machismo*, but he couldn't help but feel like he needed to step up and be the man of the family. He thought caring for his mother and little sisters was his duty. I tried to say otherwise, seeing the turmoil it caused him, but nothing worked, so I stepped back and supported him.

"What you and Javier had is something I could only wish I had a sliver of with Rosie and I," I said.

She raised her hand, shaking her head. "I see it in your eyes. Your heart does not lie," she waved her finger in my face. "Don't mess it up," she said sternly.

I reassured her I had no intention to. Her features softened at that. I went to help around with whatever was needed. The outside was quiet for a moment until I heard muffled shouts and footsteps through the back patio. My heart rate spiked when I recognized the voices.

"It's true! Victor's back!" Four heads appeared in the doorway. "Victor!" They all ran to me.

I couldn't do anything but welcome their hugs.

"Our honorary Mexican is back!" Maria shouted. She was five years younger than Luis and had recently graduated from college with a degree in literature.

After giving all the girls long overdue hugs, we all sat around the patio table to eat. It was great being back. The chaos that surrounded the table never made me feel so at home.

"What's new? Luis could only tell me so much, but he tends to exaggerate, so I'd like to hear directly from the source," I cracked a smile, hoping to get updated on what happened in the past year.

The table laughed at the jab that Luis was nothing but what's called a *chismoso.*

"Sofia has a boyfriend!" Isa announced.

I chuckled to myself, knowing the fifteen-year-old couldn't keep a secret.

The sudden news of her older sister was shocking, though I was not as shocked as Luis was based on how the vein on his forehead popped out at the discovery. It was obvious he was protective of his sisters, but sometimes I wondered how much stress he put on himself.

"Ma, you said she wasn't going to say anything," Sofia leaned over towards her mother.

"I said I was ninety-five percent sure," she raised her hands in defense.

"Why wasn't I made aware of this, *hermanita*?" Luis leaned on the table with his elbows, folding his hands, emphasizing the nickname she despised to annoy her.

"Because you'll overreact, just like when Maria introduced Angel to us," she crossed her arms over her chest, rolling her eyes.

Sofia was the third child and second daughter of the Sosa family. She was currently attending UIUC and studying marine biology or chemistry— her mind kept changing. Now back home for the seemingly long holiday, it was a joy to experience her easygoing and captivating nature.

"I can't be blamed for that. Someone has to make sure my little sisters' are treated right," he defended. "And if they're not, it's up to me to beat the shit out of them," he explained, causing the girls to groan.

Like I said—internalized machismo.

"Don't worry, Sofi. Luis is just looking out for you, and I'm sure he's a great guy," I tried to calm the fire, and by how her cheeks blushed, I could tell she appreciated it.

"Thank you, Victor."

"Do you have a girlfriend?" Valentina spoke up. She was the second youngest. Her teeth flashed with a new set of braces, and she got a new pair of glasses. At thirteen, she was the same age as Luis when he got his braces.

"No, not at the moment, Vale," I laughed.

She narrowed her gaze. "Sure, an attractive twenty-eight-year-old millionaire doesn't have a girlfriend," she rolled her eyes. "So believable," she exaggerated as she got up to grab more food while her mother scolded her.

I was shocked to hear her say that, but considering she had just become a teenager, maybe I shouldn't have been surprised.

"Well, now, since that topic is brought up," Maria pointed the conversation back to me. "Why *aren't* you dating anyone?" She cocked a brow.

"Work is more important, I guess," I shrugged. "I've been focusing on expanding the business."

"Sure, blame work, but who's this Rosie?" She set her fork down. "Luis talks too loud," she added at my taken-aback face.

I sent my best friend a look before opening my mouth. "She's the woman who won the grant last Saturday; she runs her own business," I explained. "She dropped off some lunch to thank me the other day." I wanted to keep my answer short, hoping I didn't give away too much information so they couldn't find her.

"Oh my gosh, she's so pretty!" Isa gasped, staring at her phone.

I sat dumbfounded.

Today's generation will never fail to amaze me at how fast they can find something online. All the girls beckoned her to pass the phone around, each cooing and agreeing on her beauty.

"*¿Hecho de Hilo, ah, Mexicana?*" Alma asked. "She's cute," she said, and her approval meant a lot.

"So you did the right thing and asked her out, right?" Elena asked.

"No, as much as I'd like to," I said before they all booed. "I would like to get to know her first," I explained.

"Respectful, but you gotta grow some hair on your chest," Maria spoke up. "A pretty girl like that is not going to be available much longer," she waved her fork in the air.

The rest of the Sosa family agreed.

While it wasn't fun to be bombarded with questions about your love life, hearing some feedback and opinions was nice. Because they were right about one thing—my window to ask Rosie out was dwindling, and I had to make sure I had a chance.

Was I going to take it, though?

Chapter 8

Rosie

"You want apple pie-flavored Oreos?" I raised a brow in confusion.

"Yes! They're seasonal and were just released for fall. If not, peanut butter ones are fine," Luna spoke into the phone.

I could hear the pots and pans clanging as she prepared for dinner. It was her turn to cook dinner tonight, leaving me to do our weekly grocery run. That job was usually left to me since I actually checked the prices and didn't throw whatever I wanted in the cart. The last time Luna ran the errand, she went almost two-hundred dollars over budget. I was flabbergasted and learned that my best friend couldn't be trusted when she was left unattended in a store full of food.

"Okay, why would they make apple pie? That doesn't pair with chocolate," I shook my head, turning down the snack aisle, a quarter of one side taken up by the famous sandwich cookie. I stepped back, searching for the supposed apple pie-flavored cookies. "You better like them," I sighed, finding the pack and staring at them weirdly before placing them in the cart.

"You sound like my mother," she responded with a laugh.

"They're five dollars, and we're on a budget," I turned back to the shelves, trying to find another snack to cure my chocolate cravings. "Is there anything else you want?" I asked, ensuring I had everything I needed before walking down the aisle.

"No, I'm okay," she answered. "Don't forget the rice."

"Alright, I'll be home soon," I said before hanging up.

Grocery shopping at night was the best thing. Hardly anyone crowded the aisles, the lines were short, and the workers barely acknowledged the customers, considering they were probably at the end of their eight-hour shift.

As I rounded into the next aisle, I almost bumped into another person, and an apology quickly slipped out of my mouth just as I did.

"Sorry," a low voice chuckled.

I paused at the sound of Victor's voice.

"Oh, Rosie, hi," he greeted, licking his lips as a smile appeared when he realized it was me.

I blushed, my heart beating a mile a minute. Seeing him again after such a short time was both unexpected and thrilling. I fell frozen—shocked— that out of all the nights, I'd be running into him while grocery shopping. But I held my composure.

"Victor, it's good to see you again," I grinned. "Sorry I almost trampled you with my cart," I laughed.

"Well, it wouldn't be the first time you ran into me," he joked, turning his head slightly.

"If anything, you trampled me. You're a lot taller," I shot back in amusement.

The corner of his eyes crinkled.

I took that opportunity to search his eyes, the dark color twinkling under the fluorescent lights. For a second, I wondered if his eyes were brighter because he was looking at me, if it were even possible. I hummed to myself and felt my heart thump against my chest as I briefly contemplated the what-ifs.

"This wouldn't do any damage to you," I gestured to the shopping cart I had been pushing around for the last thirty minutes, bringing myself back to reality.

"You're probably right," he smirked, his eyes scanning over me. His gaze followed the stitchwork of my patchwork cardigan. "Thank you again for the food," he said, eyes tracing back to me. "It was one of the best meals I've had," he complimented.

My heart skipped a beat, and I couldn't help the grin grow on my lips. I tugged on my sleeve as I let out a sound of contentment. "I'm glad to hear that. Nothing makes me prouder than knowing something I created has made someone happy," I replied. And it was true. From crocheting to cooking, I loved making people happy.

"I know the feeling," he hummed.

"Y'know, it's kinda weird to see you here," I said, deciding to voice my thoughts to make our conversation last longer. "I'd always imagine you shop at Whole Foods or something," I humored.

He was rich. He dressed the part with his tailored suit, driving his nice and expensive car, and I'm sure he lived in a luxurious penthouse along the lake. But shopping in a local grocery store? No, it didn't add up.

The corner of his eyes crinkled again. "Even for me, that place is too expensive. Besides, I like the produce from here better," he shrugged.

I dropped my gaze at the movement and noticed the bag of tomatoes in his hand.

"I'm gonna try my hand at making Mexican rice," he explained, raising the bag slightly so I could see better. "Been a while, and my friend who usually tells me what to do is currently asleep, so I'm feigning on my own with the rice selection."

"I could help with that," I offered without giving it another thought. "I was actually just going to get more rice," I gestured to where the item would be.

"Thanks," he smiled before falling into step with me. His long legs moved swiftly beside me.

I wondered how tall he was, maybe over six feet, based on how my head almost matched his shoulder.

After we located the rice and I explained why jasmine rice was better than anything else, I was growing a little sad that we would depart again. Maybe we weren't meant to stick around in each other's lives. But that didn't mean I couldn't make the most of it.

"Is that all you need?" I questioned.

"Yeah, only two things on my list," he nodded, the tomatoes and rice in one hand.

"You came to the store for two things and actually left with just that?" I cocked a brow.

"Yeah?" He laughed. "Do you not do that?" He tipped his head to the side, looking at me like I was the crazy one.

"No, I'm always remembering something I need, or my roommate texts me asking for a different thing than she already asked for," I joked, walking towards the check-out. I glanced between my cart full of groceries and his two items. "You should go first since you only have two items," I said, leaving some space to let him walk through.

"No, please, ladies first," he gestured for me to go.

I smiled, thanking him again. By the time I loaded my groceries in the cart, Victor had paid for his items. Once again, we fell in step with each other. Silence engulfed us as we walked to our cars, and oddly enough, I didn't mind it.

"It was nice seeing you again, Victor," I walked in the direction of my car, the wheels squeaking against the pavement and the bags rustling as the cart bumped against the cracks on the surface.

"I enjoyed running into you. And thank you for helping with the rice," he expressed his gratitude, shoving his free hand into his pocket. Such a simple move, yet it made him look so attractive.

"No problem. What are you planning on eating with it?" I asked, chewing on my lip as I stared at him. But I stopped when his eyes darkened slightly, his gaze brushing over my mouth. Suddenly, there was a flutter in my stomach, low in my abdomen.

Glancing away as a slight blush appeared, I waited for him to answer.

"Beef fajitas," he stated.

"Ah, date night tonight?" I raised my brows, not stopping myself, and asked him a personal question.

"No, just dinner," he answered, something glinting in his gaze.

I glanced down, the corner of my mouth curving upward. It felt good knowing he wasn't dating anyone. I made it to my car, unlocking the trunk before I turned to him, leaning against the cart handle.

"It's nice to see a man who can cook," I started.

"It's a basic human skill. That shouldn't be impressive, Rosie," he said my name. The way it just rolled off his tongue made my knees buckle.

"That is true," I thought, finding my composure again. "Unfortunately, not many men in my life have known how to cook," I added.

However, there were only two men in my life and both were irrelevant now.

"Well, now you know one more," he said with a smile.

"I do," I hummed, glancing at my groceries and feeling reluctant to end the conversation. "What do you like to make?" I raised a brow. I mentally congratulated myself on my question, happy I could talk to him longer.

"Hmm," he furrowed his brows in thought. "That's a tough question," he smiled as he glanced up.

"It's not that hard," I shook my head, gulping at the way his Adam's apple bobbed.

"What do you like to cook, then?" He teased, looking at me.

I paused.

Well, shit.

"Fine, there are a lot of things I enjoy making," I answered truthfully. "I think I could narrow it to a top five," I smirked.

He cocked a brow in amusement. "Five? All the dishes you've cooked in your lifetime and five can fit perfectly on your list?" He narrowed his gaze in a teasing manner.

"Yes, you can't?" I raised a brow enticingly.

"Oh, I can," he nodded.

I laughed. "Okay then," I pursed my lips. "We'll have to show each other someday," I offered.

"For sure," he hummed, glancing over his shoulder where I assumed his car was. "Goodnight, Rosie, drive safe," he bid, backing away.

"Goodnight, Victor."

Chapter 9

Rosie

I was in the back, grabbing some inventory before I heaved it over to the front of the shop. Weekly inventory was my favorite job. Restocking the yarn was satisfying, and knowing how much customers bought from us gave me pride. Yet, this week, I wasn't focused at all. I couldn't stop thinking about Victor.

How much of a coincidence was it that we were at the same grocery store? At the same time? Walking in the same aisle? It felt like fate, but…I shook my head to clear my thoughts. I didn't want to get ahead of myself fantasizing about some man, but just thinking his name ignited something deep inside me.

He had it all—CEO, billionaire, philanthropist. Literally Tony Stark without the suit of armor.

My only knowledge of that was when Summer made Luna and I spend our free weekend binge-watching the entire Marvel Cinematic Universe in release order. Apparently, they come in a different order? Beats me. I was busy working on new releases for the shop, so the only thing I got out of it was the whole Iron Man line—and that I would die for Loki.

But while Victor had the title, the money, and the looks for me to be on my knees for him. It's intimidating.

He was intimidating.

Not because he had wealth and status but because my feelings for him were powerful. He was pulling me in with his charm, his kindness, and his wicked good looks. I was already distracted just because I thought of him.

I needed to remember to focus on my business.

"Rosie! You have a visitor!" Luna shouted from the front.

I paused as I placed a yellow yarn on the shelf.

A visitor?

I rushed to finish the inventory, stacking the empty boxes together haphazardly. I smoothed my hands over my hair, placing it strategically over my shoulders. I adjusted the sleeves of my cardigan as I walked towards the front.

Keeping my head up, I inhaled deeply before my gaze caught the beautiful sight of brown eyes. I watched as his gaze flickered over my outfit. Every day, I wore a piece that I crocheted myself, partly to show the customers what could be made with our yarn but also because I loved my work.

He seemed to also.

"Victor, I wasn't expecting you," I tipped my head to the side, offering a small smile. "What can Hecho de Hilo do for you?"

"Hi," he smiled. "I'm not here for business. I just wanted to drop this off," he held out a bag.

I nodded as curiosity piqued my interest.

"This is number five on my list," he explained.

I furrowed my brows, only to realize a few seconds later. My heart fluttered at the thought that he went out of his way to show me one of his favorite meals to cook.

"Number five?" Luna furrowed her brows, leaning over the counter as she listened in on our conversation. Shooting her a look, she got the message, holding her hands up in defense before she made her way to the back.

"I can't wait to try it," I grinned, reaching out to grab the bag from him. Our fingers brushed, and those sparks shot up my arm. I shook the feeling off as I peeked inside. "What is it?"

"Fried chicken," he rolled his lips together. "Some sides with it too."

"That's sweet of you. Thank you, Victor," I let my arm drop before gesturing behind me. "Would you want to join me for dinner? We're closing, Luna and Summer are heading to a movie. I was going to stay until I got inventory done, but I could always do that tomorrow," I grinned.

His gaze brightened, "I'd love to."

"We're heading out now. What'd I miss?" Luna was checking her watch, glancing between us, a brow raising in interest.

"Victor's going to join me for dinner," I answered, her eyes widening in excitement.

"Well, you two have fun," Luna had a knowing tone in her voice, her lips pressing together to conceal her excitement. "Summer and I will get going. Don't want to miss the previews," she cocked a brow knowingly as she rubbed her palms together. "Summer! Let's go!" She shouted towards the back, the sound of the back door opening.

"I'm coming! God, can't you let a girl go to the bathroom? The movie is almost three hours long, and I'm not missing *anything*," she emphasized, coming to a halt at the sight of Victor. "Victor, hey!" She greeted him. "Nice to see you again," she smiled, throwing her purse over her shoulder.

"Good to see you too, Summer," he nodded, tucking his hands into his pockets.

The girls said goodbye, the door shutting behind them. The store was quiet, and it didn't feel awkward, even with just the two of us.

"Summer is taking Luna out to see a new superhero movie, couldn't tell you if it was DC or Marvel," I shook my head.

"Not a big fan of superheroes?" He chuckled.

"I admire them from afar," I sucked in a breath. "Kinda hard to tell what's going on with all the movies and shows coming out. Summer tries to get me in line, but I can't do it," I laughed.

He followed suit, the corner of his eyes crinkling. "I get it. I tried to keep up but got lost around the first or second movie," he said.

"Tell me about it," I rolled my eyes, walking towards the back of the break room. "You can come in," I nodded. "We can share," I offered, grabbing some utensils. "And eat on the roof."

"Great, that sounds perfect," he hummed.

I led him to the door leading to the roof. It was a small stairwell that opened to another level.

"I didn't realize there was another floor up here," he glanced around the small space, particularly the decorated door.

"Yeah, this is where I host our crochet classes," I stopped in front of the door painted in Hecho de Hilo's colors with yarn, photos, and small decorations glued on the wood. "This is the only part we have access to upstairs. The other door connects to the building next door. I don't pay rent there, so I don't have the keys," I shrugged before pointing to the second door straight across from us; it was bare and boring. Most importantly, locked. "What I would do to it, though," I muttered, but Victor still caught what I said.

"What would you do?" He asked.

"It's not important," I shook my head, opening the door to the roof. "Just a dream I've had for a while."

"Sounds like it's important," he offered. "I'd like to hear it," he fell into step with me as we approached the picnic bench.

I contemplated but decided to voice my idea to him.

"If I rented that building, I would open a ceramics shop," I started, sitting in front of him. "It'd be perfect having it right next door," I inhaled as I looked over the ledge, picturing what it would be like. "But the rent is too expensive," I frowned, snapping out of my daydream. "Let alone the downpayment for both buildings."

Knowing I could potentially pay for the downpayment with the grant money if Mr. Jones kept the farm, I felt like I had it right at my fingertips. It was only a matter of waiting.

He nodded, and I caught him running his eyes over my cardigan again. I fixed the sleeves again. It was hot pink and had daisies. I was proud of the design and remember it becoming popular on our social media page. But did he think it was too much? Childlike? I would take personal offense if he didn't like it.

"I like your sweater," he gestured to it.

I mentally relaxed, my face heating up at his compliment.

"When I first heard about crocheting and your shop, I honestly was picturing grandma's house," he joked.

"Crocheting is not what it used to be," I began, pulling items out of the bag. "You can make more than just chunky, itchy sweaters," I raised a brow, a smirk growing.

"You're quite talented, Rosie," he gazed at me, eyes cascading with the most genuine look, causing my cheeks to grow redder.

Calm down.

"Thank you," I tucked a strand of hair behind my ear, clearing my throat. "A lot of people don't consider crocheting to be a talent or even a form of art, but I love to prove them wrong," I shrugged.

It was considered more of a craft. When people hear the word "craft" they thought of children finger-painting. While many crafts like crochet tend to be more of a hobby than a profession, it made sense why many people didn't understand the skill it took. Regardless, it was refreshing to see the definition of it change. And it meant a whole lot more knowing I was one of the ones to do that.

"I like the attitude," he chuckled. "But if ceramics is your dream, then why crocheting first?" He asked, helping me open the container of chicken.

"A crochet shop was more viable at the time, so that's why I opened it. I figured if I worked hard, I could finally save up enough to rent the space next door. I'd have classes daily, taught in English and Spanish, and open studio hours so anyone could come in. It'd be a safe and educational space for my community," I explained.

Hecho de Hilo was already a dedicated space for my community. It was safe and welcoming. I knew that was what I wanted—something for people like me to share. And to grow that space into another business? Especially in the heart of my community, where the art and culture were rich.

I couldn't wait to be there.

"Just like your business now," he connected the dots. "Why ceramics specifically, though? What about it drew you in?" His eyes glimmered with interest that made my stomach flutter with butterflies.

"There's just something about having a blob of nothing and forging it into something you want. You have control, and if you mess up, you can start over or mend your mistake," I hummed, smiling down at the ground. I had given so many questions thought, and my answers just poured out of me.

"And what about crochet?"

"I guess it has the same idea," I laughed, realizing there was a connection.

"When I read your profile, you opened when you were eighteen. How did you even come up with an idea at that age?" He grabbed a napkin before twirling the fork in his hand.

"I've been selling my own creations since high school, so I guess I started young. Thankfully, I had my sister's support," I felt my heart warm at the thought of her.

~

"We're sorry, Miss Martinez, but if your sister continues to sell unauthorized merchandise on school property, we'll have no choice but to expel her. It violates a multitude of codes," the principal tried to reason.

"So what I'm hearing is your school is trying to diminish a child's entrepreneurial spirit?" Bianca arched a brow, her acrylics clicking on the chair's wooden arm.

The principal frowned. "No, we are simply trying to control the potential of gang formation. You have to understand," he defended.

My sister rolled her eyes. "Are you fucking kidding me?! She's selling crocheted scarves and hats! Do you not want your students to be warm during the winter? Buy necessities that are handmade for a bargained price?" She leaned forward, slamming her hand against the desk.

"Not at all," he gulped. "How about this? Rosa can continue to sell her products, but it has to be across the street," he offered.

She crossed her arms over her chest, shaking her head. "And have the cops arrest her for selling without a license? It's safe for her to sell here. Her peers come up to her during lunch or passing periods, there's no disturbance during class hours, she offers deliveries for larger orders at their homes, and she doesn't sell anything affiliated with 'gang formation,'" she said, using air quotations. "Fuck the stupid school codes. If we all were to abide by them, then I'm sure you would know about the violation of in-office romances," she rose to her feet, the principal's eyes widening in shock at the accusation.

"Ma'am, I suggest you watch your tone. You have no idea what you're talking about," he stood abruptly, shoving a finger in her face.

"I'm sure the rest of the PTA and I are aware of what happened between you and the secretary in the west hallway," she tipped her head to the side, batting her lashes.

"You," he clenched his jaw before shaking his head, coming to a conclusion. "Fine, Rosa can continue to sell on school property, but if any fights come up with this, then it'll be shut down."

"What a great compromise," she smiled brightly. "Thank you for your time. I'll see you at the next meeting. C'mon, Rosita," she waved me over, grabbing my hand.

~

I reminisced before I looked back at Victor, wondering what kind of dreams and ambitions a multi-millionaire had. "What about you?"

"What about me?" He smiled, confused.

"What's your dream?" I hinted.

He wiped his mouth and shook his head. "I wouldn't necessarily call it a dream," he said. "It's something I've been working on for the past year, Project Regenerate," he named. "I want to try and give our society another chance," he shrugged.

"That's very ambitious. What does it consist of?" I leaned forward on the table.

"It's more or less creating a space for my top engineers and scientists to work on solutions and build resources to end climate change. This facility will be the best of the best in the country and eventually the world," he stated, his gaze warming when he noticed I took interest.

"Wow, the world huh?" I raised my brows. "You're trying to save the world from extinction, and I'm just selling yarn," I laughed at myself, the irony of it all.

"If it weren't for businesses like yours, Rosie, people would be spending too much time worrying about extinction," he countered.

My heart skipped a beat.

"I'm trying to find a way for people to live, but you give them a reason to live," he complimented, his smile genuine.

I guess he was right. With my focus on my community, I did more than just sell yarn.

"I don't know how to respond to that," I noted, my cheeks growing warm. "Thank you, though," I nodded. "I know I get in my head sometimes, but it's nice to hear my worth from someone else," I exhaled.

"Anytime, Rosie."

Chapter 10

Victor

Rosie was brilliant.

She had taken something simple as opening a yarn shop and turned it into something irreplaceable—a haven for her community. A business that added to the already rich culture and art of the city. It wasn't something that could be so easily mimicked.

I was entranced by her.

Her voice, her words, her lips, the way she tucked a strand of hair behind her ear anytime she was nervous, the sparkle in her eyes when she talked about her business—beauty didn't exist until her.

My gaze flicked over her collarbone when she shrugged off her cardigan and set it on the table. Her skin looked so delicate, and her body's shape so alluring.

"You know fall is approaching when it's cold in the morning and hot in the evening," she sighed, reaching for the lanyard around her neck and grabbing a hair clip, swiftly throwing her hair up and out of her face.

The movement pulled me out of my daze. I watched the way her fingers ran through her soft, silky hair, her bangs falling out of the collected pieces, resting against the curves of her face. I ran my gaze down, gulping at the sight of the skin on her neck. I wanted to reach out and touch her, graze my fingers against her warm flesh, feel as goosebumps trickled along it, the soft noises she would make as I continued…

"I love the end of summer," she adjusted in her seat, the sun glowing against her skin, utterly oblivious to my own iniquitous thoughts. "It reminds me of when my sister would take me to the park, and we'd play soccer. It was the perfect temperature to stay out there for hours," she smiled and stared out over the ledge, crossing and resting her arms on the table as she closed her eyes, letting the remaining rays of the golden hour kiss the high points of her face.

I momentarily trained my gaze on her, allowing my mind to absorb her just as her skin was to the sun. It melted my heart to picture her playing with her sister, taking me back to a moment in my childhood.

"I used to do the same with my best friend. Our dads would take us to the park, and they'd have to bribe us just to go home," I chuckled, following her gaze out over the ledge of the rooftop.

Humming in amusement, she turned back to look at me. "The only bribe to ever work on me as a kid was popsicles," she laughed, shifting in her seat. Every time she did, I caught a waft of raspberries and jasmine.

I never liked raspberries, but I was starting to think they deserved a second chance.

"What did they bribe you with?" She blew out a breath, her eyes running over me.

I couldn't help but smile. "Ice cream. We used to go crazy for it," I hummed before I gazed back down at our empty plates. My mind traced to what led to this moment in the first place.

The last time I cooked for someone…*shit*, I couldn't even remember. Regardless, I hadn't had the urge to until I ran into Rosie that night at the grocery store. Fate was on my side, pulling me back into her life, and I had my second chance.

I tried not to give it too much thought a few days later, going through my pantry and finding the ingredients for fried chicken. Before I knew it, I walked into her store, handing her the meal that took me two hours to make.

And here we were.

Where we were meant to be.

"There's this ice cream cart in the park nearby. We should go sometime," she said, almost stopping when she realized what she implied.

I smiled. "I'd like that."

We gazed at each other, our irises filled with curiosity and interest.

I wanted to study her eyes, to find out if they were truly made up of the beautiful dark chocolate brown I saw from afar or if she had light brown specks that added dimension to them, making it seem like the irises were made up of craters.

Her eyes were a world undiscovered, waiting for others to explore the stunning formation.

A car's horn went off, and we jumped out of our daze before silently agreeing to clean up. Our arms brushed momentarily, and suddenly, her bracelet was stuck to my sleeve.

Letting out a laugh, I maneuvered so we sat on the same side. I sucked in a breath when I saw how bad it was and gently grabbed her wrist. "Here," I offered, and she held out her wrist so I could see better.

"This always gets caught in things," she laughed.

"Why wear it then?" I focused on getting ourselves untangled.

"I can always do that, but it's very sentimental to me," she licked her lips. "I feel incomplete without it," she explained.

I felt her pulse against my thumb, and it was racing fast. Her skin was warm against mine, the scent of her perfume lingering, and I knew it would stick to me once I let go.

"It was gifted to you," I said, hoping it was her grandmother or someone and not her boyfriend.

"My sister did for my sweet sixteen," she licked her lips.

I caught her gaze and sensed something behind that story, but I didn't push.

"I've been collecting charms since."

I hummed, managing to get the chain unhooked from my sleeve. Letting go of her, she thanked me, scooting away just an inch to give some semblance of space. But the heat of her radiated off on me.

"Some have been gifted to me, but most I've made myself," she touched them, smiling. The sentiment was evident, and it made my heart warm.

"Through ceramics?" I asked, my heart beating against my chest each second.

"Yeah, I enjoy pottery mainly, but I love making charms," she blushed, glancing at me briefly before she focused back on her bracelet. "They all represent someone or something important to me," she began. "For Luna, a bi pride flag, a crescent moon, and a book. For Summer, a paintbrush, the orange infinity stone, and a lesbian pride flag," she moved the bracelet around her wrist, allowing me to see each and every one. The attention to detail was unbelievable. "And for Bianca, a bee, a lipstick, and a musical note," she pressed her lips together in a smile.

"What about you? Which ones represent you?" I questioned, hoping she made room for herself on it.

She turned the bracelet around, revealing more. "I have a ball of yarn, for obvious reasons," she cracked a grin. "A monarch butterfly since I love that they represent hope and a rose," she explained.

My gaze softened. Part of me wondered what happened in her life to make hope one of her symbols. But I kept my mouth shut. I moved my attention back to the craftsmanship, observing the detail. "Did you use polymer clay to make them?"

The different colors of clay created such a vibrant contrast against one another. Each charm was smaller than a penny, but the details were clear.

"Yeah," she seemed taken aback by the specificity but continued. "It's kinda tricky since they're small, but keeping my ceramics skills up is helpful," she trailed.

"Until you open your shop," I said, ending her thought.

"Yeah, until then," she said solemnly.

"I'm sure that day will be soon," I genuinely said.

"Thank you," she turned her head to hide her blush, but I could still see the tinge of pink spread across her cheeks. "I hope we both reach our dreams, me with my ceramics shop and you with saving the planet," she grinned.

"Me too."

We stayed up on the roof until the sun set. The night sky settled over us, and apartment lights nearby turned on.

Once we returned downstairs, I said, "Thank you for dinner. I enjoyed our conversation."

The shop had closed, the lights off, save for a few. But it was quiet.

"Your fried chicken was phenomenal," she pressed her lips together in a smile. She held the door open while I stepped outside. "It's nice to see that a man can cook; it makes him more attractive," she said, pulling her bottom lip between her teeth.

I felt my cheeks heat up at the compliment. "What did I say about knowing how to cook being the bare minimum?" I raised a brow with amusement.

"There's a difference between knowing the basics and knowing how to cook something delicious," she raised her hands in defense.

"Thank you," I hummed.

She stood before me and seemed hesitant as she stared at me, her eyes darting to my lips.

I froze.

Did she feel the same way as me?

"Goodnight, Victor," she bid, leaning against the door, but she hesitated again. I was going to ask if she was alright until she reached up, placed her hand on my shoulder, and kissed my cheek. The gesture was small and quick, but it made my smile grow. "Drive safe," she pulled away, a sheepish grin on her lips.

"Goodnight, Rosie," I managed to say.

She tipped her head, her cheeks pink when she stepped back into the store, locking it.

I felt dazed as I began walking to my car. My hand reached up to caress my cheek, the feel of her soft lips lingering and the wave of her scent crashing over me when she came closer was making its imprint in my memory. I'd only spent a few hours with her, but I was already falling. I wasn't supposed to be falling, but I was falling *hard*.

Chapter 11

Rosie

Saturday soon came, and I was back sitting across from Bianca. The minutes counted down to an hour, and they seemed to fly faster with Luna and Summer talking nonstop on either side of me. I couldn't decide if the car ride was worse or better.

Thankfully, most of my attention swarmed with memories of Victor and I's dinner. I recalled how easy it was to talk to him. No matter who I would speak to, especially if it were someone I wanted to impress, I would doubt myself over any word that came out and feel like an idiot. But with him, that wasn't an issue. My sentences and questions came out smoothly, and we engaged in the conversation. Not to mention, I couldn't help but notice he kept staring at me with an intensity like he wanted me.

The look was subtle, but it made me shake to my core, and I blushed at the mere thought. Even our short entanglement had my heart beating uncontrollably. All the details leading up to the end of our shared night gave me the courage and security to kiss him, but the cowardly little me backed out at the last minute and opted for his cheek.

Even though it was a small gesture, I couldn't help the way I would fight back a smile at the mere thought of it.

"I finished reading the chapters you sent me last week for your new book, Luna, but when did Gabriel become Gabriella?" Bianca's muffled voice drowned me out of my thoughts, and I redirected my attention to the conversation. "Did I miss something?" She scrunched her brows together at a timid Luna.

I raised my brows in interest, pushing my distractions to the back of my head.

Luna was never shy or timid.

"No. I decided I wanted the love interest to be a woman. I'm going back and making sure all of the Gabriels are Gabriellas," she laughed awkwardly, scratching her head. "What do you think about that?" She placed her hand in her lap, looking at all of us expectantly.

"I think it's great!" Bianca smiled. "I'm already die-hard for Gabriella," she encouraged her, her tone genuine.

"I can't wait to read the final product," I said, bumping my shoulder with hers.

"Thanks, I think this is the right direction, but now I'm kinda worried about how my parents will react once they see what this book is about," she sighed. "It's one thing to be a romance writer, but a queer romance writer?"

I frowned at her fears. She shouldn't have to worry about that. Her only focus should be finishing her book, not the opinion of her parents or anyone else, for that matter.

"Don't think about that now," Summer butted in. "We need more sapphic romance authors," she smiled. "I, for one, am loving it," she winked as Luna nodded, letting out a sigh of relief.

"Keep up the good work, Luna. Me and the other inmates are excited and can't wait for the next chapter," Bianca grinned. "Now tell me, que es el chisme?" She scrunched her shoulders up in excitement.

"Rosie had a dinner date with the CEO of Romano Tech."

"Nothing's been going on."

Luna and I both said at the same time.

"What?" Bianca deadpanned, her widened eyes flying to me.

"It wasn't a date," I shrunk in on myself. "We just shared a meal," I explained, trying to stop the fire before it started. But I knew it was too late the moment I met my sister's eyes and saw what was going through her mind.

"You weren't gonna tell me?" She took offense as she furrowed her brows together.

God, the number of times I've tried to keep my romantic relationships under wraps from Bianca was impossible. It wasn't that she was overprotective. She just got too excited and way in over her head. It's hard juggling her fantasies with reality.

"Because it wasn't a date! And I bet you planned our wedding, the number of kids we'll have, and their names all in the last two seconds," I retorted. She rolled her eyes, but I knew I was right. I couldn't even lie about how true it was.

"*De veras*, Rosie, don't exaggerate," she scoffed, crossing her arms over her chest. "Is it so bad I want you to find love?" She shrugged, gesturing with her hands. It was unbelievable she was trying to paint me as the bad guy.

We stared at each other for a few moments. It was times like this when we acted like tried and true siblings. The pettiness that coated the atmosphere anytime we covered topics on my romances, her ex-boyfriend, my financial situation, and hell, even her current situation of being in prison. Those were things we rarely ever discussed—especially the middle two.

"No, but nothing is going on between me and him. We ran into each other at the grocery store and realized we both like to cook, so he brought one of his favorite meals," I explained, toning down the exact details. "It's a friendly thing," I stated firmly, hoping she got the message.

"Well, then tell me about this man," she shook her hair out of her face, clearing her throat. "What does he look like? Is he cute?" She asked. She leaned back in her chair, running her tongue over her teeth.

I narrowed my gaze at her, deciding she agreed she was a bit over the top, so I gave her the benefit of the doubt. I was about to explain how handsome and tall he was until Summer beat me to it, taking the phone.

"Picture the essence of Christian Bale's Batman with the look of Rafael from *Jane the Virgin*," Summer butted in.

I cocked a brow at the specificity.

"I'm an artist. I look at a lot of references," she responded to my strange look.

It made sense.

"Totally can picture it," Bianca nodded, wholly invested in this.

"He does not look like Rafael," I shook my head, reaching over Summer to speak into the phone.

He's definitely cuter and more sculpted.

"Maybe when I meet him, I can vouch for you," Bianca wiggled her brows.

I sighed, trying to accept the route this conversation took.

"Agree with the Batman part, not gonna comment on the latter," Luna added, grabbing the phone from Summer. "He's very handsome, tall, with dark hair and eyes, a dazzling smile, nice hands, smells great, a little bit of a stubble," she looked off to the distance, a content smile on her face. "The definition of a man who you'd wanna take home but can also fuck you well," she smirked, contemplating.

"Are you sure you don't want to go out with him?" I cocked a brow.

She laughed, shaking her head.

"Don't worry, I'm not preoccupied with your lover boy right now," she batted her lashes as I studied her, making a mental note to swing back to that later. "Because I'm writing my book," she quickly added.

"Imagine all the places he can take you," Bianca jumped back in and hummed in delight. "Fancy dinner? His boat on the lake?" She bit her lip in anticipation.

"Again, not dating," I clarified. "We shared a meal once."

"If I were dating a rich CEO, I would've made sure to be taking advantage of her millions…or billions," Summer smirked, adding into this already dreadful conversation, Luna and my sister agreeing.

"*Not dating*," I emphasized for the last time. I was so glad they weren't aware I kissed him on the cheek.

It was bold, considering my gut told me to do something. And well, I did.

"We'll see about that," Luna smiled smugly, the other two humming in agreement.

I was so done already.

~

The green sign with a little alpaca on it that read "Welcome to Plains Acres" passed us as we drove down a dirt road leading to the two-thousand-acre farm that provided the yarn for my business. It was located about an hour from Bianca, so we used the day to get as much inventory as possible.

"You think Bianca will like Victor?" Luna asked from her spot in the passenger's seat.

"Who's to say we'd even be in each other's lives by the time she comes out?" I asked parking at the end of the road. "I don't want to get my hopes up that Bianca will be out soon, knowing the prison system," I sighed, unbuckling my seatbelt. "But then again, why would it matter if he meets her?"

"Who's to say you guys won't be dating by then?" Summer cocked a brow, a giddy smile on her face as she walked out of the car. "I'm rooting for you guys," she grinned.

"Thanks, Summer," I wrapped an arm around her shoulders, deciding to ignore the possibility that Victor and I could date. "Now, let's get this new inventory loaded so we can get back home. I'm thinking *tacos dorados* for dinner tonight?" I suggested, and they all hummed.

Just as we reached the farmhouse, the screen door opened, and an older man with graying hair and dark skin appeared. The smile on his face and his signature Plains Acres dad hat gave away that it was no other than Mr. Jones.

He was such a lovable and respectable man. My longest business partner and a good friend, too.

"Girls! Welcome back!" Mr. Jones greeted us. "Can't believe it's been two weeks already," he grinned, hugging the three of us.

"Time never stops, especially when you're running a business," I shrugged.

He was quick to agree.

"Yet, there's always time to enjoy a quick meal before y'all hit the road again," he beamed, and the three of us weren't about to deny the goodness of Mr. Jones's cooking.

"Can't disagree with the man!" Luna cheered, letting him take the lead back to the house.

"And how's Jackson doing?" Summer questioned, springing a new conversation. "Place seems quiet. Is he around?" She joked.

"Oh, the boy is doing as best he can. He's back in Wisconsin with his family," he replied. "He had a family emergency, so he rushed back. Lord knows I'm only prayin' everything's alright," he sighed, going up the steps.

"That's awful. Please give us a call once he's back so we can visit," I said as I followed him up the porch steps, thanking him when he opened the door for us. "How are you managing without him, though?"

"I got a few workers helpin' out, just not as good as him, so things are a little slow. Thankfully, my niece is visiting, and she knows her way around the place just as well as he does," he walked us into the kitchen, where the smell of his famous chili awaited us. "Now, help yourselves, girls. My little girl's probably around here somewhere," he mused, checking down the hall before he went outside.

Mr. Jones spoke fondly of his "little girl," his niece, Quinn. Even though she was a grown adult woman, she was like a daughter to him, and things like that never changed. I was always, and still was, envious of their relationship. He wasn't her biological father, but that didn't matter. He loved her unconditionally. That was something I only ever wanted.

"Earth to Rosie?" A vibrant voice spoke up, shaking me out of my daze. "I haven't seen you in four months, and you're just gonna ignore me?" She spoke again.

My eyes widened.

"Quinn!" I gasped, throwing my arms around her. "I wouldn't ignore you on purpose," I pulled away, taking her in.

Quinn Jones was a beautiful Black woman with dark skin that glowed brighter than all the stars in the midnight sky. Her hair was parted into two thick braids that reached down to her mid-back, and she wore a sage green sundress with a delicate floral design. Her cottage-esque style could put her on the cover of *Country Living*.

"You better not," she hugged me one more time. "So word on the street is that you got a new man?" She raised her brows.

I shot Luna a look.

"Can you blame me? This is good chisme," she shrugged. "You never have anything going on in your love life."

I rolled my eyes like I didn't run an entire business that had me jumping ropes to stay afloat. But I guess that wasn't interesting enough.

"Don't worry, I was gonna find out sooner or later," Quinn said as she led me back to sit down. "Now spill," she urged me, and so I did.

I told her everything from how I'm *not* dating Victor to our found love of cooking.

"This man sounds *hot*," Quinn emphasized the last word. "You guys had a romantic dinner on the roof, and he touched your wrist?" She smirked, shimmying her shoulders. "The bar is literally on the floor, but the floor is *hot*," she joked.

I threw my head back in laughter.

"Even his name is hot, Victor Romano," she rolled the r's for even more emphasis.

"He looks hotter in person," Luna added.

I gave her another look, and she shrugged, raising her hands in defense. I turned back to Quinn, continuing our conversation. We enjoyed our meal for the next half-hour until it was time to help Mr. Jones load up our inventory.

"You guys go ahead. I'm gonna talk to Mr. Jones for a bit," I waved my two friends off, and they both shrugged, stepping into the car. "Can't believe you're selling this farm," I sucked in a breath, scanning over the wide span of plains where the alpacas and other livestock were grazing.

"Now, now, not unless you can stop me," he chuckled.

I pressed my lips in a tight smile, attempting to find the humor in it, but failed.

"Why are you doing it? Willing to not sell because of me, it seems pointless," I furrowed my brows.

"I've supplied for many businesses in my lifetime, but it wasn't until I met you that I saw how passionate a person can be about their own creation, the life they're building for themselves," he gestured with his hands, signaling for me to take a step towards the fence. "Even if that passion barely scrapes to pay the bills or your employees," he added.

I nodded.

"You're resourceful, Miss Martinez, but I want to give you enough time to plan. This contract I'm working out with the buyer allows me to pull out of the deal until the end of November. I want to use every minute I have to know what I'm doing is the right thing, and I need you to help me with that," he explained.

"By making the presentation," I said.

He nodded.

"Wow, I really don't know what to say." My hands became clammy. "So you're willing to not sell for me?" I realized.

"I'm willing to postpone," he clarified. "Dear, one business owner to another, this is something that I've been planning for a while. Running a farm isn't like it used to be, I'm afraid to say it, but we've been struggling," he began. "I'm getting older, too, and I don't want to say anything to Quinn. She's been studying hard at school, and I know she'll drop everything for this place if given the chance. It's a sacrifice I don't want her to make," he inhaled before releasing it.

I stared at the grass in shock. I hadn't even realized business was rough for a successful man like Mr. Jones. All two thousand acres, all the dozens of wonderful employees, the big beautiful house he built for his family. It was the picture-perfect dream. Still, there was so much struggle behind it.

I didn't like the feeling that bubbled in my stomach.

"I guess I should say thank you for letting me get my orders straight," I hummed as he patted my shoulder. "But it still doesn't make sense. You have a successful farm."

He sucked in a breath, taking his cap off, before he opened his mouth to speak, "We've been losing business, many clients are not renewing their contracts, and we're just getting by," he shook his head. "I didn't want to worry you, so I kept my mouth shut."

I understood.

"So selling this farm will be your saving grace."

I didn't want to look at the bigger picture. I wanted to stay in my little bubble of ignorance for a little while and prioritize myself. But I couldn't.

"It will, but I haven't worked in this field for forty years to be kicked out in a short time. I have a plan, and you're a big part of it. You're the most deserving one out of all the people I've worked with," he complimented.

I blushed.

"Well, I hope it takes you a little longer than until November to sell. Good day, Mr. Jones."

I bid him goodbye before I walked towards the car. Luna immediately asked me what we talked about, and I explained briefly. The two of them reassured me that everything would work out in the end. I nodded before starting the car and took a deep breath before making a U-turn onto the dirt road.

No pressure.

Chapter 12

Victor

Today, I spent time in meetings. I oversaw our current projects, touched base with the CFO to ensure our budget ran smoothly in the last quarter, and approved new hires. It was only the middle of the day, and I'd already thought about Rosie a million times.

"Goodnight, Victor. Drive safe."

Her sweet, angelic voice repeatedly rang through my ears. Her gentle hand was placed on my shoulder, perfume engulfed my nose, and soft lips pressed against my cheek.

I wanted to see her again and knew the only way would be to cook again. I was contemplating what meal I wanted to cook next. I was clearly overthinking it, but regardless, I wanted it to be perfect.

"Someone's in a good mood," Ari's voice kicked me out of my daze.

My smile quickly fell, and I turned to find her sitting at her desk, a smirk plastered on her face.

"Don't let me be the one to ruin it. Happy looks great on you, boss," she said, turning to type something on her computer.

"Thanks," I softened my features, returning to my office.

Shutting the door behind me, I sat calmly in my chair. My mind raced back to my previous thought process.

I've cooked for the past few years because I needed to eat. However, I have always kept that skill alive partly because I just enjoyed it. Chopping vegetables, stirring sauces, and the smell of home-cooked food unlocked the nostalgia of cooking with my mom. When she passed, I stopped for a little and never cooked for anyone. But now Rosie inspired me to fall back.

That meant whatever I was cooking needed to be right for the person who inspired me. Leading to my dilemma…what do I make?

I leaned back in my chair, spinning around to look out the window.

It was overcast today, and the sun was hiding away. People wore light sweaters and long sleeves as the light wind made the beautiful sixty-degree weather colder than intended.

September in Chicago was barely cold, with some days hitting the eighties. While others prepared their warm soups and dishes for the harsh weather, Chicagoans still lived out the last few days of summer.

I decided to check the weather, hoping I could plan my next dish for Rosie around the temperature that day. A few days from now, it should be a little chilly, similar to today. I felt myself relax when an idea popped into my head.

Something classic and warm.

A knock interrupted me just as I placed my phone on the desk. I didn't even get the chance to grant entrance to whoever it was before they popped their head in. I kept my face straight when Luis walked in.

"So, Ari tells me you're in a good mood," he cracked a grin, shutting the door behind him. "I have an itch that has something to do with your dinner date you had with Rosie," he smirked, and I rolled my eyes.

I decided to tell him about the dinner we shared, hoping he would see it in a platonic way like I had. But man, was I wrong.

He "bet" that Rosie and I would be dating by the end of the year, claiming I owe him one hundred dollars if that happened.

I didn't want to tell him I hoped that would be the case, too. I wanted him to believe he would win out on a Benjamin from me.

"It wasn't a date," I argued, my attention moving to my computer screen where I had emails waiting for me.

"You cooked her one of your favorite meals and brought it to her work, where you shared it," he deadpanned, standing in front of me at my desk. "If we're being technical, you're already married," his lips curved, and smugness spread across his face.

"Only under your terms," I shot. "I only brought the meal as a friend, nothing more," I sighed, not having the emotional capacity to deal with another one of his romantic interpretations.

"Fine, you shared a meal with a friend, but it doesn't hide the fact that you have a crush on her," he shoved his hands into his pockets.

"I don't have a crush," I exhaled, shaking my head.

Since when did we go back to middle school, pointing out the girls we liked as we walked to fourth period?

"I'm gonna ignore your denial for a second," he pressed his lips together. "You like Rosie, and you share a love for cooking, so why not use that as a way to ask her out? The worst she can do is say no," he shrugged.

Ah, yes. Not only was Luis an idealist, but he was also an absolute hopeless romantic. Whether it was a date I had in the past or a simple conversation I held with a girl at a bar, he never stopped himself from picturing how our love story would go. It was truly unique how his mind worked.

"And the best thing she can say is yes," he added after I didn't respond.

"If I admit I like her, will you stop?" I glanced up at him, cocking a brow.

"No," he shook his head, another smile spreading across his mouth. "But that's all I need," he winked before he turned and left, walking triumphantly.

"Close the door on your way out," I shouted after him, and he flipped me off as he did.

I answered a call, and my receptionist's voice greeted me.

"Sir, your one o'clock is here," they said.

Right.

My meeting with Jones.

I had been so occupied thinking about Rosie that my looming lunch plans with him had slipped my mind. I've entirely pushed Project Regenerate to the side, and now I was going to have to sit through lunch and kiss some ass in hopes that I moved this deal along.

Letting out a sigh, the elevator doors opened.

There he was, sitting on the couch in the waiting room dressed in a plaid button-up tucked into a pair of dark-washed jeans, his hat in his hands. He looked out of place compared to the others walking around in business attire, but based on the person I grew to know—he had a hell of a lot more business expertise than any of them.

"Miles, thank you for coming all this way," I greeted him, reaching out my hand.

He gave me a firm shake, the corners of his eyes crinkling as he smiled. "Thank you for inviting me. It's not often I get a reason to come to the city," he grinned.

I gestured for him to follow me to the VIP lounge on the twelfth floor, a private area for executives only. Consisting of a fine dining hall, private conference rooms, and many other luxury amenities, it was my way of pushing company morale.

"I hope this is not your way of persuading me to sell my farm to you, young man," he looked around the area.

The dim lighting, leather sofas, carpeted floors, and a bar with black granite made it a relaxing sight.

"If it were that easy, you'd already be signing," I hummed.

One of the hostesses led us farther back to where the seating was. As we took our seats, I ordered our finest scotch.

"So, if you claim your luxurious VIP lounge isn't your game to persuade me, why am I here?" He accused. "I didn't drive four hours for nothing," he sent me a pointed look.

I smiled, dropping my chin to my chest. "To work out a plan between us," I said, glancing at him. "We've been back and forth the last month and a half. I believe it's time we make a conclusive agreement," I stated.

He hummed. "And that agreement would be signing my name on the contract."

"It's what was proposed from the start," I said. "Romano Tech came to you because we saw an opportunity, and you agreed because it's obvious you see something in us."

He narrowed his gaze. "I'm aware. But I'm not going into an eighteen-million-dollar deal lightly. This farm is my baby, and I gotta make sure it's taken care of after I'm gone," he explained.

"Right," I pressed my lips together. "It will be. We're going to make sure it is."

"Very good then."

I grinned.

Once our meals were ordered, the conversation changed, mainly because he took the lead. I did my best to take the reins back, but this man could talk.

"I never married," he said. "I grew up taking care of my sister. She was all I had after our parents died. That's when I bought the land for the farm," he continued. "I grew my business alongside my best friend. Who would've thought he'd fall in love with my sister, though," he cackled. "They got married quickly and had Quinn not too long after," he reminisced.

I nodded, partially enjoying the heartfelt story.

"Boy, were they happy," he hummed. "It wasn't too long after, though, that her daddy passed away. We lost a best friend, husband, and father that day," he grew solemn. "Since then, I helped raise my niece like she was my own."

"I'm sorry for your loss. He was a brother to you," I said, leaning back in my seat.

"He was," he smiled. "It's important to remember them, all the good things, sometimes the bad. That's how we keep them alive," he stated.

I agreed. My mind traced back to my mom.

"That's enough backstory," he chuckled. "I know you're a little impatient, so I'll break the news to you," he clasped his hands over his stomach as he leaned back in his seat. "I won't give you a final decision until the contract deadline."

I faltered. "That won't be until the end of November."

"Exactly."

"May I ask why?"

"There are a few reasons. There's the matter of relocating our livestock. It's important to find good homes for them. I want to ensure my employees have enough time to look for other opportunities," he listed. "I also have a matter of private interest to remember. Depending on how that goes, I can back out of the deal with just a say," he concluded.

My blood rushed cold. "Of course, Miles. If that's your choice to wait until the deadline, then by all means," I cleared my throat.

"Thank you," he smiled.

We stood up from the table, descending back to the ground floor.

"Thank you for the lunch. Compliments to the chef," he grinned.

"No problem, as always, give us a call if anything comes up," I forced a light-hearted voice, hiding the blatant disappointment in my stomach.

"I will," he said as he shook my hand, bid farewell to the receptionist, and walked out the doors.

Great.

My year-long plans have been pushed three months behind. I let out a breath and lost my composure when I entered the elevator again. At this point, there was nothing to do besides let time take its course.

Still, the stress grew.

There was a point in my life where I had hit rock bottom, and right now, it felt like I was edging my way towards that point again.

I'm not losing hope just yet, though.

Chapter 13

Victor

I had to see Rosie. After that entire lunch with Jones and an overly stressful day, I knew it would do me good.

The bell over the door signaled my arrival, and the store was filled with people. Luna and Summer were ringing out customers. Their eyes widened when they saw me, and their attention spanned over to Rosie, who caught my gaze.

She clearly wasn't expecting me, but she said goodbye to the shopper she was helping before walking over to me.

"Rosie, hi," I exhaled, shoving my hands into my pockets.

"Victor," she greeted, her eyes sparkling. "What brings you here?" She rubbed her hands together, shoving them in the pockets of a rainbow checkered cardigan I was assuming she made herself, and the softness of the color complimented her well.

"I would be lying if I said something important," I smiled. "I just wanted to see you," I admitted, hoping I didn't sound too desperate.

"Oh," her face relaxed, and she pondered for a second. "Really?" She seemed to second-guess, scrunching her nose in the cutest way possible.

I nodded.

She blushed. "I have a break. Do you want to join me for a drink?" She pointed towards the back.

I agreed, following her after she turned to Luna and Summer, letting them know she was taking her fifteen.

Opening the breakroom, I noted its dullness, something I recalled from the first time I came here. It was a complete contrast to the store out front. The state of it was pretty banged up, and I was guessing Rosie paid more than it was worth. But I kept my mouth shut, not saying anything when she handed me a soda.

We found ourselves sitting on the roof again, the sun rising higher towards the west, and we were quiet. We felt content and natural, just like the first time.

"I have something to confess," I opened my mouth, deciding to break the silence. "When you were talking about ceramics, I failed to mention that I've also dabbled in that art," I trailed.

She gazed at me intently.

"You're kidding?" Her eyes lit up as she turned to face me. "Why didn't you say anything?"

"I liked listening to you talk about it. You obviously have a thing for teaching," I mused while her cheeks reddened. "I didn't want to ruin it," I explained.

She nodded.

"That's sweet," she smiled. "How long?"

I felt my heart pound as she stepped closer to me, our shoulders just inches apart, and if I moved, they would brush together. I could practically smell her if I moved my head.

Raspberries and jasmine.

"Since I was a kid, my grandparents were sculptors, and they taught me. I did a little bit of pottery, too," I stated. "Don't think I would be good as a teacher, though," I chuckled, licking my lips.

"What's your favorite type?"

"Sculpting," I answered. I briefly thought back to how I would make figurines as presents for my parents and friends. "But I've cut back on it since I started the company," I added. "What about you?"

"A little bit of each," she said after sipping her drink. "I do agree with you, though. I miss being able to make something whenever, but," she trailed off, her fingers brushing her bracelet as she glanced at the door that led to her shop.

"Life gets in the way," I finished, understanding what she meant.

She turned to face me as she beamed. Something glinted in her eyes, and it was more that she didn't say that I understood.

"Strangely, we have a lot in common," she hummed, pushing hair out of her face. "We both care for the environment, we have our own businesses, we love to cook, and now we both enjoy ceramics," she pondered, running her teeth over her lips. "There has to be something we disagree on," she laughed.

The more I discovered the interests Rosie and I shared, the more I realized that's precisely what was pulling me to her in the first place, like two peas in a pod.

"If you think pineapple belongs on pizza, then that's our thing," I chucked.

"It does," she smirked, a humorous look spreading across her features. "You don't think it does?" She asked after my beat of silence.

"You're kidding," I deadpanned when I realized she was being serious. "It's a fruit," I elaborated.

She furrowed her brows like I was crazy for stating the obvious.

"Tomatoes are a fruit, yet they're a big part of the pizza," she argued, and I turned away in shock.

"Not the same," I shook my head. As much as this discovery disheartened me, I couldn't help the smile that grew on my lips.

"Agree to disagree," she kept my gaze, a smirk covering her mouth.

I wanted to reach out and run my thumb over her plump pink lips, to dip my head down and feel as our lips met for the first time. The feeling of the afternoon sun beating down on us, its warmth complimenting the heat we felt coming off each other's bodies.

"I don't know," I narrowed my gaze at her, speaking to distract myself from my thoughts. "Pineapple pizza better not be your top dish," I grinned.

"Maybe it is," she glanced away, hiding a smirk. "Have you finished your list?"

"I've been working on it," I answered. "Fried chicken was number five, though."

"I'm tempted to know your top dish," she rolled her lips together. "My top dish is breakfast burritos, by the way," she added. "You seemed to be stressing out at the possibility it was Hawaiian pizza," she raised her hands, giggling.

"I'm glad to know it's a sensible meal," I grinned.

"So I told you mine, what's yours?" She rested her arms on the ledge.

"I don't know," I sucked in a breath. "I want that to be a surprise," I teased.

She narrowed her gaze at me. "What if I don't like surprises?"

"Then maybe I'll have to make it for you," I responded, taking a chance.

Her brows shot up the slightest bit before her lips curled. "Hmm, I think you have yourself a deal," she said, her interest piqued. "Should we set a time and place for this secret you can't wait to unveil?" She grinned wickedly.

"I think we should," I hummed.

We set a date for the end of the week—dinner at my place. We finished our drinks before returning downstairs, Rosie's break ending.

She stopped at the top of the stairs before she opened her mouth to speak. "If I come over and you're making pineapple pizza, you have another thing coming," she cocked a brow, pointing at me.

"Oh, I think I'll be prepared," I flashed my teeth, anticipation growing.

The end of the week couldn't come sooner.

~

Rosie

The bundle of nerves in my belly grew at my upcoming dinner date with Victor. I was invited to his place, where he would cook for me. I never expected he'd ask me out, and even more, I never expected I'd say yes.

"So what was so important that you had to take your fifteen-minute break early?" Luna appeared behind me, causing me to shriek.

I had been standing by the door, watching to make sure Victor got to his car safely (not because seeing the way he walked did things to me). I pressed a hand to my chest as I turned to face my best friend, sending her a look of annoyance.

"Did I scare you?" She bit her lip teasingly as she rocked back on her heels. "He is a fascinating, *attractive* specimen," she followed my gaze, but Victor had already driven away.

"Shut up," I shook my head, moving away from the entrance. "You didn't have to scare me like that," I exhaled, shaking the remaining adrenaline off me.

"Oh, I didn't mean to, but I'm not going to apologize," she giggled. "I've never seen you like this, so what was so important?" She repeated her question.

"Victor wanted a friend to talk to, I guess," I shrugged, fixing things on the already perfected shelf. "We shared a conversation while drinking sodas. Turns out he likes ceramics too, and he hates pineapple pizza," I grinned.

I never considered what my perfect man would look like or who he would be. The idea of that was too distracting with everything I had going on. I tried to push it away, but Victor appeared like a prince waiting to sweep me off my feet whenever my mind slipped. The more I thought about it, the more tempting it became.

"He's right, pineapple doesn't belong on pizza," Luna shook her head as she stated her opinion, Summer jumping in to agree with her.

"Why do you think we always get pepperoni and sausage?" Summer added, placing a hand on her hip as she stood from behind the counter. "Did you talk about anything else?" She rounded the counter before she hopped on, crossing a knee over the other.

"He kinda asked me out on a date," I trailed, the two gasping in unison.

"I knew it! You owe me five bucks," Luna waved her hand out. Summer rolled her eyes, but she pulled out a fiver.

"You're betting money?" I looked at them with concern.

If I had a nickel for the number of times my friends bet on my love life, I'd have one. But honestly, I think that's more than enough to be gambled on.

"I thought Victor was going to ask you out next week," Summer explained. "I guess he likes you more than I thought," she sighed, watching solemnly as Luna stuffed the bill in her pocket.

I widened my gaze at her, a little hurt by her comment.

"That's a good thing! Sorry," she was quick to correct based on my expression.

"To be honest, it's not even a date. After the meal he brought for us to share, he wanted to do that again with his favorite meal, just at his home," I elaborated, aware that I could be misinterpreting it, but their smiles grew wider at that.

"Oh, girl, he's in love with you!" Luna clapped her hands together in excitement.

"He is," Summer backs her up, pursing her lips.

"Don't get my hopes up," I groaned, stepping around the corner to the next aisle to escape this conversation.

"Joking, but not really," Luna pressed her lips together, following me. "He obviously likes you a lot if he's finding a way to impress you. First the fried chicken, and now he's cooking his *favorite* meal for you, that's big!" She cheered, grabbing my shoulders.

"He invited you to his house, too. I think you're only kidding yourself if he only sees you as a friend," Summer pointed out. "It's okay to be excited; you're going on a first date!" She hopped off the counter and joined us. "Victor is an acts of service type of man. Enjoy it and delve into it because I think you like him too," she stood beside Luna.

I gulped at the thought. I haven't had a crush since high school, and even then, I was a twenty-four-year-old woman with a lot on her plate. I didn't have time to have a crush, let alone be in a relationship.

Just thinking about all the wonderful dates, all the kisses and cuddles, all the best laughs and jokes hurt my brain. But the more my best friends stared at me with those lovesick eyes, the more I felt my heart swell at those possibilities, and I knew they were right.

I, Rosie Martinez, had a crush on Victor Romano.

Chapter 14

Victor

Today was finally the day of my date with Rosie. After enduring an agonizing week of work, I finally ran into my final last hours until I could go home and prep any last-minute things on my mental list.

Everything was set and ready in the fridge. I had a nice bottle of wine that paired perfectly with the dish, my apartment was already cleaned, and I had her address to pick her up at seven.

Now, if only I could get Jones to move his stance slightly, I would call this an absolute perfect day.

"All the livestock live here, from chickens to alpacas," Miles waved around a vast land area.

I shoved my hands into my pockets, following him along the fence line as my gaze ran out to the expansive plains of different farm animals. A few sheep and goats were grazing right by us, and numerous sounds came from them. I couldn't help but stare back at one who was looking at me.

"If I decide to sell, I'm hoping they'll go to a nice home in Oregon," he smiled, leaning on the wooden fence.

"Still not changing your mind?" My attention was pulled away from my staring contest with the goat as I turned to face him. I didn't want to be desperate, but he made it hard.

Especially when he let out a belly laugh.

Miles Jones was the only partner I've worked with where I felt I didn't have them in the palm of my hand.

I've built a reputation where people respected me, not because I was an ass, but because I was honest. I tried to always be respectful, but the moment someone lost their respect for me, all bets were off.

Yet, he has not given me a reason to do that, and it only forced me to work ten times harder, which I accepted as a challenge.

"Victor, son, this contract is not set in stone," he shook his head.

I sighed before pressing my lips in a tight line, going along with what he said.

"Until the end of November. Just be glad I'm allowing you to come down here and draft some blueprints for whatever you're planning on doing," he patted my shoulder before walking back towards the house.

The end of November.

Fuck, I've been working on finding a place for Project Regenerate for the past year. After Luis finally put this farm on our map not even two months ago. I couldn't rip my eyes away. All two thousand acres and our options were limitless in what we could do.

"Thank you, Miles," I said, watching him walk away.

I turned to our team that accompanied us today, allowing them to get to work before I walked over to Luis.

"We're never gonna get him to change his mind, are we?" He turned to me after noticing my appearance and said goodbye to a baby lamb.

"Doesn't seem like it," I shook my head. "But I have an off feeling," I chewed on my lip, my eyes squinting from the sun's bright rays. "This place is too beautiful, too lush to build over," I second-guessed.

"What are you talking about?" Luis waved his hand, standing up from his crouching position. "We're planning on building an entire campus run on green energy. Do you know what that would do for our business?" He gripped my shoulder pretty firmly, shaking me in the process. "For *the* world?" He raised his brows.

"I'm the CEO. Of course, I'm aware," I rolled my eyes. "You seemed to have found this place out of nowhere, that's all," I exhaled. "Where'd you even find it?" I asked.

While our current headquarters was in the city, having a location in a rural area would be ideal. There would be no distractions and an optimized space. It would be an opportunity too good to pass up on. Still, my question has lingered in my mind for the past few weeks—where the hell did Luis find this supposed gem?

"I was dropping Sofia off at UIUC. There was a billboard posted near the expressway. I got the number, and now we're here," he gestured around him. "Miles seemed pretty happy that I called. My guess is this farm isn't doing so well," he sucked in a breath, spreading his arms wide on either side of him on the fence.

"You think he's in debt?" I stepped next to him.

"I have an itch. No one gives up a family business that easily, especially one as loved as this one," he answered.

I frowned. The guilt in me weighed heavier. As much as I wanted to be done with Project Regenerate and finally put it into action, I knew it needed to be done right, not by buying off of a respectable man who didn't want to sell in the first place.

"Hey, look, if Miles didn't want to sell, would the farm be marketed for such a reasonable price? He knows what he's worth," he shrugged. "And what he'll get out of it if Romano Tech buys the farm," he hit the back of his hand against my chest.

I stared at him.

"Still, *we* know it won't be breaking the bank. I mean, eighteen million for all of this?" He spread his arms wide, barely scratching just how big this place was. "That's a steal," he added.

I nodded, tempted to agree.

And there's the last factor. Money. Did it make me feel good that one of the biggest reasons we decided to buy out Plains Acres was the price tag? No, fuck no. It felt so shitty, but putting Luis's assumptions into the equation, Miles was willing to sell the farm if that meant retiring financially well off. He would be more inclined to seal the deal once November ends.

I couldn't turn my back on it. Romano Tech needed this, and frankly, so did I.

"I'll agree with you just this once, but let's not stop looking 'cause we have a few months until this deal is closed. Let's use that time, yeah?" I checked in with him.

He hummed.

"You got it, boss. I'll set up a meeting with my team. But don't set your eyes off this place just yet," he smirked. "I can feel it in the palm of my hands already," he chuckled.

"You're so weird," I shook my head in defeat. I was about to make another remark when my phone buzzed.

Rosie

Anything I can bring for tonight?

I grinned; my heart skipped a beat as I stared at the message. Her name read on the top of the screen as I quickly typed a reply. I had a few hours until I picked up Rosie for dinner. There was enough cow manure and fruitless negotiations to fill up my day. I couldn't wait until my night was filled with mind-nurturing conversations and a plate of comfort food.

"I'm gonna say bye to Miles, and then we're heading out," I said, shoveling my phone back into my pocket.

Luis had a knowing smirk on his face. "Wouldn't want to be late for your date, now do you?" He wiggled his brows, straightening up as he followed me. "It's fine that you canceled our movie night, by the way," he pursed his lips, shrugging. "No hard feelings."

Luis and I tried to squeeze a movie night in at least once a month. It wasn't a whirlwind night; we usually watched whatever new movie was released on our chosen streaming service, joined by some takeout. It was an enjoyable night; he was my best friend, after all, but I figured I could cancel one night.

"Just invite Ari. You guys usually do something," I said, hoping to solve his problem.

"She said no," he sighed.

I shook my head, turning away from him.

"She mentioned she was going out with a 'friend,'" he used air quotes.

"Is she not allowed to have other friends?" I cocked a brow.

"She *does* have other friends," he clarified. "But I don't know, something about this one seemed different, like she was surprisingly excited to go out this time around," he furrowed his brows.

"Maybe she finally met someone who melted her ice-cold heart," I joked.

"You think she has a date too? She usually tells me about those," he pondered.

"So what will you do now that your only friends have plans?" I tipped my head to the side.

"I'll figure it out. I'll probably check on what the girls are doing at home," he shrugged. "But, tomorrow, we're hanging out, and you're going to tell me how your date went," he punched my shoulder before walking to his car. "Good luck, Vic!" He shouted before stepping into his car.

God, he was annoying.

Chapter 15

Rosie

"He's here!" Luna shouted. The sound of her voice made my heart start beating faster as I struggled to close my purse.

"And he looks good!" Summer added before her footsteps were heard through the apartment. She ran across the living room to answer the buzzer.

They decided to stake out at the front window, watching and waiting until Victor showed up.

I found their patience amusing, but their ability to become overly excited was slightly annoying.

"Hurry up, Rosie!" Luna screamed again, but she was louder, considering she was in my room now.

"You do realize we live in a one-thousand-square-foot apartment. There's no need to shout," I giggled, throwing my purse over my shoulder. "You and Summer are way too enthusiastic for this. It's a dinner date, nothing more," I said, shaking out my hands in a calming manner.

"Umm, correction, you're going to his house so he can cook for you. This is a first date. Of course, we're excited!" Summer was looking through the peephole, her voice bouncing off the wood door.

"While I admitted that I like him, I wouldn't get your hopes up. I'm not interested in dating and have too much going on. I think we'll be better off as friends," I stated, my best friends rolling their eyes at me.

It was a whirlwind of emotions after I acknowledged my true feelings for the handsome CEO, but I knew I couldn't let it go further. Going on a date was one thing that I already opened my mind to. An entire relationship, though? My heart was swelling with the simplest idea of it, but my brain decided to stay shut on even the possibility. And right now, I wanted to listen to my head.

"Don't say that. You enjoy being with Victor. I don't know why you're fighting this," Luna raised her brows, hands on her hips.

"Totally," Summer agreed, turning her head to face me. "Besides, a distraction wouldn't be so bad," she suggested as I blew out a breath. "You've got so much going on with the store and Bianca. It would be good to have someone you can just *be* with," she offered.

"It will be a bad thing, and I have a deadline coming up. Let's just focus on this date, okay? It's a pretty big step for me, so can you guys just mark this as a win?" I sighed, adjusting the hem of my sweater, just as a knock sounded on the door.

"Of course," Luna rushed to agree while Summer ran to the door. "Good luck, okay?" She whispered to me.

"Victor! We've been expecting you," Summer grinned as she opened the door.

"Ladies," he greeted, a kind smile appearing on his face that only grew when his attention drew to me. "Rosie, hi," his eyes sparkled over the warm lighting of the apartment.

I couldn't help but warm at how he said my name, a heat creeping up my neck.

"Hi," I took in his simple outfit, a white tee with jeans. It was so casual. I was kind of shocked to see him in that. "I'll be going now. You guys have fun," I turned to my friends, who were grinning like schoolgirls.

"Oh, we will, but hopefully not as fun as you two," Summer smirked, wiggling her finger at us while she pushed me out of the apartment.

"Be safe!" They shouted in unison right as they shut the door behind us.

I blinked back in surprise, the feeling in my stomach shifting between nerves and excitement as I glanced at Victor.

"Your friends are funny," he mused once we began to make our way down the stairwell. "And they clearly care about you," he added.

"They're funny but annoying at times. Then again, who's friend isn't annoying at times, y'know?" I asked.

He blew out a laugh in agreement.

"Tell me about it. They seemed to have an eventful night ahead of themselves, though." He noted the living room decked out in blankets, snacks littered on the coffee table, and a movie paused on the TV.

"Oh yeah, Luna asked Summer to watch the Spider-Man movies. She has all of them on DVD, and she was really excited when Luna asked," I smiled.

Was it odd that Luna asked out of the blue? Yes, but she said she was getting into her Andrew Garfield phase and wanted to know what was up.

"So, still not planning on telling me what we're having for dinner tonight?"

"That's a surprise," he smirked, opening the car door for me.

I thanked him and noticed how clean the interior was. I also noticed how much it smelled like him. I kept my thoughts to myself as he came in on the other side and started the car.

We made small talk during the ride until he turned the corner and reached his building.

I knew he lived deeper in the city, dead center in the wealthier areas, but as we pulled up to the building, my eyes couldn't even make out its height.

"You live here?" I gaped, looking up as much as possible through the closed window. I stared at the ongoing glass panels that made up the structure. "To be honest, I thought you lived in the Sears Tower, being so rich and all," I sat back in the seat as he pulled into the parking garage.

"I don't think that'll be the right investment," he chuckled as he pulled into the parking garage.

"I honestly can't tell if you're joking, but I'm amused," I smirked, glancing at all the luxury sports cars parked in their respective spots.

Oh, to be rich.

We kept the same energy going as we laughed while we walked into the tenant's hallway, skipping the lobby and taking the elevator to a high level.

"Woah," I gasped once the door opened, the shock still in me when he unlocked his door.

Everything was *so manly*, yet it wasn't the typical billionaire playboy penthouse with sleek furniture made of the finest leather where everything was either black or a *really* dark gray. No, this was warm and welcoming.

The place opened into an open living room and dining room off to the left with different platform levels. The walls alternated between navy blue and charcoal gray. A huge brown leather sectional was in the middle of the living room with a massive TV, and copious amounts of pillows were strategically placed on the cushions. A huge plush rug broke off the area, making it all that more inviting.

As I stared at the bookshelves aligned against the wall that led to the kitchen, I was enticed by the photos that seemed to decorate the surfaces.

"This is not at all what I imagined," I shook my head in disbelief.

"What were you expecting?" He mused, shoving his hands in his pockets as he made his way down the few steps of the entrance.

I mindlessly followed him, my eyes scanning the things that adorned the shelves. "I don't know, but this feels like you. It's a beautiful place, Victor." I turned to look at him, finding him with a smile on his face. "May I look?" I gestured to the photos, and he nodded, offering his hand out. I gladly took the opportunity to step closer.

The first photo showed a woman and a young boy. Both were smiling at the camera while she held him in her arms.

"Is that your mom?" I asked, my features softening as I studied the young woman with dark brown hair and eyes and a nose like Victor's. "She's pretty," I smiled.

"Yeah, she was," he sighed.

I couldn't ignore the use of the past tense. "I'm sorry," I frowned, dropping my hands and playing with my charm bracelet. "I lost my mom too," I gulped, recounting the events that happened *that* night. "She seemed lovely," I added.

He nodded.

"She loved to cook," he started. "She taught me everything I know, and cooking her recipes feels like she's still here." He stared at the photo with adoration and heartache.

My heart skipped a beat. "She clearly taught you well," I grinned. "And I anticipate tonight's dish will be good," I licked my lips. "Any chance I get to know now?" I cocked a brow.

"Follow me," he nodded towards the kitchen. "We're making ravioli tonight," he stated, a gleam in his eyes.

"Oh," I hummed.

"I made some bruschetta as an appetizer," he said, pulling a tray from the fridge. The golden brown pieces of bread with cubed red juicy tomatoes placed on top begged to be eaten. "If you'd like, I have some wine," he said.

I grinned, asking for some before two glasses were placed in front of me. "Thank you for inviting me," I held out my glass for a toast. "I'm already having a great time."

"Me too," he clicked his glass with mine before taking a sip. "Have you ever had fresh ravioli?" He questioned, his hands resting on either side of him on the counter as he faced me.

I shook my head. "The closest I've ever gotten was taking a bite from Summer's plate at Olive Garden," I answered.

He winced at my response. "Nothing compares to real ravioli," he beamed. "Or any pasta, for that matter," he began, turning around to grab a chilled blob of dough from the fridge.

"Maybe you could show me then," I hiked my shoulders up, a sheepish grin on my face.

His gaze brightened before he agreed. "All you need is eggs and flour," he splayed it out on the counter after sprinkling some flour.

"That easy?" I leaned forward in interest. "Now, why is ravioli your favorite dish?" I asked, sipping from my glass.

"It's the first thing I ever learned to cook," he answered.

"I can't wait to try it," I said, watching him knead the dough.

I stared in awe as he kneaded it until it was plump and soft, the veins on his forearms protruding as he used the palm of his hand to push the dough together. It was clear he knew what he was doing, and I didn't think I found anything more attractive than in that moment. My eyes began to roam up his arms, his shirt sleeves strained against his biceps. I wondered what they would look like with my thighs hooked over them, my...

"Rosie?"

"I'm sorry, what?" I blinked repeatedly, putting my attention back to him, and I tried so hard to conceal my blush.

"Are you even paying attention?" He pondered. There was a teasing smirk on his face, and for my own sanity, I told myself he didn't notice the staring.

"I'm paying attention," I failed at an attempt to smile without my cheeks turning even redder. "I'm studying the technique, that's all," I shrugged and almost choked on air after realizing what I had said.

"Do you want to give it a try?" He asked, stepping away from the counter.

I made my way over to him, washing and drying my hands before placing them on the dough.

"C'mere," he stepped away from the counter, giving me enough space to stand between his arms. He put his hands on top of mine. His skin was soft, but I could see the noticeable burns and cuts on his fingers—cooking will do that to you. He looked over my shoulder to see, his chin brushing the top of my head, and my shoulder blades grazed his chest. "Is this okay?"

I nodded. How couldn't this be okay with the way I could feel the burning heat radiating off of him? Our bodies weren't pressed together, but he was so close that I could just step back, and I would feel *all* of him. But no, I couldn't do that. If he was giving us some distance, there was a clear reason why, and I wasn't going to disregard that boundary.

"I've never made pasta before. I always use the premade stuff." I started a conversation when his hands moved against mine, leading me to knead the dough properly.

"That stuff is disgusting. I haven't had store-bought pasta since I was seven," he grimaced.

"Since you were seven?!" I exclaimed, throwing my head back to look at him. Only I miscalculated, and my head rested against his chest. His broad and firm chest.

Oh my god.

"Other kids at school would always eat Kraft mac and cheese, and I begged my parents to buy some from the store. I took one bite, spit it out, and started crying," he chuckled at the memory.

I laughed, melting at the thought of seven-year-old Victor crying over mac and cheese. "Aww, that's adorable! Please tell me they said you weren't going to like it?" I hoped it would be the cherry on top of the story.

"Yes. My mom then prompted me to teach me how to make my own macaroni," he stated, something changing in his eyes.

"What was she like?" I asked.

"She was everything. Kind, compassionate, funny, smart," he sighed. "She was a nurse, and she loved helping people. She was actually kind of the reason I went into environmental engineering. She always said, "You know you're doing well if you're helping others,'" he reminisced.

"That's beautiful," I felt tears prick at my eyes, partially feeling jealous but also content that he shared this with me. My mother only cared about one person, and it wasn't Bianca or me. "I could tell she loved you a lot," I glanced up at him, which seemed to spark something inside him.

"Yeah, she did," he pulled away. "The dough is done," he cleared his throat and patted the freshly kneaded dough before reaching below one of the cabinets and pulling out a mixing bowl. "It's gonna rest for a bit," he settled beside me.

"It feels like I'm part of a cooking show," I leaned against the counter. "I'm entirely entertained right now," I smirked.

He blushed.

"It's a very hands-on experience."

"What better way to learn?" He shrugged, his gaze darting to my lips.

I paused, thinking back to my friend's words. Maybe I did need a distraction. Maybe I should open my mind to the thought of starting a relationship with the guy I like. Perhaps I should stop fighting it and listen to what my heart wanted for the first time.

Without overthinking, I reached up and pressed my lips against his. I quickly forgot my stance of not needing a distraction and not wanting a relationship.

Everything faded except for him.

He seemed taken aback, but his hands quickly found their place on my hips.

I leaned back as he deepened the kiss and placed both my hands on his face. I didn't care if my hands were covered in flour and I'd most likely left prints on his cheeks or if he did the same on my sweater.

Our lips molded against one another, causing my chest to burn as I desperately ached for more. The way my body contorted against his, begging to become one, was not far from a cry of desire, of passion…of love. No, it was too soon. I was getting ahead of myself. Knowing I was starting to let my heart take too much control, I pulled away.

"I think I was too scared to admit how much I wanted to kiss you before," I sheepishly said, licking my lips. "Or the fact that we just started being friends."

"I could say the same," he responded, resting his forehead against mine. "But I think we're past just being friends," he chuckled.

"Definitely past that," I smirked. "This moment was too perfect to miss," I nudged my nose with his as I wrapped my arms around his neck. "I really like you, Victor."

"I really like you too, Rosie," he replied.

"I'm so glad I went to the grocery store that night," I glanced up.

He chuckled. "Me too," he said before dipping to kiss me again.

~

I kissed Victor goodbye, inserting my keys in the knob before I leaned over for one more kiss. I couldn't stop smiling as I entered the apartment, setting my keys and purse down just as I shut the door.

"So, how'd the date go?" Luna asked, wiggling her brows.

The TV was paused in the middle of Tobey Maguire fighting off a villain in the movie, and I stared at the two girls breathing heavily on the couch.

"I feel like you guys already know," I squinted at them, not catching their bluff.

"We totally did not listen by the door and see you kiss Victor through the peephole," Summer waved off, scoffing. "Ow," she rubbed her arm after Luna punched her.

"Well?!" Luna turned to me.

"I did kiss him!" I squealed. "And we're dating now!" I bit my lip, not able to contain my smile.

"So, what did you guys do?"

"He made ravioli!" I pressed a hand to my chest. "Victor Romano can cook, and he made ravioli for me!" I exclaimed.

They shared my joy, kneeling on the cushions to face me.

"There's nothing hotter than a man who knows how to cook," Luna shook her head.

"I know, I was-," my phone ringing cut me off, the screen lighting up with an unknown number. I gulped as I answered, not expecting to hear from anyone at this hour. "Hello?"

"Rosie, it's Maritza. I know it's late, and I'm gonna get in real big trouble, but you need to know that Bianca was stabbed. She was sent to the medical ward, but I don't know how bad it was," she sucked in a breath, her words rapid and hushed. "I don't know how it happened, but it ended badly. I'll try to call again. I gotta go," she ended before hanging up.

"Wait! Is she going to be okay? I-," I dropped my hand, the phone clattering on the floor, and I felt my knees give out, the door being the only thing stopping me as I slid to the floor, panic setting in. "She was stabbed," I shook my head, tears spilling down my face. "She was stabbed," I repeated, my heart rate increasing.

Summer and Luna jumped on their feet.

"Woah, woah, deep breaths, Rosie," Luna kneeled in front of me.

I could feel her, but I could only picture the possible scenarios that led to this.

Was she trying to defend a friend? Was she pushed? Was it the creepy inmate? Did someone provoke her?

"I'm calling the number back. I'll try to get a hold of Maritza," Summer said, picking up the phone from the floor.

"I don't want her to die," I shook my head, sobbing as I curled in on myself. "I can't lose her," I cried.

Luna nodded. "She's not gonna die, so you're not gonna lose her," she rubbed her hands up and down from my knees to my ankles, trying to calm me down.

"But-I-I, she's hurt," I trembled, the words struggling to come out.

"It's gonna be fine, Rosie. Deep breaths," she encouraged, glancing back at Summer, who had the phone pressed to her ear.

I really hoped it was.

Chapter 16

Rosie

Summer couldn't get a hold of the number. No one answered. We figured it was contraband and didn't want to get Maritza into trouble.

She was a friend of Bianca's and a current inmate at the Greenville Correctional Institution. I met her a few times over the phone. She's helped Bianca in more ways than I can count.

I tried to consider myself lucky. Loved ones didn't usually receive a call if inmates got hurt. I would know, remembering the time Bianca was sent to solitary and I wasn't even aware until I visited her. Even with that experience, knowing the emotional turmoil, I still felt terrible.

After Luna managed to calm me through my anxiety attack and once I was able to think clearly again, I knew I needed to distract myself. So that's how I ended up back at Hecho de Hilo at midnight.

I wiped my cheeks as I continued staring at my notebook, which contained the instructions for a custom order I was working on. Part of it was illegible now, my tears splatting on the pages and smudging the ink. Everything was going perfectly, but of course, it all had to come toppling down in an instant.

I pushed my hair out of my face and rested my elbows on the table. I inhaled deeply, counting to four before holding for four and finally letting out for four. And repeated. I felt myself calm down just a bit, my heart rate easing.

The room was quiet except for my sniffles, and I was about to return to work when my phone rang.

I jumped in anticipation, thinking it was an update.

It was Victor.

"Victor," I forced a smile, hoping my voice didn't sound like I was crying. "What are you doing up? It's late."

"I was about to sleep, but I wanted to hear your voice first," he said through the phone, and my heart skipped a beat.

I squeezed my eyes shut as I melted, more tears pouring down my face. I wanted to indulge in my new boyfriend calling me just to say sweet nothings to me, but the looming dread of Bianca's health towered over me.

She should be here with me.

I wanted to imagine we'd be sitting on the couch watching a show while I recounted my date with Victor. I would answer his call, and she'd send me a thumbs up as I made my way to my room. Instead, I was fighting the urge to cry as I spoke to him.

"That's sweet," I hummed, but my voice cracked at the end, and I winced.

"Rosie," he began. "Are you crying?"

"No," I denied, but my voice raised an octave as I strained.

"Where are you?" He pressed.

I could hear the shuffling of bed sheets and the sounds of his feet pacing around his room. I choked back a sob, my emotional state sending me into overload at his kind gesture to check on me.

"At work," I answered, dropping my head into my hand.

"I'll be there in twenty minutes, don't move," he ordered before he hung up.

Twenty minutes later, I had cried out whatever I needed to before he arrived. I rinsed my face with cold water, making sure my eyes weren't red or puffy, but when I unlocked the door and let him inside, he knew I was hurt.

His brows furrowed as he wiped my tears away with his thumb. His mouth twitched, and I knew he was curious about why I was crying at one in the morning.

"Can you just hug me?" I asked, too scared to let myself speak before I revealed the real reason.

He seemed confused at my request, another sob raking through me, and his gaze softened. He whispered my name as he pulled me into his chest. He quickly embraced me, his strong arms wrapping around my shoulders, his touch sending more tears down my face.

We stood there for a few minutes, his hand rubbing soothing circles on my back until my crying calmed down enough that I could breathe properly again.

"What happened?" He asked, his voice rumbling through his chest and vibrating against my face.

"I don't know how to explain," my answer was muffled as I lifted my head and rested my chin on his chest.

"Take your time," he reassured.

"Thank you," I glanced down, turning around to lead him to the break room. "You didn't have to come all the way here to check on me, but the sentiment means a lot," I forced a small smile.

"I didn't have to, but I wanted to," he said, sitting next to me at the table and reaching for my hand.

I squeezed his hand, blinking more tears away. I tried to find the words, but everything piled in my head, thoughts consuming the possibility of the worst. Wiping my eyes with my sleeves as I held back my sobs.

He didn't say anything. His arm wrapped around me, and while he was just looking at me, I didn't find it weird that he was. Usually, staring caused me immense stress, but his was….comforting.

I felt the tension fall behind my eyes as I smiled mentally before my thoughts loomed into darkness again. I hesitated. Should I tell him, or shouldn't I? I opened my mouth to speak; his dark brown eyes bore into mine, and all I could find was sincerity and curiosity.

"It's my sister," I began, biting my lip as I felt the tears press on.

"It's okay, deep breaths," he guided me through my breathing and didn't continue until I had relaxed. "One word at a time."

"My sister, she's hurt," I muttered, shifting in my seat. "I don't know how bad," I forced out.

Her black hair was splayed on the tile, her lifeless eyes staring at me as she lay cold on the bathroom floor.

"Is there someone you can call?" He questioned, leaning forward in his seat.

"No," I answered, clapping a hand over my mouth to suppress the sobs. "I don't know. Her friend called me but can't call back because she's in prison, and they won't tell me what's going on!" I began hyperventilating, my mind wandering back to the phone call I received a few hours ago.

"Come here," he beckoned me over.

I stood up before he pulled me into his lap. I settled quickly, his warmth nuzzling me in, and I couldn't stop the thought forming in the back of my head about how perfectly I fit with him.

"I just," I let out a frustrated sigh, resting my cheek on his shoulder, my hand playing with the material of his shirt. "She's been there seven years already, on charges that shouldn't even run that long, and she's all I have left," I paused, taking a deep breath. "Every time I get a call, my heart rate picks up. I only get one hour with her twice a month, and it's never enough. I haven't hugged her since she's been there, and I'm afraid I never will again."

My mind raced back to the day she was arrested, the last time I hugged her.

~

"I don't think Ms. Lopez cares if you have a B in AP Lit. Hasn't she been tutoring you for the test in May?" I asked, turning the corner to Bianca and I's apartment as Luna and I biked home from school.

"Yeah, but she's been hounding me since she wants me to get into a good school," she sighed. "Stanford and Columbia have been on my list, but they're so expensive," she frowned. "I don't think my parents could afford it."

"Tell me about it. Even UW-Madison is closer, but I see Bianca already stressed about it," I sucked in a breath, my gaze ripping to the numerous police cars parked in front of our building.

My heart plummeted, and I quickly hopped off my bike, running to see what was happening. As I stepped closer, my worst fear came true.

"Bianca?!" I screamed when I caught sight of her in cuffs, being escorted to a police car. "What's going on? Where's Julio?"

"¡Rosita!" Her eyes widened. "Go with Luna, call her parents," she ordered. "I'll explain everything," she reassured, but her eyes were glossed over, and the officer tugged on her harder to get her moving.

"No! Please don't take her!" I felt panic set in, tears streaming down my face as I acted on instinct, moving around them to wrap my arms around

my sister, preventing her from being moved. "Tell me what's going on?!" I cried, looking up at her.

She wouldn't meet my gaze, the afternoon sun casting a glow on her so that even with her disheveled makeup, she still looked beautiful. But her eyes bore with regret and fear. Her lips quivered, and she only looked down when I asked.

"You have to let go of me, Rosie. This will only end worse," she sniffled.

The officer decided to intervene, gripping Bianca harder, but I only pulled my weight, keeping her where she was.

"I'm not letting go," I shoved my face into her shirt, tears staining the thin material. "Not until you tell me what's going on," I begged, my sobs racking through my body, only drawing more attention from the neighbors.

Another officer came up behind me, using all his strength to pull me off, but I held my ground.

"I'm not letting go!" My voice cracked as I was sent into hysterics, my knees giving out, and I fell to the ground, but I wrapped my legs around Bianca like a child clinging to their mother on their first day of school. "She's all I have left! Please!"

"We need child services. There's a minor in distress," a third officer called over the dispatch. "Kid, you're testing our patience right now. Listen to your sister. Things will only get worse from here on out if you don't cooperate," he warned.

I froze, my cheek pressed against Bianca's thigh, and I squeezed my limbs around her harder, the force almost sending her toppling down if it weren't for the officer's tiger grip on her.

"Chiquita, por favor," she whimpered, eyes closed as she begged. "You have to let me go," she shook her head.

"I don't want to," I hiccuped. "Why are they doing this?" I stared at *the ground, my vision blurry from my tears.*

"Because I made bad choices," she inhaled, her voice hovering over me. "I'm sorry, Rosita." She broke out sobbing, tears splattering on the ground, and I felt as one fell on my face. "I'm sorry," she repeated pleadingly.

An empty feeling sank in my stomach, my mind racing to all the clues splayed out in front of me the past few years. All the late nights, the surplus of cash, the secretive whispers between her and her boyfriend—it all made sense now.

I finally let go, a fourth cop pulling me up as numbness consumed me. She and Luna helped me to the steps of the neighboring building. I sat frozen, my eyes fixated on the pavement.

The sounds of the police sirens, the sounds of the officers shouting orders, the barks of the police dogs coming from inside our apartment, and the commotion of the bystanders were all drowned out.

I didn't even watch as they took Bianca away.

~

"What's the name of the prison?" Victor whispered, the heat of his lips on my forehead pulling me out of my daze.

"It's located in Greenville," I sighed, not thinking much of it. "I'm sorry if I sprung too much onto you. I haven't been put in a position like this in a while," I gulped, wiping my eyes.

"Never apologize," he kissed the top of my head. "I want to be here for you, whatever you need," he cupped my face, searching my eyes for understanding.

I nuzzled into his touch, my eyelids fluttering closed. For a moment, I let everything slip away, only focusing on him. I allowed my head to rest entirely on his chest, the steady rate of his heart calming me.

"Do you want me to drop you off at home?" He asked. "Or do you want to spend the night at my place?"

My ears perked at that, and I responded, "Your place, if that's okay."

Before we got up, he sent me the tiniest, most reassuring smile. He then helped me collect my things and close up shop.

Soon, we were back in his car and driving to his apartment. Walking back into his place, it still felt warm and welcoming.

I was brushing my teeth in the guest room's ensuite when he returned, handing me a T-shirt and some sweatpants. I changed into them, finding comfort in the lingering scent of his cologne.

Afterward, I stood by the bed, my fingers brushing the comforter. My heart sat heavy with the thought of Bianca. I inhaled, wanting to push the worry aside for a little bit to sleep, but I wasn't sure how I could.

Victor stood at the foot of the bed, asking me if I needed anything else. I contemplated before I spoke. "Stay, please," I reached for his hand.

He sent me a small smile before we crawled into bed. His presence felt warm and welcoming, like his home, drawing me closer as I scooted until I was cuddled against his chest. The similar rhythm of his heart and his breathing lulled me to sleep that night.

Chapter 17

Victor

Rosie woke up crying the following morning.

Her sobs filled the guest room, and it took an hour to get her calmed down. Her well-rested sleep ended once her mind flashed back to the events that had occurred the previous night. Now, she claimed she wanted to go back to work.

Something I was against, but through her tear-soaked eyes, I didn't want to argue.

"It's a little cold this morning. Do you want your jeans?" I asked, sitting in front of her on the bed.

"I'll just wear these," she whispered, referring to the sweats I had given to her last night, arms crossed out in front of her as she sat up under the covers.

"You haven't eaten since last night, and if you're going to be working, you need breakfast," I proposed. I didn't want to sound pushy, but I was worried.

She inhaled deeply, averting my gaze. "I'm too nervous to eat," she chewed on her lip. "Besides, I ate pretty well last night. It should hold me over for the day," she reassured me, but I didn't buy it.

"Eat a little bit, just a piece of toast," I offered. "I know you're nervous, but you need the energy," I reasoned.

She thought it over for a moment before nodding. "Okay."

"Thank you," I leaned over and kissed her forehead before I left her to get ready.

She came to the kitchen a few moments later, my shirt still on her, and I felt my heart leap in my chest, but it sank a moment later at the sight of her red eyes.

I was about to open my mouth to speak, but her arms wrapped around my waist stopped me.

"Thank you," she said against my chest. "For being here," she added, turning her head, her cheek rubbing against my shirt.

"It's nothing, Rosie. I want to be here for you," I tucked a strand of hair behind her ear. "Are you sure you want to go to work?" I asked again as she pulled away.

"Business is not gonna run itself," she smiled before grabbing my toast on a plate and taking a bite out. "Luna said she'll take me to work," she swallowed.

"Okay, that's no problem. I'll drop you off at your place then."

She smiled genuinely for the first time this morning before she stepped forward to kiss me.

I kissed her back briefly. It was short but said everything that needed to be said.

Warm, welcoming, reassuring.

Driving her back to the apartment was silent but comfortable.

I walked her to her door, where Luna was waiting for us, and I got another look at her tear-stained face. "If you need anything, call me, okay?" I cupped her face with my hands, wishing her a good day before I kissed her goodbye.

"I got her from here," Luna helped her into the apartment. "Thank you, Victor," she pressed her lips together in a smile, her arms wrapped around her best friend.

"For sure," I tipped my head as the door closed. I turned and made my way back to my car to get to work as well.

Still, I worried about her. I knew there was something I could do, but not knowing how to go about it led me to stand in front of Ari.

"What do you know about blackmail?" I asked her, stopping before her desk.

She straightened, her face serious as always. "What do you want to know?" She moved her attention to me.

Ari was fascinated with true crime, a small detail she shared in passing a few Halloweens ago when she wore bloody knife earrings to work.

I smiled, grateful for my fantastic assistant. "I need to make a light threat," I shrugged.

"A light threat?" She cocked a brow, folding her arms over her chest. "To whom?"

"The warden at Greenville Correctional Institution," I answered. "There's been a situation, and he needs to be reminded of what happens when the protocol isn't followed," I elaborated and watched as a smirk grew on her face.

"And what is this "light threat"?" She used air quotes, her mocking tone slipping through. I regretted asking for a moment, but I didn't back down. "Does that matter? Can you just get me some information?" I brushed off.

She licked her lips, humming as she nodded. "Or you can call him," she scrunched her shoulders up. "He's afraid of you, y'know? I don't think he believes the whole "kind boss" thing," she used the air quotes again. "It's funny if you think about it," she snorted.

I paused. "He's afraid of the guy who built a garden in the prison? He's backward in more ways than one," I rolled my eyes. "Thanks again, Ari," I dismissed before walking to my office.

"Sure thing, boss," she called after me before returning to work.

I shut the door behind me, pulled out my phone, and promptly got to Ari's advice.

The line rang a few times before he picked up.

"Mr. Romano, it is a pleasure to hear from you, although a surprise as we don't have any meetings planned?" He pondered through the phone, acting like he wasn't a malicious ass that disregarded the well-being of his inmates' families and loved ones.

I wished I could punch him through the phone.

"I'm aware. I'm calling because it was brought to my attention that one of your inmates was injured during a fight, and she still hasn't been put in contact with her family. Am I correct?" I asked. I heard the gobsmack sound through the phone, anger bubbling in my stomach.

"Sir, how were you even made aware of this?" His chair squeaked through the phone, probably struggling to sit up.

I let go of a tense breath, unclenching my fists. "I supply green energy for your facility, and I'm going to make sure I'm aware of what's going on," I raised a brow, stating matter of fact. "Would you please put Miss Martinez in contact with her sister?" I tipped my head to the side in disbelief that I had to call in the first place.

"That's not protocol," he excused, his words jumbling together.

"We both know that's bullshit, people were hurt, and their families should know if they're okay," I gritted. "I thought Romano Tech partnered with a competent prison, or am I mistaken?"

"Of course, you are, Mr. Romano! I'll grab Miss Martinez immediately.

Our best medical staff attended to her, and will make a full recovery," he spoke quickly, struggling not to stammer.

Relief filled me. "Don't tell me, tell her sister."

"Of course," he blew out a breath, his voice raising an octave. "So sorry again, Greenville Correctional Institution is happy to be working with Romano Tech," he sounded insincere, but that didn't matter.

As long as Bianca would be okay, that meant Rosie was too.

I hung up, feeling better. About to check my emails, my phone buzzed. My body relaxed as I read Rosie's name on the screen.

Rosie

Nothing from the prison yet, hoping I'll hear something before lunch. Thanks again for everything though.

I chewed on my lip, hoping she would get a call soon.

~

Rosie

"I don't need to go home!" I argued. "I can't stay there and twiddle my thumbs all day worrying about my sister. At least here I can worry and work," I huffed, shaking my head as I reorganized the yarn on the shelves.

"We're just worried for you, that's all," Luna softened her voice.

I inhaled and exhaled. I knew I was being a little harsh, but I was so angry.

This morning, I could barely muster out a word, but now that my mind was processing my emotions, all I felt was anger and regret.

I couldn't stop thinking about Bianca. I couldn't stop thinking about how I only knew her situation because of her friend. I couldn't stop thinking about how there was nothing that I could do.

I was frustrated at being helpless.

"I'm sure the prison will call soon," Summer tried to reassure.

I nodded. "I hope so," I picked at the yarn in my hand, the burnt orange one that was one of my favorites.

Bianca said it was ugly when I first showed it to her, but it was one of the top sellers in the fall.

I felt tears prick in my eyes at the memory.

"I want to see her," I pulled my lips together to suppress a sob. Just like that, I was back to being sad. "Even just to demand they let me know how she is," I sniffled.

"We can do that," Luna agreed. "We're getting an influx of customers now," she winced when she noticed the crowd gathering at the door. "Should I tell them we're closed due to an emergency?" She placed a hand on my shoulder.

"I don't know," I glanced down, that feeling bubbling in my stomach and not the good kind.

Maybe I should've eaten breakfast.

"How about we stay for another hour? If we don't hear anything by then, we'll close and go," Summer suggested.

"Okay," I wiped my tears.

That was a good idea. It was logical. Right now, that's what I needed.

"Great," Luna pressed her lips in a small smile. "Refresh in the back. We'll take care of everything," she patted my back before guiding me to the break room.

I was left with the soft buzz of the light in the breakroom before I sat down at the table. Pulling out my phone, I sent Victor a quick message. I smiled softly when he replied.

Victor

Let's hope. Let me know if you need anything. Anytime, Rosie :)

I made my way to the bathroom, checking on my appearance when my phone began to buzz again.

Expecting it to be from Victor, I was shocked to see it was the prison.

Chapter 18

Rosie

"Hello?" I chewed on my fingernail, waiting anxiously to hear a voice.

"*¿Rosita?*" Bianca's voice sounded hoarse as my name fell from her lips.

My shoulders eased with a newfound relief, but my heart dropped at the weakness in her tone.

"Bee?" I asked. "You're alive?" I gasped, resting a hand on my forehead.

"I am," she laughed lightly. "How are you doing?"

"I should be asking you that. You were stabbed!" I exclaimed, pacing around the bathroom.

I wanted to jump through the phone and assess the situation myself. My lack of a medical degree be damned. I needed to see for myself that she was alive and hug her until I knew she was going to make it.

For now, her voice would do.

"Prison life, *mija*. The doctor said I would've died if the infliction was two inches to the right," she hummed, talking like it was a walk in the park.

"What happened?" I gulped, my throat dry as the anticipation clawed into me.

"Wrong place at the wrong time," she answered.

I gulped, blinking my tears away as I glanced up.

"Didn't even see it coming. The guards speculate I was a target, but who knows," she hummed, her raspy voice causing strain. "They're all a bunch of gossips anyway," she sucked in a breath before it pulled into a fit of coughs.

I heard her chug some water over the phone, the coughs dying.

"I might be put in solitary for my own protection," she mentioned after a pause.

My heart stopped.

"That's bullshit. You didn't do anything wrong," I felt my lip wobble, my eyes training on the shakiness in my hand. "They need to put whoever *stabbed* you in there, not you!" I yelled, my chest heaving with each breath.

"I'm going to be fine. Nothing I haven't been through before," her calm state made me stress more. "I'm going to make it, Rosie, okay?" Her voice found some strength, giving me the tiniest ounce of reassurance. "The warden said you can call me whenever you'd like while I'm in recovery," she said lightheartedly.

I nodded, tears spilling down my face.

"Kinda strange. Wonder what has them in a good mood to be following protocol," she scoffed, continuing after my silence. "Unless they were threatened," she pondered.

"I don't care. I need to talk to the warden. They can't put you back in there," I said, focusing on what she had told me.

"You can try, but I'm sure they're going to find a way regardless," she sighed. "I'm tired, okay? Call me back later. I love you," she said.

"Okay," I whispered, lips trembling. "I love you too," I attempted to sound firm but failed.

I hung up, staring down at the phone in my hands. I slowly reached for the doorknob, but my mind couldn't quite process that's what I was doing. Before I knew it, I opened Victor's message.

It wasn't a second later that he replied he'd be right over.

Me

Can you come to the shop please?

I was sitting on the roof, sipping on some tea Summer made for me after I told them the news. My eyes were dry from crying so much, and the crisp wind didn't make it any better.

The sound of the roof door tore my attention towards it, and I found Victor standing there, concern written all over his face. I turned my body to face him before I crumpled.

"They're putting her in solitary," the words left me on autopilot just as the tears slipped out. "I-I can't," I squeezed my eyes shut, Victor immediately pulling me into his arms. "I can't keep going like this," I shook my head, sobbing into his chest.

He stayed silent, running his hand over my head, coaxing me as he sat on the picnic table beside me.

I tried to calm my sobs, focusing on the beating of his heart and the smell of his cologne. I forced my attention to the numerous sounds in the streets, but all my worries made themselves front and center of my thoughts.

"I need you to say something, anything but this right now," I cried. "Please, I just can't," I doubled over, clutching his shirt. "Can you tell me something about yourself?" I questioned, fear setting in me like I was asking for something big.

"Okay," he responded, his hand brushing over my hair. His voice was so gentle and soft as he continued. "Besides store-bought pasta, store-bought marinara sauce is a monstrosity."

I blinked in content, my face relaxing just a bit.

"My family's from Sicily, and I've visited every year until my grandparents passed away, and my mom couldn't bear going back," he stated, a hint of sorrow filling his tone.

I often wondered what it would be like to visit where my parents came from in Mexico, but I have never been, so I couldn't miss it, unlike him.

"I think lemon desserts are the best," he added, changing to a positive tone.

I was glad to hear that, as I agreed wholeheartedly. Victor seemed like a lemon dessert type of guy.

"I don't get the hype with superhero movies, and I think anyone who takes offense should get a life," he said, followed by a chuckle.

Oh, Summer would love to hear that.

"I find astrology fascinating. I have no knowledge of it, though, and given a chance to go to space, I would turn it down in an instant," he reached his hand up and wiped my tears before he started rubbing small circles on my cheek, soothing me to look at him. "My favorite animal is a rhino because they were my mom's favorite. She thought they were adorable," he smiled, glancing down at me.

My cries quieted down, and I thanked him softly. I closed my eyes gently as he pressed a kiss on my lips.

He handed me my mug, my frame still wrapped in his arms.

My mind was distracted from the obvious. The newfound facts I learned about this man filled my brain with more questions than I could process. I used this opportunity to focus on the warm sensations surrounding me—the smooth liquid of the tea soothing my throat and the heat radiating from Victor.

But even then, it was impossible.

In the back of my head, I knew I needed to find a lawyer. The search for one had been endless. Most either didn't want to bother taking Bianca's case, or they were charging an arm and a leg for their services.

Maybe I could get in touch with Maritza soon. I chewed on my lip, contemplating. I hadn't heard from her since she called, and I was starting to wonder if I could get more info from her.

Inhaling deeply, I sipped my tea, nestling into Victor's side as we watched over the roof. I kept telling myself I'd worry about it tomorrow, weighing on the positive that my sister would survive.

~

Victor

I kissed Rosie goodbye before I had to head back to work.

We spent an hour on the roof, sitting in silence.

It was strange the amount of silence we find ourselves in.

I've known her for roughly two weeks and have been dating for two days, yet I felt more comfortable around her than others I've known for years. I found that to be a good thing.

Once I got into my car, I tried not to dwell on the fact that I was still working with an incompetent person, but I knew that problem would be handled the moment I dialed the warden's number.

"This wasn't what we agreed on," I began when he answered, and I could hear him scoff.

"You have no power over what goes on over here, Romano. This is always the solution to issues like these," he grumbled.

I've met the man a handful of times, and I could count how many times he's told me otherwise.

Incompetence made you your own enemy.

"How long do you plan on keeping Miss Martinez in solitary then?" I cocked a brow.

He sighed, the creak in his old chair sounding through the call. "As long as needed until she is safe to go into gen pop again," he explained.

"You do realize that it's illegal to keep an inmate in solitary confinement for more than ten consecutive days, right?" I narrowed my gaze.

The audacity.

"Oh, I'm sorry, I didn't realize you worked in the prison system," he scoffed. "Stay in your lane, Romano," he spat.

I could practically see the cocky smirk he had on his face.

"I don't, but I work close enough to know that a publication from The Chicago Tribune about this incident could bite you in the ass," I sucked in a sharp breath.

He paused, another creak coming from his crusty chair. His smirk was gone. "You're bluffing," he gulped.

"*Prison sends inmate to solitary confinement after being stabbed by fellow inmates,*" I smiled wickedly. "The press would *love* to know which prison caused this and who exactly allowed such a cruel thing," I stated.

"What do you suggest we do then?" He sighed.

"Send the other inmate to max security. That's standard protocol, *something* you should already be aware of."

"I'll see to getting it done, but this better be the last call from you, Romano," he warned.

I laughed through the phone. "Then don't do anything you shouldn't be doing," I said before hanging up.

Chapter 19

Rosie

As much as the dread of knowing Bianca might be sent to solitary ate away at me, and knowing that I couldn't do anything to help weighed me down, I kept myself busy by returning to work.

That's what I've always done.

It was the only thing I could do.

Continue to work my ass off in hopes that I'll profit enough money one day to afford a good lawyer to get my sister out of that hell. All the late nights and endless struggle would all be worth it if that meant I could have her back with me.

Where she belonged.

The sound of my phone ringing shocked me out of my headspace, and when I answered, I stopped stocking the shelves.

My heart sank when my gaze briefly read the prison's contact.

"Miss Martinez," the warden greeted after me.

"I wasn't expecting a call so suddenly. Is my sister okay?" I gulped, squeezing the phone as I leaned against the shelves.

I glanced over to Luna and Summer, who tended to the customers at the checkout. Their faces were filled with concern, but I sent them a reassuring look before I walked towards the corner window for some privacy.

"I wanted to personally call you and let you know that Bianca won't be placed in solitary; she'll continue to recover in the medical wing," the warden answered. "As for the other inmates, they will be transferred to a maximum-security prison tomorrow. You can come visit your sister like usual on Saturday," he explained.

A quivering smile appeared as I inhaled and exhaled deeply, relief swarming through me.

Thank you.

"What changed?" I asked, happy tears streaming down my face.

"Let's just say you have a guardian angel watching over you," he said lightheartedly before he hung up.

I dropped my gaze as I furrowed my brows. I turned around to glance at my friends. I loved how strong-willed they can be, but I knew they weren't the angel watching over me. I licked my lips in thought, my eyes scanning over the street at an empty parking space, and I couldn't help but wonder if it was him.

It wasn't a reach, and as much as I was thankful, an unpleasant feeling grew in my stomach.

I blew out a breath, shaking the nerves out of me. I turned and walked over to the girls just as the last customer walked out.

The past twenty-four hours were intense, and I was just glad it ended on a good note.

~

"How do you feel?" Victor greeted me after he let me inside his apartment.

His apartment still held that inviting warmth. The lights were dim, creating such a cozy ambiance.

We were meeting for dinner, another meal he cooked per his request. It was only our second day as a couple, yet it felt much longer.

Contentment and anxiety both lingered in my body. I was happy I was in a relationship that felt promising, *exciting*. But I was nervous that we were moving too fast and hadn't stopped to discuss important things.

I looped my arm around his waist and placed my bag on the hook. "Better, the warden called. She won't be put in solitary," I smiled genuinely, searching his eyes for any sign of shock.

He grinned, placing his arm over my shoulders. "I'm glad to hear that. Are you hungry?" He asked, guiding me into the kitchen.

"I could eat," I said, feeling my stomach rumble as the sweet herby aroma entered my nose. On top of the fact that I only ate a piece of toast today and a small lunch. "What's on the menu tonight?"

"This is number two on my list. It's the best comfort food," he reasoned, pulling two bowls out of the cabinet.

"Grilled cheese and tomato soup," I stated, glancing at the simple meal ready to be devoured. "You know how to make things look good," I smiled, leaning into his side as I hugged him.

I enjoyed being close to Victor, and he seemed to enjoy it too. As I inhaled his woody cologne, I couldn't help but feel a pang in my heart as I thought back to my assumption earlier.

"Plating the food is one of the fun parts," he hummed, handing me my plate before we walked to the dining table, where we sat next to each other.

"Victor, can I ask you something?" I pulled my lip between my teeth.

"Anything, Rosie," he turned his attention towards me.

"Are you why Bianca contacted me and why she won't be going into solitary?" I fidgeted my fingers on the table. "The warden said I had a guardian angel watching over me. You and the girls are the only ones who know what's going on," I trailed, staring at the food.

I wasn't sure if I wanted it to be true.

He didn't respond right away, pausing before he spoke. "I work with the prison your sister is at. Romano Tech gifted renewable energy to many state prisons and opened gardens for the inmates," he explained. "I know the warden personally, and I figured getting to him directly would help," he placed a hand on my knee. "Did I do something wrong, Rosie?" He furrowed his brow.

"I don't know," I exhaled. "On the one hand, I'm very thankful for you," I offered a small smile. "But I can't stop this feeling gnawing at me," I wrapped my arms around my stomach. "It was so easy for you just to call him up and change his mind," I laughed in disbelief. "They didn't even bother calling me," I added, feeling tears prick my eyes.

"I didn't mean to hurt you, Rosie. I'm sorry," he reached up, wiping a tear away.

His sincere words and soft touch made my following words much harder to say.

"Victor, I know you want to help me, but I want you to stop what you're doing," I confessed shakingly. "I've dealt with the warden before. I've dealt with Bianca being in prison. I know how to survive it, so I can't let you swoop in and fix everything," I rolled my lips together, glancing away before I looked back and was met with a face of confusion.

"I don't understand," he shook his head. "I want to help you, and I can, but you don't want me to?" He licked his lips, eyes searching mine.

Those big, beautiful brown eyes that were so hard to resist, I could fall in.

"I do, but this is just complicated," I averted my gaze. "The first time

Bianca was in solitary, I was a mess," I squeezed my eyes shut as the memories flashed back. "Same thing as before. No answers, no news. I even got turned away when I went to visit her. I couldn't eat, I couldn't sleep, I couldn't do anything but worry. She was there for almost two weeks," I felt tears prick in my eyes.

Luna and Summer tried so hard to get me to do anything. But I didn't have the urge to until I saw her again.

"I went to visit her for the first time, and she was gone," I gulped. "She wasn't the same person I saw before, and she hasn't been the same," I sniffled, bringing my sleeve up to wipe my eyes. "I tried to pull my savings together, but none was enough for a lawyer. I still can't help but blame myself for everything she's gone through," I struggled to say.

The knock on the door, the flashing red and blue lights, Bianca clinging to me as we heard our mother scream in agony…

"Why do you blame yourself?" He wondered.

"I'm so thankful you stopped her going through that again," I ignored his question. "But you have to understand that it's hard to process. All the grief I went through those two weeks, I was *helpless*, and here you come in like a white knight saving the day," I heaved.

"Is that what you think of me, Rosie?" His face fell, his hand loosening on my knee. "I don't want you to think I'm doing this to fuel my ego. I do it because I care for you, and I can only imagine how hard it is to have your only family locked away. I'm sorry if I crossed a line, but you can't expect me not to do anything knowing I can help," he breathed deeply.

I didn't have much of an intention to word it the way I did. But I knew how I said it was how I felt.

How many stories are about the prince saving the princess? The hero saving the damsel in distress?

I wasn't a princess or a damsel.

"That's the problem, Victor," I looked up at him with a teary gaze. "You can choose to help or not," I shook my head, tears spilling. "I've been stuck with the cards I'd been dealt my entire life, and so far, I've been doing just fine. I know you want to help. I know you have the power and money to do so, but I can't let you do that. I can't ask you to do that," I sighed.

"I understand, but I want you to know you can ask me anything. I would do *anything* for you, Rosie," he reached to cup my jaw.

I melted in his touch.

Because is what you feel for me, the same way I feel for you?

"Why?" I gulped.

"Because I care," he answered, but part of me knew that wasn't the entire truth.

"You've done too much for me, though," I shrugged away from his touch. "We haven't even been dating for a week," I breathed, running a hand through my hair. "In the past day, you've saved my sister more than I could ever. You're so much more capable than I am, and it's kinda scary," I shook my head.

It was true.

I started my business at eighteen, straight out of high school. Six years later, I'm barely profiting in the five-figure range.

Victor though?

He started his company at twenty-two after college. He built his business in the first two years and has since created a billion-dollar empire.

Power, money, capability.

Something Victor had and I didn't.

"I don't want you to be scared of me. I'd never do anything to hurt you," he reached for my face. "I don't want you to think you're incapable,

Rosie. You do so much for your community, and you're still standing after everything you've been through. What will it take me to convince you that you're the reason you've come this far?" He begged, voice cracking slightly. He wiped my tears away with his thumb.

I nuzzled into his hand. I wanted to give in and let him save me, but it wasn't right. It wouldn't be fair to me.

"I don't think you're the right person to convince me," I looked up at him. "I need time to think," I stood up abruptly.

I didn't look back, I couldn't do it.

If I was going to get into a relationship with a powerful man like Victor, it needed to be on the right terms—not like this.

"Rosie," he called after me, following me into the living room.

"Please, I need space," I grabbed my bag. "I'll call you when I can think straight," I gulped, tears welling in my eyes.

He exhaled, tipping his head down. "Okay, take all the time you need," he stepped back, shoving his hands into his pockets. He looked so hurt, so remorseful.

I wanted to tell him it wasn't his fault, and he only tried to do good for me. But it wasn't my fault either because I needed to do right by myself.

Chapter 20

Victor

I never thought I'd be so bad at a relationship that the first serious one I ever was in ended before it started. Yet, here I was a day after Rosie and I had our "fight."

I didn't want to categorize it as an argument. Nothing was said in vain, and we weren't angry with each other. We just had a discussion that resulted in us going on a break.

A break after a day of becoming official.

Fuck, it hurt more to say it. It also hurt that my attempts to help Rosie didn't work out as I intended, but I didn't want to push her away by starting a problem that didn't exist. I crossed a boundary, a huge one. And I wasn't sure how to fix things.

A knock sounded through my office before it opened, and my thoughts were forced aside.

"Heading out for lunch, I figured you and I could get a sandwich from that shop you like? Eat it by the lake," Luis entered my office, leaning against the door frame.

I inhaled, contemplating it before I nodded, thinking I could use the pick-me-up.

Deli Kings was a local favorite downtown. It had been a while since

I'd gone, and considering the beautiful weather, there was no more perfect pairing.

We sat near the planetarium, finding a spot in the sun. It felt like those days we would ride our bikes out here after school. Eating the huge deli sandwiches we bought on the way and leaving just as the sun set, knowing we would face the wrath of our mothers for being late.

"So what's got you down in the dumps?" Luis asked just as he bit into his sandwich.

"Why do you think I'm sad?" I shrugged off, wondering if I wasn't hiding my emotions as well as I thought.

"You're wallowing like a puppy," he stated. "So what's the deal? Got in a fight with your girlfriend or something?" He turned to face me.

"Or something," I raised my brows. "I think I fucked things up with Rosie," I admitted.

"Damn, already?" He furrowed his brows.

Wincing at his outburst, I realized it sounded worse than I thought.

"It hasn't even been a week. What could you have possibly done?"

"I overstepped a boundary even though my actions were well intended," I blew out a breath. "I apologized, but she said she needs time to think things over," I added. "She's scared at how capable I am and asked me not to do anything to help her." It hurt to say it, to acknowledge that what I did was wrong, but then I think back to her words.

"*I don't think you're the right person to convince me.*"

I had hurt her, and I couldn't take it back. There wasn't even a situation I played out in which things didn't end up the way they did.

"Because you're rich or because you're white?" Luis stated.

"I think a little bit of both," I glanced out onto the lake. "I enjoy spending time with Rosie even though it's only been a short while. I want to get to know her more. I truly think she's the woman I'm spending the rest of my life with," I felt my shoulders relax at the mere thought of a future with her. "But I just don't know how I cannot do *anything*," I grimaced, exhaling.

"You just have to respect her wishes," Luis began. "I know you mean well, and your intentions are good, but look at it from her perspective," he pointed out. "You're a white man, although sometimes that Sicilian glow makes you look more Mexican than me," he tried a joke that made me smile. "She's dealt with a lot of prejudice in her life. I'm sure it leaves a nasty taste in her mouth when you come in to save the day," he concluded. "Some things she needs to face on her own even if you're her boyfriend now."

Luis was right.

I hated admitting it, but fuck.

"Talk to Rosie and tell her you're sorry but mention you're still here if she needs anything because you care about her," he said.

I nodded. "Thanks, Luis," I reached out to pat his shoulder.

"Anytime, Vic," he mimicked my motions.

We finished our lunch, and I felt better knowing there was a possibility I could get my girl back.

~

Rosie

I focused on the clay smoothing against my palms. The stubby walls of the bowl I was molding formed slowly. Since Victor and I last talked, I've resorted to spending a lot of my time at the ceramics shop twenty minutes from my apartment.

Ceramics have always been my escape; if I mess up, I can start over and shape it into something new. That small semblance of control distracted me from all my life's problems. The only issue was when my need for an escape happened in the middle of the night when everything was closed. Leading me to find solace in working on commissions for the shop. Thankfully, it was daytime now, and I can rationally release my frustrations.

"I've been taking care of myself for the last seven years. I run my own business, pay my bills, fight my own battles," I grew angry, my hand curling into a fist, and I didn't realize the clay smushed together until it was seeping through my fingers. I stared at the mess I made, my heart wrenching as my anger left. "To think he was different," I frowned, a sting forming in my eyes. "He *is* different."

Maybe that's why it hurt.

I liked him more than enough to start a relationship, which I never thought I'd find someone I'd want to let in that way. I never thought I could enjoy spending time with someone as much as I do with him.

Our conversations, our shared views of the world, our common interests. The way he made me laugh, made me feel more secure in his embrace, the happiness I felt watching him cook—even just that once.

He made me feel heard.

Even when he crossed a boundary, he never made me feel like I made the wrong choice. He gave me space, and now he was giving me time. If he hadn't done that and weren't so understanding, then maybe it'd be easier to choose.

"That doesn't look like a bowl."

I yelped at the familiar voice and turned to find Luna leaning against the table beside me. Her arms crossed over her chest when I glanced up.

"Unless it's a decomposed bowl. It won't hold my cereal." Summer brushed past her and took a seat at an empty pottery wheel.

"It's not—I'm not—I got distracted," I fumbled over my words, throwing the smashed clay onto the wheel as I inhaled. "How'd you even know I was here?"

"Because we love you and know you."

"Tracked your phone."

Summer and Luna said at the same time. Summer narrowed her gaze at her, receiving an honest look.

"Does this have something to do with the fact that you got into a fight with your obnoxiously hot boyfriend?" Luna cocked a brow.

"I'm gay, but even I can realize he's hot," Summer added.

I cracked a smile.

"Ah! I made her smile!" She straightened up, pointing at me.

"It wasn't a fight, just a discussion that ended in a mutual break," I blew out a breath, moving a flyaway with the back of my hand. "I know he means well, but he should've asked me first, right?" I sighed, scraping the clay off my hands. "I'm grateful, but why do I feel so disgusted?"

"That's fair. We've all had our fair share of white people, specifically men, thinking they're doing us a favor. But Victor is different," Luna offered.

I cocked a brow at her, hoping she would elaborate. While I knew what made Victor different, I wanted to see if I was looking through rose-tinted lenses.

"You haven't been as stressed in the two weeks you've known him. You dropped your closing routine to *eat*. I swear, the number of meals you skip because of work is insane," she raised her hands in disbelief.

I frowned, afraid to admit it.

"And you take more breaks," Summer pointed. "I mean, didn't you say your screen time went up? You're always texting Victor now," she grinned. "Always smiling at your phone."

I averted my gaze. It only went up like five percent.

"Or what about how happy you are when you cook now," Luna added. "Just knowing he loves to cook too makes you love it even more."

"Yeah, earlier this week, you were smiling while chopping carrots. You hate carrots," Summer emphasized.

I felt my cheeks heat up.

"You care about him," Luna began. "You value his opinions and his thoughts. Especially with that corny top-five list thing you have going on," she sighed. "But he also cares about you."

"He's impacted your life in little ways, so why not let him help you out in a bigger way?" Summer added, a smile on her face.

"So what? Do I just let him? What does that say about me if I do?" I asked, glancing between the two of them.

Did that make me weak? Did that make me the princess who needed saving or the damsel in distress?

"If you want or need the help," she answered. "It should be up to you to ask him for it. He shouldn't just assume," Luna said.

I nodded, understanding what she was getting at.

"But would it be so wrong that he's helping you with your sister?" She shrugged.

"I'm sure he would get points with Bianca if she knew he was helping her because he cares about you," Summer smiled.

"I know he's a partner with the prison, I know he has the money to get an excellent lawyer, and I know he would most likely jump at the chance to help me get Bianca out, but," I felt tears prick at my eyes. "Why? Why is it that until I met him, my problems couldn't be solved? I've been working my ass off to get to where I am now."

Summer quickly leaned over, engulfing me in her arms. "It's okay," she rubbed my back.

"I've done everything right. I paid off my loans, and I've gotten out of debt many times, but no matter how much I keep getting closer, the finish line moves," I wiped my eyes with the back of my hands. "I want nothing more than for Bianca to be free, but I can't do it knowing Victor would have that over me," I sniffled.

"Oh, Rosie," Luna cooed. "He doesn't have to help, not if you don't want to, okay?" She crouched down to look at me. "Based on what you said, it seems that he understands."

"Yeah, talk to Victor. I'm sure you can work on that boundary together," Summer pressed her cheek to my shoulder. "You're in control, Rosie," she reached around, patting my shoulder.

I nodded, reaffirming what they told me.

I was in control.

~

I wrung my fingers together as I walked over to the ledge of the roof.

Victor stood beside me.

I had invited him over after work. With my friend's advice, I was ready to talk to him. I was hopeful.

"I won't say I'm not grateful because I am," I began. "You clearly care for me because you helped my sister," I reached for his hand, my heart melting when his fingers curled before I squeezed it lightly. Taking a deep breath, I prepared for my next words, observing his features carefully. "But I think you should only help me if I ask for it, especially with my business and my sister," I let out a breath. "I know you come from a good place, but you have to understand it's a little intimidating that you can fix things so easily, and it should be up to me whether or not I want that help."

He stayed quiet for a moment.

I searched his eyes for any sign of disagreement but didn't find any.

"I understand," he nodded, a smile forming. "I'm sorry again for overstepping," he apologized. "I didn't realize I was hurting you," he brushed his thumb over the back of my hand.

"Thank you," I stepped closer. "You're very sweet, you know that?" I raised a brow.

"You're adorable," he chuckled, straightening up and towering over me, his hands cupping either side of my face. "Should we give this relationship a fresh start then?" He suggested.

"I think so," I bit my lip, stepping on my tippy toes to reach up and kiss him.

Our lips melted against each other's, his touch igniting something in my lower half. The moment felt new, still as exciting as our first kiss.

I wrapped my arms around his neck, playing with the hair on the nape of his neck. I moaned against his lips, tasting the fresh mint off his tongue. I arched my back, melting into his body and allowing his heat to engulf me. My tightened hold on his shoulders caused his hands to slip down, exploring me just as his hand nestled into the curve of my back, fitting perfectly. I moved my head, Victor following me with ease.

It was clear I was taking the lead in this kiss. I felt secure about that, and Victor enjoyed it, too, especially as he groaned when I tugged on his hair.

I had reservations about getting into a relationship with a man like Victor, but after today, all those were washed away.

I was in control.

Chapter 21

Victor

"I got the dishes," I stacked our plates together as I walked over to the sink before rolling my sleeves up.

"Thanks," Rosie smiled. "So who's *chiles rellenos* are better? Mine or Mrs. Sosa's?" She stood up, leaning against the counter by the sink.

"By far yours," I answered. "Just don't tell Luis. He'll skin me alive," I chuckled, though my tone rang with a warning.

"I won't," she turned around to finish cleaning up the table. "My numbers one and four are off my list. What's next on your list?" She placed a hand on her hip.

We were still sharing our favorite meals to make, and it was a fun process. Not much had happened since the night we started over. Our relationship was new, and this common interest has become our favorite thing to do. It was our way of getting to know each other.

"Baked potato soup is fourth on my list. But I only like making it for the holidays," I stated. "Maybe in December," I mused.

"Sounds perfect," she reached over to kiss me.

"Aww." A high-pitched squeal was heard from the entrance of the kitchen.

We pulled away to find Luna leaning against the archway, her face smitten as she stared at us.

"Hi, Luna," I greeted over my shoulder.

She responded with a gentle "hi," her voice teasing.

"You missed dinner. There's some chile rellenos on the stove," Rosie pointed to her left.

"I know, I was getting in the flow with my book, but I've reached a roadblock. I'm going out to get some inspiration," she responded.

I heard her keys jingle and the movement of her bag rustling. I was about to wish her a goodnight when Rosie stopped her.

"It's late," Rosie stated with a firm tone.

I stopped and turned around to find her with a face full of worry and her arms crossed over her chest.

"I'll be fine," Luna shrugged, reassuring her. "Besides, I'm meeting a friend," she added, turning to walk towards the door, but Rosie followed her.

"What friend?"

"A friend I met online," she blew out a breath. "They're taking me to a poetry bar," she specified. "I'm going to be alright. You have my location, and I have my self-defense alarm—trust my judgment," she cocked a brow, and this time, she crossed her arms over her chest.

I became busy with the dishes again, hoping my presence wasn't too distracting.

"Okay," Rosie sighed as she retreated, realizing she was being a bit too overprotective. "Be safe."

"I will, bye *Mom*," Luna said.

I could hear the smirk on her face and laughed to myself as I listened to the door shut. Wiping my hands, I found Rosie standing in the living room, staring at the door like she was waiting for Luna to return.

"It's sweet that you care," I came up behind her, kissing behind her ear as I wrapped my arms around her, hoping she'd realize we had the apartment to ourselves.

"I just get worried. Luna doesn't go out much," she inhaled, leaning back into my embrace.

The smell of raspberries and jasmine filled my nose again, and it took everything in me not to let my impulses take over.

"And now it's like she's going out every day," she led us to the couch, her hands on mine. "I don't know who she goes with, and I feel like she's purposely keeping it a secret from me," she frowned, taking a seat and nestling into my side.

"Do you think she's doing anything to harm herself?" I asked, rubbing her knee.

"No, but still. I can't help but let my mind wander. The last time I was lied to, Bianca got arrested," she chewed on her lip. "I don't want to think the worst," she exhaled, shaking her head.

"What about Summer?"

"I worry about her all the time," she managed to smile, but her eyes didn't meet. "She's always going to art exhibits, hikes, searching for the perfect scenery, and clubbing with a few classmates from school. But I've met her friends, and she has a family who would kill for her," she answered. "Luna's family barely knows what's going on in her life, as much as she tries to include them in it," her face fell again. "Sometimes, I feel like I'm the only one in her corner."

"I'm sure once she's ready, she'll tell you everything," I licked my lips, reaching up to caress her chin. "She knows she has an amazing friend by her side."

"You're right," she nuzzled deeper into me. "Do you want to watch a movie?" She changed topics.

I nodded, handing her the remote.

The movie we decided on was playing on the screen, but about an hour into the run time, I couldn't tell you what it was.

I was too focused on the way Rosie's lips moved against mine, the softness of her lips, and the sweet taste of the lemonade that lingered on her tongue. I didn't know what was playing, but I sure as hell knew I enjoyed kissing Rosie.

Her legs were splayed over my lap, her hands running through my hair, tugging on the strands that only made me lean further.

My hands cradled her body close to mine, one hand caressing up her thigh and hip and the other on her neck, guiding her head to move as I pleased. I swiped my tongue over her bottom lip, her mouth opening as she granted me access.

A light moan escaped her mouth when our tongues meshed, exploring each other for the first time. She pressed her chest against mine, my hold on her hip tightening as I pulled her closer.

It was unbelievable to think I was making out with the woman I was falling for on her couch. I felt like a teenager all over again, and the budding emotions of our new-found relationship were thrilling.

We pulled away, our foreheads resting against each other's. We were breathless, eyes dazed, our noses brushing as we leaned in for one more kiss.

She pulled away, getting up to get some water.

My gaze was fixated on her as everything about her was so captivating.

The flutter of her lashes, the rise and fall of her chest, the movement of her tan legs as she walked—she was indescribable.

"If you keep looking at me like that, we're not gonna finish the movie," she warned when she appeared in front of me with a glass of water.

"How am I looking at you?" I asked, taking the water from her. I allowed my laugh to escape me when she grew flustered.

"You know what I mean," she fell back on the couch.

"What movie did we even pick?" I asked, staring at the screen, unable to recall the scene playing.

She shrugged. "I do have something in mind we could do," she straightened up, cradling her glass on her lap.

"What is it?" I took a sip of my water, listening.

"I want to see you sculpt," she smiled.

My lips curved upward when the idea slipped past her lips. "Sculpt what exactly?"

"I'll get the stuff," her eyes lit up.

I watched her shoot up and run to her room before she came out a few moments later.

Buckets of sculpting clay were in her hand, and a box of tools in the other. "Sculpt whatever you want, and then I'll do the same. Like a sculpting date," she rolled her lips together when she met my gaze.

"Sounds like fun," I agreed.

A second movie played in the background while we worked on our projects. The makeshift divider kept our privacy, and about an hour and a half later, we were done.

We moved the divider out of the way but kept our designs hidden by some shoeboxes.

"Ready?" She asked, chewing on her lip.

I nodded, placing my hand on the shoebox before I lifted it, revealing my creation.

"Woah," she sucked in a breath when her gaze fell on it. "A rose?" Her gaze softened.

"For you," I smiled. It was a small replica of the real thing. I picked it up and held it out gently, aware it wasn't dried.

"Wow, Victor, it's beautiful," she gasped, leaning in to look at the detail up close.

A few strands fell in front of her face, framing her features. The smile on her face was cute as she traced her finger along the edge of the clay, her scent drifting to my nose at her close proximity.

I was happy studying her, so much so that I had to force myself to speak again.

"What did you make?" I asked after she looked at mine for a few minutes.

"Here," she blushed, revealing hers. She slid it over to me.

I traced my fingers over the design, careful not to mess it up but enough to feel each groove and rough edge. "R+V in a heart," I smiled.

"It's carved into a tree," she pointed.

I nodded, noticing the detail. It was a flat piece of clay with the rough grooves of tree bark carved in. Plus, the detail of an R + V surrounded by a heart with an arrow was added.

"I thought we could hang it up somewhere," she suggested.

"I love it."

We spent the next hour cuddled on the couch, *actually* watching the movie until it was time for me to leave.

"I'll text you when I get home," I smiled down at her, my hands resting on her waist and hers wrapped around my neck. I leaned in for one last peck before we pulled away.

"Goodnight, Victor," she grinned before heading back inside.

Chapter 22

Rosie

Things were good between Victor and me now. Our boundaries were established, and the budding relationship bliss was able to resume. Not only that, but Bianca was making a full recovery, and I was able to visit her the past week. Although her mood hadn't been the best, with good reason, I've been trying to make myself available for her—as best as I could be considering the entire situation.

According to her, though, her preferred medicine was me gossiping about my CEO boyfriend. Usually, I would refrain, but from my excitement about being with Victor and her state, I gave in. I told her all about our first date, our sculpting date, our shared love of food, and my growing feelings for the raven-haired man. On top of everything he did to help her out.

Which Summer was right about. That did earn him points with Bianca.

With life inching to a new normal, I walked through the lobby of Romano Tech. Greeting the receptionist, they signed me in before I headed up. The elevators dinged open to the floor, and Ari smiled at me when I walked past her, letting me know Victor was in his office. I grinned as I knocked on his door, hearing a "come in" before I walked inside.

He was surprised to see me but stood up to greet me with a kiss.

"What did you bring?" He glanced at the bag in my hand.

"Number five on my list," I grinned. I almost knew the entirety of his list, so I figured it'd only be fair to find a way to catch up with him. "Although I didn't make it myself because I had no time, I craved it. So this is from my favorite restaurant," I explained.

Nothing better than tamales from Dahlia's.

"I feel like that's cheating," he chuckled, pulling me in by my waist.

"Is it? How about one day I make them for you then?" I circled my arm around his shoulders.

"I'd like that," he said, cupping the side of my face. "I'm gonna kiss you, okay?" He looked into my eyes.

I nodded, licking my lips in anticipation. Our lips met, and warmth exploded in me. I was obsessed with kissing Victor.

His lips felt like kissing the stars. The idea of being able to kiss a man so amazing felt out of reach, but growing closer only made me burn with such passion that the moment we touched felt like I was on fire.

I giggled when his hand ran over my low back, slowly easing its way down, and I gasped when he groped my ass. My skirt lifted, creating a draft on the back of my thighs.

"Fuck, do that again," I curled up against him, biting my lip.

"You liked that?" He leaned back, staring at me. His lips were shiny from my gloss, and the sight only made me want to devour him more.

"Mhmm," I nodded.

He smirked.

"C'mere," he practically growled, walking towards the couch where he sat back, pulling me with him until I straddled him. "Much better," he cupped my face, pulling me back in for a kiss.

I felt so dirty making out with the CEO in his office. This was supposed to be an innocent thing: meeting my boyfriend for lunch, not making out with him when I should be keeping time to get back to work.

Eh, who cares?

I grabbed either side of his face, moving my lips against his as I pleased. Getting into it, I moved my lips down his neck, listening to the sounds that left his lips, smirking when I shushed him when he got too loud.

Who knows who was listening outside?

"You'd be screaming if you were in my position," he threatened, making me bubble on the inside.

"Promise?" I asked seriously.

His eyes flashed darker. "Promise," he squeezed my ass, causing me to bite down on my lip to muffle a moan.

Last time, our make-out session was so innocent. It was a new experience that we wanted to savor and step into gently. It was exploring a new territory, but this?

This wasn't sweet. We weren't taking our time, and we weren't soft or gentle. We were hungry for each other, desperate to discover all the deepest parts as our lips melted together, our hands running over each curve, groping each bundle of flesh, nipping at our most sensitive points. Drawn between the line of want and need.

It was maddening and thrilling.

I dipped my head to kiss him again, one of his hands sliding up to hold the small of my back. I grabbed his chin, guiding his head in the position I wanted as our lips danced together. I felt his tongue swipe my lower lip, my mouth opened, and I was able to taste his mintiness. I moaned, pressing my chest against his, my lower body sliding down, and I found myself straddling his waist.

His hands slid down, resuming their position on my hips. The force of his hold made me move involuntarily, my hips rocking back and forth. His pants tightened, and I could feel him harden against my thigh.

I tensed slightly.

"Do you want to keep going?" He asked, noticing my state and loosening his hold on my waist.

"Yes."

That was all the confirmation we needed to continue.

His lips found home on my mouth as I sat up, my hand trailing down the side of his neck. I towered over him, gaining control of the kiss. His head fell back against the cushions, his neck becoming exposed, and I could feel his pulse against my thumb.

I moaned into his mouth when his hand reached up, pushing the hair out of my face, his other hand sliding down my back. A shudder fell from my lips when his fingers grazed the exposed skin from my side, a delightful feeling it was. I was glad he kept his hand there.

Curling my fingers around the strands of his hair, I tugged slightly, earning a groan from him, and I took that as an opportunity to slip my tongue in, exploring his mouth. I loved the taste of Victor—peppermint. I got lost in him.

We didn't even process how much time had passed until sirens sounded outside, their blaring noise pulling us apart.

I inhaled, making up for my lack of oxygen as I relaxed in Victor's lap, my hands resting on his chest. Passing him a smile, I wondered how he could look at me with such admiration when I knew I looked like a mess from our makeout session.

"So much for eating our lunch," he glanced at the forgotten bag on his desk. He ran his hands up my thighs.

"You're the one who groped my ass," I stated matter-of-factly, placing my hands on top of his as I reached down to peck near his mouth. "It's entirely your fault," I licked my lips, clasping my hands behind his neck.

"You asked me to do it again," he pointed, arching a brow.

My face turned red. "I guess you're right," I hummed, my gaze raking over his face and seeing how much of my lipgloss smeared off. "Maybe it was a bad idea to wear lip gloss today," I pinched his chin, moving his head around to see the damage we caused.

Thanks to me, the terracotta-tinted gloss was all over his mouth and neck.

"But you look good in this color," I complimented, my stomach doing somersaults.

He laughed. "You wear it better. You look so sexy," he ran his hand up my thigh before settling on my hip.

The heat on my cheeks grew.

"Before you seduce me again, we should have our lunch," I changed the subject. "But we need to clean ourselves," I said, reaching for some wipes in my bag.

I began to clean Victor's face, my touch gentle as I wiped, and I could feel his gaze on me, his hands simply resting on my hips. Cleaning the lipgloss off of him was intimate. It was nice.

"There," I set the wipe aside, moving a loose strand of his hair out of the way before sliding off him. I grabbed my compact mirror and a new wipe, beginning to swipe the smudged color. Now, with bare lips, I turned to look at him only to see he was already staring at me.

"You're so pretty," he said, pinching my chin.

I turned bashful, rolling my lips together before my teeth caught my bottom lip.

"You're doing it again," he smirked, reaching up to pull my lip from between my teeth. "I think you know exactly what you're doing," he accused me.

"I don't know what you're talking about," I feigned innocence. Before he could respond, I silenced him with a kiss, one he tried to deepen, but I pulled away. "You're cute," I said.

He grinned in response.

"I'm never buying from this brand again," I sighed, looking at the dirty makeup wipes. "Long-lasting and non-transferable my ass."

"Terrible advertising," he tsked.

"Yup." I tilted his head back to make sure there was no staining, and the sight of his Adam's apple bobbing made me water. "Oh shit," I was quickly distracted when I saw a huge stained blotch on the collar of his white button-down.

"What's wrong?"

"I got some on your shirt. I'm sorry," I tried to dab it off, but it had already set. "Wow, this lipgloss is just getting worse, and it even got on your undershirt," I scoffed. "You think the people at your meeting will notice?" I chewed on my lip, growing nervous.

"Don't worry about it, Rosie, I always keep spare in here," he reassured.

I blew out a breath of relief, dropping my forehead to his shoulder. I stood up and watched him walk over to a cupboard on the other side of his office, where a few spare shirts were.

He took one out and began unbuttoning his shirt.

I couldn't help but look.

There he was, just shrugging it off, the thin white tee straining against his muscles before he ripped that off, too.

Fuck me.

Victor Romano, *my boyfriend*, was shirtless in front of me. His chest and abs were dusted with hair. The expanse of his chest, his pecs. He looked like he was made out of marble.

I was a blushing mess at the sight of him half-naked.

"You okay, Rosie?" He smirked.

I loved and hated that he used my ability to become flustered easily as a weapon.

"Can I touch you?" I blurted out the question. I wanted to take in all of him today.

"C'mere," he took a few steps to grab my hand, and I walked around the couch to meet him. He slowly guided my hand to meet his chest.

I squeaked at the contact and gaped up at him. "Are you sure you're not a sculpture brought to life?" I asked, finding the courage to place my other hand on him. I slowly ran my hands over his chest, my fingers tickled by the hair as I laughed out of disbelief. "You are the most beautiful person I've ever seen," I stared, amazed, my hands spreading down his sides and up his abs, tracing my fingers over each dip and crevice.

"You should look in a mirror."

"Let me take in your beauty, Victor," I studied him before leaning forward and pressing my lips right where his heart was. "Thank you," I closed my eyes, slightly melting into him for a moment.

"Don't thank me, Rosie," he chuckled.

"It's an intimate moment, and I'm happy it's with you," I said.

His gaze softened at that. "Then it's the perfect time to give you something," he walked over to his desk and pulled something out of his drawer. "Here," he handed me a small red box with a bow.

"What?" I furrowed my brows, laughing before opening it to find two little polymer charms: a rhino and a ravioli. "I love it," I gasped, pulling them out. It matched perfectly with the style of my other charms, and the clasp was the right kind of gold. It was perfect. "But how?"

"I kinda asked Luna and Summer for help, and they told me the materials you use when making them. I followed their instructions and made them myself," he answered.

I immediately wrapped my arms around him.

"We've been going out for a little bit, and I don't know, it felt right," he smiled.

I grinned. "It's perfect," I quickly latched them onto my bracelet, and they fit right in. "The attention to detail is insane, thank you," I rolled my lips together as I traced over the delicate design.

"You're welcome," he wrapped an arm around me before pressing his lips against mine. "I gotta go, but later tonight, how about you stay the night? And we could have a game night," he suggested.

"That sounds like fun. I'll bring UNO," I said, pressing my hands against his chest.

"Great, see you later, Rosie," he pressed a kiss on my temple before he walked out of the office.

Chapter 23

Rosie

"Packing?" Luna entered my room and watched me shove my pajamas into an overnight bag. Realization dawned on her, a loud gasp escaping her mouth. "You're staying the night at Victor's," she smirked, quickly walking over to my bed before plopping on it.

"He invited me over. We're having a game night," I explained, walking over to my dresser to grab my lotion and deodorant.

The nerves in my stomach were bubbling even though this wasn't the first time I'd spent the night at his place.

"Are you planning on taking your relationship to the next level?" She suggestively shimmied her shoulders.

I sent her a disapproving look. "We're only going to play board games. It's a date night," I stated. "I'm bringing UNO."

She winced.

I glanced at her with furrowed brows.

"You get pretty competitive with UNO," she said. "You think he's ready for that? You need to cross a certain level of intimacy before you bring out the competitive sides," she joked.

My eyes widened at that, a blush creeping up my cheeks as I thought back to earlier today, but I pushed the thought aside. "UNO *is* supposed to be competitive. Besides, we've been making out like crazy," I pressed my lips together to suppress a grin.

"Now you're just telling me?!" She gasped, shooting up from my bed.

"We were in his office earlier today. I met him for lunch, and one thing led to another," I hiked my shoulders up as I tried to downplay it.

"You were in his office! That's why you were late?!" She gasped, placing her hands on my shoulders. "Oh my *fucking* God, Rosie! This is the type of gossip I need to be aware of!"

"Actually, I was late because of traffic," I clarified.

"That doesn't matter! I needed to know the moment you came back."

"It's all new. If you had told me I'd be making out with my boyfriend in his office a month ago, I wouldn't believe you," I snorted, reasoning. "Sometimes it's hard to realize this is my reality."

"Understandable, you're enjoying the new relationship bliss. And you've never been in a serious relationship," she said with a softened look. "I think you're also seriously horny, and I'm praying that you get dicked down tonight," she crossed her fingers.

I sighed. "Just an innocent game night."

"Yeah, well, being alone together, playing highly competitive games," she trailed, raising her brows. "No doubt you'll get turned on. Who knows what you'll do to each other," she suggested.

"And you know this because?" I cocked a brow.

"I'm a professional erotica writer. I know what leads to sex," she shrugged.

"How's that going, by the way?" I asked, staring at my bag to make sure everything was packed.

"Oh, ya know," her cheeks became red. "Been focusing on writing the sex scenes, trying to expand my imagination," she backed away awkwardly, waving me off. "Who would've thought a sapphic romance would be the dirtiest thing I ever wrote? Not me, for sure, as I have *never* slept with a woman," she leaned against the door jamb. "Complete and total lack of experience with the same sex as a bisexual woman," she continued to talk in the hall before she shut her bedroom door.

I stared at her closed door, blinking slowly as I tried to recall what had happened. Something was up with Luna. I knew she was stressed about her book, not telling her family about the contents of the book, feeling guilty that she wasn't going to represent the bi community properly in her writing, and feeling her own doubt about her sexuality.

This was uncharted territory for her, but I hated that she was shutting me out. I was so tempted to go over and beg her to let me know what was happening, but I thought back to her words.

This was my first serious relationship, and she was happy for me. So I grabbed my bag and shouted a quick goodbye before leaving to have a date night with my boyfriend.

~

"UNO!" I raced to place my second to last card on the deck. Not giving Victor a second to pull his hand back.

The game had become intense.

I forgot how much of a sore winner I could be when it came to UNO, and I wasn't about to lose my winning streak. I held my last card in my hand, smiling deviously as I sat back on my heels. I had a red seven clutched against my chest to prevent Victor from peeking.

He had his chance to win at checkers.

"There's no way. I literally gave you plus fours back-to-back five minutes ago," he deadpanned, looking at the four cards in his hands.

"There are two types of people in this world: the ones that are good at board games and those that are *great* at card games," I winked. "Make your move, Romano," making sure to roll my r's.

My plan to distract him with the seductive tone worked. His eyes trained on my lips as I smirked, pulling my lip between my teeth.

"That's how it's gonna be, Martinez?" He raised his eyebrows, eyes darkening as they trailed back up to meet mine.

Those beautiful dark irises.

I felt myself growing hot despite wearing a tank top and sleep shorts.

"It's already been since checkers. You know what you did," I glared at him.

"All I remember is beating you fair and square."

"That's exactly what I'm doing here, so place the card," I said, my heart pounding with anticipation.

"Very well," he glanced at his cards before picking one, slowly placing it on top of my blue three.

He placed a red three.

"I win!" I shot my hand out to put my winning card on top of his. "Feel what it's like to lose!" I leaned forward, teasing him.

"You're a gracious winner," he leaned back on his hands, his gaze briefly dropping to my cleavage, my boobs practically pouring out of my tank top.

I blushed as I leaned back, cautiously fixing the straps.

"You owe me a pity kiss," he raised his brows.

I laughed before grabbing his face and pressing my lips on his.

He gave me one after I sorely lost to checkers. I don't think I'll ever get over that, so it was only fair that I returned the gesture.

I did happily as I threaded my fingers through his hair, the luscious strands perfect for me to grab onto. I smirked into the kiss when he groaned as I tugged on his hair, and he reciprocated by pulling me into his lap.

"Does the winner want her prize yet?" He smirked against my skin as he began kissing my throat.

I moaned as my eyes fluttered close, my arms wrapping around his shoulders. I ground my hips against him, feeling his erection against me. I had to stifle a gasp, muttering, "What's the prize?"

"Whatever she wishes," he looked me in the eyes, my body melting, and I could've finished at the sight of him.

His gaze lured me in, our lips crashing together as his arms wrapped around me, picking us both off the ground until we settled on the couch. My fingers threaded through his hair as his lips trailed down my neck, my breath heavy as everything turned hot.

He kissed along my collarbone. His gentle touch felt a thousand times more powerful with the pleasure it brought me. He continued, trailing farther down, and pressed his lips on the soft tissue of the tops of my breasts, a shudder escaping me.

I moaned, my hand running along his arm that was wrapped around me as he reached back up to kiss my lips. I scratched my nails along his forearm, feeling his muscles clench underneath my touch. His fingers dug into my side as he held me closer.

My body was sensitive to Victor and to him only. I experienced more pleasure in the days we've been dating than the rest of my life. His affection was addictive.

And I wanted more.

I reached for his hand on my side, sliding it down my thigh and stopping right before it dipped between my legs.

He pulled away, gaze searching mine.

I nodded, squeezing his wrist.

This was what I wanted.

He kissed along my jaw, my hand reaching for his shoulder. He pushed my thighs apart, his hand brushing over my clothed pussy before he reached up to my waistband. He stopped his kisses for a second, watching me as he slipped his hand into my panties.

I shivered, his slender fingers working their way between my wet folds. The feeling was indescribable, and I could only think about how much better it felt than I imagined. A whimper escaped me as he brushed a finger over my clit, my hand pressing against his chest as I closed my legs around him.

"Be good, beautiful," the nickname rolled off his tongue.

I felt my heart skip against my rib cage, but I complied, my knees falling open.

He slowly circled his finger on my clit, allowing the pleasure to build up. He encouraged me to breathe, wanting those sweet noises to slip past my lips, and he was more than glad when I clutched onto the material of his shirt.

I let my head drop to his shoulder when his middle finger slipped lower, teasing my entrance before he slipped inside. It was a new sensation, my walls clenching around him, drawing him deeper, but he pulled his finger out. Confused, I wanted to protest, but this time, he placed two fingers in—his middle and ring finger.

He reached deeper, and his fingertips brushed against me until my eyes rolled to the back of my head.

"You're doing so good," he said, kissing me. "Tell me how much you like it."

"I like it so much," I breathed out.

The palm of his hand created friction with my clit. I felt dazed as I searched for his lips, and I enjoyed the pleasure he made with just his hand. I pressed my chest forward, and my nipples hardened as they rubbed against my shirt. I threw my head back, my hand curling around his neck as I urged his head towards my chest, needing to feel a new sensation.

The feeling of his smirk against my chest brought butterflies to my tummy. Like he read my mind, he reached down, wrapping his lips around my sensitive peak through the cotton of my shirt. He repeated the action on the other.

I felt the pressure build in my lower belly, my walls drawing his fingers further into me, and it was almost embarrassing at how wet I was. I wished for release, my hips beginning to grind against his hand, his fingers never stopping their rhythm.

"I'm gonna—" I gasped, clutching to his strong shoulders as I hid my face in his neck, the knot snapping as I came undone. I shivered against him, knees touching as I closed my thighs around his hand.

He slowed his movements, the heat of his stare on me as he watched me, a smirk on his face as he helped me come down from my high.

I made a sound, batting my eyes open to gaze at him. My skin was flushed, and I involuntarily squeezed around his hand that was still nestled between my legs.

"You really do know how to treat a winner," I stifled a laugh, breathing heavily.

Chapter 24

Victor

I laughed at her joke, nipping at the soft tissue of the tops of her breasts, and licked along her neck until I sealed it with a passionate kiss on her lips. I slowly slipped my hand out from between her legs, earning a moan from her.

She threaded her fingers through my hair, arching into my body.

Having just given her an orgasm, I felt my chest swell with pride. Especially the moment I slipped my hand inside her panties—she was soaked.

After our hot and heavy moments in my office, I needed more of her. I could've kissed her all night, but she wanted to go further, and I was content with giving her what she wanted. After fingering her and watching her come undone, I was aware of what heaven was. The sight was a masterpiece now embedded in my brain.

I had her to thank for that.

"I don't think I ever came that hard before," she took a deep breath. "I need another minute," she giggled, pressing her back to the couch cushions.

I left her on the couch and walked towards the kitchen to get a glass of water. When I came back, she was resting, her chest falling and rising heavily.

"That orgasm tired me out. I'm ready for bed," she smiled, face flushed.

I handed her the water, a soft look on my face. "Let's head to bed then."

Once we were in bed, Rosie's body curled against mine. My hand slid around her waist as I pulled her into my lap, and I rested against the headboard. A giggle escaped her beautiful lips, and I smiled before kissing her.

She moaned, running her hand up my chest and cupping my jaw as she deepened it. Her thighs rested on either side of me, and she began to rock her hips back and forth.

I hissed when her heat rubbed against me, my cock growing hard, and I felt her devious smirk against my lips. I gasped when she ground harder, my hands flying to her waist, stopping her before I warned, "Don't start what you can't finish."

"Later then," she said, nipping my bottom lip. "You are a man of many talents," she cupped my cheek as she leaned forward to kiss me once more before settling under the covers.

Our relationship was still new. We've only been dating for two weeks, but it hasn't felt like it. I've been learning about her in more ways than one, and it felt like a blessing every day.

As our relationship moved into the more physical aspects, I couldn't help but love how Rosie felt comfortable expressing her desires. The woman she became when things got heated was sexy, confident, and fierce. It was a privilege to see her like that.

"I was simply just rewarding the winner. You did win the majority after all," I smirked, tracing the curves of her face.

"Well, the victor is very satisfied," she licked her lips before they rolled into a smile. "And she will graciously accept any more offerings in a short while," she added, her cheeks tinting pink.

"Good to know. Just say the word, and I'll happily grant her wish," I pinched her chin, unable to resist giving her another kiss.

If I could kiss Rosie for the rest of my life, I would do anything to ensure that.

Nothing felt more gentle and passionate than her kisses. Her kisses were starting to feel like a home we were building together. One I would never want to leave.

We stayed in bed, allowing our lips to move against the other's as we desired.

After a mini make-out session, we were finally resting in bed.

My arm wrapped around her, her face nestled on my chest.

"I wanted to ask you," I licked my lips. "Would you accompany me to a gala in two weeks? It's a fundraiser for an anti-deforestation organization," I elaborated.

She didn't answer right away, her shoulders tensing and her fingers curling into a fist as she contemplated.

In the short while we've been dating, we haven't gone out as a couple. Most of our dates consisted of us having dinner together or staying in. We were both content with it being just us, and Rosie never voiced anything different.

Sometimes, I wondered if that was another reason we gravitated toward each other—our distaste for socializing. We were both in business, so it came naturally in professional settings. I've seen how she won all the executives over at the grant benefit, but outside that?

We were introverted.

So I wasn't sure how she would feel about going as my plus one.

"I-" she started but quickly stopped, letting out a heavy sigh.

"You have time to think about it," I stopped her, rubbing her arm. "All you have to do is show yourself and stand by my side. Of course, it's a great networking opportunity if you're interested, but don't feel pressured," I kissed the top of her head.

She seemed to process it better once I added the networking opportunity.

"I'll think about it," she responded. "If I go, that means I need a dress. Maybe Luna or Summer have one," she spaced out, talking to herself.

"I know a good place for a dress. I'll call the owner tomorrow, and she'll take care of it whenever you decide to go," I said.

She glanced at me, puzzled. "You know a lot of people," she sighed, rubbing her thumb in circles on the stubble on my chest.

"It comes with the job. I'm sure you know a lot of people, too," I said, and I felt her nod.

"Not as many as you, but thanks for inviting me. I'll be sure to think of it," she stated, kissing my jaw. "When do you need confirmation?"

"There's no deadline. Just make sure there's enough time to get a dress," I hummed.

"Okay," she pressed a smile. "I'll let you know."

We didn't stay up much longer after that. But it was truly one of the best sleeps I've ever had.

Chapter 25

Rosie

"This is insane," Luna gaped at the luxurious shopping center in the northern suburbs of Chicago. "I mean, look at this place," she pulled her sunglasses over her head to get a better look. "You know you're in a rich neighborhood when they don't have a roof in their mall," she gestured at the bright blue sky.

The sunny sky hovering over us in the almost empty shopping center felt odd. The white and gray modern architecture fed into its high economic status.

When I told Victor I wanted to go with him to the gala, I wasn't expecting him to send me to one of the wealthiest shopping malls in Chicago. The best shopping mall I've ever been to was the Super Mall on Pulaski in Little Village, but *this*?

This was a Hallmark filming location.

All the crisp lines and open space were new. I couldn't stop thinking how different this place was compared to my usual navigating through the busy and packed aisles where I bought bargain items in Spanish at the Super Mall.

While I would prefer my routine of listening to *Los Tigres del Norte* over the speakers, I was hopeful for a good experience walking through the sparse place as light jazz music played.

"You think they have a dollar store nearby?" Summer asked, bundling in her thick coat as the heavy fall breeze blew around us. The pause that enveloped us after her words made her add, "I wanted to see if we could get some snacks after."

"We'll just get some brunch at that place down the street," Luna shrugged.

"Victor said this lady will help us," I stated, refocusing on what was at hand as my eyes followed a brown pomeranian nestled in its owner's bag. "How much do you even think a dress here will cost?"

"I'll say more than a thousand," Luna hummed.

I raised my brows, figuring that was the case.

We stepped inside, finding the place to be grand and bright. The cream-carpeted floors were warm and welcoming, the huge chandelier in the center added to its high-end feel, the floral design with touches of baby blue on the wallpaper gave a hint of dimension to the minimalist decor, and the multitudes of dresses hung up on racks screamed this was a fancy place.

I sucked in a breath. I was grateful that Victor offered to pay, happy that he was pleased to do so, but it didn't stop it from feeling a tad weird.

"Welcome to Bella's. I'm Bella, the owner of this boutique. How can I help, ladies?" A woman who looked to be in her mid-thirties appeared. Wearing a sleek black dress and red-bottom heels, her long blonde hair in a high ponytail. She was magnificent.

"Hi, I'm looking for a dress for a gala I'm attending with my boyfriend next weekend. His name is Victor Romano," I smiled, remembering Victor told me to tell Bella he sent me here. It amazed me the way her eyes widened, face brightening.

"You must be Miss Martinez," she flashed me her pearly, perfectly straight, white teeth and snapped her fingers. Like magic, two sales assistants came out of nowhere, one of them holding champagne in their hands. "We've been expecting you. It's so lovely to meet you," she graciously walked over, grabbing my hand and shaking it with poise.

"Oh, thank you," I blushed. "You sure know how to treat a customer," I grinned awkwardly.

"Only for the best," she placed her hands delicately on my shoulders, guiding me to the back, where a seating area with blue suede couches and a fitting room was located. "I asked Mr. Romano to give me a hint of your taste, and we laid out a few options," she gestured to the clothing rack packed with more than a few options. "But we have the entire store to try on," she smirked.

"And the boyfriend delivers," Luna beamed, walking over to the rack and instantly picking out a dress. "You should try this one first," she grabbed an emerald green dress made of tulle.

"I'll leave you and your friends to it," Bella stepped back. "If you need any assistance, I'll be at the counter," she pointed to the middle of the store. "Enjoy yourselves."

"So, what are we waiting for?" Summer asked, picking up a flute of champagne and sipping it as she sat on the large plush sofa.

I pressed a smile on my lips, looking forward to the night I would spend with my boyfriend, and figured I needed to make sure I had the perfect dress. After not having a quince or going to prom, this was my first time trying on formal dresses.

Knowing this was my first experience, my uneasiness was pushed to the side, and for the next hour, I tried on fourteen different dresses. None of them caught my attention, though, which was discouraging.

I inhaled, Luna zipping me up for the fifteenth time before I stepped out, walking onto the platform in front of the mirror.

It was a sheeny material of red, like luminescence, with a sweetheart neckline. It made my boobs pop, and it cinched at my waist, completely forming with my hips as well. The fit was tight, a size too small, but the girls insisted I try it on. I stared at the dress warily, my mind whirring, but I couldn't figure out why.

"It looks good. It's sexy," Summer shimmied her shoulders from behind me.

The comment irked me, but still, I didn't know why.

"I feel like Bianca would wear this," Luna pointed out, her forehead creased in thought. "Actually, you kinda look like Bianca in that dress," she mentioned.

I stared at myself in the mirror, and it finally hit me. I didn't look like Bianca. I looked like my mother. I ran my hands down my sides, gulping at the memory that began to wash over me.

~

"Rosa, Bianca, esto es Gerardo, es mi novio," my mother announced. She was wearing a bright red dress that clung to her body. A few sizes too small, but that was her style. According to her, it made her look better, considering her boobs were about to pop at any moment. "Vamos a vivir con él en su casa," she added.

Tears clouded my vision as I disagreed when she sent my sister and me to pack our things.

"¡No! ¡No quiero ir!" I screeched, tears pouring down my face. My sobs filled the small apartment as I wailed on the floor.

"Listen to your mother!" The strange man yelled at me, his large hand

wrapping around my arm, and I froze, my lip quivering as I stared at him in fear.

"Don't yell at her!" Bianca ripped me away from him and shielded me. He paused and gazed at her. I couldn't discard the way he looked at her. "We don't even know this man," she turned to our mother, who only rolled her eyes in response.

"Chiquita, vas a aprender que cuando me escuches, todo va hacer más fácil," he grinned maliciously.

I felt the hairs on Bianca's arms rise.

~

"Rosie, are you okay?" Summer's voice popped up.

I looked up to find her concerned face in the mirror.

"Yeah, I'm fine," I shook the chills away. "I just think this color washes me out," I shrugged.

"Look, I didn't want to say it," Luna raised her hands.

I laughed.

"So I'm glad you did," she grinned in the mirror. "I did find this one," she stood up and pulled one from the rack.

My eyes widened, a smile instantly washing over my face, and I completely forgot about that memory for a moment.

This dress was the one.

"Let's try it," I nodded, Summer cheering from her seat.

~

After dropping Luna and Summer off, I drove back to Victor's apartment.

The warmth and modern architecture were welcoming to those who paid to live here, yet so intimidating to those who didn't.

Like me.

Thankfully, the doorman and staff knew who I was.

I knocked on the door, and Victor greeted me. He opened it with a kiss on my cheek. We walked back to the couch, where he was working on his laptop.

"How'd it go?" He asked, pulling me to cuddle his side.

"Good, weird day today," I shrugged, leaning back into his hold. "Never felt richer," I joked.

He smiled, rubbing my arm. "I'm guessing Bella went all out with her hospitality," he stated.

"A switch flipped when she found out I was your girlfriend," I gestured the action, smiling. "The dresses were beautiful, and the quince section was calling my name," I added, rubbing my shin. "But I did find a dress."

"Can I see?" He held me tighter, his eyes gleaming.

I patted his cheek, pressing a kiss to the other one. "Nope," I grinned. "It's a surprise," I repeated what he always told me.

He playfully rolled his eyes before returning to me, his expression softening. "But you're sure you're fine?" He nuzzled his nose along my neck.

"Just thinking," I answered, giving in to his worry. "Don't really wanna talk about it," I sighed.

Once we got back, that short-lived moment in the dress shop ended. My mind went back to that memory, causing a flood of all the ones that happened after that, which ultimately led to *that* night.

"Do you want to take your mind off of it?" He asked.

"I'm not really in the mood for that either," I frowned.

"Wasn't talking about that," he chuckled. "Tell me what you want to do to distract yourself," he pressed.

"I usually go to the ceramics studio, but they're closed," I chewed on my lip. "It helps," I said.

"There is an entire ceramics studio in the building if you recall, I mentioned it that one night," he cocked a brow.

I turned my head to face him. "Oh yeah," I realized. He had mentioned it so quickly in passing that I didn't even register it. "Is it open?"

"It's always open and should be empty, too, considering the time," he stated, glancing at his watch.

"Can we please go?" I sat up.

He nodded.

We both stood up from the couch before I grabbed my sweater, and he grabbed his keys.

Having not been here before, I was shocked to see the underground open space. Entirely modernized with its cool color palette, the endless hallway lit up to reveal rooms of anything and everything. There was a dance studio, a library, a gym, and an art studio. As the lights continued to turn on, each room was revealed, the glass walls allowing any visitor to see inside.

I almost fainted at the sight of the studio. It was an artist's dream, and I eagerly pulled Victor along. I scanned along the shelves, finding one of my favorite types of clay.

"Have you ever done pottery before?" I asked, remembering he told me he preferred sculpting when it came to ceramics.

"I took Luis's sister once," he recalled. "But that was just painting," he explained.

"Aww, that's cute," I smiled. "Did she invite you?"

"It was so many years ago," he answered. "Maria hadn't come out yet, and I was the only one who knew after I caught her kissing her partner goodbye when I picked her up from school," he smiled at the memory. "I kept my mouth shut, and luckily, Luis put me in charge as a chaperone when he heard his little sister had a date," he chuckled. "She was so mad."

"That's the sweetest story I ever heard," I pressed a hand to my chest, feeling it beat against my palm. "But couldn't you have left them there? Lie to Luis?" I was partially curious. If I were forced to go on a chaperoned date with two teenagers who clearly didn't want me there, I would've made sure to come up with something.

"That was the plan until Maria texted me in a panic that Luis wanted photo evidence of my presence," he chuckled. "I had to run back to the place. So much for getting some dinner that night."

"You had fun though, didn't you?"

"Yeah, seeing some budding young love was cute," he mused. "They've been dating for eight years now," he added.

I gasped. "I'm already obsessed with them," I grinned. "It's cute that you care about them," I added, causing him to blush. "Like family," I hinted.

Something washed over his face. "They are my family," he said. "They were there for me after my mom died, and I'll forever be grateful for them," he hummed.

"What about your dad?" I questioned. I instantly regretted it when he stilled. "I'm sorry, you don't have to answer that," I shook my head, placing my hand on his and squeezing it.

"He was a good father and husband until he chose not to be," he stated.

I rolled my lips together. "It's funny how parents have that choice, isn't it?" I said. Each one of his words hit hard.

He glanced at me, our eyes meeting. He reached up with his hand, slowly cupping my face, his thumb running over my cheekbone.

"Yeah, it's funny," the corner of his lip curved upward.

I reached up on my tippy toes to kiss him.

"Tell me all about pottery," he pulled away, a smile appearing on his face. "Pretend I'm your student in one of your classes who knows nothing," he hummed, changing the subject.

I mentally thanked him for it as I bounced on the balls of my feet, rubbing my hands together.

"As any ceramicist knows, you always have to wedge the clay, " I rolled the clay out of the plastic bag, heaving a sigh at the weight. "It's a total workout, and my arms would be jacked like yours if I did it more often," I said, grabbing the wire to section the clay off.

"Once you open your ceramics studio, I'm sure you'll be able to beat me in an arm wrestling contest," he smirked.

I sent him an amused look.

"What are we making?" He asked.

"Okay, so tonight, how about we make matching mugs!" I gasped at the sudden idea. "Yes, we're totally doing that!" I clapped my hands together. "Anyway, tonight we're doing pottery, which is a type of ceramic," I began while measuring the clay correctly. "Ceramics is a broader term with many different ways to do it. From making tiles, sculptures, porcelain—and that's just brushing the surface," I listed, and I turned to look at him, pausing midway. "What?" I smiled before I realized I was rambling to an expert.

He gazed at me with the kindest smile, his eyes dazzling with something I couldn't place. But I knew his look gave me butterflies.

"Nothing," he shrugged. "Continue, please," he gestured.

I stared for a moment before I did.

"So, pottery is when you make a vessel. Bowls, mugs, vases, that's pottery," I explained as he listened. "Now, I need you to wedge this clay to remove the air bubbles. Put your pasta-making skills to work," I patted the section of clay.

Victor was a pro already. Between his pasta-making and sculpture background, he knew what he was doing, and he looked damn good while doing it.

I absentmindedly bit my lip when the vein on his forearm protruded more than usual, his biceps flexing. I paid no mind to the clay, ensuring it was properly wedged. I was distracted.

"That should be good," he placed a large hand on the wedged clay.

I thought how amazing it felt when he had that exact hand on my…

"Rosie?"

"Wow," I sucked in a breath, ridding my head of impure thoughts. "That was the fastest I've ever seen someone wedge clay before."

"I don't think you were focusing on my speed," he smirked.

I felt my cheeks blush. "I was focusing on your *technique*," I argued.

He chuckled in response. "Keep telling yourself that," he pinched my chin, pecking my lips.

"I will," I hummed, grabbing the clay and walking to one of the wheels. "Shall we do that cliché?"

"What cliché?" He tipped his head to the side.

"This one," I placed the clay in the middle of the wheel, reaching for his hand and guiding him to sit on the stool before I pulled another behind him, straddling the seat as I attempted to reach around him. "This is not going to work," I laughed, realizing I couldn't guide him if his broad shoulders blocked my view. "Your shoulders are too built," I smirked, my gaze following him as he stood until he towered over me.

"Here," he guided me to sit in the front before he sat on the stool behind me, scooting as close as he could until my back pressed against his chest.

His chin rested on my shoulder, and his arms wrapped around my middle. "Much better," he grinned, pressing a kiss behind my ear.

"This is amazing," I confessed.

He hummed in agreement. "So what's first?" He asked.

I gestured for him to give me his hands.

"First, we gotta make sure the clay is centered," I placed his hands on the ball, starting the wheel slowly. "Then, we wet our hands," I guided him to the water bowl. "And we begin," I placed his hands on the clay ball, increasing the wheel's speed. "Make sure to lean a little forward. Keep your elbows tight," I felt him press up against me further, the rhythm of his heart beating against my back, and I felt my breathing relax. "Now, start to squeeze it a bit," I glanced at him, his warm breath fanning my cheek, and I inhaled the woody scent of his cologne. I leaned back, sighing out contently.

"Feeling distracted?"

"Very much," I nodded. "Thank you, Victor," I pressed my forehead against his, both of us becoming unaware of the clay spinning endlessly on the wheel, my foot still pressed on the pedal.

But none of that mattered. I just cared that I found a new distraction, one as equally sculpted but more comforting than ceramics.

None other than Victor Romano.

Chapter 26

Victor

"Victor!" Luna greeted me when she opened the door. "Rosie is almost ready. You can wait inside," she grabbed my arm and pulled me into the apartment.

"Luna, it's nice to see you again," I greeted, shoving my hands in my pockets once I adjusted from being manhandled.

For a small woman, she was strong.

"You seem dressed up. Do you have plans tonight?" I asked.

She seemed to freeze up at that. "Oh yeah," she waved off. "Summer wants to go to an art museum. She needs some inspo before her final, and she's kinda stressed about it even though she has a month and a half left," she scratched the back of her head, avoiding my gaze.

I stared at her in confusion.

Her bubbly and confident personality was gone and replaced with a flustered mess. It was odd.

Though, I didn't question it.

"Which one? I'm friends with one of the curators at The Art Institute, and I could probably get you two on a private tour," I offered.

Her eyes widened. "That won't be necessary," she shook her hands in front of her. "Thanks, but no thanks," she reassured. "Summer kinda prefers to be with her inner thoughts. I'm just going 'cause she had a spare ticket," she explained. "I'm gonna go check on Rosie," she gestured towards the hall before hurrying in that direction.

I couldn't help but smile at the similarities between her and Luis. Both could talk your ear off and make you fall in love with their witty nature. It was good Rosie had someone like Luna. I couldn't be more glad.

Not even a minute later, Rosie rounded the corner with a bright smile. She was radiant.

I didn't even know where to begin to describe her beauty. It was so indescribable that I even began to wonder if she was real. It wasn't until she grabbed my offered hand that I knew she was.

"You look amazing," I cracked a laugh, in complete disbelief that she's mine. "Wow," I took her in for a second time.

Her hair was in big, glamorous waves that reached down her back. Her makeup was subtle but more than usual since she seemed to sparkle whenever the light caught her.

And her dress?

I fought hard to keep my thoughts pure with the way the silky fabric clung to her like a second skin, and the slit running up her upper thigh was teasing me so hard. The deep purple color complimented her so well. She was such a double threat—brilliant and beautiful.

"Thank you," she blushed. "You look rather handsome yourself," she smiled, placing a hand on my chest and reaching up to kiss me.

"Thanks," I smiled, resting my hand on the small of her back, my thumb brushing over her bare skin, and I felt her shiver.

"Have fun, you guys," Luna spoke, handing Rosie a black fur wrap.

She seemed eager to have us leave, but I didn't pay much attention; I had the most beautiful woman beside me.

Once we made it downstairs, I opened the passenger door, her hand firmly in mine as she stepped into the car. I followed, rounding the car before I slipped into the driver's seat.

Our conversation was light as I drove into the city where the gala was being held.

Her hand stayed in mine over the center console, her thumb brushing over my skin to calm herself. She smiled when I grabbed her hand, kissing it as I silently told her tonight would be fine.

We arrived at the museum, and the valet opened Rosie's door, helping her out of the car. Then, she grabbed my offering hand and slipped her arm through mine.

Her eyes were bright but quickly widened when her line of sight followed straight ahead of us and up the hundreds of stairs where hundreds of people were going up the steps.

"You okay?" I asked, placing my hand on top of hers.

"Yeah, I am," she nodded. "It's a lot of steps," she pointed, a smile blooming.

I chuckled.

"I'm not kidding. These are tall heels," she added with a joking tone.

I raised a brow. "I don't believe you since you looked this place up a week ago," I stated matter of factly. "You would've known not to wear heels if you couldn't do it," I reasoned.

She blew out a heavy breath.

"We can go home right now," I said.

She shook her head. "There's more people than I expected, but it's okay," she pressed. "If I'm not okay, I'll let you know," she proposed.

I agreed.

We walked up the staircase. Rosie was perfectly graceful and did not miss a step. We reached the top, where giant banners and lights decorate the open space. Staff was dressed in uniform suits, holding out silver trays of hors d'oeuvres and glasses of champagne.

"This is definitely something," Rosie took it all in. "I've never seen so much production value go into a gala," she made note of the theme. The banquet hall was decorated to look exactly like a forest. "It's insane," she looked up. Watching her act like this was cute, taking in all the details. That's what made her so brilliant; she knew what to look for to see the whole picture.

"They claim it boosts donations," I explained. "We should find our seat," I gestured to the banquet room where the main event occurred.

The attendants were allowed to mingle after the basic run-through of the event, the dinner, and other spokespersons. It was probably the most exciting thing to do during events like this.

I was enjoying the night, getting to introduce Rosie to everyone.

While she was nervous, she greeted everyone charismatically. They were enamored by her already.

We were in the middle of a conversation, Rosie slipping out a joke that caused everyone to laugh when a slow song came on. Most of the group departed, coupling off onto the dance floor when it was just us left.

"Would you like to dance?" I asked.

She stared out onto the dance floor, her eyes shining with something. "Sure," she grinned sheepishly, sliding her hand into mine as we made our way to the center of the room.

We fell perfectly in sync with the slow beat, our chests pressed together, our hands bound.

It was bliss.

~

Rosie

"I never picked you for a dancer," I glanced up at Victor; one of my hands rested on his shoulder, and the other held onto his. I knew my cheeks were red, and the intimacy of dancing and being close was more intense than I had thought. Chills ran up my spine as his other hand rested on the small of my back, his thumb circling against the exposed skin—it was perfect.

When he picked me up today, I was nervous. Galas and events weren't my cup of tea, but just like the grant benefit I attended back in September, I knew what opportunities lay in places like these. I would regret it if I missed out on it, so I always pushed through. I went on autopilot, somehow letting my entrepreneurial side take over while the rest of me hid. But right now, as I was in Victor's presence, I could live with all of me present.

And it was great.

"Why?" He pondered.

"You say you never like coming to these events. A dancer would take any opportunity to dance," I shrugged as I explained.

"Is this really considered dancing, though?" He glanced around before his gaze closed in on us. "We're just stepping back and forth," he smiled.

I rolled my eyes playfully. "You're not stiff," I added, noticing his calm and smooth composure. "A good dancer has the posture and the elegance. That's you," I smiled, toying with the lapel on his suit. "And that makes you very hot," I licked my lips.

"You're a good dancer, too," he complimented, pulling me closer to him. "Where did you learn?"

"Bianca taught me," I smiled. It was a sweet truth, but the full story was about my mom being too busy trying to find a man to teach me. My sister learned early on that teaching a four-year-old to dance was the best way to distract her from her mother's neglect.

"What about you?" I asked, distracting myself from the bad memory.

"Luis actually did," he stated.

My eyes widened. "Wait, what?" My smile grew, not believing him. I knew Luis was his best friend, but learning how deep their love and care for one another ran was cute.

"His family was always inviting us to parties, and my family had to learn at some point," he shrugged, acting like it wasn't the most adorable, heart-warming, sweetest thing ever.

"That's so cute! Do you think he can give Luna lessons? Bianca tried teaching her, but she really needs the help," I joked. My best friend lacked both rhythm and coordination.

"I'll see, but I'm afraid to ask because I know that'll fuel his ego," he snorted. "It'll take a while before he comes down from that."

"Am I fueling your ego when I say I am even more attracted to you than I was before?" I raised my eyebrows suggestively. "Now I know I won't have to go find another partner when the time comes to dance," I smirked.

"I'm glad Luis's overbearing teaching has paid off," he hummed.

I grinned, leaning up to kiss him as we continued to dance. My head rested on his chest, his thumb circling lazily on the small of my back, and our hands intertwined. We fit perfectly, and it felt like bliss.

After a few songs, we returned to our table so I could rest my feet.

I was pretty skilled in wearing high heels, but even the most seasoned heel wearer couldn't last a few hours when dancing was thrown in the mix.

"I'll feel it tomorrow. I haven't worn heels in such a long time," I blew out a breath. I was going to say something else, but I stopped when someone approached the table. My nerves grew again as I recited my greeting, but I've made enough introductions this evening to last me a lifetime. I was fine.

"You two are such a lovely couple. It's nice to see you finally settle down, Victor," an older blonde woman smiled deviously at us before her attention turned to him.

"Abigail Taylor, this is Rosie Martinez, owner of Hecho de Hilo," he introduced me to her.

I pressed my lips in a smile and held out my hand.

"What an interesting name," she hummed, shaking my hand. "What is the business?"

"A crochet shop," I answered, turning off the voice that told me to laugh at her comment about my business's name. "We're based in a neighborhood outside of Pilsen," I added.

She seemed to have found the answer to her unasked question. "We don't see many of those around nowadays, and it seems a bit unethical, doesn't it? All those fibers creating pollution?" She pondered.

I gulped.

"Hecho de Hilo is one of the greenest businesses out there," Victor butted in. "Rosie is a remarkable businesswoman. I'm sure you can learn a lot from her," he said, his attention being drawn by a person waving him down. "I'll catch up with you later, Taylor, but please, sit down. Rosie has one of the most extraordinary minds out there," he said with the brightest smile I ever saw.

My heart beat against my rib cage. I didn't want him to go, but the reassuring look he passed was all I needed.

"Mr. Romano sure does catch the eye of anyone, doesn't he?" She joked as we watched him greet the group of people.

"He has charm," I replied, a content look on my face as I studied him.

"One of the things I like about him," I specified. "Thank you for taking the time to talk with me. I've admired your work for many years."

Abigail Taylor was one of the most influential philanthropists out there. A self-made woman who single-handedly started the government's project for cleaning up plastic in the ocean and created an organization to help third-world countries fight natural disasters. Of course, she owned a jewelry brand where you can adopt a turtle with each purchase. She doesn't even like being referred to by her first name.

She was *that* cool.

"How kind of you," she grinned. "Now tell me, what makes you develop an eco-friendly crochet shop?" She asked.

I felt my shoulders relax as I began telling her.

We talked for a good twenty minutes, and she asked me basic questions about where I had learned and how I had become so skilled in my work.

It was a good conversation.

"How do you not get burned out, dear? I'm tired just by you telling me!" She laughed.

I suppressed a laugh and hiked my shoulders. "When you have a dream you want, you'll do anything to make it, even if it gets tiring," I stated honestly. "I just remind myself what I'm working towards," I shrugged, sipping my champagne.

"Owning your own business is a big dream. I'm glad you made it," she tilted her lips in a light smile.

"Well, actually, my dream is to open a ceramics shop," I explained. "I view my crochet shop as a gateway to that," I rolled my lips together, praying I didn't lose her on that.

"Hmm, interesting. Will this also be an eco-friendly business?" She asked, her eyes glimmering as I reeled her back in.

"Kinda, that's a work in progress. Really, what I hope to do is open a studio for my community and offer materials to educate people on how pottery can be an eco-conscious hobby. The source material is still being worked on. I want something local, but many businesses don't wish to work for someone like me," I gestured to myself.

"What kind of educational material?" She didn't seem phased by my last words.

I was juggling if I liked that or not.

"Oh, my best friends, Luna and Summer, wrote manuals for Hecho de Hilo and made the illustrations. We partner with a second-hand bookstore owner who makes the actual books. I'm hoping to bring her on with this," I smiled.

"So how does a pottery class become eco-friendly?" She questioned, running her fingers over her mouth.

I chewed on my lip before answering. "While pottery may not be the most eco-friendly hobby out there, the little things are what count, right?" I tried to shake off my nerves as I began listing a few things. "Making sure the material provider is eco-conscious and uses environmentally friendly devices, not using gas kilns, reusing clay that hasn't been fired yet," I said.

The way she hummed to my words, nodding every few moments, I hoped she was paying attention.

"Very interesting. Do you have any investors lined up for this business?" She sipped from her glass.

"No," I blushed, feeling like I was falling even more behind. "I barely have the funding to start it. Everything I make goes to Hecho de Hilo. While it's not my dream, it's still my baby, and I want to make sure it's taken care of," I explained, pressing my hands to my heart.

I love Hecho de Hilo with all my heart, and to think of pushing it aside hurts. I couldn't do that.

"Understood," she nodded. "Why don't you give me your number? I want to get in contact with you." She reached into her bag and pulled out a business card.

I did the same.

I stared at the juxtaposition of our cards, hers a sleek white with a geometric design and mine a bright, vivid splash of design that spoke to my business.

We were different in every possible way, but why did it make me so insecure?

I shook the feeling off and gladly took her card.

"I hope to talk to you soon. In the meantime, draft up a business plan for your ceramics shop," she stood, pointing at me before she turned around.

Victor was on his way back, a soft smile on his face as Taylor stopped him, hand on his arm as she said something to him. His eyes darted back to me with such admiration before he grinned at her, kissing her on the cheek before walking back to me.

"Everything went well, it seems," he grabbed my hand, matching my big smile.

"I think so," I glanced down at the table. "Ah, the adrenaline," I rubbed my arm, shaking off the lingering jitters. "I think she liked my idea for my ceramics shop. What did she tell you?"

"She said I was a lucky man," he grinned, his other hand stroking my arm comfortingly. "Do you want to get out of here?" He asked, glancing at his watch.

"And go where?" I stared at him, puzzled.

"Away from here, I spoke to who I needed to, and you networked," he answered. "Unless you want to stay," he said, searching my eyes for any sign of disagreement.

"No, I'm good," I beamed. "Let's go back to my place," I agreed, squeezing his hand as we stood up.

"Good," he kissed my hand, leading me towards the back exit where few were standing.

There was a dark hall with another staircase that led to the front entrance, just secluded.

"Where are we going?" I giggled, looking over my shoulder as the music and the lights faded.

"Just follow me," he chuckled.

We rounded a corner, the setting feeling oddly familiar, and it was confirmed when he pressed me against the wall. Just like the first night we met, but this time, we were making out, our lips pressed together in a heated kiss.

"I've been wanting to kiss you all night," he said against my lips, my mind dazed as I chased his lips.

"Mhmm," I moaned when he dipped his head down again. "If you think this is going to lead to more than just kissing, you have the wrong idea, sir," I chuckled against his lips.

"Are you implying you want to call me "sir"?" He grinned, pulling away. His hand slid around my waist, his hips pressed against my abdomen.

I could feel *him* against me.

"Haha, you're funny," I rested my head against the wall, a distance created between our bodies. "There's only one thing I'll call you," I looped my fingers through his belt loops, forcing him to step closer to me.

"Oh, yeah?" He raised a brow. "What's that?" He cupped my cheek, running his thumb along my skin.

I nuzzled deep into his touch.

"*Mine.*"

His gaze glossed over with darkness, a smirk spreading across his face.

"It has a nice ring to it," he hummed, dipping his head down, his nose rubbing against mine before he kissed down my neck and jaw. "But it sounds so much better when I'm saying it to you," he grinned.

I gasped when he sucked on the sweet spot behind my ear. "*Fuck,*" I held onto his strong shoulders, my body curving into his as he continued to press kisses along my body. My neck, my collarbone, and dipping down the neckline of my chest before I stopped him. "I really want you, Victor," I breathed. "But not here," I implied.

He pulled away, breathless, and his hair tousled slightly due to my part. But he smiled, nodding as he grabbed my hand. We made our way to the valet, making sure to "adjust" ourselves along the way.

Chapter 27

Rosie

"Luna is spending the night at her friend's place, so we have the apartment to ourselves," I said, tucking a strand of hair behind my ear, glancing out the window before I stared back at our interlocked hands resting in his lap.

After we came out from our mini rendezvous, we acted completely composed while the valet brought the car around. Now, the car ride had been silent until this point, filled with anticipation.

"I thought she was going to an art museum with Summer?" He glanced at me with a quirked brow. His hand squeezed mine slightly in an unconscious manner.

"Wait, really?" I laughed. "That's odd," I furrowed my brows. "I don't know why she's keeping it a secret," I grinned, smoothing my hand over my skirt before I crossed one knee over the other, leaning towards him. "Besides, Summer's at home working on her art final."

"You don't seem worried about her spending the night," he said while flipping on his signal as he pulled onto my street.

"Mainly because she seems happy. I don't want to get in the way of that," I shook my head. I haven't seen Luna this happy in a while, and I'm patient enough to let her tell me on her own.

Once we made it back inside my apartment, I flipped the switch on, leading him to my bedroom.

"These heels are a devil in disguise. I don't know how I made it through the night," I smirked, sitting on my bed.

I briefly remembered how I used to steal Bianca's heels, which she would wear for her "classes"—my curiosity was always at its peak.

I slowly took off my jewelry, placing it on my nightstand. I could sense Victor staring at me, and I was met with his gaze running over me when I turned around, his shoulder leaning against the door frame.

"What?" I furrowed my brows, a smile reaching me. As I waited for his response, I reached down to strap off my heels, but he beat me to it.

He kneeled before me. "You're so beautiful," he whispered, his fingers dancing down my leg and wrapping around my ankle as he pulled off my shoe, my foot breathing in relief. "Did you know that?" He glanced up at me, his eyes so full of *something*.

My heart skipped a beat when I guessed what it was.

"Yes," I hummed. "You tell me all the time," I sighed, licking my lips when he placed his hands on my knees, spreading them wide.

"Because you need to understand your beauty, Rosie," he lifted my right leg, placed my calf on his shoulder, and kissed the exposed skin softly. "You say I'm a work of art, sculpted by the gods. But no," he whispered, shaking his head, a grin on his face when he grabbed me by the hips and dragged me so my ass was hanging off the bed. "You're the sculpture, carved and curated by the powerful creatures above, and I'm the one blessed to have you," he pushed the fabric of my dress away. "Tell me, and I'll worship you as you deserve."

"Please."

He smirked before he reached his hands under my dress, pulling my thong off and throwing it over his shoulder. He reached between my legs, his stubble tickling the delicate skin, making me shudder. He kissed down my thigh, his hands pushing the material of my dress further up. The cool air hit between my legs, but the heat of his kisses warmed me up as he traced his lips closer to my aching pussy, teasing me until I was begging for him.

My hand reached for his hair, guiding his mouth to my center. The moment he swiped a long stripe between my folds, I closed my eyes, my shoulders relaxing as I let out a heavy sigh.

He wrapped his lips around my clit and used his tongue to circle it, earning a trail of moans from me. His hands held the material of my dress out of the way while also holding my thighs open, his fingers digging into my flesh to hold me down.

"Oh my god," I gasped as his warm breath blew on my delicate skin.

It was such a simple move, but the shocks it was sending me up my back and down my legs were pushing me over the edge. I tugged on his hair, needing more.

"I'm," I gasped, resting back against the mattress, one of my hands leaving his head of hair to reach above my head. My body was losing control from the pleasure I was feeling. Electricity coursed through my veins, the cool silk of my dress turning warm against my hot body.

I reached down to grab onto one of his hands, his other kneading the flesh of my ass as he continued his assault on my clit. I raked my nails down his arm, my other hand coming down as I began to play with my breast over my dress, the friction creating enough buzz that excited me.

The mixed sensations allowed that pressure to build until it toppled over.

"*Fuck*," I cursed.

His movements slowed but didn't stop.

Something he knew I enjoyed.

The soft sensations allowed my orgasm to trail out, creating a transition of immense pleasure to a gentle touch.

He pressed a few kisses around my clit before letting go of my hips, reaching for my hand, and pressing a loving kiss to the back of it. His gaze stayed on mine as he kissed his way up my body. The only thing I could offer to him was my dazed smile before he hovered above me.

"How are you feeling?" He asked.

"You're good at that," I reached up to play with an out-of-place hair before I reached up and kissed him before I maneuvered our bodies so I straddled his waist.

His hands found home with mine, his lips moving against my mouth in the most gentle kiss I've ever felt.

I groaned at the taste of me when our tongues melded together before I moved to stand. Breaking apart, I guided him to follow me.

Standing in the middle of my room, I kept my gaze on him as I grabbed my hair and moved it to the side. I turned around, showing off the zipper in the back, and glanced back at him.

"You sure?"

"More than anything, you?" I bit my lip.

He gleamed. "Yes, more than anything," he responded, his hands brushing over the exposed skin of my back. His fingers found the zipper, and the room was filled with the sound of it coming undone.

I sucked in a breath at the draft that hit me, but his lingering heat quickly warmed me up. I let my hands fall to my sides and allowed the dress to pool at my feet. I slowly turned to face him, and his eyes scanned over my naked figure.

This was the first time I was completely naked in front of him. In all of our previous physical moments, I had kept my shirt or shorts on. It was a thrilling feeling to be able to be vulnerable in front of the person you trusted the most.

"I'll always be right," his breath hitched. "You are beautiful, Rosie," he beamed, his eyes casting over with both lust and admiration.

I couldn't help but blush, taking a step towards him. "You're overdressed," I smirked.

"That won't be a problem much longer," he stated, guiding me to sit back on the bed.

I leaned back on my hands. I watched intently as he began to undress himself.

Beginning with his jacket, he took off his shoes, untucked his shirt, and teased me with each button he took off.

Soon, Victor was naked before me.

I stood up. I bit down on my lip as I grinned before running my hands over each crevice and dip of his abdomen. My skin was tickled by the hair on his body, and I let out a small giggle, the excitement growing before I reached up to kiss him.

Our skin touched as we leaned into each other, the heat of our bodies sending a new wave of intensity.

I pulled away, grabbed a condom from my nightstand, and handed it to him. I went to my bed, watching as he rolled it on.

He crawled over me, settling between my legs. He slid his thumb along my lip, tracing the plump pink skin before our lips touched again.

I moaned, raking my hands down his body until he reached between us, grabbing one of them and bringing it up beside my head as he threaded our fingers together. The coolness of the sheets pressing against the top of my hand was a complete juxtaposition of his warmth radiating against my palm.

He rubbed the tip of his cock against my clit, my toes curling and my eyes fluttering open to watch him.

I wanted to see him as he entered me, and the sight of him blessed me as he guided himself slowly into my slick walls. I welcomed the feeling, my thighs opening wider to let his hips come completely flush against mine.

"Fuck," I threw my head back, squeezing his hand.

"So perfect," he said slowly, squeezing my hand back. He reached for my other hand, mirroring the same action as before.

His large hands had mine pinned down, his hips slowly beginning to move while I rested my calves on his hips, allowing him to take control.

"You okay?" He asked.

I opened my eyes to find him staring at me with such desire and care.

"Yes, please don't stop." I lifted my head to nuzzle my nose against his before it fell back against my pillow when he reached that favorable spot. My walls clenched around him.

He groaned, his head dropping to my chest. "Keep doing that, and I won't last long," he mumbled against my skin.

I smirked, doing it again.

He squeezed my hands as a warning.

"Feels too good," I said innocently when he looked back up. "I wanna touch you," I requested, and he nodded, kissing me before he let me go.

I immediately ran my hands over his shoulders, raking my nails down his skin, kissing him desperately. The continuous feel of his cock dragging along my aching walls had the bubbling feeling in my stomach grow. Running my hands through his hair, I threw my head back as he left wet, sloppy kisses along my throat.

His mouth reached over my breasts, his tongue swirling around my hardened peaks. The feeling of his teeth grazing over the delicate tissue made me shudder, my legs squeezing around him. I began grinding my hips against his, my clit enjoying the friction as the familiar feeling began to grow.

"Victor," I moaned his name, my nails running over his ass when he hit my g-spot. My eyes rolled to the back of my head.

It was indescribable—the feeling of his mouth on my breasts, his pelvis rubbing against my already sensitive clit, and his throbbing cock piercing through my dripping pussy.

He only coaxed my attention back to him when he whispered my name in my ear. His hand ran along the sides of my thigh, the teasing feeling sending currents up my body.

"I'm not gonna last long," I said with a flushed face.

"Let go, beautiful," he encouraged.

That's all I needed before I did.

My lashes fluttered closed, and I wrapped my legs around his waist. I hid my face in his shoulder as I cried out in pleasure, the sensation causing my walls to clench around him.

He stilled. The way I wrapped around him prevented him from doing anything but to come too. He held himself up with arms at either side of me, his head dropping as he let out a low moan.

I sighed out in contentment, my limbs unraveling from his.

He pulled out, disposing of the condom before he nestled on the bed, waiting for me to nuzzle next to him.

I happily nestled beside him, attempting to catch my breath. "It was really sexy seeing you work your way through those people. Instantly charming them with your words and your smile," I trailed my hand up his chest before I kissed his lips.

"What about you?" He smiled, running his fingers along my back, his arm resting behind his head.

"What about me?" I questioned, holding my head up.

"You had Taylor wrapped around your finger," he smirked, resting his hand on the small of my back. "She loved you," he kissed my cheek when I turned away, blushing. "I'm seriously proud of you. I know it was a lot to come out there, but I hope you can see that it was worth it," he kissed my shoulder.

"She did, didn't she," I hummed, deciding to agree for once. "It was definitely worth it," I grinned as he pulled me in for another kiss, his praises continuing as we went under the sheets for another round.

Chapter 28

Victor

One thing I loved about my apartment was the soundproofing. Mornings and nights were quiet—empty of cars honking, sirens wailing, and people shouting. But as I stirred awake, the muffled noise against the window quickly annoyed me.

I shifted, my arm tightened around Rosie's body. I paused, a smile forming as the sounds drowned out.

She stirred, her hand moving to slide over mine as she sighed. Her movements signaled her woken state, and she subconsciously rubbed her ass against my pelvis, a notable groan escaping my lips, and the tiny smirk on her face told me it wasn't an accident.

"Please tell me you're not going to work today," she groaned, scrunching her eyes and reaching back to tangle her fingers in my hair.

"It's Saturday," I pressed a kiss to her shoulder. "Are you?" I asked, knowing Hecho de Hilo was open all week. I never understood how she did it, and I wondered when she last had a day off.

"Summer's opening, she can handle it. I'll probably go in after lunch," she yawned, scooting closer to me. "You're so warm," she sighed contently.

I swore my heart could've burst.

"I'd ask for a good morning kiss, but I'm not one for morning breath,"

I joked.

She hummed in agreement.

People in movies always seemed never to mind it, and I could never wrap my head around it. Though staring at Rosie's relaxed state, her messy hair, and her soft cheeks, it was tempting to disregard it.

"Don't worry, I have an extra toothbrush," she patted my cheek, slapping my temptation away before she got up, pulling me with her.

My brows furrowed. While I did want to kiss her, desperately so, I didn't want to get out of bed. I tried to stay in, defend my ground, but the moment the sheet slipped over her ass, and she was walking around naked in front of me, I stood up.

"So soon?" I questioned while pulling my boxers on.

"Well, I want that good morning kiss, and I have other plans that involve kissing," she wiggled her brows, pulling a shirt over her head before we walked to the bathroom together.

The fabric and color looked familiar, and that's when I realized it was the shirt I lent her the time she stayed over after our first date.

"I forgot you kept it," I tugged on the material, letting it flow back against her frame.

"Yeah," she sheepishly shrugged. "It brings me comfort," she batted her lashes while she handed me a toothbrush.

"You look cute in it."

She beamed, cheeks flushing pink before she began brushing her teeth.

The second our breaths were fresh, I pulled her into a kiss, my arms wrapping around her waist and hers around my neck.

We both moaned against the other, the kiss growing heated until she pulled away, licking her lips.

"Mhmm, minty," she smiled up at me. "One more, please," she puckered her lips, reaching up with her tiptoes.

She was so cute, and there was no way I could say no to her.

"Wanna go back to bed?" She suggested, pulling away and tracing shapes on my skin, a knowing look on her face.

She giggled when I picked her up, taking us back to her room before I threw her on the bed. Her face was beaming when she glanced up at me, but that didn't stop her from throwing my shirt off her.

Last night was our first time together. It was intimate and loving, but now that I had a taste of her, I felt like it would never be enough.

I slid my hand up her thigh, her hand pumping me as she kissed my neck. I used my finger to rub her clit, small gasps escaping her while she began to grind on my hand.

"Fuck, I want to come with you in me," she whined, hand cupping my face as she bit on her lip—I could've finished right there. "Please," she pecked my lips, nuzzling her nose against mine while she continued to grind on my hand.

"After," I groaned, feeling her slick grow on my hand. "Be patient," I whispered, nipping at her ear.

She shuddered under my touch, nodding profusely.

"How many fingers?"

"Two," she gasped when I circled my finger over her opening.

"Like this?" I smirked, earning a reaction from her as I slipped my middle and ring finger into her, using my palm to rub against her clit.

"Oh, god, *yes*," she threw her head back, hand clutching my shoulder.

The movement in her hips didn't stop, and it was amazing to see her lose control with just my fingers. She was so sensitive.

I kissed along her throat, sucking on her soft skin.

Last night, I had some self-control, but right now, I didn't feel remorse as I left a red mark right on her neck.

She owned plenty of turtlenecks anyway.

I soothed the forming bruise with my tongue, her moans echoing in my ear. The sounds radiated to my core, making my already hard cock ache with precum.

"You're squeezing my fingers, beautiful," I glanced down where her pussy was sucking my fingers into her, the wet sounds filling the space of her room.

She whined when I brushed over the rough patch inside her, sending goosebumps over her skin. Her knees buckled in, her walls clenching around my fingers again, but I used my arm to spread her legs wide again.

"Patience," I reminded.

She complied, keeping her thighs splayed out for me while I continued moving my hand.

My palm rubbed against her swollen bud while my fingers continued to work their way into her, the repetitive movements sending her over the edge.

"Victor," she squeezed around me, her hips grinding against my hand.

My movements slowed, allowing her to ride out her orgasm. "Atta girl," I said against her ear, watching as she relaxed against me.

I slipped my fingers out of her, spreading them apart to see her wetness glisten in the morning light.

She watched expectedly, her eyes widening when I placed them in my mouth.

The taste of her landed on my tongue, and I pulled away with a groan. "Sweet," I smiled before I placed my fingers on her bottom lip. Her mouth opened as she got a taste of herself, too.

"Mhmm," she moaned after letting go, her body straightening up as she grabbed the back of my head.

Our mouths meshed together in a passionate kiss.

Wrapping my arm around her waist, I slid her onto my lap. My throbbing cock teased at her entrance, causing me to moan.

"I need you inside me *now*," she pleaded.

"Fuck," I groaned, reaching for a condom on the nightstand.

She rubbed herself against my tip, relieving herself for a split moment until I rolled the condom on. Not a second later, she was sliding onto me. Her hands were on my shoulders to stabilize herself, and she began bouncing on my cock.

"Lie back," she placed her hands on my chest.

I followed her request, and my hands found a place on her knee, giving her some stability before she began to rock her hips back and forth, grinding on me. I told myself this was heaven, having the most gorgeous woman riding my cock, her breasts bouncing as she moved.

Nothing was better than that.

"Oh god," she moaned, throwing her head back. "I'm not gonna last long."

Heat crept up my neck as I felt my ego fill with pride. I was quickly distracted, though, when she clenched around me. My eyes fluttered closed at the feel of her slick walls coating me. She gripped onto me, hips rocking back and forth as she used me to get herself off, but in reality, I wasn't far behind her.

I sat up, wrapping my arms around her before I flipped us over, my cock hitting an angle it didn't before, her eyes rolling to the back of her head when I began to thrust deeper. I had one hand hooked under her knee, the other hand caressing her thigh while I kissed along her throat.

"Kiss me," she muttered, grabbing my face and locking our lips together.

Our tongues explored each other ravenously. Soon, we were both coming together. Our heads fell, chests heaving, and our breaths exhausted.

I rested on the pillow beside her head. The feeling of her nose nuzzling along my cheek brought a smile to my face, and it only grew as a soft giggle erupted from her.

She peppered kisses along my throat while I pulled out of her. Her eyes trained on me as I removed the condom, dumping it in the trash.

I crawled back over, kissing whatever I craved, my lips lingering on the red mark on her neck that she still hadn't noticed.

"I was thinking of making breakfast," she said, running her fingers through my hair.

"What did you have in mind?" I lifted my head, smiling down at her.

~

Rosie

Spending the day with Victor must've been the best day of my life.

We woke up, brushed our teeth, had sex, made breakfast together, and now we were back in my room fucking again.

I'd be happy to live like this for the rest of my life.

Beyond happy.

"Okay, don't stop," I gasped, holding myself up with my arms while Victor gripped my hips tightly.

His cock was dragging in and out of me so deep and hard I couldn't help the moans coming from me.

I had experienced two orgasms today, and he was already pushing me towards another.

Fucking missionary and me on top offered two different angles his cock hit inside me.

But him behind?

Oh my god.

My hands fisted the sheets, and I couldn't see what was in front of me from the way my eyes rolled to the back of my head every time he brushed that spot inside me.

And he did so many times.

"I'm gonna come again," I gasped, walls clenching around him as I let go, his name slipping from my mouth. My shoulders relaxed against the mattress, and I felt as he followed suit, his cock twitching inside me as he released into the condom.

He moaned, spreading my ass as he pulled out, discarding the condom.

I moved to my back just as he collapsed beside me.

We were both out of breath, our chests heaving like crazy. His hand lazily massaged my skin while I let my fingers trace the curves of his face.

I was the first to speak. "I need a break after that," I cracked a weak smile, gazing into his eyes.

"I agree."

We stayed like that for a moment before we decided to get dressed again—this time in loungewear.

I was so thankful I still had his shirt and pants from when I first slept at his house. While I did miss wearing his shirt, the way the fabric expanded over his broad chest and shoulders looked so good on him.

God, Rosie, you just had sex with this man.

Getting my dirty thoughts out of my head, I returned my attention to the TV where *Malcolm in the Middle* was playing.

"Why don't you take the day off?" He suddenly proposed.

"I would, but I have to ensure I have the inventory down and finalized before we go for our shipment next week. I also have a meeting with the bookstore owner. We're recycling the current books and updating them," I explained.

It wasn't an extensive list, but I knew I would feel better if I got them off my radar.

"Oh, and I'm hosting a late-night brainstorm with the girls. We're coming up with new releases for next year!" I grinned, but it dropped when I realized he had probably asked because he wanted to spend the day with me. "Sorry."

"Don't be," he rubbed my arm, reassuring me. "My only concern is when did you last take a day off?" He rubbed my jaw with his thumb.

"I have days off," I said. "We're closed eleven days out of the year, thirteen if you include Christmas Eve and New Year's Eve," I pointed out. "I technically had a day off this month already."

"You spent the entire day working, though. The store might've been closed, but you were still there," he responded.

I frowned.

"Federal holidays don't count."

"Well, there's things to do," I shrugged. "I can't not work for a day. Things would go haywire," I tried to reason.

"Even on the days you visit your sister, you work?" He wondered.

"I go early, and we only have an hour. I'm back after lunch," I explained.

"So you haven't taken a day off since you started working?" He cocked a brow. "What about your birthday? Aren't you burned out?" He threw out the questions as they hit me.

I knew he was worried, so I took a calming breath before answering.

"No. The girls and a few regulars celebrate in the shop with a cake that Señora Rivera makes. And I can't afford to be burned out, so I don't," I shrugged, trying to keep my tone as calm as possible. "What about you? Have you ever taken a day off?"

"I try my best not to work weekends and take a day off during the year just to do *nothing*. I trust that my employees will cover things. I come back, and things are running smoother than ever because I gave myself a break," he elaborated.

I didn't respond.

"No one deserves a break more than you," he said.

"I can't just call off. I have things to do."

"You're the boss. You can do whatever you want."

I caved in.

I messaged the bookstore owner. She thankfully understood and was grateful since she had something come up. Then Summer and Luna were relieved I came to my senses, thanking Victor over the phone.

"So you were right," I laughed, dropping my phone. "This feels weird," I stilled. "It's one thing to have a lazy morning, but the *entire* day?" My brows raised.

He rolled over in laughter.

"What do we do?"

"That's the beauty of it, Rosie," he grabbed me, pulling me into his side. "Whatever you want," he smirked.

"Anything?" I smirked, looking up at him.

"Anything," he smiled.

I grabbed the back of his neck, smashing our lips together. I figured I could be productive in one way, at least.

Chapter 29

Rosie

I was a changed woman. Taking a day off and having sex whenever with my boyfriend.

It had only been a few days since my first day off in a while, but that, on top of the endless sex with Victor, was making me happier than I could imagine.

I smiled to myself as I thought about this morning, Victor and I making out on the counter in the kitchen, so close to finishing what we started earlier in bed, until Luna walked in.

She nearly screamed the walls off the place before she ran back into her room.

It was funny, but it ruined the mood.

Our laughs stayed quiet as we fixed our clothes and hair, returning our attention to the pancakes we were making.

While I was disappointed our morning got cut short and we had to depart due to work, I looked forward to lunch.

I became more comfortable walking through the Romano Tech building and greeted the receptionist before I went to the elevator.

I couldn't contain my excitement as I stepped onto the main floor and found Ari typing on her computer.

"Hey, Ari," I waved, catching her attention.

She pressed her lips in a smile, waving slightly at me.

"Good to see you, Rosie."

I was so glad that "Miss Martinez" was dropped after conversing with her a few times.

"He's in his office," she tipped her head towards the closed door, answering my unasked question.

"Thanks," I grinned. "Did you get a haircut?" I pointed, noticing something was different about her, but I couldn't figure it out.

She shook her head.

"Anything new?" I questioned.

Her face was glowing, eyes beaming, skin flushed.

"Just same old me," she shrugged, letting out a small laugh, her cheeks tinting slightly pink.

"You seem happier. I can see it in your eyes," I nodded, finally realizing it.

"Hmm, guess I never noticed that," she tucked a strand of hair behind her ear. "I am happier," she gleamed. "Thanks."

"Anytime!" I grinned before I walked towards Victor's office.

I knocked before opening the door, finding him working on his computer.

God, why was he so hot?

Our gazes met as he passed me a small smile.

"You made it," he pushed away from his desk, standing up and meeting me halfway.

"I brought lunch," I held the bag and kissed him. "Burgers and fries," I hummed as he led me over to the small couch in his office.

"Good, because I'm starving," he sat down and pulled me into his lap.

I felt my face heat up.

Even though there was enough room for us, he wanted me close.

"I got the chili cheese fries. They looked delicious on the menu," I said, my breath hitching as he kissed along my neck. "Are you sure you're hungry for food?" I cracked a grin, my lower half aching as his hand slid under my dress.

"I don't know, what's on the menu?"

"What do you want?" I bit my lip in anticipation.

"Fuck, don't do that," he groaned, his thumb reaching up to pull it from my teeth.

"Why?" I grinned. "You love it."

"Exactly," he chuckled, turning my head to kiss along my jaw. "I've noticed you wear dresses each time you visit me at my office," he said between kisses, his fingers tugging on the fabric.

I feigned innocence. "Guess that just works out in our favor, purely coincidence," I smiled.

"You've visited me numerous times in the month and a half we've been dating," he stated pointedly. "But I'm gonna choose to believe you don't have other motives, mostly because I need to be inside you," he breathed against my ear, his hot breath fanning against my skin.

My hands worked on untucking his shirt from his pants, my nails raking over his firm abdomen while I got his belt unbuckled and reached into his pants.

His hand pushed the fabric of my dress away, his hand dipping into my panties.

We both sucked in a breath as we began touching each other—my hand pumping him slowly and his finger working against my wet folds.

"I can't believe we're going to have sex in your office," I whispered, shaking with excitement. "This is a huge step up from making out," I humored.

"You're so—" he breathed out a chuckle, but he quickly swallowed it when I caressed his balls.

"Were you saying something?" I smirked as I whispered in his ear.

"These walls used to be innocent before you walked into my life," he managed to say, hand clenching my waist.

"My office has never been christened, if you wanna be even," I suggested, gasping when his finger rubbed over my clit, my other hand clutching his shoulder. "*Fuck.* You really have to show off like that, huh?" I furrowed my brows from the pleasure.

He worked two fingers in me, beginning to pump them in and out of me.

"You're one to talk," he referred to my hand, still working on his cock.

"Enough showing off," I said, pulling my hand away from him and laying back on the couch.

Once he had a condom on, he placed his hands under my knees, pressing them into my shoulders while he lined up at my entrance.

"Oh, wow," I gasped, holding onto his shirt as I watched him sink into me.

He stilled for a moment before he began moving.

We were both mesmerized by the way he was stretching my walls. Seeing how perfectly we fit together was amazing—our bodies joining like two pieces of clay. It never got old.

"Touch yourself," he instructed.

I followed his command, reaching my hand between us as I began rubbing my clit in slow circles.

The added sensation shot electricity up me, and I clenched around him.

He moaned at the feeling, pulling out completely before slipping back in.

I whimpered at the feeling of every inch of him brushing against my walls.

"You take me so well."

I blushed, but my body reacted by fluttering around his cock. "I'm so glad I'm the only girl you've ever brought in here," I expressed truthfully, keeping my gaze on him.

"You'll be the first and the last," he leaned down and whispered in my ear, his cock hitting deep in me, sending me to my climax.

Following me, we stayed on the couch like breathless fools until we mustered enough strength to get dressed.

"You okay?" He asked as he buckled his pants.

I bit my lip, nodding as I leaned in for a kiss.

"Mhmm, I just know getting back to my car will be a trip," I chuckled, a post-coital sheen plastered on my skin.

"I could carry you if you'd like," he mildly joked.

"I'll be fine, but I would like to spend the night with you, continuing what just happened?" I asked, clasping my hands behind his neck.

"You're still horny?" He cocked a brow, amusement spread across his features. "You want my cock that bad, huh?" He nuzzled his nose against mine.

"I'm mature enough to admit it. I'm *desperate*," I emphasized, leaning against him. "Give me a little bit more to hold me off until then?" I pucker my lips, reaching for a kiss.

"What happened not even five minutes ago should hold you off, but I'm feeling generous, so here," he licked his lips before he leaned, pressing our lips together.

I moaned against him, my hands sliding to frame his face as he deepened the kiss.

Just then, my phone rang.

"God, if it's spam, I swear," I shook my head, pulling my phone from my purse.

The contact made my heart stop.

"Rosie?" He called after me, noticing my change in demeanor, but I ignored him when I answered.

"Maritza?" I stilled. "What is it? Is Bianca okay?" I stepped away from him.

I prayed everything was fine. The aching feeling in my gut already told me what to expect, but I didn't want to let my heart believe it. I swallowed hard, chewing on my lip as I paced in anticipation.

"No, she got hurt real bad."

The worry in her voice was loud and clear.

"That psycho, the one that got sent to max, one of her other crazy ass friends wanted to get back at Bianca for what she did," she sighed.

Oh no.

"She got her messed up big time while in the library. No one was there to help. They put her in solitary for her own protection. I'm sorry, Rosie," she apologized before hanging up.

What? Didn't they learn from last time?

It felt like I couldn't breathe.

I clutched my throat, the air wanting to come out, but I couldn't get anything. My chest was frozen. I couldn't see; everything was blurry in front of me. All my senses left my body, and I could barely hear Victor as he called my name.

Chapter 30

Rosie

"In and out, Rosie. In and out," Victor rubbed my back, squeezing my hand with the other while I tried to focus on my breathing. "It's just you and me, okay?" He moved so he was kneeling in front of me.

I focused my gaze on him, staring at his sharp features. My eyes cast over his dark brown ones, and I tried so hard to get lost in them, but my mind kept thinking about my sister.

She could be dead because of you.

"I want you to name five things for me, name them, and describe them in detail. Can you do that for me?" He searched my eyes, worry embedded in his features by the crease between his eyebrows.

I nodded, my body still shaking as I began to look around his office.

A Rubik's cube on his desk, solved as always. The red side was faced up, and I could only see the blue and yellow faces from here.

The bag of cheeseburgers was still on the desk, wholly forgotten after our quick session.

The painting on the wall was huge with black and gray splatter paint adorning it, shades of blue scattered between. There was a particularly big splotch on the right upper-hand corner that looked like Patrick Starr.

Victor laughed at that and told me to continue, the hand rubbing my back slowing in its movements, but his warmth remained.

A glass trophy that looked like it was plucked right out of the earth with its rough edges and natural form, the plaque reading "Most Generous Philanthropist: Victor Romano".

"That's cool," I shivered, my teeth chattering as my body reacted to the panic coursing through me.

One more, I tried to focus.

"A photo, right on the bookshelf. There are three people: a lady, a man, and a boy. They're standing somewhere, maybe outside, but they look happy. The lady is pressing her cheek against the boy while the man looks at them lovingly," I sucked in a breath as I slowly gained control of it. "It's you and your parents. You're happy," I pointed, realization dawning on me.

He nodded, stroking a hand over my head. "Yeah, I was," he reminisced. "You did great," he cooed, pulling me into his arms. "How do you feel?"

"Scared," I admitted, taking in a big inhale. "Bianca's friend called me from the prison. They cornered her and hurt her, and now she's in solitary," my throat hitched as I exhaled, tears blurring my gaze again. I bit on my lip as I tried to swallow the sobs.

He stood up, sitting beside me on the couch. "I'm sorry, Rosie," he embraced me. "They should have put the other person in there for what they did."

"You know the prison system isn't smart. They barely know what sympathy is. I'm only aware of what happened because of Bianca's friend. God, she's already done so much for Bianca and me," I sighed, guilt consuming me.

I shouldn't have to keep relying on people.

"She wants to help because she also knows the pain," he responded, wiping my tears away. "I'm sure she would want someone to tell her if she was in your position," he reasoned.

I nodded.

"I know, but if something happens to her, on top of Bianca?" I shuddered. "I can't," I let out a defeated sigh.

All I wanted was my sister back, safe, with me.

He allowed me to cry into his chest, my tears staining the material, but he didn't care.

"Rosie, do you get panic attacks every time something like this happens?" He asked, pulling away so he could look at me.

I sniffled. "I wish I could say not all the time, but when I fear something bad is going to happen to her, I do," I answered.

Looking away, I frowned, knowing I didn't tell the whole truth.

"I tend to think the worst. Her being in prison doesn't help," I shook my head, glancing down. "But I've been dealing with them most of my life. I'll be fine," I shrugged, passing a smile, though he didn't look convinced.

We were facing each other now on the couch, our knees touching and hands intertwined.

He licked his lips in thought before speaking.

"Just because you're used to it doesn't mean you have to endure it," he frowned, tucking a strand of hair behind my ear. "Why do you have panic attacks, Rosie? What happened?" He sounded so concerned, so terrified.

I knew he was wondering what exact moment made all of this start. I never talked about it, rarely with Luna.

Summer and Quinn only knew the basic details.

Even Bianca and I try not to mention it.

I only imagined telling Victor once we were *really* serious, but now it seemed like sooner was better than later.

"Because of my stepdad," I felt my eyes water at the memory of him.

"They didn't start until he came into our lives," I choked out a sob.

Victor quickly pulled me into his embrace.

"What did he do?" His tone sounded strained, like he was controlling himself. That was proven correct by the way his jaw ticked when I glanced up to look at him.

"He was abusive. Anything we'd do would trigger him. That would send me into those attacks, which he didn't like, but because Bianca didn't want him to hurt me, she always took the beatings," I squeezed my eyes shut.

"I said no TV!" He yelled, raising a hand at my sister. "Do you pay the bills in this house?!"

I was hiding in the corner, my heart beating against my chest. The strain in my chest told me I couldn't breathe. The more the tears streamed down my face, the more I realized he was hurting her.

"Rosie was having an attack! The TV distracts her!"

I accidentally tracked mud in the house earlier, and it sent me into complete panic. She cleaned the mess up while I sat on the couch, hoping I'd calm down. But he walked in before then.

"It's all in her fucking head!" He threw her to the side before he searched for me. "I thought I told you to stop with this bullshit!" He pointed a crooked finger at me.

My eyes widened at the sight of him charging towards me, sending me into another wave of panic.

"No!" Bianca shouted, stepping between me and him.

"Part of me felt like he knew what would send me into an attack just so he had a reason to hurt Bianca, knowing she would always protect me from that," I played with a loose thread of my sweater. "I hated him so much," I gulped. "I was only seven when I wished he was dead."

I searched Victor's eyes.

There was no pity, no fear, just *understanding*.

While his expression made me feel a little better, the thought still loomed in my mind: what kind of child wishes death on someone?

"Was your mom aware of any of this?" He squeezed my hand.

"She didn't care. In her eyes, he gave us the world," I shrugged.

"*¿Y por qué estás llorando?" My mom placed a hand on her hip.*

"*He hurts Bianca! He doesn't love us!" I cried, clutching my mother's leg.*

"*Ay, deveras, Rosa," she scoffed, throwing the dish towel on the counter. "Maybe if you stopped crying all the time, he wouldn't hurt her," she raised a brow.*

I stilled, lip quivering, and tried to stop the tears from falling.

She bent down, grabbing me on the shoulders. "Do you like living in a nice house?" She shook me.

"*Yes," I heard my voice crack and chewed on my lip to stop it.*

"*Do you like having food on the table? Clothes on your back?" She cocked a brow.*

"*Yeah," I stared at the ground. "But we were okay before," I whined.*

"*Porque estaba trabajando, pero ahora, tenemos Gerardo para que nos cuide," she rubbed my shoulders. "No me gusta que estés chillando, por favor," she rolled her eyes before standing up. "¿Oyistes?"*

"*Sí," I frowned, wiping my eyes.*

"There was no love in that house besides Bianca and I," I forced a smile. I've always loved my sister, and there wouldn't be a day I don't.

"You've always had your sister," he stroked my hair.

"Until I *only* had her," I responded.

"*Señora, perdón, pero tu esposo no sobrevive," the officer took his cap off as he told the news to my mother.*

Her knees instantly gave out as she wailed.

"¡Gerardo!" She screamed, hands clutching to her heart. "¡Mi amor!"

I stared at her before turning to Bianca.

Her arm wrapped around me, and she just stared into space, the blue and red lights flashing on her face.

A single tear ran down her cheek.

I could've sworn I saw the corner of her mouth peak up.

"He was walking home from the store, a car ran into him and killed him instantly," I recounted.

A single tear fell down my face.

"I was thirteen at the time. I could still hear my mother's cries," I huffed out. "She blamed me for his death," my voice cracked.

I burrowed myself deeper into Victor.

"How could you possibly have anything to do with it?" He scoffed.

"¡Es tu culpa!" She shouted, jutting a finger in my face.

The police were long gone, and my mother was too hysterical to go to the hospital. They gave up after a while, leaving us in the house.

"¡Por un pinche pastel!" She screamed, grabbing the unfrosted cake and throwing it across the room.

It landed on the sliding door before it crumbled to the floor.

I was crying now, too. My back pressed to the wall as she continued to yell at me.

"¡Basta!" Bianca ripped my mother away from me.

She was older now, tougher, stronger.

"You need to calm down, Ma!" She grabbed our mother by the shoulders, pushing her into the other room.

My weak and fragile mother didn't try to fight.

She spent the rest of the night crying.

"He was at the store because I needed some peanut butter for a cake I was making for her," I explained, a hum following as I gulped. "We were going to celebrate her birthday that night," I chewed on the inside of my cheek.

"¿Quieres ayudarnos?" I questioned, glancing between my stepfather and Bianca.

"Claro," he shrugged. "You're my daughters. I want to help," he smiled.

I blinked in shock.

This wasn't the man who spent all his time yelling at us. The man who abused us for years.

He was a stranger.

"We need peanut butter, though," Bianca said from the other side of the kitchen, her arms crossed over her chest.

"No problem with that," he smiled, hiking his shoulders up. "I'll go get it at the store. You guys start," he patted my shoulder.

I stared at my sister in shock, but she was staring at him while he grabbed his jacket and wallet and made his way out the door for the last time.

"I thought things would change, but because of me, he died," I hid my face in my hands.

"Rosie, you have to understand that it's not your fault," he pushed my hands away from my face, tucking my hair behind my ears. "He made that choice to go to the store, and he was hit that night. It could've happened to anyone."

I looked up at the ceiling, pressing my lips together.

Everyone in my life told me that.

I have not believed a single one because the rest wouldn't have happened if they were telling the truth.

"*I was the one who wanted to bake a peanut butter cake, I was the one who finished the peanut butter the night before because I wanted a snack, I was the reason he had to go to the store, I was the reason he was out there that night, so that means I was the reason my mom decided to end her life the next day*," I said.

Another fit of sobs racked through me as my shoulders shook.

"*¿Ma?" I asked, knocking on the bathroom door.*

I opened it to find her there.

Her black hair was splayed against the tile. Her eyes wide open as she stared back at me. Her hand was holding an empty bottle of pills.

Dead and cold.

"Rosie, what are you doing?" Bianca rounded the corner, finding me frozen. "Rosie?" She questioned before walking over to me, a gasp escaping her lips before she hurried to shut the door.

"That was the last time I saw her."

"You shouldn't have had to find your mother like that, but that wasn't your fault, Rosie," he gently pinched my chin, urging me to look at him.

"That's not all, though," I forced myself to continue.

He nodded, telling me it was okay.

"After losing both our parents, we were almost homeless. CPS wanted to take me, but Luna's family took us instead. Bianca then quit school and got a job to provide the moment she turned eighteen, against Luna's parent's wishes," I grabbed Victor's hand, finding comfort in the action. "They got into a lot of arguments."

"*¡¿Qué chingados vas hacer sin trabajo?! ¡¿Sin educación?!" Luna's mom shouted.*

I was crying my eyes out in Luna's room, my head resting in her lap while her fingers were running through my hair to try and calm me down.

But even the yells could be heard through the walls.

"¡Yo lo resolveré!" Bianca shouted back. "¡Es mi hermana, mi familia!"

"¡Nosotros estamos tratando de ayudarte. ¿Por qué no ves eso?" Luna's father asked.

"¡No quiero ayuda! I can do this on my own," she gritted.

"Okay! Fine! Pero, Rosa is staying here until you figure out what to do!"

"Fine!"

I squeezed my eyes shut, wondering why Bianca was choosing this. But the sound of the front door slamming told me everything I needed to know.

"She got a job at a club, bartending, I thought," I gulped.

"This is our place?" I gasped.

My eyes worked their way around the small apartment, which had a kitchen to my left and a living room to my right, with a hallway leading down to who knows where.

"Yup, and you get your own room!" Bianca clapped her hands together. "What do you think?"

"How did you afford this?" I asked, checking inside all the cabinets.

"I'm making a steady income now, remember?" She laughed, throwing her arm around my shoulder with a bright smile. "It's just you and me now, Rosita," she kissed my cheek. "I'm taking care of us."

"I figured we were set. We were *happy*," I smiled weakly.

Victor passed me a small one.

"I started high school and was making plans to go to college. Bianca was smiling again, and then she met Julio," I gulped. "I liked Julio," I nodded, tracing my thumb along the veins of his hands.

"What?!" I gasped, ripping open the present. "You got me the new iPad?!" I jumped up, showing off the brand-new box to my sister and her boyfriend.

"Julio, I said no expensive gifts," Bianca whispered.

"She is always watching unboxing videos online. I had to get it for her," he shrugged.

"Now I can plan out all my stuff for my future ceramics shop! Designing the logo, researching a place, creating my website!" I clutched the box to my chest. "Thank you!" I jumped and wrapped my arms around him.

He chuckled as he returned the hug, but Bianca didn't share the sentiment.

"Maybe use it to write an amazing college essay to get you into a good school," Bianca raised a brow. "An education is just as important as starting a business."

"Ay, preciosa, she has that entrepreneurial spirit. Isn't that what you're always saying?" He nudged her shoulder.

"Yes, but she should also have an inquisitive spirit," she reaffirmed, staring at me.

"I'll work on the college stuff, too," I sighed, rolling my eyes. "I promise," I stated.

"Okay," she blew out a breath.

"I'll be in my room. Luna is gonna flip!" I ran down the hall before shutting the door.

"I truly thought he was the best. I thought my sister found her forever," I felt tears prick in my eyes again. "But beneath the warm, charismatic surface laid a manipulative, money-hungry man."

"You said you'd keep it out of the house," Bianca whispered. "I don't want Rosie to find out," she was talking to Julio.

I furrowed my brows, staying hidden in the hall.

"It's just for a few months. A friend needs them in a safe place while he's doing other business, alright?" He said. "Besides, we'll get a major cut from it."

"A few months?!" She softly shouted. "You expect me to keep cocaine in my house for a few months?!"

My eyes widened.

"Watch that tone with me. I'm already making sacrifices for you, for Rosie," his voice got harsh. There was a pause and some rustling before he added, "You love me, right?"

"Right," she whispered, straining.

"I never thought she'd commit a crime, but I figured he had something to do with it," I exhaled. "I knew she was lying to protect me, but ultimately that failed when she got arrested."

"What happened after? You were still a minor, weren't you?" He asked.

I nodded.

"Mr. and Mrs. Garcia, thank you for taking the time to talk at such short notice," the social worker offered a small smile. "We're aware Bianca's arrest was hard on Rosie. We just want to ask a few questions to make this process easier."

"Whatever you need," Mr. Garcia said.

"Were you aware of any of the crimes Ms. Martinez committed?"

"We aren't even aware what crimes she's charged with," Mrs. Garcia answered.

The social worker nodded, lifting the page. "The police report states a Class 1 Felony, possession with intent, and a Class A Misdemeanor, solicitation of a sexual act," she read from the report.

"Ay dios mio," Mrs. Garcia shook her head.

My gaze fell on the social worker.

"She was a prostitute?" My heart sank. "I asked her about the drugs, and she said she got rid of them," I shook my head, not caring if I said the wrong thing.

It was the truth.

"You knew, mija?" Mr. Garcia asked.

"I heard her and Julio talk in the kitchen. The drugs were his, not hers," I shook my head. "And she worked as a bartender," I ran a hand through my hair. "You have the wrong person!"

"We're currently investigating Mr. Ramirez, but it appears he fled. Right now, the evidence shows that the drugs were in Miss Martinez's possession. The lease is under her name," she sucked in a breath. "As for her job, there was no record of her being a bartender. She was a dancer at a nightclub downtown a year ago until she began soliciting. Those are the charges," she explained, clasping her hands together on the table.

I kept thinking back to my sister, telling me she made terrible choices. As much as I wanted to deny she was innocent, there was no proof. I sat back on the couch, defeated.

"How long will she be in jail?" I mustered the courage to ask.

"Fifteen years," the social worker answered. "That's also why I'm here," she added. "You're a few months away from turning eighteen and there are a few options for who will care for you until then."

"No need," Mrs. Garcia butted in. "She'll stay with us for as long as she needs," she squeezed my hand.

I glanced down, tears slipping from my eyes as I squeezed her hand back.

I sucked in a breath.

"It feels like that night started a domino effect, like that one choice I made could've prevented it all from happening," I frowned. "It's stupid, but that's how I've always thought."

"It's not stupid," Victor spoke up. "You felt like it was your responsibility,

and it's hard to change that way," he said. "Even after everything you told me, I know it wasn't your fault. You were just a child," he wiped a stray tear. "You couldn't have possibly known what would've happened."

"But," I began.

He shook his head. "You want to disagree, I know, but hear me out," he offered. "Your stepdad chose to go to the store. Your mother made the choice, a long time ago, to love her husband more than her own daughters. And your sister chose to go down a path that wasn't good for her because she didn't know any better," he said. "If they had known what the outcomes would've been, I'm sure they would've made different choices, too," his gaze was light.

I melted into his touch before I allowed myself to crack again, wrapping my arms tightly around him.

A newfound relief filled me as I cried it out.

I think I believed what he said.

I couldn't change what happened that night, what my mother chose, or Bianca's path.

But maybe I could control my present so my future was brighter.

Chapter 31

Victor

After Rosie told me everything, we decided it would be best to take the rest of the day off. She was cuddled on the couch in my apartment, feet tucked under her while I was in the kitchen making tea.

"This should help," I handed her the mug filled with peppermint tea. "How are you feeling now?" I sat beside her, my mug in my hand.

Her gaze was kept on the ceramic in her hand, the one we had made together the night she went dress shopping. It was pink with a simple design. Mine was purple. I hoped it brought her comfort.

Swallowing her tea, she set the mug on the table before she wrapped her arms around her legs, resting her chin on her knees. "I want to go visit Bianca, but I can't," she had tears in her eyes. "I don't know what to do," she hid her face before she moved, wrapping her arms around me.

I kissed the top of her head as I embraced her, pulling her into my lap. Hugging her was a comfort I never knew could be possible. Even when I comforted her, her warmth never ceased to fill that part of myself I never knew needed to be complete.

"Hey," I cooed, running a hand through her hair. "We're gonna figure it out," I reassured.

She nodded against my chest before she pulled away, staring into my eyes. There was reluctance in her gaze, but her lip wobbled with worry. "Victor, I think I need your help," she squeezed my hands. "Call the warden; she can't be in solitary and not get treated. Please?"

My face softened. Knowing she was asking me to do something like that after everything only exemplified how scared she was. I didn't want to see her scared.

"Of course, Rosie, I will," I said, caressing her cheek. "I'll do anything you need," I kissed her head again before pulling away. I kept a hand on her while I reached for my phone, quickly dialing the number.

Rosie sat in anticipation when she heard the warden pick up. Her fingers wrapped around my hand, her other hand on my forearm as she listened in. The hostile tone in the warden's voice made her grip tighten on me, and she didn't relax until I hung up, letting her know her sister would be safe and transported to a hospital.

Her tears dried as she stared at me. The tension in her brows melted away, her head bowing slightly in disbelief. "Thank you," she sniffled, hooking her arms around my neck. "That was unbelievable, thank you," she repeated and framed my face with her hands, her forehead pressed against mine.

"Anything, Rosie," I inhaled.

I love you.

My heart flipped as I said that in my head. But it didn't feel like the right time to say it out loud. Right now, it was enough to have her relax in my arms.

We headed to bed for the night, our bodies entangled under the sheets.

Her head rested in the crook of my shoulder, her fingers tracing patterns on my chest. "Can I ask you something?" She licked her lips.

I hummed.

"Earlier today, how did you know the right thing to say? About making choices?" She reached for my hand. "What happened?" Her brows drew together in worry.

"Nothing extreme," I shrugged, turning my head to look at her.

"Does it regard your dad?"

I nodded. "Remember when I told you he chose to stop being a good husband and father?" I referred to the same night we made our mugs.

She hummed.

"I was seventeen when my mom got diagnosed with ovarian cancer," I started, remembering the day.

"I'm afraid the cancer is stage two," the doctor sighed, breaking the news.

My mom pressed a hand to her mouth, silent sobs racking through her. The paper she was sitting on crinkled under her movement. My dad stood up, quickly pulling her into a hug.

I moved my attention to the floor, my fingers toying with the material of my sweatpants. I felt a strain in the back of my eyes, but I forced it away, not wanting to sadden my mom further.

"I know it's hard to process, but there's still hope at this stage," the doctor continued.

"What do you suggest?" My mother perked up, wiping her eyes with a tissue.

"We can remove the tumor, along with performing a hysterectomy. We would follow through with chemo," she explained.

I listened, trying to navigate the plan she laid out for us. I kept telling myself there was a solution: many people beat the illness and lived long, happy lives with their loved ones.

I shifted so I was leaning against the headboard. "The surgery was scheduled two weeks later, and that's when my dad started changing," I reached for her hand.

She sat next to me and pulled our hands into her lap while she massaged my fingers, reminding me she was there.

I carried the hot tea over to my mom, holding it as she drank it so she didn't burn herself.

"Thank you, cuoricino," she reached out to pinch my cheek.

I smiled, setting the mug down next to me. "Are you sure you want me to go?" I asked, checking my watch and making sure I had enough time to get to the school. "I'll wait until Dad comes back," I sat on the coffee table.

"Go, it's your senior year, and you have a baseball game to go to," she argued. "I don't want you to be late," she said.

I sighed. "It's just a game. You're recovering from major surgery," I countered. "I should be here until Dad comes back."

While it was the first game of my final season, I didn't want to abandon my mother for it.

She noticed my reluctance, her eyes widening before she pointed to the door. "Go," she sterned.

I nodded, finally agreeing. My dad did say he'd be back in ten minutes.

"Have fun, come back with a win," she kissed my cheek when I reached down.

"I came home from my game and found out he didn't come home from work at all," I stated. "He claimed his meeting ran late, but I found out he chose to stay because he didn't want to come home to help his wife," I clenched my jaw, still angry about it. "Luis's mom was eight months pregnant and still managed to check up on her after she realized my mom was home alone," I pointed out.

I felt my fingers curl into a fist with my other hand, the frustration of the memories piling up, but Rosie's voice pulled me out of that.

"Was your mother mad at your dad?"

"She claimed she was fine on the couch watching TV, but I knew she needed the help," I shook my head, glancing at our intertwined hands. I could never imagine not rushing home to tend to her.

Growing up made me realize how vulnerable my mother must've felt, and it only hurt more knowing my dad wasn't there for her.

I cleared my throat, pushing the thought aside. "Once she healed, she began chemo. It was hard adjusting. Between school, baseball, and taking care of her," I sucked in a breath. "I thought my dad would help with more than the bills, but he used that as an excuse to be at work for long hours."

Rosie scooted up, resting her head on my shoulder and rubbing my arm tenderly.

"I was waiting for things to get better, but they never did," I gulped.

"Right now, all we can do is continue chemo."

We found ourselves in the doctor's office again, and her scan came back positive. Somehow, the cancer came back.

My mom was sitting next to me in the chair because she was too weak to get up on the exam table. She was pale, her skin loose as she lost muscle over the last few months, the scarf she had on her head covered her shaved head, and her grip on my hand was almost nonexistent.

"How many rounds this time?" I asked. I usually stayed quiet during the appointments, but my dad hadn't shown the effort to be here, so I stepped up as the emotional support.

"I'm not doing any more rounds," my mother stated, stopping the doctor.

I turned to look at her like she had lost her mind.

"I know," she pressed her lips together, glancing at me. "I'm so tired. If

the cancer came back, then that means it's aggressive," she tried to squeeze my hand. "I just want to live the rest of my life with my loved ones," she looked at the doctor. "I'm done."

I wanted to argue, but looking into her eyes, I shut my mouth.

"You didn't want her to stop fighting," Rosie had sat up, kneeling before me.

I shook my head. "She accepted her chances," I stated.

"Ay, Mia, por favor," Alma scolded when my mother tried to get something off the high shelf. "We're here to help you. Please go sit," she held her by the arms, leading her back to the couch.

"I want to help," she sighed, but the heaviness in her voice proved she wasn't capable of helping. "I'm not entirely useless," she grunted when she sat back down, the shake in her limbs evident.

"This is your party. You're just going to sit here and relax," Alma rubbed her shoulder. "Besides, we're just setting up," she brushed her off before walking back into the kitchen.

"You just had a baby," my mother huffed, pinching the bridge of her nose, sending her good friend a glare.

"Luis is taking care of her right now," she reassured me while she pulled something out of the oven. "I'm here to help you," she gestured to my mom.

I watched from my spot at the fridge, filling a glass before walking to the couch. "Here," I said gently and held it in front of her, holding the straw so she could sip.

Even holding a glass of water was too heavy for her.

"I got her, mijo. Go see how Luis is doing," Alma ordered me to do.

I nodded, walking through the guest bedroom, where Luis was changing Elena's diaper. I shut the door behind me, my face falling as I walked across the room.

"My dad isn't coming," I bit the inside of my cheek. I looked out the window where his car should be in the garage. Instead, I found Javier outside with his daughters, getting the tables ready before the guests arrived. "It's her party to celebrate her life before she dies, and he's not even here," I shook my head.

"What was his excuse this time?" Luis cradled his little sister in his arms.

"He stopped giving one," I gulped, clenching my fists by my sides. "He doesn't care anymore."

"I want to disagree, but I can't lie to you," he sucked in a breath, standing beside me. "You know you have family with us, right?" He asked, glancing at me.

"I know," I nodded.

I thought for a second, contemplating. I had a month until high school graduation. I was supposed to be leaving for college in the summer, but I didn't know how I would do that if she didn't have anyone to take care of her.

"Don't think about not graduating," Luis spoke up.

I furrowed my brows.

"I know that look. You've been thinking about it since she decided not to do chemo anymore," he explained.

I rolled my eyes. "She needs me," I reasoned. "I know she has you guys, but I know she wants her husband out of anyone," I swallowed the ache in my throat. "If he doesn't want to be here, I need to be here for her," I glanced at my feet.

"Did you graduate?" Rosie furrowed her brows, confusion written across her face.

"I did," I said, that strain in the back of my eyes forming again.

"The cancer has advanced. She doesn't have much time," the doctor pressed her lips together. "It's time to say your goodbyes," she bid, leaving me alone in the room.

I stared at her unconscious body, the machine monitoring her heart rate and blood pressure. I leaned over, reaching for her hand. The tears didn't start pouring over until I felt how cold it was.

I stayed like that while Alma and Javier came to say goodbye. They tried contacting my dad, but by that time, he had left. He took everything and left.

Luis came in, placing a hand on my shoulder before he hugged me.

I wasn't aware I had still been crying when a sob escaped me.

"I'm sorry," he said after a beat. "Do you want me to stay?" He asked.

I shook my head.

He nodded before standing up, walking around to the bed's other side before kissing my mom's forehead.

It was just her and I again for one last time.

"She died an hour later," I said, feeling a tear fall down my face.

Rosie reached up to wipe it, her own eyes brimming with tears.

"My mom made the choice not to do chemo anymore, and my dad made the choice to leave," I said. "I've wished to go back and fight against it, with both of their choices, but I realized I had no control over it. They decided for themselves. My mom, thankfully, found peace with that choice. My dad," I trailed. "I'll never know," I chewed on my lip.

"Oh, Victor," she gasped, wrapping her arms around me. "Your mother was so brave," she sniffled. "As for your dad, I wish things had turned out differently, but you're right. He made a choice," she said solemnly.

"Thank you, Rosie," I offered a small smile. "I wish you could've met her," I swallowed the lump in my throat. "She would've loved you," I tucked a strand of her hair behind her ear.

She blushed. "Me too," she hummed.

~

"Have a good day at work, okay?" Rosie reached up on her toes to kiss me on the lips.

I placed my hand on the small of her back, leaning down to reach her. I hummed, pulling away before wishing her the same. I gazed at her with a newfound admiration.

Yesterday was a heavy day, but now we knew we were here for each other. It was a great feeling.

Shortly after she left my apartment, I headed to the office.

Now, halfway through the day, I felt my phone ring. Checking the ID, I was surprised to hear from Abigail Taylor. I greeted her, walking over to the window of my office.

"I'm doing good, Victor. Listen, I'm calling to confirm our lunch later this week. I was also wondering if you could bring Rosie along because I would love to hear more from her," I could hear her smile over the phone. "What do you think?"

I was beyond happy to hear the words come out of her mouth. This was beyond good news with everything that happened to Rosie in the past few days. I rolled my lips to suppress my excitement. "Sure thing, I'll pass the news on to Rosie. See you then," I ended before hanging up.

I confirmed my calendar with Ari before heading off to my next meeting. The news I had for Rosie kept circling in my head. I had a few hours left until dinner with her.

Tonight, Luna and Summer were joining. Mainly to distract Rosie until she is able to visit her sister.

I was glad the rest of the day ran faster, and soon, I was in her apartment, throwing the cut-up brussel sprouts in the pan.

"I thought you hated brussel sprouts," she came up behind me, her hand curling around my waist.

I smiled, welcoming her touch as I began sauteeing the vegetable. "Uncooked, but once you add butter and bacon to it, it's delicious," I smiled, wrapping my arm around her shoulders.

She nodded with a smile, checking on the main dish.

"Any updates on Bianca?" I asked. It had been a day since I called the warden. It was agreed she'd be sent to a hospital. I was relieved she was being taken care of professionally.

"I called her today," she slowly said, her eyes still sad, but she was managing better than I expected, so I was hoping she received good news. "She's stable for the extent of her injuries. There was a lot of bruising on her internal organs; her eye socket was almost fractured, but they did break her nose. She's going to be in the hospital for two weeks," she stated. "I talked to the warden, and I can visit her on Thanksgiving for the full day," she softly smiled. "Thank you, Victor," she pressed her cheek against my chest, leaning into me.

"Those are extensive injuries, but I'm glad she'll pull through. She's strong," I kissed the top of her head. "Do you want me to drive you or come along?"

She shook her head. "No, it's okay. As much as I'd love for you to meet her, I don't want your first meeting to be with her in the hospital," she explained.

"No worries, let me know how it goes," I reassured.

She reached up to peck my lips before pulling away, but her hand lingered, massaging the strands of hair on the nape of my neck. She gazed admirably at me, her eyes studying my features.

"You okay?" My lips curled softly.

"I'm just happy where we are," she hiked her shoulders up. "Thank you for telling me about your mom. It means a lot," she squeezed my hand.

My heart jumped, and I chuckled lightly. "Same here," I framed her face with my hands. "I'm glad we shared it," I said.

We leaned down to kiss again, our lips brushing against each other. It had only been a day since we last shared a passionate kiss. I hadn't realized how much I had longed for them, and now, I only wanted it to last forever.

Unfortunately, the timer went off, alerting us the dish was done.

"Since you'll be with Bianca all day on Thanksgiving, do you want to have dinner for ourselves another day?" I asked.

Her eyes brightened before she agreed, reaching up to kiss my cheek. "Sounds perfect!" She squeezed my arm playfully. "How was work, by the way?" She turned off the stove, gathering the silverware for the table.

"Same old," I started. "Abigail Taylor called," I led on, which caught her interest. "We have a lunch meeting later this week, but she wanted me to bring you along to discuss your ideas more," I smirked, loving how she lit up.

"Oh my god, really?!" She gasped, hands clasping over her mouth.

"I'm serious," I laughed. "What do you think?" I pulled her in close by her waist.

"That I have the best boyfriend in the world," she grinned, falling into my arms. "I can't thank you enough."

"You've thanked me plenty," I cooed.

"How about a kiss, just to seal it?" She suggested.

"Works for me," I hummed before we met in the middle.

Chapter 32

Rosie

Victor rubbed my shoulder reassuringly, his hand running across my neck and rubbing the soft spot on my nape, soothing me immensely. The day of Taylor's lunch meeting had arrived, and my nerves were getting the best of me.

My first visit with Bianca was also close, and I'm sure that's what was adding to the anxiety. I tried not to overthink, knowing whatever I thought would be worse than her actual state.

But now I had dinner with Taylor. Hopefully, she can jumpstart my dream, and then maybe I can finally make enough money to get a lawyer good enough to get my sister out of prison.

"Are you sure this is fine?" I asked, staring down at my outfit—simple and paired with a crocheted sweater to showcase my talent. It felt out of place now.

"You look professional, and you are beautiful, Rosie. Please don't stress out," he kissed my temple, pulling me to his side. "You did good when you talked with her at the gala. It'll be like that today," he said.

"Kiss for good luck?" I asked.

He smiled down at me, cupping my face before he enveloped his lips with mine.

I melted into his touch, tilting my head to the side to deepen it, my lips chasing his as he pulled away.

"No, one more," I pleaded, and I heard him chuckle before he pecked my lips.

"Just because I know you'll do amazing, I'll make sure to have a little something extra for you tonight," he smirked.

My knees felt weak.

"Give me a hint?" I touched his hand on my face.

"No, I need you focused," he nodded toward the host before giving them our reservation.

They led us down the multiple tables, the area surprisingly empty for it being lunch.

Victor's hand never left mine as we were seated. He pulled out my chair, his hands resting on my shoulders as he leaned in from behind me, his lips brushing my ear.

"Breathe, I'm right next to you, okay?" He pressed his lips to my cheek before sitting down.

"Thank you," I exhaled, reaching for his hand over the table.

Thankfully, he was sitting perpendicular to me.

A few minutes later, Taylor showed up. Dressed so sophisticated and fierce.

I took in a breath, smiling and standing as she came over.

"Thank you so much for including me in your lunch with Victor today," I shook her hand.

Her grip was firm, and she wore a pantsuit that radiated power and dominance.

"Anything for Victor's special someone," she glanced at him, smiling before we sat back down. "I'm very eager to learn more about you. I was telling my partners about your idea, and they seem to be on board to be investors as well," she smirked, her eyebrows raising in praise.

I grinned, gathering my thoughts just as the waiter came to take our order.

So far, so good.

The conversation flowed with some small talk here and there until the attention turned back to me.

Taylor asked me about my business plan for the ceramics shop, and while it was still a work in progress—due to me trying to finish my presentation for Mr. Jones on time—I had my ideas down.

"You have the foundation fixated with your ideas, but what will this ceramics shop be named?" She hummed, sipping her water in the most poised way possible.

"I was thinking of *Ceramicá de la Vida*," I answered, proud to say the name out loud. "It translates to 'ceramics of life,'" I explained.

She nodded, glancing down at her plate. "Seems like people could get confused easily," she pointed out.

I furrowed my brows, noting the change in atmosphere. "Not really. Hecho de Hilo gets many customers who don't speak Spanish, and they love the individuality and expression of culture," I smiled, an off feeling forming in my stomach. "They also don't mind learning the proper pronunciation."

"Don't worry, I get it. People value culture; it's what's trending right now," she waved off, her laugh only causing that feeling to sink deeper. "Where do you want to locate this? I was thinking somewhere close to Lake Shore Drive, where there is lots of traffic," she suggested.

I cringed on the inside, glancing at Victor warringly.

He sent me a reassuring look.

I didn't like disagreeing with people, especially potential investors. But

I had to say what was on my mind, right?

"I actually have a spot in mind," I began. "Right next to Hecho de Hilo. I've been eyeing it since I leased the first building. Customers can hop between shops, and most of my clientele live nearby, so it's convenient and accessible to them. I want to ensure I'm putting my community first," I explained.

"Of course," she said after a beat of silence. She pressed her lips together like she was holding back something to say. "But we don't want to drive out new customers," she turned the conversation, making an excellent point.

"Hecho de Hilo gets a lot of tourists because of the rich culture in our neighborhood. Considering that ceramics have a deep history in Mexico and based on the market research I've done, opening the shop next door would be best," I shuddered, nervous about how she would react. Obviously, I wanted to bring in as many new customers as possible. What kind of entrepreneur was I?

"We don't want to erase history, you're right," she agreed, although not that enthusiastically. "I'll contact a realtor to see how the building is holding up. Until then, finish up that business proposal. As far as I can see, I'm impressed." she hummed, flashing me a grin. However, she kept glancing at Victor as if looking for approval.

I chose to ignore it.

"That's great!" I exclaimed. "Thank you so much, Ms. Taylor."

She waved me off, a composed laugh escaping her.

I beamed at Victor, relief filling me and telling me it went better than expected. Now, I could enjoy a fine dining experience while listening to Victor and Taylor continue the conversation.

"I tried to get into the business with my sister, but she's too dramatic for everything. It's a blessing she decided to go into pharmaceuticals," she laughed, Victor joining in.

I smiled softly, noting that it was his fake laugh. Forced and more throaty. My grin widened when I turned to Taylor, seeing her ego fueled as my boyfriend laughed.

"Do you have any siblings, dear?" She asked, directing me.

"I have an older sister," I answered.

"What does she do?"

My eyes widened slightly. "She's between jobs right now, but her passion is dancing. I'm hoping she'll find something like that," I hiked my shoulders, nodding. I used my go-to lie when someone asked about Bianca, and I didn't want to explain why she was in prison.

"Sounds like your parents made very creative people," she hummed. "What about you, Victor? I noticed you rarely talk about family," she realized.

"I'm an only child," Victor said, hand next to mine, and he subtly touched my wrist with his finger.

I felt my body warm up at the gentle brush, my eyes darting to his hand and my heartbeat picking up just knowing he was there. I had to roll my lips together to stop the smile from forming.

"My mom said I was more than enough," he chuckled, hand moving away.

I felt my heart melt at his words.

I glanced at Victor for a brief moment, picturing his mother carrying him in her arms as a baby. It was sweet, and for some reason, it made me love him more, knowing his mom loved him so dearly.

Oh my.

I said I love Victor.

I could feel my cheeks heat up as I stared at the napkin in my lap. I inhaled slightly, clearing my thoughts when I reached for my water.

Who would've thought the moment I realized I was in love with my boyfriend was because of something he said in passing about being an only child?

Keeping the thought to myself, I waited until lunch was over, and we walked back to his car.

Our hands were linked, my other arm wrapped around his as I nuzzled myself into his heat.

"How do you feel?" He asked, voice vibrating against the top of my head.

"Good, I did feel like I was losing Taylor for a bit, but I think I was too nervous," I stated.

"You were perfect," he placed his hand on top of mine. "Were you okay though? You did seem a little flushed towards the end of lunch," he searched my gaze.

"I got distracted," I inhaled as we entered the car. "I made a realization when you were talking about your mom," I leaned back against the seat, anxiety swarming, but I pushed it down. "I love you, Victor," I turned slowly to look at him.

The words took a minute to process, but a smile spread across his face, his hand reaching up to touch my face.

"I love you, Rosie," he repeated.

I broke into a grin, nuzzling into his touch before we leaned over the console, our lips meeting in the middle. I swiped my lip over his bottom lip, his mouth opening slightly, and our tongues melded, the smokey taste of his whiskey mixing with the floral taste of my wine. I never liked the taste of whiskey, but on Victor, *fuck*, it tasted so delectable.

His hand glided over my back, and I leaned further across the console.

He moaned when I tugged on his hair, and my hands had found their home in his luscious strands way before. His other hand slid over my ass and underneath my thigh, his fingers digging into the flesh.

My hand reached out to grab the driver's seat, our thoughts linking as he eased me over the console, my leg swinging to straddle his lap. I hummed as I seated myself on top of him, earning a muffled groan.

We continued to make out like love-sick teenagers in a car, the air growing hot and sweaty, but none of it mattered. Our only focus was on each other, the hot feeling of our skins melting together, our salvia mixing as we poured our love into one another.

It was our first kiss after we said I love you, and it felt exactly that way. Never had I felt a kiss filled with such passion.

I loved Victor Romano with all my heart.

Chapter 33

Rosie

I sucked in a breath as the guard led me to the room. I can't remember the last time I was ever in a hospital, and I hated that now it was because Bianca was in here.

Bracing myself, I rounded the corner, the guard gesturing to the room before they stepped back.

"Oh my god, Bee," I immediately started crying at the sight of bandages on her face and the purple bruises littered on her arms.

"Rosie, I'm fine," she reassured, reaching for me.

I sucked in a breath at the moment, realizing it would be the first time I had held her in so long. I hesitated, scared the guard would take the moment away from me, but feeling her warmth radiate against my skin as our hands touched took me back to when we were young.

It was like her protectiveness wrapped around me.

"I missed you," I sobbed, gently sitting on the bed. "I'm so sorry."

"Rosita," she rubbed my hand with her thumb. "I'm alive," she smiled, although weakly. "I'm a tough girl," she smirked. "I will be fine in a few weeks, no doubt."

"I know we don't talk about it; you always shut me down, but I'm going to use the money I won from the grant and the money I saved to get a good lawyer," I confessed. "I've been researching and found a pretty good one. She's won many cases like yours and cut their prison time in half. You can be free, Bee," I sighed, clinging to her hand.

"No," she shook her head, immediately frowning. "You're not giving up your dream for me," she argued.

"I'm not giving it up. I'm postponing it. I can't stand you being here anymore. It's killing you! You don't deserve this. We both know you're innocent."

"Don't do that," she laughed, wincing at the end. "I made choices that got me in this, and I'm dealing with the consequences by doing my time. Eight more years, we've said it before. Remember when it was fifteen years?" She cocked a brow. "I'm not letting you sacrifice everything you worked for. That's not fair," she pointed.

"No," I disagreed. "It's my money, so it's my choice," I gritted. "I can't do this anymore," I cried, glancing at my lap.

I felt like such a kid again. The waterworks were uncontrollable, the harsh squeezing of my eyes shut to prevent them, yet they still found their way through. I was that little girl Bianca always had to console—the one she always had to protect.

"You can because we're both strong. Isn't our love getting us by? I survived solitary once. I got stabbed, and now this? We've been through so much that wasn't even the tip of the iceberg," she yanked on my hand to grab my attention. "You gotta pull yourself together, Rosie, 'cause if you can't, then why should I?" She reasoned.

I bit down on my lip.

"I don't know," I answered honestly. "Everything is just changing. I might have a potential investor, but I have a feeling, and I don't want to get my hopes up," I frowned, letting the negativity take over. "Mr. Jones's presentation deadline is looming, and while it's done, what happens if it doesn't work? I don't know how we will keep Hecho de Hilo open if he decides to sell. I don't know what I'm going to do," I let everything topple out of me. "If I can't save my business, at least let me help you."

"This is my fight," she squeezed my hand.

"The money is there, though," I tried to reason.

She shook her head.

"No," she reaffirmed. "It's there for your business, not for me. If you find the money another way, a *legal* way, then we can talk. But not this way, Rosita," she searched my eyes for understanding.

"Okay," I nodded.

"C'mere," she opened her arms.

I stilled.

"My right side isn't so bad," she explained.

I smiled lightly, rounding the bed to the right side before nestling gently beside her.

She placed my head on her chest.

I cried when she began running her fingers through my hair, just like when we were kids.

The soft beat of her heart sounded like home. The feeling of her nails scratching against my scalp sent me through a field of memories.

Bianca was more than my sister. She was like my mom.

The thought made me cry harder.

"It's okay," she cooed, pressing her lips to my forehead. She let me cry, filling the room with my sobs and the sound of the monitor until she spoke again. "Tell me about your boyfriend," she mumbled.

"I love him," I confessed, sniffling.

"What?" She gasped, her voice still soft.

"I know," I smiled, feeling a tinge of happiness through the sadness I felt right now. "He said it back."

"My baby sister's in love!" She rejoiced, clutching me as tight as she could.

"Yeah," I said.

"You don't sound so happy about it," she shifted, her chin brushing my forehead.

"I am, truly, it's just," I inhaled. "Everything is changing so fast, I'm worried we're diving into the deep end without proper precaution. I don't want to get my hopes up."

"Has he done anything to tell you he's not the one for you?" She asked.

"No, he's perfect. But after everything that happened in the beginning, even now," I began, referring to everything he's done to help Bianca. "I don't want to feel like a damsel," I huffed. Even after all this time, I was still insecure about it.

"You're not a damsel," she reassured. "How many times have you saved your own ass? I think it's about time you have a strong, handsome man in your corner," she smirked. "There's nothing wrong with asking for help, y'know?"

"I know, and he has helped. I'm forever grateful," I pressed my lips together.

"So what's the problem?"

"I don't know," I admitted. "I love him. He's the first man I've ever loved," I nuzzled into her shoulder. "I never felt this way before. I never experienced so much joy in my life," I hummed. "But what if I don't deserve it?"

"What if," she hummed. "You can't second-guess what the outcome of anything will be because you don't know!"

"But what if I want this to be my forever?"

"Then allow yourself to let it be, Rosie," she exhaled. "Don't think, just *feel*."

~

"YOU'RE IN LOVE WITH HIM!" Luna and Quinn squealed at the same time, both of them grabbing me by the arms and shaking me.

"This is the best thing I ever heard!" Luna sighed in contentment, sitting back on her haunches.

"Our little baby is in love," Quinn cooed.

"I'm really happy for you, Rosie," Summer hugged me.

I smiled down, unable to control my blush.

After I spent the entire Thanksgiving with Bianca, I wanted to make sure I told the girls the news at our annual Friendsgiving.

Quinn had driven up to Chicago for this very night, bringing Mr. Jones's famous roasted potatoes.

Once we had eaten all the delicious food, we gathered in the living room, dressed in our pajamas and covered with numerous blankets while watching *The Sisterhood of Traveling Pants*.

"Does he know?" Summer smiled, clasping her hands together.

"Yeah, we told each other the other day," I tucked a strand of hair behind my ear. "Then we made out in his car for like twenty minutes," I grinned sheepishly, the girls squealing in excitement, their hands shooting out to shake me even harder. "This is good, right?" I asked, chewing on my lip.

While Bianca told me just to feel, I needed some second opinions.

"Uh, yeah?" Luna said, her face plastered with a look of offense that

I still held some doubt. "Who cares if you've only been dating for almost two months?" She shrugged, reassuring me.

"Yeah, you're in a serious relationship with him. You both know that. Do you see a future with Victor?" Summer wondered.

"I mean, yeah," I nodded, thinking about it. "I want to marry him," I played with the fringe of the blanket. "And I want to have kids with him," I smiled. "Yesterday, when I visited Bianca, she knocked some sense into me. I think I'm starting to understand that it's okay for me to want those things, especially with him," I blushed.

"Ah, I knew you guys were going to last," Summer clutched her hands to her chest. "I can't wait!" She wiggled on her spot on the couch.

"Oh my gosh! I'm so glad this happened right before our Friendsgiving!" Quinn squealed. "If I were back at school, I would've missed this."

"Don't worry, Luna would've texted you before I had the chance to tell you directly," I reassured.

Luna just shrugged. "*Soy una chismosa*, what can you do?" She raised her hands in defense.

I rolled my eyes playfully.

"Regardless," Quinn held a hand out. "This is the best news I have heard in a while. I'm so glad you're finally getting dicked down," she had such an adoring look on her face, but her words did not match it whatsoever.

"Quinn," I gaped at her.

"I wasn't going to say it, but we've all been praying," Summer interrupted.

I didn't know if I was more shocked to hear what she said or hear her *say* it.

"You've always been tense, for good reason," she shrugged. "But Victor is a distraction and a stress relief for you, in more ways than one," she smirked towards the end. "We're all happy."

"I wasn't *that* stressed," I trailed, avoiding their gaze.

"Mhmm," Quinn shook her head. "Stress is literally your toxic friend," she stated, the girls humming along.

"Thanks for being happy for me," I smiled. "I really love you all," I pulled them in for a group hug.

Chapter 34

Victor

Rosie was coming over tonight for our intimate Thanksgiving dinner.

I was reviewing my recipe in my head, gathering the ingredients before the doorbell rang. I smiled as I made my way to the door, greeting her with a kiss. Pulling away, I noticed three reusable grocery bags in her hand and a brown one clutched to her chest.

"Are you sure you're cooking a meal and not a feast?" I grinned before taking the big ones from her as we returned to the kitchen.

We agreed to make a few dishes each to share, but this seemed excessive. Although, I was intrigued to know what she had planned.

"I just wanted to be prepared," she shrugged. "I also brought ingredients for a pumpkin pie," she smiled. "I know we're not great at baking, but I figured it would be fun."

"You seriously have that much faith in us?" I cocked a brow.

While Rosie and I were avid cooks, leave the title of "baker" at the bottom of the list. We've never baked something, so the thought alone worried me, but it could be fun.

"What's in the bag?" I asked, glancing at the brown paper bag she held, different from the blue ones containing food.

"I know our anniversary isn't for another few days, but I wanted to give it to you early," she smirked, holding out the bag for me to grab.

"Rosie," I smiled before I grabbed it from her hands, peeking inside to find a crocheted plushie. "It's a rhino," I cooed, pulling it out of the bag, my gaze softening as I stared at its black dots for eyes.

"Since they're your mom's favorite," she explained. "I made him after that day," she pressed her hands together, taking in my reaction. "And when you told me about her last week, it only made it more sentimental," she blushed.

"I love it, thank you," I pulled her in for a hug, pressing a kiss to her temple. "You're amazing," I reached down to kiss her lips.

"It's nothing. I wanted to make something special since you made me these," she said, touching the two charms on her wrist. "Now we match," she hummed, touching my chest.

"We do," I looped my arm around her waist. "Are you hungry?" I asked.

She nodded, glancing at the stove to see what I was making. "What are you going to make?"

"A roast and potatoes, it's already in the oven," I gestured. "Easy and somewhat classic. Also, some green beans," I said. "How long does your meal take to cook?"

"Not long," she shrugged. "You have spaghetti, right? I'm just going to make the sauce, and then I can cook the chicken breast," she smiled.

"I was worried it was going to be too little for us, but I'm second-guessing," I laughed.

"Me too," she started unpacking the groceries, mainly fresh vegetables and a bag of chicken breast. "Do you want to help prep the veggies?" She suggested, and I nodded. "Oh, and the pasta," she turned to me expectedly.

I directed her to the batch I had prepared for her.

"Thanks," she kissed my jaw before washing the produce.

We began working together in sync, with some light music playing in the background, but the prominent noise was the sounds of peppers roasting on the stove and vegetables being chopped on the cutting board.

I checked on the roast before shutting the oven door when I turned my attention to Rosie. I watched her shake the seasoning into a blender, take the poblano peppers she was roasting on the stove earlier, and throw them in before she started the blender.

The contents mixed, creating a light green sauce.

I pressed my hand against her stomach, pulling her closer as I rested my chin on her shoulder. "So, what kind of pasta is this?" I pressed a kiss on her throat, and she nuzzled closer to me.

"Green spaghetti, made with poblano peppers," she grinned, shutting off the blender and removing the lid. "Sorry if the air was spicy a while ago," she pressed her lips together before she turned around and wrapped her arms around my neck, making sure her poblano-covered hand didn't touch me.

"It wasn't too bad," I grinned, nuzzling my nose against hers.

Slowly, she leaned up, pressing her lips against mine. Our lips molded together like they've done so many times before. It was pure muscle memory at this point, and nothing felt better than having her in my arms and tasting her.

"Mhmm," she pulled away in a soft moan. "I love kissing you, but the food," she had an internal conflict, but with her dazed mind, she reached forward.

My mind still lingered on the kiss to notice it, too, but we were too late.

She had accidentally pressed the start button on the blender.

The green sauce splattered all over us, the hot pan hissing at the direct hit, and I heard it splash against the cabinets, too.

"Don't open your eyes!" Rosie shouted.

I stifled a laugh but listened.

"Oh god," she groaned, searching for a towel.

"Hang on," I stopped her, remembering where I had placed a clean dish towel before I led her to the sink next to us. "Got it?"

She hummed in response while I turned on the faucet.

We rinsed our eyes, thankful it didn't burn too much. Once we were cleansed of the spice, I made sure the stove was off before I glanced at the mess.

"Well, that made a mess," her brows rose, looking at the fucked up cabinets and floor.

It was everywhere.

"You go shower. I'll clean this up," I pushed her toward the bedroom, but she shook her head.

"How about we clean ourselves up together?" She placed her hands on my waist, leaning against me, a look in her eyes.

"Even better solution," I grinned, cupping her cheek and pecking her lips.

She turned away with a giggle, grabbing my hand and pulling us down the hall and into my room until we reached the bathroom. She was undressing while I turned the water on. Her hands flew to the hem of my shirt, wanting it off.

The moment we were bare in front of each other, we reached for a kiss. My hands flew to cradle her head while hers rested on my sides. We pulled apart, stepping into the shower to get cleaned.

As I rinsed myself off, I watched Rosie.

She was beautiful, *relaxed*. Her eyes were closed, allowing the water to wet her hair. The rest of her features were light. There weren't any creases between her brows, her jaw was slack, and her breath was even.

Knowing how stressed she was, I wanted to ensure she cared for herself. Over the two months of our relationship, it was nice to see her prioritizing it. Even more when I noticed she allowed herself to let go around me.

The level of intimacy it gave off was more profound than anything before. I loved her more because of it.

She wiped her eyes, blinking them open to find me staring at her. She only smiled sheepishly, one that I returned.

I stepped in front of her and grabbed the shampoo, lathering it in my hands before threading my fingers through her hair and massaging her scalp.

She watched my movements intently, her gaze soft as she let me wash her hair. Her eyelids fell close again, her hands resting on my abdomen gently as she leaned into me slightly. A heavy sigh escaped her when I pulled my hand away.

I took the shower head off the wall, being careful not to hit her face as I washed the shampoo out.

"I could've done it myself," she said as soon as I finished.

"You looked so cute, though," I beamed, pinching her chin.

She shook her head, snorting out a laugh. "You're too sweet," she reached up on her tippy toes, wrapping her arms around my neck until we managed to be face to face. "I wanna wash your hair now."

"Can you reach?" I asked, wrapping my arms around her waist.

She gasped, offended at my question. "I'm not short!"

I chuckled, my hold loosening as she leaned away from me. "You are to me."

"I'm average height, and you know it," she raised a brow.

"Okay, okay," I let my laughs die down. "I'm playing," I defended.

"You better be," she pressed her lips together to suppress a smile as she grabbed the shampoo bottle.

~

Rosie

After our shower, we settled in bed for a little bit until our stomachs were begging for food. We managed to clean the kitchen and finish cooking our dinner.

Between our shared meal and shower, I enjoyed the intimacy. I was comfortable around Victor. I was able to be myself.

"This Thanksgiving had me beat," I sighed. "I wonder if there's a way to condense it all," I tucked my feet under me as I sat on the couch.

Victor turned the TV on, but he glanced at me. "Maybe next year we can host," he suggested.

My heart fluttered. "Really?" I blushed.

"Yeah."

My mind quickly wondered just how much he thought about our relationship. How much did he consider besides hosting a holiday dinner together?

"Do you think about the future? Our future?" I decided to ask.

"All the time," he answered. "I'm happy with you, and I want us to have a future together," he grabbed my hand, pressing his lips to the top.

"Me too," I grinned sheepishly. "But what about marriage, kids, our businesses?" I scooted closer.

"I have my hopes, but really, all that matters to me is that you're in it," he reassured, rubbing my hand.

"What if I want to get married?" I asked.

"Then let's get married."

"What if I wanted kids? More than one."

"However many you want."

"I always wanted a house with a big yard."

"As long as it's fenced," he countered, a playful glint in his eyes.

"I don't plan on stepping down from my business," I said, chewing my lip.

"I don't expect you to," he answered.

We stared at each other with such admiration.

I loved this man, and right now, I think I love him even more.

"I love you," he smiled, pinching my chin as he ran his thumb over my bottom lip.

"I love you too," I cradled his arm.

We shared a brief but loving kiss. We were growing as a couple, becoming more secure, and that flutter in my stomach was still there.

"Today was a lot of fun, but I wish you tried the pasta," I pulled away, pouting.

The one dish we couldn't salvage.

He kissed my forehead. "Maybe we can try tomorrow," he suggested.

"Or next week," I countered. "It is our two-month anniversary," I pointed out. "We can have another dinner to celebrate."

"Next week's no good. I have something special planned for us," he smirked.

My eyes widened in anticipation.

"What is it?" I licked my lips excitedly.

"Rosie, we've been dating for almost two months. At this point, you should know I'm not going to tell you," he deadpanned.

I rolled my eyes playfully before leaning in *really* close to him. "Just a tiny clue," I inched my fingers close together in front of his face.

He grabbed my hand, pushing it away as he laughed. "Go down to Bella's. She'll help you out," he said.

"Victor, I can't have you buy me another dress," I shook my head. "That's too much," I declined.

"Nothing is ever too much, okay? You're the woman I love. I want to make sure you have the perfect dress because I want the night to be perfect," he kissed the top of my hand.

I couldn't help but blush before agreeing.

We sat there together until my eyes couldn't keep open anymore. We went to sleep in each other's arms, and the only thought in my head was that it was him and us.

Nothing that I could imagine could ever ruin this perfect bliss.

Chapter 35

Rosie

The end of November appeared out of nowhere.

While my presentation for Mr. Jones was done and emailed to him a few days ago, the idea that I actually exist on the day that makes or breaks my future was unreal.

I spent the entire day anxious, watching the clock like a hawk.

Mr. Jones said he'd call me around lunch since he knew that's when I was available.

So here I was during my lunch break, sitting on the roof and trying to enjoy a nice breezy day. I had my sandwich out in front of me, but my knee shook in anticipation as I stared at my phone.

I exhaled and glanced at the sky just as my phone went off.

I was quick to answer.

"Hi, Rosie, how are you doing?" Mr. Jones greeted me.

"Hi, Mr. Jones. I think we both know how I'm doing," I answered truthfully, laughing.

He chuckled slightly. "I know, dear. I didn't want to keep you waiting long, but the buyer just left with the contract. I'm sorry, Rosie, but I decided to go forth and sell the farm," Mr. Jones said on the phone. "I hope you understand. From one small business to another, it's hard to keep up with all the costs," he sighed. "I wanted to stay open, but I can't."

My heart stopped. I sucked in a breath, nodding subconsciously, my voice trying to catch up and get the words out of my mouth.

"I understand, Mr. Jones. I wish there were another way, but I understand," I tried not to make my voice crack, but it did. "When will the farm be closed?" I gulped.

My real meaning behind the question was—how long will it be until Hecho de Hilo closes?

"Thank you. I know it's hard. So, I made sure to save enough inventory to last you six months," he stated.

I chewed on my lip.

"Hopefully, by then, you'll find something out."

My heart plummeted again.

Six months?

I had six months to find another supplier, six months to ration inventory, six months to figure shit out. Was I going to be able to do it? Where else can I find an in-state, eco-friendly, ethically-raised alpaca farm? Then again, I did it once. Who's to say I can't do it again?

Deep breath, Rosie.

"What will happen to the alpacas? What will happen to you?" I rationalized by asking questions before I began to go into full panic mode.

"Don't you worry about us. The alpacas are going to a new home in Oregon, and I'm going to a new home in Florida!" He cackled. "It's about damn time I retired," he hummed.

I laughed along.

At least one of us was going to get a happy ending.

"And what about the farm?" I chewed on my lip nervously.

"Oh, sweetie, it's being turned into a warehouse or something, I don't know," he sighed. "I think an environmental engineering campus. A tech corporation bought it," he shrugged. "Beats me."

My eyes widened instantly, and my heartbeat picked up.

It couldn't be.

"Do you happen to have the name?" I found myself saying before I could stop.

Please don't let it be.

"Sure, let me get it," I heard shuffling on the other side before he cleared his throat. "Romano Tech, I could send you a picture of the card if you'd like," he offered.

I shook my head. "No, thank you, I got the name."

"Okay, good luck, Rosie. I wish you all the best," he said.

A weak smile appeared on my face. "Thank you, Mr. Jones. Truly," I stated before I hung up.

I set my phone down next to me before I hid my face in my hands, letting tears run down my cheeks.

Everything I worked for the past seven years would be gone in six months. My chances of opening Ceramicá de la Vida and getting Bianca out were done. I cried harder at the thought. After everything I fought for, I couldn't win in the end. My sleeves were soaked, the wool piling slightly as it absorbed my tears.

How did I not know Victor was trying to buy the farm?

It was so obvious looking back, but not once did I connect the lines.

The man I loved would get his dream while mine would be left in the dust.

Wiping my eyes, I tried to think.

Suddenly, I remembered.

"I'd do anything for you, Rosie."

Victor's words rang, and I couldn't stop thinking about them. I loved him more than anything. I truly hoped he meant those words because I knew what I was about to do was a big ask. Especially with our anniversary dinner approaching.

Chapter 36

Victor

Rosie looked fantastic tonight. Her hair was done perfectly, the gold of her jewelry shone each time the light reflected off of it, and the dress she wore was so fucking gorgeous.

I was utterly in love with this woman. Everything I had planned tonight had to be perfect for her. It was a month-long process, but it would all be worth it just to see the look on her face.

We held hands as we walked down the street, our fingers locked together, and her other hand wrapped around my wrist as she leaned into me.

"Are we there yet?" She asked, glancing up at me.

"Hang on," I smirked before I came to a stop. "We're here."

"An Italian Restaurant?" She gazed up at the front of the building.

I nodded.

"Are you sure they're better cooks than you?" She cracked a smile. "Cause I'm all for heading home and having my own personal chef," she batted her lashes.

"You'll have me all to yourself soon," I smirked. "Trust me, okay?" I beckoned her over towards the door.

She pressed her lips together, glancing at the building again. There was some reluctance in her gaze when I said that, and my brows furrowed in confusion, but she nodded.

"I know you, beautiful. I wanted the night to be special, so I did a little planning," I opened the restaurant door for her.

She walked inside, a gasp escaping her as she took it all in.

Moody lighting, soft classical music playing by a band, velvet seats, and no one in sight. Except for the required staff, that is. But the rest of the space was hidden, large burgundy curtains blocking out the empty tables and booths, leaving just one table in the middle for us.

"You bought the entire night for me?" She glanced back at me.

I met her with a smile on my face. "Of course," I grabbed her hand and kissed the top of it before I pulled out her chair for her to sit. "I love you, Rosie," I kissed her cheek.

She smiled widely, a blush appearing across her face.

"This must've been expensive," she chuckled, still in disbelief. "If this is for a two-month anniversary, I don't know what to expect for a year," she grinned at me before her composure fell for a split moment.

I noticed, though, the way she gulped down a sudden weight. I couldn't question it until a waiter came out and poured us a glass of white wine, her favorite.

We clinked our glasses together, my gaze on hers.

"Are-"

"How was work?" She asked, cutting me off.

I smiled. "Work was good. I closed that deal for the project." Plains Acres was finally mine, and I could finally prioritize my dream. "Construction begins next month, and the campus will be open by August of next year," I elaborated, reaching over to grab her hand.

"That's amazing," she hummed, pressing her lips in a tight smile. "You worked really hard. I'm happy you're achieving your dream," she squeezed my hand lightly, her gaze dropping to her plate.

"What's wrong?"

She rubbed the back of her neck, inhaling slightly. "I'm just stressed with work," she exhaled, rolling her lips together. "But I don't want to talk about that," she said. "We're celebrating."

"Okay," I squeezed her hand. I didn't want to drop it. I wanted to know what was bugging her and fix it so she would no longer be stressed. But what kind of boyfriend would that make me after what we've been through at the beginning?

"I need to know how you got this place, though," she pressed a smile. "No one's ever done anything like this for me," she sighed, looking around us, her gaze falling on the live band.

"I know the owner. I worked in a favor," I shrugged. "I wanted tonight to be special."

"It is," she agreed.

Once the discussion of work was off the table, we delved into a conversation. But still, something was off.

Rosie looked sad. She was stressed, but she was also down. The emotion pushed through more as her eyes were filled with sorrow. Her smile never reached her gaze either.

"How is everyone?" I asked, hoping I could pinpoint the reason for her sadness.

"Bianca should be out of the hospital in a week," she began. "I'm glad she's healing, but thinking about her going back," she closed her eyes for a brief moment.

I reached over the table to grab her hand again.

"I can't wait for you to meet her someday," she inhaled, pressing a smile forward. "She already loves you."

"I can't wait to meet her, too," I grinned.

From what she told me about her sister, I knew she was strong and capable like her. I also knew I had her to thank for protecting the woman I loved all those years.

"Besides her, Summer is enjoying her winter break," she tucked a strand of hair behind her ear. "Quinn is on vacation with her mom in California, and Luna is writing her book like always," she said.

I listened intently. "I'm glad to hear that. When's Luna's deadline again?"

She had mentioned in passing how she's been stressed about the deadline.

I couldn't begin to imagine where to start with writing a novel.

"I think April," she answered, scrunching her brows in thought.

I noticed she tended to do that when she was confused. It's one of the cutest things I've ever seen her do.

"But I could be mistaken," she bit on the inside of her cheek. She smiled lightly when the waiter came out with our food. "How are Luis and his family?" She dove into her plate of pasta.

"Luis is trying to find a girlfriend, but no luck," I chuckled.

He's been single most of his life. From taking care of his sisters and his mom after his dad passed away, he didn't have time for a girlfriend. But as of recently, he's been putting himself out there more. However, no one was meeting his standards of being family-oriented, charismatic, and honest.

I think he was close to giving up.

"I'd hook him up with Luna, but one, I think that's too much chaos, and two, Luna doesn't seem interested in men anymore," she hummed.

I laughed, reaching my glass out. "To having chaotic best friends," I clinked it with hers.

"What about his sisters and his mom?"

"Maria is doing good. She recently moved in with her partner, which Luis is not happy about," I emphasized.

"That is so adorable, though. He's such a protective brother," she cooed, her face warming, and for a second, her eyes matched her smile.

"More like overbearing."

I was an only child, so I couldn't judge how one wanted to act when their sibling moved out, *but* growing up alongside the Sosa sisters—Luis needed to take a few steps back.

"Sofia is also on winter break. She won't stop talking about her first semester back at college," I continued. "Isa is plotting a way to convince her mom she should have a sweet sixteen. I'm sure Luis already paid for it, but their mother doesn't want her to be spoiled since she had a quince last year," I chuckled. "Vale is focusing on school, and Elena got an A on her spelling test," I explained. "Alma is also doing good."

Spending time with the Sosa family reminded me what having a family truly meant. It reminded me of the good times I shared with my parents. It reminded me that I could be happy, and every time I glanced at the girl in front of me, that feeling only solidified.

"That's so nice. I hope to meet them someday soon," she pressed a hand to her heart.

"They can't wait either. Every time I go, they ask more questions about you than me," I hummed.

"Really?" She blushed.

"Really."

We ate our dinner, enjoying the quiet and secluded evening until it was time to leave. After thanking the owner for a lovely evening and sending him an extra tip, we found ourselves in the car.

I knew Rosie was still blue, but I wanted to ensure we were in my apartment's comfort and privacy before I said anything.

She took off her heels and headed straight to the bedroom while she got ready for bed.

I unbuttoned my shirt in my room, slowly undressing and watching her while she also got undressed.

Her naked frame was still breathtaking, and I was awestruck, but the deep-seated feeling in my gut prevented me from truly appreciating her beauty.

Pulling one of my shirts over her head, she sighed as she walked to the bathroom. She brushed her hair, the soft bristles running through her long, thick strands.

I changed into my sleepwear before I joined her in the bathroom. She acknowledged my presence, but she still stayed quiet. I went on to brush my teeth and wash my face. By the time I was done, she was patting her face dry.

I stepped behind her, her gaze meeting mine in the mirror as I wrapped my arms around her middle.

"You know I love you, right?" I asked, pressing a long kiss to her cheek.

She nodded, pressing her lips in a line as her hands reached up to run along my arms, her body leaning into me.

"I know," she gulped.

"What's wrong, beautiful?" I reached up, running my thumb along her jaw.

"I'm fine," she said, but her voice cracked.

"Hey, it's okay," I stepped back, allowing her to turn to face me. "Come here," I beckoned, allowing her to embrace me.

She started crying, her sobs raking through her body as she clutched onto me.

I picked her up with ease, carrying her over to the bed. I rested against the headboard, pulling her into my lap.

After a few moments of crying, she sniffled, lifting her head and wiping her eyes. She stared at the ceiling, a few tears cascading down her cheeks as she squeezed her eyes shut. She inhaled, licking her lips before looking at me.

"You know how I've mentioned that I supply my wool from a farm in southern Illinois?" She knelt next to me on the bed, arms crossed over her chest insecurely.

I nodded, my hand placed on her thigh.

"Well, I found out today that the farm is being sold to a major tech corporation," she kissed her teeth, staring at the duvet.

I was about to ask which one it was until it dawned on me. "Plains Acres was your supplier?"

"Shocking, right?" She laughed, using the back of her thumb to wipe her tears.

I didn't join in.

"You've been sad because of that."

She nodded.

"I'm calling Jones right now to tell him I'm pulling out of the deal," I stood up, searching for my phone, but her hand wrapped around my wrist stopped me.

"You're not going to do that," she shook her head.

"Rosie, the farm is being sold. You're losing your main supplier," I reasoned, crawling back on the bed. "What's going to happen to your business?"

"Unless I find another supplier in six months, I'm closing," she hiked her shoulders up, and tears welled in her eyes.

"Not unless I pull out of the deal. I can always find another location," I tried to reassure, reaching up to wipe a stray tear.

"But your dream," she sniffled, tipping her head to the side. "You worked too hard for this."

"And you haven't?" I scoffed.

"I know," she chewed on the inside of her cheek. "I thought about asking you to pull out of the deal, but you should've seen how you got so excited when you talked about how you got the contract signed today," she grabbed my hand and reached forward to touch my cheek. "It's just too big of an ask. I can't do it," she licked her lips.

"That's because-" I began.

"I can't do it, Victor. You've worked too hard to get where you're at," she squeezed her eyes shut, stopping me. "I'll look for another place. I'll save up. But you need to know I can't ask you of this. It's just too much."

"No, nothing is ever too much," I reaffirmed. "I don't care if it takes another year to start this project. You mean so much more than that," I framed her face. "I love you, Rosa Martinez," I shook my head, gazing into her eyes as I tried to wipe the tears from them.

They kept falling, though.

"I love how hardworking you are, I love the passion that fuels you, and I love how strong-willed you are. I don't want you to give up on your dream because of me," I stated.

She leaned up, interlocking her hands behind my neck. She pressed her lips against mine, and for a brief moment, I got lost in it.

Our lips meshed together like they always did. Warm, welcoming, *home.*

She pulled away, pressing her forehead against mine.

"We are two sides of the same coin," she chuckled out a breath, licking her lips. "You want to fix the situation with the snap of your fingers because you can. You think everything will be fine. But I only see this unleashing Pandora's box of problems," she shook her head.

I furrowed my brows in confusion.

"Since the moment you came into my life, things have gotten better," she began. "I've learned to love—physically, emotionally," she grinned, running her hands through my hair. "My business was thriving thanks to you, yet everything else was toppling down behind me," she sucked in a breath. "Bianca almost died twice, and now I'm losing my business and my dream. As easily as you can fix my problems, I can't live knowing I would only make it because I had a strong man swoop in to save poor me," she gulped. "And I think down the line, you'd grow to resent me if you lost an opportunity like the one you'd been working so hard for the last year."

"I wouldn't be saving you. I would never resent you," I argued. I pulled her close to me like I was afraid if I let her go, she'd believe I would resent her.

"Maybe I would. I need to work this out alone," she squeezed my hands.

"What are you saying?" I shook my head.

"I'm asking you not to do anything. I just want your support while I work things out," she explained, pulling back so I could see her face. "I don't want to lose you. I'm already losing everything," she shook her head against me. "I love you, and it would mean a lot if we just pushed this under the bridge and moved on with our lives," she sucked in a breath.

I stared at her, searching her face for any sign of second-guessing, but I was met with the most sincere look I've ever seen.

Moving my hands to her waist, I gulped. "If that's what you want, Rosie," I forced a smile, but I'm sure, like with her earlier, it didn't meet my eyes.

She let out a sigh of relief, her lips curving upward before she leaned in to kiss me again.

Rosie caused my senses to go haywire. Her body melted against mine, and her hands ran over my chest as we landed on the mattress. It was clear she wanted to have sex, but right now, I wasn't sure if that's what I wanted.

"Rosie," I breathed, my hands finding home on her hips as I tried to push her off gently.

Everything about tonight wasn't right. The farm, the contract, her wish. I couldn't.

"Wait," I managed with enough force to push her off without hurting her. "I'm sorry, I can't," I closed my eyes, rolling onto my back.

"Hey, it's okay," she reached for my hand. "I'm sorry, I got caught up in the moment. I wanted the distraction," she licked her lips, glancing away in embarrassment.

"Don't apologize," I shook my head. "It's been a tough night, we should call it," I suggested.

She nodded after a long pause, sliding her legs out from under her before pulling the sheets over her.

We cuddled for a bit before she turned to her side, away from me.

I placed a hand on her arm, stopping her.

She looked at me, and her eyes met mine even in the dark.

"I'm here, Rosie, okay?" I said. "I'm not going anywhere unless you ask otherwise," I brushed my thumb over the top of her hand.

"I know," she smiled softly.

I inhaled deeply, gazing at the ceiling.

Happy anniversary, I guess.

Chapter 37

Rosie

I sat alone in the office, my eyes straining after staring at the computer screen. My spreadsheet of potential vendors was opened up. I kept it just in case anything were ever to happen. Anytime I would pass on the expressway in the middle of nowhere, I would always find myself jotting down their contact info to add to my list.

Luna and Summer were taking care of the front, whereas I was in here calling people all day.

I was halfway through my list, which was filled with red after they told me they weren't looking to do business with anyone. Now, I was on my next call.

"Hecho de Hilo?" The woman butchered the name horribly.

I inhaled before responding with the correct pronunciation. "The H's are silent," I stated.

"Ah, I see. Well, what a creative name," she hummed. "But I'm sorry, sweetie, we're not looking for new clients," she stated.

"That's okay, thanks for your time," I hung up the phone, throwing my head in my hands.

If I had a nickel for every time someone said they don't do business with "people like me" or are currently "unavailable," I would have a yacht.

After crossing out that farm's name, I dialed the next phone number until Luna arrived.

"Any luck?" She crossed her arms over her chest, leaning against the door jam.

I shook my head.

"Nothing?" Her eyes widened, her hands coming over her mouth as she approached me. "How many have you called?" She peered over my shoulder and hissed at the amount of red on the screen.

"I think if we changed our name to Made of Yarn, we'd be back in business," I half-joked, but even my tone didn't reach it.

"Borning ass name," she playfully shoved my shoulder. "One of them has to want to do business with us. It's statistically improbable," she said.

I cocked a brow at her. "How would you know? You failed stats in school," I stated.

She waved me off. "I just do," she shrugged. "So Victor didn't even offer to back out of the deal?" She placed a hand on her hip.

"He did, but I told him not to," I leaned over the desk. "He was too excited about working on his project. I couldn't let him give up on his dream for mine," I shut my eyes. "It was supposed to be a romantic night, and I completely ruined it," I sighed.

The dinner was romantic. I truly enjoyed it. But after we came back to his apartment, I tried, really tried to keep my composure. But Victor saw right through me.

The moment he asked me what was wrong, I broke.

Everything leading up to that dinner was me preparing how I would ask him. I was so nervous about it, I couldn't think. But watching how his eyes lit up about sealing the deal with Mr. Jones—my heart dropped.

Still, it fluttered with such pride and joy for him.

I knew I had to work my way out of this one like I always did. But if I couldn't, which was highly probable. I didn't want to lose Victor in the process, too.

Was I stupid?

"Why, though?" She furrowed her brows.

"I was scared, I guess. Scared that he would resent me if he gave up on his dream. Scared that I wouldn't be able to get ahead without his help."

"You need to let go of that insecurity, Rosie," she sighed, shaking her head.

I nodded.

"You've worked so hard for everything you have. You have a man waiting to give you the world. Why not let him?"

"Because then I'd have the weight of the world on me, and it's heavy," I felt tears prick in my eyes.

"I know," she rubbed my shoulder reassuringly. "We're closing in an hour. Summer and I were thinking we could order in and have a movie night, all your picks," she grinned as I glanced up at her.

"You're the best," I wrapped my arms around her. "Thank you."

After Luna left, I stared at the screen.

It was evident that Hecho de Hilo was going to close.

I glanced around my desk and caught sight of a familiar business card. White and sleek.

Running my finger over the embossed number, I ran my tongue over my teeth before I dialed the number.

"Hi, Abigail Taylor. It's Rosie Martinez, owner of Hecho de Hilo?" I asked once, and she answered.

There was silence before she replied. "Ah, yes, how are you?"

I sucked in a breath. It was time to be honest or proud. I decided to be honest. "Not so great. I was hoping we could continue our discussion and maybe finalize the future of Ceramicá de la Vida?"

"Oh, yeah, that," she said point blankly.

My heart dropped.

"Listen, Rosie. I understand you're a brilliant and talented young woman, but I must say I gave you the wrong impression during our lunch meeting. I don't think we would work out as partners. I'm so sorry. I know you have high expectations for the future, and I hope you reach them, dear," she hummed. "Goodbye," she was quick to hang up.

I stayed still for a while, the phone still in my hand as I stared in disbelief. Gaining my composure, I inhaled, biting my lip before I let myself go again.

I hid my face in my hands, allowing my sobs to pull through, not caring if Luna or Summer came rushing in.

Rock-bottom was officially my state of mind. That aching feeling in my gut returned, taunting me like a nagging voice saying, "I told you so."

I didn't know how to make it stop.

Chapter 38

Victor

"She's upstairs," Summer said the moment I walked through the doors of Hecho de Hilo.

"Thanks," I bid, tipping her a smile.

I walked further down, passing the first aisle.

The shop had a few clients browsing through the remaining aisles, most picking through the yarn while another bunch was queued up.

I met Luna at the door leading to the roof, where she pulled out the stopper and opened the door for me.

"Just so you know, things aren't going so great," Luna sucked in a breath and leaned against the open door. "A lot of suppliers rejected her application," she frowned, her brows pinching in worry.

"Already?" I furrowed my brows, shoving my hands into my pockets.

It hadn't even been a full forty-eight hours. Most applications take weeks, so it doesn't make sense that many have declined already.

"Yeah, just so you're prepared when you go up," she nodded.

"Thanks for letting me know," I breathed out before going up the steps.

I followed down the hall, rounding to the other flight of stairs. The door to the roof was open, and I allowed the nippy air to bite me as I walked through.

"Rosie?" I called out, finding her sitting at the picnic table bundled in a thick sweater she made.

She turned around, happy to see me, but her eyes didn't match her smile. "Hi," she sniffled as I stepped closer, allowing me to see her red eyes. She bundled her legs in a blanket, but she was cold when I reached out to touch her.

I sat beside her. "C'mere, beautiful," I opened my arms, allowing her to fall into me as she began to weep.

"They all said no," she cried against my coat, her fingers curling around the material, clinging on so tight the skin over her knuckles strained. "I thought I'd have a fighting chance," she shook her head.

"What can I do to help? There has to be something," I wondered, cupping her face, attempting to warm her rosy cheeks.

"I don't know," she shook her head, completely defeated.

The look in her eyes felt so familiar. She had been fighting for so long, and after all the obstacles she endured, *this* seemed to be the last straw. But there was still that glimmer lurking in her irises—she wasn't ready to give up.

"Even Taylor backed out of investing in my other business," she said, wiping her eyes and lashes soaked with tears.

I reached up to wipe her tears as my eyes widened. "Why?"

"Apparently, she gave me the wrong impression," she rubbed her lips together. She moved the blanket in her lap, bowing her head as she played with the fringe.

I made a sound of disapproval. "She's not worth it," I tucked her head under my chin. "I'm sorry, Rosie," I kissed her hair.

"At least now I know," she muttered against the wool of my coat. "But it's back to the drawing boards," she pulled away, letting out a weak laugh, her gaze heavy.

"I can spend the rest of the day here," I suggested.

"It's okay. I'll probably take a break from calling," she said. "I'll be working on Winter Drive stuff anyway," she reassured me.

I nodded. "Just call me if you change your mind," I pinched her chin.

"I will," she offered a smile.

I stood up, letting her grab my hand as we returned inside. The heating of the building engulfed us. I stayed briefly, letting her return to work before kissing her goodbye.

She may not have given up yet, but I wasn't sure how much more she could take until she did. Still, I didn't know how to help without messing up again. There had to be another way.

~

"Hi, *mijo*," Alma greeted me when I opened the door to my apartment. She pulled me in for a hug.

Sunday dinner was being hosted at my place this time around. It was refreshing having loved ones over at my house. While I would've loved to have Rosie with me, she wasn't feeling up to it. Thankfully, the Sosas understood, hoping they'd meet the love of my life very soon.

"How are you guys?" I hugged each one of them.

"We're good," Alma answered.

"How's Rosie holding up?" Luis stepped into the apartment, slapping my shoulder in greeting.

"She's managing," I answered. I stepped back as the seven-member family piled in, shrugging their coats off. I had the dining table set with a few appetizers that I knew were the girls' favorites.

"Is it true her business is closing down?" Vale asked, watching as her little sister rushed to the pigs in a blanket.

"If she can't find another supplier," I explained, smiling to see Luis grab onto Elena before she made a mess.

"Can't you help her? You're her rich boyfriend," Sofia cocked a brow, taking her seat by the window.

The sun had set already, even though it was barely seven, but the full moon in the night sky allowed for a beautiful glimmer on the lake, its light shining bright.

"I can, and I do, but she doesn't want me to," I explained, pulling out Alma's seat at the head of the table. I excused myself to get the main dish out of the oven, but I could hear their conversation from the kitchen.

"That's bullshit," Isa said, but her mother scolded her. "Why not?" Her attention was turned to me when I came back with food.

"She doesn't want me to help. As much as I love her, she can be a little proud," I explained. "And frankly, I don't want to overstep," I added. As much as I wanted to help, I didn't want Rosie to overthink it and send herself into another downslope.

"*Pues*, let's eat," Luis cut the tension.

We all agreed, dishes being passed around, and when we began to eat, it was nice to receive compliments about my cooking. Especially now that I knew Rosie wasn't just being polite.

After dinner, Alma sent Luis to do the dishes, and I cut into the key lime pie she had brought for dessert. The conversation was enjoyable, just like any of our other Sunday dinners. And, like usual, my mind would drift to Rosie.

Just as I was wondering about her, Elena spoke up, getting up from her seat and wandering over to the couch in the living room. "What's this?"

She found the crocheted rhino nestled in the corner.

My gaze softened. Rosie tended to keep it there so she had something to hug while we were watching a movie. It was unspoken that the couch was its home.

"Rosie made that for me for our anniversary," I said.

"What's his name?" She squeezed him, a smile on her face.

"He doesn't have one," I shrugged. Thinking of a name never came up. I didn't even think of what pronouns to refer to, but I guess it was a he, according to her.

"Can I name him?" Her eyes sparkled like she was awarded the highest, most honorable duty.

"Go for it," I smirked.

She glanced in thought for a moment before looking back at me. "Tuffy, because he's tough," she hugged him tight.

Everyone around the table cooed in agreement as she returned with him in her arms.

"This is very cute," Alma reached over, studying the craftsmanship. "She's talented," her gaze softened.

"She makes sweaters, too, right? Like she teaches classes?" Maria questioned.

"She does, in Spanish and English," I stated. "She actually made something pretty cool last week," I stood up, remembering she left the finished product.

I walked to my room, grabbing the light yellow cardigan from the chair. The movement caused the air around me to shift, and my nose instantly filled with raspberries and jasmine. The smile appearing on my face couldn't be helped.

Maria's attention was drawn to me when I came back, her arm reaching out as I handed her the cardigan. Her eyes widened in shock as she studied the stitch and design. "Do you know how hard it is to make this stitch?" She raised a brow. "Let alone making it into a cardigan," she scoffed in amazement.

"Let me see," Sofia and Isa leaned over, wanting to look closer.

"This is a jasmine stitch. If she's teaching that, then that means she's skilled," she pointed.

"She'll appreciate the compliment, thanks," I hummed.

"Let me add," she held up her hand. "You need to help your girlfriend save her business so her talent isn't wasted," she gestured to the cardigan and Tuffy. "You're really just gonna stand back and not do anything?" She crossed her arms over her chest.

The aggressiveness in her voice was uncanny, but I didn't falter—we both knew she was right.

"I'm aware, but what can I do without completely disregarding her boundaries?" I asked the question plaguing my mind the last few days.

"Well, *mijo*, just cause she said you can't fix it doesn't mean we can't," Alma smirked.

My gaze narrowed in curiosity, her words drawing the attention of her daughters, who seemed to understand what she said. I was intrigued and asked, "What did you have in mind?"

Chapter 39

Rosie

Bianca was out of the hospital and back in prison. Some would say it was bittersweet, but honestly, it was more bitter than sweet.

But I pushed that aside as she sat in front of me. Her hair was pulled back in a braid this time, and her bruises healed more, but anyone looking at her could tell she went through a lot.

It had been a week since I found out Mr. Jones was going to sell the farm, a week after Victor and I's anniversary dinner.

I wanted to push off seeing Bianca, not wanting her to see me in this state. But it had been too long, and I missed her. This visit was supposed to be a positive one, at least as much as we could've had it, but I found myself sitting in my chair and glancing to my right to see the girl I saw a few months ago introduce her boyfriend to her mom. It made me think about how hopeful I was that long ago. There was so much to look forward to, but now I was losing my dream.

"What's wrong, Rosita?" My sister cooed, noticing my demeanor right away.

I shook my head, about to say I was okay, but my voice immediately cracked.

"I'm losing Hecho de Hilo," I sucked in a breath before explaining everything that led up to that moment.

"Oh my gosh, I'm so sorry," she frowned.

Her sympathy was all I needed to break.

"It hurts," I clenched my chest, my grip on the phone tightening. "I never thought things would end up like this," I wiped the tears from my eyes, my body shaking. "I've worked my entire damn life, and *this* is how things end up?" I seethed.

"Let it out, *mija*," Bianca reached forward, pressing her fingers against the glass. She had always comforted and protected me, so her being behind that glass again made everything much more painful.

I sensed the heavy sound of footsteps behind me, our gazes reaching up to see a rather unamused guard.

"Everything alright here? Not gonna have to escort you out now, am I?" The guard cocked a brow as she stared at me, hands placed on her hips.

"My sister is going through heartbreak. It's very complicated, but she's losing her business," Bianca shouted so the guard could hear, and that seemed to gather the attention of everyone around us.

"That asshole!" One of the inmates shouted, and mumbles of agreement could be heard around.

In the small parted room where eight inmates gather at a time, plus their relatives and the two guards posted, roughly twenty people were in the room. All of their eyes were on me as they took my side.

"You should slash his tires!" One person shouted.

My lips curved into a smile.

"Make *him* lose his business," another one screamed.

The noises of the inmates and relatives quieted down, mainly after the guards threatened to have everyone kicked out. But their support could be heard a mile away.

I pressed a hand over my mouth to suppress a laugh. As much as I loved the enthusiasm, it did bring a smile to my face as they thought I was heartbroken over a boy.

"Can I please see my sister? She needs me," Bianca turned to the guard.

She held her gaze for a while. "Rules are rules, inmate. She'll be fine," she readjusted her belt before returning to her post.

I pressed my lips together, another rack of sobs coming out as I cried harder. Of course, she said no. My sister hurried to console me verbally—shushing me, whispering encouraging words—but nothing was helping. I couldn't control it. I heard as she sighed in defeat, unsure of what to do. I so wanted to suck it up and let her know I would be fine, yet, there was no bone in me that would allow that.

The sight of a defeated Bianca and the complete mess that was me caused a kind mother in the section next to us to scoot her chair over, wrapping her arms around me.

I inhaled. Her warm scent reminded me of my mom when we were small, before she stopped prioritizing us and Gerardo came into our lives. I found myself nuzzling against her shoulder; her jacket's softness invited me, and I felt like a child finally being soothed.

"It's okay, *mijita*, cry it all out. And once you do, pick yourself up and fight," she rubbed my arm.

"I don't know if I can," I shook my head, squeezing my eyes shut. "Everyone keeps telling me no," I exhaled shakingly.

"Rosita," Bianca called my name.

I looked over.

"You're going to get through this, okay? You're going to save your business. You know why?" She cocked a brow, a knowing smirk on her face. "Remember the day you told me you weren't going to college?"

I did.

~

My knee bounced in my seat as Bianca approached the chair.

She waved as she sat down, reaching for the phone while I mirrored her. "Hi, baby," she smiled. "How are—"

"I'm not going to college," I confessed, deciding to get it done and over with. My palms were sweaty, and my heart raced with each passing second of silence.

"That's a good one, Rosita," Bianca laughed.

Even though the skin around her eyes crinkled, her smile entranced everyone, and her beauty still radiated even with her current state—her light was slowly diminishing.

She had been in prison for a month.

While she told me she had made a few friends, I couldn't imagine how hard it was adjusting to a place like this. So I showed up.

I've been taking the bus down so I could visit her. I had to wake up early to get here during visiting hours, but it was worth it, especially since I got to see her with news to share.

"I'm being serious," I met her gaze.

The smile wiped off her face. Her eyes turned cold. She leaned in, jaw clenched, and I thought I saw our mother for a second.

"Rosita, que estas pensando, you're going to college," her eyes flashed with fury.

I gulped.

"No," I stood my ground. "I thought about this alot. I'm not going."

"You're throwing your life away if you don't get an education," she

gritted. "Look where that got me," she gestured to her beige clothing and around her.

"I realize that, but I've learned enough from high school to get me where I need to be, where I want to be. I'm going to start a business. I have a space available to rent just out of the city, so it isn't so expensive. I signed a contract with a farmer to source my materials and have all the legal stuff ready. Luna and I even got an apartment to move in after graduation," I took a sharp breath. "I just need your support," I pressed my lips together.

"What even is this business?" She sighed, leaning back in her chair. "And with what money?"

"My college fund," I answered.

Her eyes widened.

"Rosita," her tone was laced with warning. "I worked hard to save that money for your future. It was intended for you to go to a good school," she gritted. "What happened to UW-Madison?" She hiked her shoulders up.

"It's my future. I can do what I want with the money," I glanced down. "Besides, I got the acceptance letter," I glanced at the floor. "I didn't get in."

"Mijita," she sighed. "I'm sorry, but what about your backup schools?" She tipped her head to the side, her voice softening.

"I don't want to go to any of them," I dismissed. "So if I'm not going to college, I'll use the money how I want," I reaffirmed.

"Not opening a business. If this has to do with your little side hustle in school, you can do that at college," she pointed out.

I rolled my eyes.

"You're not doing this, Rosie," she pleaded, her voice faltering with fear.

I was tempted to listen, but I had to focus on what this meant for my future.

"It's not that, this is a crochet shop. Luna and I will manage it, and we'll also hire another person. I plan to host weekly classes offered in English and Spanish for customers who want to learn, with a ten-dollar fee. I'm also opening commissions, and we just launched on social media to bring in clients from there," I smiled, feeling proud.

"You have faith that this is gonna work?" She raised a brow. "What about your pottery? I thought you wanted to do that?"

"I do, and I am, just not now," I shrugged. "Ceramics is more complicated, more expensive. I'll save money from this business, and in about ten years, I'll have enough to finally buy the building and the one next to it to open a ceramics shop," I explained.

She stared at me as she let out a breath. Her features softened before she spoke. "Look at you, that entrepreneurial spirit never left now, did it?" She cracked a smile.

"No, so what do you think?" I chewed on my lip nervously.

"I'm proud of you," she nodded. "You seem to have everything planned, and I'll support you. But promise me one thing," she raised a finger.

I nodded.

"If this doesn't work in a year and you haven't made a livable income, you're gonna apply for school," she looked me straight in the eyes.

My lips curved up in a smile.

"Deal."

~

"You managed to grow a successful business in less than a year. Sure, you're not making millions, but you're setting up a community for us. All the Latinos who worked so hard their entire lives can now find some joy in accessible hobbies. I don't think Hecho de Hilo is leaving anytime soon," she raised a brow, a reassuring glint in her eye.

I raised my head from the woman's shoulder, wiping my eyes with a tissue she handed me.

The kind lady rubbed my shoulder encouragingly, sending a reassuring look towards Bianca.

"Wait, you own Hecho de Hilo?" A small kid came up to me.

I nodded, fidgeting with the tissue in my hand. A smile appeared on my face as I stared at the adorable little boy.

His toothy grin poked out the most on his pinchable face when he spoke. "Santa said he had to go to your shop to make Ralph," he held up a green dino plushie.

I remembered it from last year.

Glancing over to see his dad smiling at us, I still remember the day he came in with the letter from Santa asking for an extremely specific green brachiosaurus. He was relieved once Summer sketched him up, and I began crocheting him.

Ralph was a little busted up now, but he was still there.

"Santa did seem desperate. All the elves didn't know how to crochet," I laughed, and the kid's smile grew wider.

"I love him!" He hugged him tight.

I cooed. "He loves you too. Ralph told me he couldn't wait to meet his new best friend," I patted the top of Ralph's head before the boy ran back to his father.

"You see, Rosie? You've built something unique, and that wasn't easy. You have a community now. Maybe instead of figuring out how you will do this yourself, you should ask for help. It's hard to let yourself do it, but you'll find a way to save Hecho de Hilo," she pressed her lips together in a soft smile.

"Thanks, Bee," I nodded. "I'll try."

A weight lifted off my shoulders that I didn't even know was there.

Chapter 40

Victor

It was late at night when I knocked on Rosie's door, hoping to find her so the plan could be set. There was a problem, though.

No one was answering.

I had messaged Rosie a few times, growing worried with each one being unanswered. Even more so when her calls wouldn't go through.

After a few more minutes of knocking, I didn't care if I was causing a disturbance. It wasn't until I felt a sense of relief when I heard the locks unclick, a very furious Luna greeting me.

"You know, knocking constantly at midnight is a disruption that could cause issues with the landlord?" She cocked a brow, her hand on her hip. She looked angry at the sight of me, but her flushed cheeks and heaving chest gave away that she was feeling another emotion.

To the naked eye, she looked pissed. But the closer you looked, it was clear she was *flustered*.

My thoughts ran past that. My main focus was on Rosie and her safety.

"Where's Rosie?" I questioned, glancing into the apartment.

It was dark, minus the dim light from the hallway. The fridge made a buzzing noise you could hear from the entryway, and the power button on the TV shone a bright enough light to notice it.

My gaze traveled to the couch, where two prints on the cushions indicated someone was previously seated.

"She's at the shop," she stated, disclosing that Rosie wasn't the one sitting there.

"At this hour?" I furrowed my brows. "Why didn't she tell me?" My heart fell slightly.

I knew she visited her sister today before heading to work. I planned to stop by for lunch, but an emergency meeting came up, and I had to cancel. While I didn't enjoy being away from her, she updated me on how she felt through text.

The last message she sent was letting me know she would take a nap at home. That's why I thought she was here.

But I was wrong.

"You know how she gets," she hiked her shoulders up, drawing my attention back to her. "She needed to finish some work," she explained. "She's also in a bad headspace, so she's trying to distract herself," she sighed before widening the door so I could come in.

"That's what I wanted to talk to her about," I began. "I don't want her to do this alone," I swallowed. "You and I agree that she doesn't deserve this, right?" I stared at her.

"Of course," she nodded. "She's too stubborn to see it, but she needs help," she added.

"I know. That's why I'm going to talk to her. I don't want her to struggle because of me," I pressed my hands towards my chest.

"She already made her choice, Victor. Do you really want to disregard that?" She crossed her arms over her chest, studying me. "As much as I disagree with her," she rolled her head.

"I'm aware, but that doesn't mean I can't make a choice, too," I inhaled.

Her gaze narrowed. "What do you have in mind then?"

~

Rosie

I woke up abruptly, pieces of tissue paper stuck to my face as I sat up. I groaned and wiped the drool off, trying to figure out what was going on.

The shop was dark besides the two lamps I had on. Their soft yellow glow illuminated my workspace.

I was trying to finish the remaining Winter Drive clothes before I became too busy to deal with anything. I grabbed my phone next to me, and my eyes bore out of my sockets as I looked at the time.

4:35 a.m.

Messages from Victor flooded in, and my heart burst as he grew worried with each one, but they stopped after a certain time. He must've fallen asleep.

After waking up from my nap, I was too delirious to message him before I decided to have dinner. My mind kept racing to everything that was toppling over and Bianca's words.

"It's hard to let yourself do it, but you're gonna find a way to save Hecho de Hilo."

I tried figuring out how I would even let people help. I tried to process it to see if I really wanted to do that.

So, figuring Victor had gone to sleep, I decided to head to the shop. But that didn't work out as I hoped when I fell asleep at the table.

Slipping off the stool, I cracked my back. Sleeping on a wooden stool over a workbench was not the comfiest, and I couldn't wait to crash into bed once I got home. Still, I cleaned up my mess, knowing future me didn't want to clean up when I came back in a few hours.

I yawned, grabbed my bag off the hook, and gave a once-over at the shop before I opened the door to close. The keys jingled in the lock before I pulled them out and shoved them into my pocket. Turning towards the apartment, I was stopped by a voice.

I shrieked, but the familiarity stopped my fight or flight from kicking in.

"Rosie," Victor's voice was calm as usual. His hand was held out, showing he meant no harm.

"Victor!" I scolded, waving my arms in front of me as I approached him. "You scared the crap out of me!" I pressed a hand to my chest. "It's four in the morning, what are you—," his embrace cut me off.

It had been almost a full day since I had felt his warmth, and I realized how much I missed it when I hugged him back.

"I didn't mean to scare you," he looked at me lovingly. "I was worried," he sighed, reaching up to cup my face, his thumb dragging over my cheekbone and his fingers curling over my neck in a gentle, nurturing manner.

I melted, my lashes fluttering as I nuzzled into his touch. "I'm sorry, I was gonna text you when I got home. I thought you had gone to sleep already," I explained, enveloping his hand with both of mine as I cradled it against my chest, showing him I was genuinely remorseful and that I was okay.

"Without a goodnight from you?" His eyes brightened, his lips curving up into a smirk.

I reached up to peck his lips before asking, "What are you doing here?"

"I came looking for you. I have something I want to show you," he nodded towards his car.

My face contorted in confusion, but I followed him to his car. I sat in the passenger's seat, twiddling my thumbs when he returned inside. "I didn't mean to worry you. How'd you find me, though?" I repeated my question before.

"Luna told me," he said as he started the car up, but he reached into the back and pulled out a brown paper bag. "You should have something to eat. It's going to be a long drive."

I felt my stomach grumble at the smell of the hot food, so I opened the bag to find a breakfast burrito.

"You're too sweet," I smiled, unwrapping it as my hunger took over. I bit into it, tasting all my favorite ingredients for a breakfast burrito—eggs, roasted potatoes, cheddar cheese, chorizo, and all the bell peppers, minus the yellow ones. "You know what would go great with this?" I swallowed my first bite, turning to Victor.

I hadn't even noticed the car started until I looked over the dash to see he had already started driving down the street, the headlights shining against the street signs.

"Hot sauce?" He smirked, reaching into the center console and pulling out a bottle of Tapatio.

"You're amazing," I reached over to pinch his chin, my fingers brushed against his stubble before I grabbed the bottle from him, opened it, and poured it on my burrito. I sat back in my seat, enjoying the taste of my breakfast as I looked out the window. That's when I recalled Victor mentioned something about a long drive.

"Where are we even going?"

"That's a surprise," he glanced over at me.

As we drove further out, the city was waking up slowly, and the sun was rising behind us. It didn't make sense for the surprise to be this far away.

Confusion ate away at me.

"Is this your way of surprising me with a weekend getaway?" I turned to face him. "I know I've been stressed and emotional lately, but a trip won't relax me," I sucked in a breath, reaching over to touch his wrist.

Many people took days off or went on vacation, but I already had a day off with Victor a few weeks ago. That was surely going to hold me over for a year at least. There was no need for him to surprise me with a getaway—if that's what he had planned.

"Rosie, it's okay. It's not a weekend getaway," he reassured me. "Trust me, okay?"

I loosened my grip on his wrist and nodded, my muscles relaxing. "Did you eat?" I asked after a beat of silence, eyeing the other half of the burrito.

"I had something before I came by," he answered with his eyes on the road.

As we kept driving south, the time on the clock changed each minute, and the view became flatter as we entered the plains with cows and horses grazing about.

The crease between my brows hardened, my mind working through clues to tell me where we were heading.

"This is the way I usually take to visit my sister or the farm," I said. "It would be another hour and a half if we were going there," I rolled my head to the side, reaching over to grab Victor's hand.

He mindlessly brought my hand up to his lips before resting our interlocked hands in his lap.

My face reddened at the gesture. "You're still not gonna give me a hint?" I asked.

He sent me a knowing look.

"What were you doing in the store so late?" He changed the subject, looking away from me and back on the road.

I sighed in defeat, leaning back in my seat as I drew my attention ahead. "I'm preparing for the Winter Drive. I was finishing up the last few items," I yawned. "Still have to call the committee group to see how things are going," I exhaled.

Victor shifted in his seat, the crease between his brows growing, and I could tell he had some reservations about my unhealthy habits when it came to work. Or rather, my unhealthy habit of taking control over everything.

Still, he said nothing, and I was grateful for that.

"Can't you ask for help with that? I'm sure a volunteer wouldn't mind making a few calls," he suggested.

"I know, but I host. It's easier if I'm the head of the committee," I responded. "But I haven't asked you about the farm. Did construction begin already?" I questioned in hopes the topic of my work would be pushed under the rug.

Also, because part of me was curious about the farm, or now, the land.

Since Mr. Jones sold the farm, I was unaware of anything happening. I don't know if the animals had been transported to their new home, if Mr. Jones had moved out, or if the place was completely demolished.

An easy phone call would let me know, but I couldn't bring myself to make it.

"No, I postponed it. I had some issues with the construction company," he cleared his throat.

I inhaled sharply, relieved to hear that.

His fingers curled around my hand, and I wasn't sure if he did that out of comfort or habit.

"How's Bianca doing?" He asked about my visit earlier when he checked his mirrors.

"She's out of the hospital. She's still recovering, but she's like seventy-five percent there," I pressed my lips together. "Her bruises are almost gone, but her internal injuries still need a few more weeks," I gulped, beginning to play with his fingers, my thumb tracing over each nail bed, each knuckle.

Touching him intimately in a non-sexual way always brought me contentment.

"I'm glad she's doing okay," he smiled, squeezing my hand. This time, I knew he had done it to tell me he was here.

I thanked him for caring about my sister before we fell silent.

Some music was playing, and we spent the next hour and a half listening to that.

I was almost drifting off, and the ride made me feel sleepy despite my lack of sleep. But I so wanted to know where we were going.

"So still no hint?" I asked when another ten minutes passed by, and all I saw was grass and corn fields.

"Well, we're here," he said, passing me a smile.

I turned to look ahead, my eyes falling on a familiar sign.

Chapter 41

Rosie

"Victor, no," I reached out on either side of me, clutching the door and the center console like that would stop him from driving further up the dirt road. I kept my gaze forward, and soon, the farmhouse I visited for the last few years came into view. "I don't want you doing this for me," I shook my head, guessing why we were here.

He chuckled. "I know," he nodded, glancing over at me.

There was no sign of remorse or regret, and no negative connotations were written across his features. He looked…happy.

"We're not here for me to ask permission, Rosie. I'm past that. The moment I found out you worked with Jones was the moment I knew I made a mistake," he began. "My team is already searching for an alternative location. This is a decision made entirely by me," he smiled. "So, will you follow me?" He opened the door, hoping I would do the same.

"Okay," I nodded, getting out of the car hesitantly.

I watched him as he walked towards the front of the vehicle before stopping, reaching out his hand for me to grab. I tucked a piece of hair behind my ear before linking our hands. I sent him an unsure look, but he looked ahead, my gaze following.

Mr. Jones was already making his way toward us with a bright smile.

I never thought I'd be so happy to see the man.

"Mr. Jones, it's good to see you," I pulled away from Victor before walking up and hugging him. "I don't understand what's going on," I let out a breathy laugh, tucking a strand of hair behind my other ear.

"Why don't we talk in the kitchen?" He offered, opening his arm as he stepped aside to let me take the lead.

The short walk to the house and into the kitchen was filled with me asking how he was doing. It wasn't until we were seated, our coats hung up in the foyer, and we had hot chocolate in our hands that we spoke.

"Victor here called me up with a difficult situation," Mr. Jones started as he leaned back in his seat. "Who would've thought the person I was selling the farm to is completely and utterly in love with you, Miss Martinez?" He belly-laughed.

I blushed, shyly glancing at Victor, whose cheeks were tinted pink.

"After some persuasion, I decided not to sell the farm," he hooked his thumbs in his suspenders, a proud smile on his face.

"But what about your retirement? Or the fact that the farm was on the brink of debt?" I pointed out two very valid reasons why he was selling in the first place.

While part of me was relieved the farm wouldn't be sold, I didn't want Mr. Jones to lose his happiness because of me.

"Oh, dear, I'm still on my way to Florida. I got my millions in the bank account where I'll spend the rest of my life on the beach drinking a nice cold beer!" He grinned. "As for the farm, Romano Tech offered to pay off the debt until we'd have her up and running like normal again," he explained.

I nodded, but there was still one question left unanswered. "Okay, so you're going to Florida, and the farm is staying. Who's going to run it?"

Mr. Jones shook his head with a smile. "To fulfill my girl's dream, Quinn will take full ownership of the farm next summer after she graduates. For now, Jackson will run it until she takes over," he elaborated.

I fell back in my chair in blissful defeat. "I'm in shock," I placed my shaky hands on the table. "I don't know what to say," I stared at the wood. The scratch marks showed how old it was and something about that only showed how irreplaceable this place was.

"How about a thank you to the handsome man right there," Mr. Jones gestured to Victor, the man in question sitting there with the kindest smile on his face, admiration drifting in his eyes as our gazes met. "A good man knows when and how to fix things," he bid before he got up and left us in the kitchen alone.

I waited until Mr. Jones left before I opened my mouth to speak. "Why didn't you just tell me this is what you had planned?" I asked, turning to face my boyfriend.

"Wouldn't be much of a surprise, would it?" He smirked, taking a sip from his mug.

I shook my head slightly, my lips curving upward. "But how? Was there really a way to back out even after the contract was signed?" I reached for his hand, my sleeve pulling up and revealing my charm bracelet. With my other hand, I began to fidget with the charms. "How much money did you give to keep the farm afloat?" I cocked a brow.

"Just to make sure costs are covered and the debt is paid off, plus enough to retire him, an even thirty million," he shrugged, amusement glinting in his eyes.

My eyes bulged out of my head.

"Romano Tech was more than happy to donate the sum, seeing as this farm already makes the world a better place," he smiled, hiking his shoulders up.

I felt tears prick in my eyes. "This was your dream, though," I wiped the first tear that fell.

"Project Regenerate was just a goal," he laughed, clasping his other hand over mine. He licked his lips, taking a deep breath in. "*You're* my dream," he confessed. "Buying the farm meant I could prioritize my dream, which is you," he added. "You're all I want in my future."

My heart soared.

I let out a shudder from the joy surging through me, and I firmed my grip around his hand to ground myself. The hand on top of mine rubbed against it and soothed me.

"I love you so fucking much," I grinned as the happy tears poured down before I wrapped my arms around him.

"I love you too," he said against my shoulder, turning his head and kissing my temple.

I mimicked him, kissing him on his cheek before I pulled away.

"I was stupid," I glanced down, grabbing the tissue he handed me and wiping my eyes. "I know I made my choice, and part of me thought it was for the best. That way, you could still have me and your dream," I gulped, sniffling.

"You deserve to have your business, Rosie, and I think you deserve to have me," he pinched my chin.

"Of course I do," I touched his cheek. "But I don't know if I deserve it. I'm still battling that," I winced.

Even though Bianca shared some words of encouragement, it wouldn't be a switch that happened instantly.

I knew I needed to open myself to help and get over my pride and stubbornness. But I think feeling grateful for what Victor did for me without also feeling guilty was a big step. The weight of losing my business was also off my shoulders, which was a plus.

"I know I'm not the right person to tell you," he captured my attention. "But I've worked with a lot of small businesses in my life, and the one thing I learned is that a lot of them are only in it for the money or the praise," he said.

I frowned, knowing he was right about that.

"But that night when we bumped into each other changed me," he continued. A smile appeared on his face. "I have never met someone with such passion and drive for something better. You were the diamond in the rough that proves what small businesses are really about," he brought my hand up to his mouth, kissing my skin. "If I have to spend the rest of my life reminding you, then I'll be the happiest man."

"I'll let you know when I believe you," I joked. My cheeks turned pink before I leaned in.

He followed, and our lips met in the middle. He tasted like chocolate, bitter and sweet. I moved my hand to entangle my fingers in his hair. I loved how he kissed me, the giddy feeling that erupted in me, like a sixth sense alerting me that I was safe, welcomed, and loved.

When his hand trailed low above my ass, I considered having sex with him right in the middle of the kitchen since it had been so long, but unfortunately—we were interrupted.

"Please don't have sex in my uncle's kitchen. We just got the floors waxed," I heard a familiar voice and pulled away from Victor as a gasp escaped my lips.

"Quinn!" I pushed away from my boyfriend, standing up and pulling her into a hug. "You're supposed to be in California. What are you doing here?" I held her by her shoulders.

She responded with a smile before opening her mouth. "Uncle Miles needed me to come down here to do some paperwork," she inhaled, her smile growing.

"You own the farm now," I said before she could. "You've been dreaming of this forever," I squealed, shaking her by the shoulders like she'd done to me many times before.

She grinned, and the excitement was evident in her eyes. "My five-year-old self would be so proud!" She cheered before her gaze went past my shoulder.

The audible gasp that left her was comical, and I wished I had seen the look on Victor's face.

"You did not say he'd be *this* hot," she deadpanned. "Mr. Romano, your looks have surpassed my expectations. It's a *pleasure* to meet you," she said, reaching across the table and offering her hand.

Just as their hands shook, he stood from his seat, a laugh escaping him.

"Thank you for not buying the farm, too. I would've hunted you down and ripped it from your hands," she smiled innocently.

"It's nice to meet you too, Quinn," he hummed, passing me a look of amusement.

She made a sound before walking back over to me, grabbing me by the hand. "Girl, you are so lucky," she whispered before she sat down at the table, wanting to catch up with everything going on.

"I know," I bit my lip to suppress my grin.

I never thought I'd consider myself lucky.

Chapter 42

Rosie

We left Plains Acres an hour ago, reaching for the drive back to Chicago. It was almost the afternoon by now. The adrenaline coursing through my veins was enough to keep me awake. I still couldn't believe what Victor did for me.

While I'd have the farm as my supplier, I wondered if it was enough. Was I going to be in the same place I've been in the last seven years, or would I make it?

"Are you sure you're not tired?" I asked, turning my head to face him and distracting myself from my thoughts.

"I'm fine," he pressed a smile. "You?"

"I'm good."

"Good, because we have one more stop," he turned in the opposite direction to my apartment. He parked in front of Hecho de Hilo.

Curiosity piqued me as I unbuckled my seatbelt and opened the door. Victor met me on the sidewalk, and we began walking towards the entrance. I hadn't left anything inside, so when he opened the door for me, I wasn't expecting to see a crowd of at least twenty people, and the entire store was decorated with streamers and balloons.

"Surprise!" They all shouted, Luna and Summer emerging as they brought me in for a hug.

"What is all of this?" I scrunch my eyebrows in confusion and delight.

"We're celebrating!" Luna answered.

"Celebrating what exactly?" I cocked a brow, still unaware of what was going on.

"You, obviously," Summer grinned.

"Me? But—" I shook my head, my lack of understanding irritating me.

"For all the work you've done, we're giving back," Luna clarified, wrapping her arms around me as she led me further into the store.

I looked back at Victor and was met with a reassuring smile.

"*Mija*, we know you've been working hard to keep this business open while trying to get your ceramics shop going," Señora Rivera pushed my attention to her. "You've always given, from the Winter Drive to the inclusive classes you provide. *Gracias por ponernos primero*," she had tears prick in her eyes, making me coo, and I wrapped my arms around her. "But now it's our turn," she squeezed my hand.

"But how?" I blinked back my tears.

"Leave that to your best friends," Luna wrapped an arm around Summer. "We knew you'd never ask for help, so we took the liberty of doing it," she smirked.

I laughed, pulling both of them in for a hug.

"We wanted to show you there's no problem asking for help, so there's a few people here who you might know," Summer smirked, gesturing for someone to come forward.

"Mr. Owens?" I gasped, seeing the older man again.

"Miss Martinez, you were right! My wife loves crochet date nights!" He grinned, wrapping his hands around mine with a huge smile.

I glanced over his shoulder, finding his wife with a light in her eyes

I had never seen before. She was also wearing a scarf that had a familiar pattern.

"The girls called me. I was beyond excited when they sent me your business plan for your ceramics shop. I was hooked the moment I read the title, but once I was done, I knew I had to invest," he stated.

My mouth opened in shock. "You're kidding, sir. You're interested?"

"Without a doubt," he patted the top of my hand.

"You guys," I turned to my best friends, my face melting from gratitude.

"Oh, honey, this is not all," Luna squeezed my arm.

"Rosie, it's nice to see you again."

Dark brown hair filled my vision.

"Luis, hi," I greeted. "Thanks for coming," I beamed. Seeing everyone come by to "celebrate" me, opening their arms to help me reach my dream, was indescribable. The feeling was indescribable.

"The other day, when Victor and the family were having dinner, we saw one of the sweaters you made," he started. "It especially caught my sister's eye," he smiled, turning and nodding someone over. "Rosie, I'd like you to meet my sister, Maria, and her partner, Angel," he introduced me to the young couple.

Maria had long dark brown hair and tan skin. She and Luis had the same eyes and nose, but her bone structure was strikingly more feminine. And her partner, Angel, was ethereal, like a literal angel. Their hair was wavy and black, and their bangs highlighted their bright green eyes.

"Rosie, it's so nice to meet you!" Maria pulled me into a tight hug. "Victor has said so much about you, dude will not shut up," she joked.

I laughed, glancing over to see my boyfriend with light pink dust on his cheeks.

"*Amor,*" Angel scolded. "Be nice," they bumped their shoulder against hers.

"Sorry," she apologized, sending Victor a glance. "I saw the cardigan you made with the jasmine stitch. I was impressed, to say the least," she smiled. "But that led me to tell Angel about your business," she licked her lips to hide her growing smile.

"I'm a huge supporter of small businesses," Angel began. "If I had known about your place sooner, I would've been a regular," they complimented. A kind smile formed on their face. "With that being said, I wanted to partner with you to bring more publicity to this business."

"Angel has three million followers on their socials and always promotes small Latino-owned and queer-friendly businesses." Maria lifted her shoulders, resting her head on her partner's shoulder and staring at them lovingly.

I felt my heart melt, knowing that's how I look at Victor.

"That's amazing," I responded. "I would love to work with you," I exhaled, shaking my hands from the excitement growing. "I honestly don't know how to believe this," I pressed a hand to my forehead.

"Well, believe it, *mija*," Señora Rivera grinned, the corner of her eyes crinkling.

"So what do you think?" Luna asked, rocking back and forth on her heels.

"I have the best community in the world," I felt the first tear slip, and both of my friends wrapped their arms around me.

"*Esta bien, es hora de celebrar,*" Señora Rivera rubbed my back as we pulled away.

I wiped a few stray tears. Victor appeared behind me as he wrapped his arm around me. I let out a heavy breath, feeling lighter than I thought I could as I leaned into his side. I glanced up at him, telling him everything

I needed to with just one look.

He looked back, saying the one thing I needed to know.

I'm here.

~

Victor

"You did all of this, didn't you?" She smirked.

I let out a laugh as I shook my head. I knew she would think I was behind the celebration her friends pulled together. "All I had to do with this was back out of the sale. The girls did everything else," I reassured.

We were lying in my bed with the curtains pulled open to look at one of the season's first snowfalls. The flurries were cascading in one of the most gentle and calm ways. The cold temperature allowed each flake to be visible even through the window.

"Still, I want to thank you," she reached up to kiss me on the cheek, her eyes darkening.

"What did you have in mind?" A smirk spread across my face.

"I think you know," she sat up, hiking her leg over my lap as she settled, straddling me. She cupped my face, reaching down to kiss me.

The intensity of the kiss was like finding the one thing I'd been longing for my entire life. The reason for my existence and the object that fueled my will to live. The kiss was more potent than all the others, the love seeping through as we pressed against each other.

I slid my hands up her thighs, around her back. The soft cotton of her pajamas rubbed against my skin, the heat of her body radiating off of her. I moaned against her mouth, her tongue slipping into mine as she began exploring me.

Her hands reached for my hair, threading her fingers through the locks and tugging on it, which earned a groan from me. She pressed her chest against mine, her pelvis grinding on top of me. She felt me grow hard, and the trail of moans that escaped her felt like music.

I wrapped my arm around her waist, laying her under me without breaking the kiss. I felt her hands glide down my chest and stomach, slipping it under my shirt before she slid it up. I allowed the shirt to come off, smirking when her gaze raked over me.

She shivered when my hand stroked her side, and it wasn't too long after that her shirt was off as well. Her hand clasped over mine when I began pinching her sensitive peak, the soft tissue of her breast hardening from the cold and my touch.

"I was supposed to be thanking you, not the other way around," she gasped when my head dipped to pay attention to her other side, her fingers immediately finding home in my hair again.

"Thank you for being the most amazing woman in the world," I muttered against her skin, pressing a kiss on the valley of her breasts, trailing up until I met her lips again.

"Victor," she panted, glancing at me. "Please, I need you," she begged.

I smiled in delight, my hand trailing down her stomach and slipping underneath the waistband of her pants and underwear.

She let out a choked gasp, her eyes on me. When I slipped a finger between her wet folds, she wrapped her hand around my wrist, and her thighs squeezed around my hand before she relaxed.

I smirked, my gaze raking over her while I began circling my finger around her clit.

"Fuck," she closed her eyes, allowing her grip on my wrist to relax.

The sound of her wetness echoed throughout the room, my finger keeping the light, lazy pace circling her sensitive bud while I dipped my head back down to kiss all over her body. Starting at her neck, then her collarbone, her chest, under her breasts, down her stomach.

I pulled my hand away, lying between her legs, and hooked my fingers around her bottoms. Sliding them down her legs, I threw the article of clothing behind me, gripping the outside of her thighs to spread them wide, allowing me the site of her beautiful glistening pussy.

"Victor, please, I want you inside of me," she stopped me, resting back on her elbows.

I hesitated, wanting to taste her so badly, but the look she gave me was hard to resist. Pressing a kiss to the inside of her knee, I crawled over her. Both of my hands rested on either side of her. A smile on my face. "You want me to fuck you?"

She nodded, rolling her lips together.

After I stripped myself and grabbed a condom, I lined myself up at her entrance.

I gripped her by the underside of her knees, bending them and pressing them to her chest. She let out a gasp, her eyes glancing up in desire while she rested her hands on the underside of her thighs.

We watched as her walls stretched around me as I entered, both of our gazes locked where we connected, and neither of us made a sound until I stopped to a hilt.

Letting go of her legs, I let them fall around my hips, my arm coming down to rest above her head. "You're so beautiful," I cupped the side of her face, running my thumb along her cheekbone.

"I love you so much," she cooed, hands running up my body and wrapping around my neck as she pulled me down to kiss me.

I moaned as I began to move my hips. "I love you too," I replied, pressing my forehead against hers.

We kissed again, allowing ourselves to get lost in the pleasure. I kept thrusting, her walls clenching with each one. When I would hit her g-spot, she'd only cling onto me tighter. We longed for a feeling like this; the events we've endured together only brought us closer.

It was evident that's what we both felt at the moment.

And soon, that feeling toppled over. Our orgasms approached together until we found ourselves catching our breath next to each other.

"That was the best way anyone's ever said thank you," I chuckled, turning to face her.

"I'll make sure to keep that in mind in the future," she smirked, rolling to face me.

Our noses brushed, and even though our bodies were covered in a sheen sweat, we craved the closeness.

Once we dressed again, I admired how she looked so at peace. Her eyes glimmer with newfound hope. But I knew something was still holding her back from feeling it entirely.

"Rosie?" I called her name.

"Hmm?" She turned to look at me.

"I know you decided this is something you need to figure out on your own, that I shouldn't interfere, but you shouldn't have to because we're in this together," I cupped her cheek. "The moment we started this relationship, it wasn't just me or you. It became us. No matter what we go through, we should do whatever we can to help the other, big or small."

She followed, but her brows pinched in curiosity. "What are you saying?" She asked.

"Let me help you with your sister," I answered. I've researched enough to know that Bianca can find justice with the right lawyer.

She stayed silent for a bit, and part of me was scared I upset her, but she blinked, her shoulders relaxing, and that look in her eyes shined brighter. "How?"

Chapter 43

Rosie

The lawyer Victor found was astounding. After a meeting with her and a sign-off with a judge, we were able to go to the prison almost a week later.

Bianca was going to be free.

A few days later, I stood beside Victor as we waited outside the gates. I played with the charms on my bracelet, the metal chains clashing against each other. It was an understatement to say I was nervous on top of being angry, excited, and *relieved*.

The last seven years were taken from Bianca. She should've been living this entire time, not behind bars. But that couldn't be changed now, and it was unbelievable to think it was over. She was able to live again. She was coming home.

Yet, with all this time to think of this day, I never knew how it would play out. I didn't know what I should do, what I should say, or where we should go after.

Victor noticed my fidgeting body; his hand delicately reached for my wrist while holding my hand with the other. He kissed my hand reassuringly before pressing it against his heart, sending me a warm smile. He didn't need to say anything. Just him being here was enough.

Just then, an alarm buzzed, the creek of the fenced gates opening. The machine that operated was humming, and suddenly, the heavy metal door a few yards in front of me opened, and my sister walked out.

She tucked her hair behind her ears, the wind blowing it in each direction. She held a bag of what she had when she came here in her hands. She waved at the guard by the door before she wrapped the hoodie tighter around herself.

The weather wasn't as cold as it was in the city, but it being December, it wasn't warm either. I was glad I brought one of my winter jackets with me.

Her pace was as quick as her internal injuries allowed, but her steps became more hurried when her gaze met mine.

A choked sob escaped me as I let go of Victor's hand, my legs moving before I could even process it, and soon I was engulfed by my sister's arms. Tears streamed down my face, the cheap material of her hoodie rubbing against my cheek. It didn't matter, though. The content sigh that left us both was enough to know this was real.

I was hugging my sister again.

"*Rosita*," Bianca inhaled. "*Mi hermanita*," she whispered, nuzzling her face in my shoulder, her hand running over my hair. She pulled away, getting a good look at my face before kissing my forehead and wrapping me back in a hug.

I was afraid I'd hurt her, so I kept my grip loose, but it was enough.

"You're here," I cried, my fingers clinging to the material of her clothes. I didn't want her to leave again. I felt like a child as I cried against her with tears of joy this time.

"I'm here," she squeezed me tighter. "I promise I'll do better," she said.

I felt my heart clench. "I know," I pulled away from her. "Let's go home, okay?" I grabbed her hands, leading us to where Victor was waiting.

Victor smiled, his eyes glancing at Bianca.

She let out a low "ooh" sound when her gaze landed on him, her mouth breaking into a grin. "So you must be the man who stole my little sister's heart," Bianca stopped before him, eyeing him once over.

He blushed. "That would be me," he smiled. "It's nice to meet you, Bianca."

"*Ay*, don't be so proper. Come here," she beckoned him over before pulling him in for a hug.

I stifled a laugh at the way Victor was taken aback, obviously not used to Bianca's bluntness, but I knew he would get used to it quickly. My face softened when she whispered something in his ear that made his lips curl softly.

They pulled away, and he nodded at her, sending her a reassuring glance. The look she had on her face when she stared at me was filled with so many emotions, but the ones that called out to me were happiness and relief. She reached out to pinch my cheek as Victor opened the door for her. Once she was settled inside, I turned to him.

"You have no idea how much this means to me," I grabbed his hand.

"I want to be there for you in any way I can," he said, taking a hold of my hand. "I'd do anything to make your life better," he said, opening the passenger door and waiting for me to go in. "And I'll continue to live every day doing so."

I reached up to kiss him.

It was soft and gentle, speaking a thousand words we had already felt.

I rolled my lips together when I pulled away, my hands resting on his abdomen before he stepped back to open my door for me.

We drove away from the prison, and something in my gut told me that would be the last time I ever came here, and I couldn't be more relieved. I reached behind me, holding onto Bianca's hand.

As we drove to the nearest burger joint, per her request, I could only see this as my future. The two of them in my life, my hopes and prospects for Hecho de Hilo to thrive and, hopefully, Ceramicá de la Vida to exist. It was a future I couldn't wait to experience.

Epilogue

Rosie

One week later

"Rosie! I'm gonna grab more hats from the back!" Luna shouted before she left.

I was busy helping a few people pick out some scarves and gloves, but I acknowledged her with a quick nod and wave.

Summer tended to the other table, where more families searched for the correct size.

We've all been up and at it since five in the morning, from setting up to opening the store for the Winter Drive. We had about three restaurants pitch in for the food, and the line was assembled after people had gotten their necessities. Plus, the customers who volunteered and the other shops were helping out, too.

It was hectic, but honestly, given all the help, I never felt so mellow.

Quinn usually came to help, but she was currently busy learning how to run a farm, so it made sense why she didn't. However, alongside our central volunteers, Luis and Ari joined in, thanks to Victor. Even the rest of the Sosas were here, and it was a blessing to have so many hands to help.

It made me emotional thinking about it.

But I've cried enough the past few months to last me a lifetime.

Someone was taking care of everything, so I allowed myself to step aside and enjoy the moment. I scanned over the shop, my eyes landing on Victor. My heart swelled at seeing him helping a few kids pick out their hats.

He looked adorable, being patient with them whether they disapproved of his color selection or asked him for the millionth time to grab the hat next to the one he already had.

Fuck, I love him.

"He sure does have a way with kids," Bianca stood beside me. "Kinda tells you how he'd be as a dad, doesn't it?" She wiggled her brows. She wrapped her arm around me.

I followed, being mindful of her still-healing injuries. I still couldn't believe she was home. In the days she's been out, I've made all her favorite food, taken her shopping for some actual clothes, and started looking for three-bedroom apartments.

I was sure she'll still take some getting used to being out, and I was sure it will be hard to navigate, but I knew I was ready for it.

Because I had her, I had my amazing friends, my community, and most importantly, *him*.

"It's too early for that, Bee," I shrugged, turning to face her. "Can we at least date for a year first?" I tipped my head.

She rolled her eyes playfully. "Fine, I'll wait," she raised her hands in defense. "But I'm positive you'll be married by year two," she smirked.

I rolled my eyes this time. "How are you feeling?" I asked.

"I'm managing, a little on my toes since I've had to watch my back for the last seven years," she looked over her shoulder. "But it's nice knowing I'm free," she grinned genuinely, and for a second, her eyes shone bright like before.

"Me too," I dropped my head to her shoulder.

An hour later, when everyone had left, the volunteers stayed huddled in the shop for some leftovers, pan dulce, and hot chocolate. There was a little bit of downtime before cleaning up.

I sat by the windows, my knee crossed over the other while I ate a white *concha*. My body leaned into Victor's side as he sat next to me.

"Are you happy?" He rested his arm on my chair's back while eating a *marranito*.

I dusted my fingers off before looking at him. The smile on my face screamed louder than I could say. "Yeah, I am," I nodded, voicing it.

Thinking about it all, I knew I was. It was the best feeling in the world.

He smiled, leaning over to kiss my temple before we returned to eating, enjoying the downtime.

I watched around the shop, finding my sister socializing with Summer and Luis, the three of them conversing. I couldn't help but notice the way Luis kept looking at my sister. I could be imagining things since I had been up for almost eight hours and was running on three hours of sleep, but I knew I had to keep my eye on him.

I shook my attention back to the crowd.

Señora Rivera was helping her grandson grab his favorite pan dulce. She was one of the customers who donated, offering to crochet a few dozen hats for the drive.

I smiled, glancing at my other loyal and amazing customers before my eyes fell on Luna talking with Ari.

They were outside, bodies pressed close.

My brows furrowed in confusion. I didn't think they were friends, let alone a couple.

I studied how they whispered at one another, smiling before they seemed to agree on something. Luna was walking back inside, heading towards the back room, leaving Ari behind.

"Did you know Luna and Ari were close?" I turned to Victor.

He seemed shocked by my question. "Ari and Luna?" He cracked a smile. "They're completely different people. I wouldn't take them for socializing in the same group."

"You're right," I agreed. "I think I'm just seeing things, I've been up since four," I yawned.

"You can always ask her afterward, too. It'd be nice if they were, but it would be shocking," he shrugged, sipping his hot chocolate.

"Maybe," I rested my head on the crook of his shoulder. I decided to leave it at that, but my mind wondered if Ari had anything to do with why Luna had been acting so weirdly. "So what's the plan for date night?" I managed to push my thoughts to the side.

"Mhm," he smirked, running his hand up and down my arm. "I was thinking of cooking you a nice warm dinner since it's so cold out," he began.

I melted at the thought of that.

"Then I'd run you a nice bath before I join you, giving you a nice massage to wash all the hard work from today," he ended, his face dipping down, and our noses brushed.

"That sounds amazing," I grinned, pecking his lips.

He smirked before kissing me thoroughly.

That feeling of home finding me, and I knew my future would be more than fine.

~

Victor

Six months later

"That should be the last of the boxes," I sighed, placing a stack of ceramic materials in the corner. I used a rag to wipe the sweat off my forehead. The AC running in the building was still not enough to cool me down.

It was a hot summer day. The intense humidity in Chicago made everything feel worse, but it didn't matter. I was happy to help the woman I loved.

"Thank you," Rosie sighed, placing her hands on my biceps while she reached up to kiss my cheek before handing me a water bottle.

I drank the cold liquid, allowing my body to cool down while she leaned against my body, her arms wrapped around me, her chest pressed against mine.

"You were lots of help," she smirked, eyes running over my body. "And you put on a good show," she winked.

I had stopped by during my lunch like usual.

However, Rosie finally had her shipments come in from her supplier today. There was lots of ceramic equipment and clay for the opening in a week.

I quickly volunteered to help her load the boxes upstairs where they needed to be for storage instead of having her struggle up the flight of stairs in this heat. The sticky air made me remove my jacket and button down, leaving me in an undershirt. I didn't realize how much of an effect it had on her.

"Was your plan to get me all naked and sweaty while doing work for you?" I pinched her chin, tilting her head back.

"Possibly, but you did say you'd do anything for me," she shrugged, batting her eyes.

She's so fucking cute.

"Obviously, but you could've asked," I cocked a brow, a smirk appearing on my lips.

"There's no fun in that, though," she moved her hands, running them over my chest and abs through the material.

I hummed before reaching down to kiss her.

She moaned before pulling away. I quickly chased after her.

There's no way we were going to stop now.

"Victor, we need to move the clay into the storage room. It's too hot for it to be out here," she moved towards the boxes. "And I need to go get the paint for the painters tomorrow," she said, but I silenced her with a kiss. She was reluctant, her mind most likely racing with her to-do list, but it only took a second for her to melt against me.

"We can do that later. Right now, I need a much-needed break," I grabbed her hand, wrapping my arms around her.

"Victor," she whined but still dragged her hand up my neck to pull me in for a kiss. "I'll give you your mandated fifteen," she joked.

"I could work with that," I smirked.

I could work with anything as long as she was right with me.

Thank you for reading!

I hope you enjoyed Rosie and Victor's story as much as I loved writing it! Their book was my leap of faith. The start of my journey and career as an author. I can't wait to see what is to come and I hope to see you there as my journey continues! Thank you so much for reading Mold My Future! Your support is graciously appreciated and admired. Who's ready for book two?!

What's next in The Fine Arts Series?

Luna's story is just beginning—*Between the Lines* will be released in 2025!

Acknowledgments

To my mom—you're the reason I grew up loving stories and romances. From watching telenovelas to being introduced to movies like *13 Going on 30* and *Maid in Manhattan*. You always said I should write a telenovela since the people at the network can't seem to come up with a new idea. At the time, I didn't know how much those words would come to mean, but now they mean everything as I begin my journey as a romance author. Thank you for being my supporter even before day one. I love you, Ma.

Para mi padre—gracias por ser comprensivo. No habría podido vivir mis sueños si no fuera por tus sacrificios. Te amo, Pa.

To my brother— thank you for always looking out for me in your own way. For teaching me to chase my ambitions and my dreams. And for always buying me food.

To Mary—thank you for being one of my beta readers and my hype woman. We share a love for spicy romance shows and hot men. Most of the time we have polarized opinions on characters and plot, but nothing is better than discussing the latest season of Bridgerton with you.

To Lizzy—thank you for being there for me when I needed you. We can talk about anything and everything, especially gossip about people at work. There isn't a competition show on Netflix I wouldn't watch with you.

To John—thank you for always making me laugh. You look out for me when you can and you have very interesting history facts I like hearing about. You're a great friend and have been a good support on this journey.

To my friends—thank you for always supporting me whenever I have a new celebrity hyperfixation, for listening to my fears and concerns about publishing my book, and seeing me for who I am. I love you all, you have no idea how much you mean to me.

To Janessa—thank you for taking the time to be a beta reader and enjoying my story. It was scary sharing it with someone who's never read my writing before but you were very supportive. Thank you for being kind.

To Tammie—thank you for helping me heal and allowing myself to blossom into the person I am today. You helped me in more ways than I can thank you for. I'm very grateful.

To Jenna—thank you for being my editor! The process was long and stressful but without you, my book wouldn't be the work it is today! You allowed me to see my story in a different perspective that changed it for the better.

To Dana—thank you for designing this cover and formatting this book! You made my book beautiful! You were so patient. I'm honestly sorry for being so nitpicky but you went above and beyond! The vision I had in my head was nowhere near the masterpiece you created! I'm obsessed!

About the Author

Ami Bella is a new and upcoming romance author who resides in Chicago, Illinois with her family. Inspired by the telenovelas she grew up watching, her writing is a concoction of drama-filled plot, romance with a hint of spice, and a lovable cast of Latino characters. Her dream is to continue to highlight the diverse Latinoamerican cultures and representation with her stories.

In her free time, she enjoys painting her nails, rewatching Cobra Kai, and endlessly shopping online without ever buying anything. She daydreams and loves to spend time with her family and friends.

Keep in touch!

Follow Ami Bella on Instagram @authoramibella!